The Stechlin

Theodor Fontane

The Stechlin

Translated with an Introduction and Notes

by

William L. Zwiebel

CAMDEN HOUSE

Copyright © 1995 by
CAMDEN HOUSE, INC.

Published by Camden House, Inc.
Drawer 2025
Columbia, SC 29202 USA

Printed on acid-free paper.
Binding materials are chosen for strength and
durability.

ISBN 1–57113–024–1

Library of Congress Cataloging-in-Publication Data

Fontane, Theodor, 1819-1898.
   [Stechlin.English]
   The Stechlin / Theodor Fontane ; translated and with an
introduction by William L. Zwiebel.
      p.   cm. -- (Studies in German literature, linguistics, and
culture)
   ISBN 1-57113-024-1 (alk. paper)
   I. Zwiebel, William L.   II. Title.   III. Series: Studies in German
literature, linguistics, and culture (Unnumbered)
PT1863.S6513 1995
833'.8--dc20
                                                                95-2917
                                                                CIP

Contents

Introduction

OF THE GERMAN novelists of the nineteenth century Theodor Fontane remains the most enduring. His chief works, written in the last two decades of a long life as a journalist, travel writer, theater critic and balladeer, represent the pinnacle of both the social novel and the novel of manners in German before the advent of Thomas Mann, whose first novel *Buddenbrooks* appeared only a year after Fontane's death in 1898.

Fontane was a descendant of the French Huguenots who took up residence in Berlin and its surrounding area, the Mark Brandenburg, in the seventeenth century. Nevertheless, although Gallic qualities such as love of witty conversation and social graces certainly mark his fiction, several generations of Prussian family tradition led him to characterize himself as a dyed-in-the-wool Prussian. During his lifetime, apart from a number of historical ballads, his most popular achievement was a five volume work devoted to the countryside of Brandenburg based on his rambles through its villages, towns and fields. Combining history, legend, art criticism and gossip, his *Excursions through the Mark Brandenburg (Wanderungen durch die Mark Brandenburg)* remain even today one of the most popular travelogues written in the German language. As a novelist Fontane's interests were similar; the primary concerns of his stories are the mores and values found in the drawing rooms and streets of Berlin and the surrounding areas of Brandenburg-Prussia. Although some of his fiction deals with earlier periods, his most famous works are those depicting contemporary Prussian society in the last three decades of the nineteenth century, the era of Wilhelmine Germany.

Der Stechlin is Fontane's testament. Well into his seventies the writer was keenly aware that on the threshold of the twentieth century Prussia, and by extension the German Empire itself, continued to cling to an outdated political and social structure. In what was essentially a modern industrialized state in which bourgeoisie and proletariat laid ever-increasing claims to economic and political supremacy, the Reich continued to be dominated by a privileged aristocratic class. Ossified values associated with the nobility still held sway in most German high government posts, and in the army an officer caste drawn almost entirely from blue-blooded families with a long-standing military code of values and sense of exclusivity continued to set the tone.

Fontane deeply admired the rich historical traditions as well as the loyalty, openness, hardiness and devotion to duty he found characteristic of the best of the Prussian nobility. But he was too much the realist not to know that as a class they had become an anachronism. Thus, in his penultimate novel, *Die Poggenpuhls* (*The Poggenpuhl Family*), he bid a whimsical farewell to the lower military aristocracy, portraying them as a comically doughty but essentially moribund caste. In *Der Stechlin* (*The Stechlin*), however, he set out to write a serious political statement, a novel which gave full measure of respect to the finer qualities of the Prussian aristocratic heritage, but which also pointed out its provincialism and morbidity and the pressing need for a total restructuring of Prussian society.

Der Stechlin is thus an essentially Prussian book. Non-German readers will learn a great deal about the values and way of life of the Junker class, the landed gentry of Brandenburg-Prussia during the salad days of the Second German Reich. That such figures would be recognized, understood and admired by his audience, was of course taken for granted by the author. After all, it was preeminently for educated Germans that Fontane wrote, readers who were steeped in most of the history of Prussia even if they did not fully share in the perquisites enjoyed by its upper classes. This means, however, that to fully understand this work, modern readers must know something about the historical background and social values which imbued Fontane's public in the late nineteenth century. It is these which this introduction and the accompanying notes seek to supply.

On January 1, 1871 the Second German Empire came into being in the Hall of Mirrors in Versailles, the most significant outcome of the War of 1870 between France and Prussia. In that conflict, through the skillful manipulation of the Prussian Chancellor, Otto von Bismarck, all German-speaking monarchies and principalities save Hapsburg Austria and the Swiss Confederation joined the Kingdom of Prussia in defending German honor against what was perceived as French political arrogance. Once victory was won, it was only natural that the coalition of German-speaking entities continue their union to create one large and powerful new state, the German Empire, the ultimate realization of those dreams of unity which had burned in many a German heart in the wake of nationalistic sentiments inspired by the Napoleonic wars. Prussia's leading role meant that the Prussian king, Wilhelm I, became German Emperor (Kaiser), theoretically the first among equals of the twenty-three German princes and kings. In practice, however, the Kaiser gradually came to be viewed as supreme. The Prussian capital, Berlin, was made capital city of the united Germany, and Bismarck, architect of the entire process, was elevated to the post of Chancellor of the Reich.

But what was the legitimacy of the Kingdom of Prussia itself? How did this small and relatively remote region in the sandy fir-covered swamps and marshes of northeastern Europe emerge as the central force of the German-speaking states, a kingdom capable of creating a coalition which defeated France and challenged Britain as the dominant power of the European world?

Compared to its European equals, Prussia's history was brief. Originally settled by Slavic Wends and later by Germans, that part of North Central Europe near the Baltic that was later to become Brandenburg-Prussia was first Christianized by monks of the French Premonstratensian and Cistercian orders in the 12th and 13th centuries. The modern Prussian state essentially began with the coming of the Hohenzollerns in 1415. In that year Friedrich von Hohenzollern, originally a Nuremburg burgrave, was appointed Margrave of the Brandenburg March (German: Mark, i.e. border territory), by the Holy Roman Emperor, who sent him to restore peace and order over the uncooperative knights and peasantry occupying that contentious and backward part of the realm. Two years later Friedrich was granted the hereditary office of Prince Elector, i.e. one of those princes responsible for choosing the Holy Roman Emperor.

Of this first Hohenzollern's successors the most famous was the Great Elector, Friedrich Wilhelm I (1620–1688), who in 1675 defeated the Swedes at the Battle of Fehrbellin near Berlin, and definitively established Brandenburg-Prussia as an independent and growing European force with a strong and capable army. As Prussian power gradually expanded to dominate all of northeastern Europe well into what is today Poland, his successor Elector Friedrich III with imperial forbearance proclaimed himself King in Prussia in 1700, thereby creating the royal house of Hohenzollern. Gradually military values, duty, obedience, subservience to authority, began to dominate the mores of the Prussian state. These were especially fostered by Friedrich Wilhelm I (1688–1740), who became known as the Soldier King, an autocratic tyrant who doubled the size of the standing army to nearly 100,000 men and unremittingly imposed strict obedience to his own personal authority in every aspect of Prussian society.

The greatest of Prussian regents, however, was his son, whom history remembers as Frederick the Great (1712–1786). Assuming the crown in 1740, Frederick expanded the highly disciplined army his father had created and put it to use in a series of wars to conquer new territories to the south and east, mostly at the expense of Maria Theresia's Austria. While continuing his father's autocratic style as a ruler, Frederick has also found his place in history, not only as a soldier but as a highly astute and sensitive personality, a flautist of considerable musical skill — he composed a number of concerti for flute and orchestra — and an enlightened philosopher king who for two years entertained and disputed daily with Voltaire at Sanssouci, his palace in Potsdam near Berlin. Under the enlightened despotism of Frederick, who took his role as regent to be that of the first servant of the state, Prussia became the most well-organized and forward-looking monarchy of Europe; with the king as its primary example, the concept of individual duty to state and society was promulgated throughout the country and essentially codified in the social and moral writings of the great Prussian philosopher, Immanuel Kant. All of that was, of course, nearly a hundred years before Fontane's novel takes place, yet as the reader will note, "the Great King" and the values associated with him, were by no means forgotten a century after his time.

In the intervening years between Frederick and the time of *Der Stechlin*, however, Prussia had fallen to the depths and risen again. During the Napoleonic era, as Queen Luise, the wife of his grand nephew Friedrich Wilhelm III admitted, "Prussia had fallen asleep on the laurels of Frederick the Great" and tasted bitter defeat at the hands of Napoleon, an episode which forms the core of one of Fontane's earlier short novels *Schach von Wuthenow* (translated in English as *A Man of Honor*). In 1813, however, following the French Emperor's disastrous Russian campaign, Prussians rose up against Bonaparte and played a significant role in his defeat, first at the Battle of the Nations in 1813 near Leipzig, and two years later at Waterloo.

Following the reordering of post-Napoleonic Europe at the Congress of Vienna in 1815, Prussia was acknowledged as a leading European power, the equal of Britain, France, Russia and in German-speaking territories, matched only by Catholic Austria to its south. Thus when in 1848 and 1849 revolution broke out in many German states, in the effort to establish a constitutional monarchy it was to the Prussian king Friedrich Wilhelm IV (1840–1852) that the representatives of the Frankfurt Parliament offered a crown. This first attempt at a democratic unified Germany floundered, however, when the king, recognizing the limits to his absolute power imposed by such an arrangement, rejected it, preferring to remain monarch by divine right of the Kingdom of Prussia rather than the head of a newly created state, chosen by a parliament of those whom he dismissed as his inferiors.

Friedrich Wilhelm's successor, his brother Wilhelm I was slow to give up such thinking as well, but under the canny manipulation of his Chancellor, Otto von Bismarck, who put his faith less in the democratic processes than in blood and iron, he was gradually compelled to see things differently and reluctantly made to accept an imperial crown. This came about in the remarkable decade between 1862 and 1871 during which Bismarck guided the affairs of the Kingdom of Prussia from its position as a local German power to the pinnacle of European might. In 1864 the Chancellor deftly employed the newly modernized and highly efficient Prussian army in cooperation with Austria to thwart the illegal territorial claims of Denmark over the North German principalities of Schleswig and Holstein. Two years later Austria was pushed out of the way as a determining force in North German politics. In 1870 it was France's turn. After ill-considered French demands on Prussian influence in European affairs evolved into a head-to-head confrontation, Bismarck was able to bring almost all the German-speaking petty states to side with Prussia against the French. Then the Iron Chancellor set the united German armies loose to defeat France in a pitifully short war whose outcome was the Second German Empire and the first step in vaulting the newly created German state to a position of power second to none in Europe.

Once a united Germany under Prussia was achieved, Europe enjoyed peace and stability as long as Bismarck and his king, now Emperor Wilhelm I, remained in power. Internally, however, the anachronistic social structure of the Reich began to make itself felt as the middle and lower classes, which had supplied the blood and iron for the success of Prussia, now began to stake their claims for social reward. It is one of the tragic ironies of history, however, that it was not Emperor Wilhelm's son, the liberal son-in-law of Queen Victoria, Friedrich Wilhelm, who died of throat cancer after a brief reign of only 100 days, but his grandson, Wilhelm II, who was to set his imprint on the future history of Prussia, Germany and the world. Vainglorious, pompous and convinced of the superiority of the Prussian-German state, German ideas and German military might, the saber-rattling Wilhelm would probably contribute more than any other single individual to the outbreak of World War I and the demolition of the German Empire.

The time of Fontane's last novel is roughly 1896. The foundation of the Reich lies twenty-five years in the past. The first German Emperor, Wilhelm I, lies in his tomb in Berlin at Castle Charlottenburg near his parents, King Friedrich Wilhelm III and Queen Luise. His grandson Wilhelm II, the infamous Kaiser Wilhelm of the Great War of 1914–1918, has been on the throne since 1888, nearly eight years. The old Iron Chancellor Bismarck, true progenitor of the Reich, has been sidelined by the young emperor since 1890, spending his last days at his estate Friedrichsruh near Hamburg. Those problems which were inherent in the social anachronism of the Reich from its creation are now becoming bitterly acute. Prominent in the background of *Der Stechlin* is the social unrest abroad in the land, the rise of the working class championed by the Social Democrats led by August Bebel (1840–1913) and the attempt to unite traditional Christian values in the sense of the Sermon on the Mount with the movement for social justice, represented by former Court Chaplain Adolph Stöcker (1835–1909) who from 1874 to 1890 led the Christian-Socialist movement.

While all the Prussians pictured here join in keen awareness of the former glory days of old Prussia under the Great Elector, Frederick the Great, or during the Wars of Liberation against Napoleon, regardless of class, it is the shared past of the events and personalities leading to the founding of the Second Reich which acts as a bond for all representatives of the elder generation in this novel. Personages such as Bismarck, Kaiser Wilhelm and Field Marshall Moltke are never far from their minds, and locations such as Düppel and Alsen, where they had fought the Danes in 1864, and Königgrätz where they had beaten the Austrians two years later, or Mars-la-Tour and St. Marie aux Chênes, where bloody engagements of the Franco-Prussian War had proven their mettle, remain vivid memories and act as a mark of pride and place for the older men of this society. Deeds on the battlefield and the disciplined order of military life in general have been a determinant part of their lives and helped to define their social identities. They are proud of their accomplishments in establishing the new German Empire and from the vantage point of their era consider the victories in which they took part — now largely forgotten footnotes in history — eternal milestones in the chronicle of European civilization. Fontane himself had recorded many of their accomplishments in several books on the Prussian wars in his lifetime.

Much of *Der Stechlin* takes place in Berlin, the capital city of the German empire, a burgeoning metropolis on the verge of the twentieth century with its horse cars, newly-built elevated railroad, and rapidly expanding industrial base. The life of the city as a whole is touched upon in various ways: an excursion on the River Spree brings the protagonists to a local beer garden, characters stroll through the Tiergarten, Berlin's central park, and admire the many church towers of the city. Although the novel dwells predominantly in the sphere of the titled, in oblique episodes Fontane presents aspects of the life of the lower classes and alludes to a number of the social problems of the era, the inability and unwillingness of the older aristocracy to take the emerging democratic processes of the Reich completely seriously, the exploitation of the serving classes by the bourgeoisie, the deterioration of class distinctions and the need for a new and egalitarian morality. With deft strokes he satirizes the cultural and intellectual ossification of members of the nobility as well as the smug self-satisfaction of the nouveau riche, while comically portraying artistic hangers-on of the upper classes. In this manner what has been characterized as a complete portrait of the age gradually emerges from the book's pages. A silent presence in the novel is the Kaiser himself. Fontane does not openly criticize Wilhelm II, but comes close to doing so in a long discussion between two of the book's chief protagonists for change concerning the Prussian past and the prospects of a German future.

Apart from Berlin, the region in which much of the novel plays is the still relatively remote lake district some thirty miles northwest of the capital, extensively described by Fontane in the *Wanderungen*. Not far from Neuruppin, the author's birthplace on Lake Ruppin, is the little town of Lindow on Lake Wutz, where stands the ruined convent which served as the model for Wutz Convent. Some ten miles east is Gransee, the closest railhead to the fictional Castle Stechlin and twenty miles further north lie the silent waters of the *Großer Stechlinsee*, the Great Stechlin Lake, which gives the novel its name. The region is in part associated with Frederick the Great. In the little town of Rheinsberg, which lies more or less at its center on the lake of the same name, stands the castle inhabited by Frederick as Crown Prince, which, following his coronation, he presented to his brother Heinrich (1726–1802), who spent the rest of his life there in a misogynist court dedicated to the pursuit of the arts and sciences and much criticism of his royal brother. Yet it will soon become clear to readers of this story, that although the Hohenzollern family ruled in Brandenburg from the fifteenth century on, they continued to be viewed as outsiders by many of the indigenous nobility who, albeit ultimately submitting to their dominance, never quite overcame their sense of priority.

This then is the historical and geographical background of *Der Stechlin*. The First World War — unthinkable at this time in its magnitude or effect — still lies two decades in the future. The era of the generation which began with the Prussia of Friedrich Wilhelm IV and shared the historical and political upheavals of the Bismarck years is approaching its end, and a new generation of aristocrats who must come to terms with the realities of a different epoch prepares to take its place. In the figure of Dubslav von Stechlin, the author has memorialized the down-to-earth old Prussian Junker of Bismarck's times, bound to values of an earlier day, warmly humane, and strongly skeptical about the changes which history has forced upon him. Dubslav's counterpart is the more elegant Count von Barby, also a Prussian nobleman, but one who because of his experiences abroad brings a certain cosmopolitan sophistication to the traditionally conservative values of the old Junker. Dubslav von Stechlin's half-sister, the superior (Domina) of a small and crumbling convent of Lutheran nuns, provides another dimension of the privileged caste, unremitting devotion to family and the old religion in the narrowest and most restrictive sense. Other members of the upper class also suggest their sense of exclusivity, inbreeding and caste consciousness. At the same time Fontane's genuine hope for the future of the Prussian nobility is depicted in Dubslav's son Woldemar and in the two daughters of Count Barby. It is their generation which will carry the Reich into the 20th century.

The very name of the elder Barby sister points to the mythical-symbolic content of the novel, revealing a fascination Fontane had long harbored for a legendary woman half human, half water sprite. It is Melusine who stands as the prime oracle of the work. In the watery origins of her name, of course, she is closely akin to the dominant symbol of the novel, Lake Stechlin, which Fontane, repeating a legend he had recounted in his *Wanderungen*, employs as a metaphor for the primary message of the novel: even the most remote corners of the world participate in the developments of the earth at large.

With the figure of the local clergyman Lorenzen, Fontane created the primary spokesman for the values he feels must ultimately carry the day, a blend of the Christianity of the Sermon on the Mount and socialism similar to that espoused at the time in Berlin by Adolph Stöcker before he turned to a strongly anti-Semitic dogma. That Woldemar's bride, who bears the simple teutonic name Armgard, inherently shares such values suggests Fontane's clear hope that the Prussia of the future, in which nobility of the sort represented by the new generation of von Stechlins will hold sway, will be a more just and democratic state. Finally, Lorenzen's tale of the arctic explorer Greeley seems to suggest that notwithstanding the dominant collective mentality of Prussian society, not only is there a greater heroism than that of the herd, but that there are times when individual acts bordering on the criminal might be justifiable — clearly a repudiation of the unthinking and duty-bound ethos of the Prussian military and even pointing ahead to the events of July 1944, when descendants of some of the characters pictured in this novel would indeed take extraordinary steps in the name of a higher good than order and legality.

The present-day reader knows of events that Fontane could not have dreamed possible. His hopes were never to be realized, and history has rendered *Der Stechlin* an almost naive pious wish. It is one of the small and ironic tragedies of the terrible age that followed, that this manifesto of a sage and humane Prussian, had its message been followed, might have led to a wiser Germany and one considerably less burdened with guilt.

Translating *Der Stechlin* has been a challenge. For one thing, the author himself, perhaps because of age, occasionally lapsed into a certain easy-going style which, had he been younger, might have been less expansive. I have not attempted to smother this tone but allowed it to emerge insofar as that is possible in another language. After all, its occasional verbosity notwithstanding, *Der Stechlin* is a product of the Victorian era, a time when wordiness was not considered as much of a stylistic transgression as today and indeed, when a finely turned somewhat, sententious phrase was considered the mark of an elegant and weighty writer. Moreover, like the English of Victoria's day, Wilhelmine German is by nature often couched in long periods, rambling sentences which occasionally try the readers' patience and now and again their sense of logic.

To retain both the tone of the age and the German ambiance so vital to the novel, I have made certain basic decisions with regard to my translation which at once mark it as such, yet I hope do neither the work nor the author an injustice.

One of these has to do with titles. German is a language rich in titles. The English military rank of Captain, for instance, is rendered in German as *Hauptmann* when the reference is to an infantry or artillery officer, but *Rittmeister* when referring to a cavalryman and *Kapitän* when applied to a seaman. Not all of these variants appear in this novel. To underscore some of these distinctions, however, and to lend the whole a clearly German flavor, I have retained many German titles throughout the text unless I felt it unwieldy or impossible. Thus words such as *Herr, Hauptmann, Frau* and other forms of address are used wherever persons bearing such rank are addressed, while their English equivalents are used to refer to the persons objectively in the narrative. In this way, the character Czako appears as *Herr Hauptmann* whenever directly addressed, but is usually referred to as "the captain" in narrative passages. I trust the reader will understand that the reference is to the same person. Certain commercial titles, which do not exist in English, I have paraphrased in English form. Thus Ministerial Assessor or Insurance Secretary, titles which sound pompous in English but were common in the caste and rank conscious Germany of the Wilhelmine era, are given in English, if for no other reason than to attempt to catch an echo of the author's whimsy at their pomposity. Similarly, the title Mamsell, obviously a corruption of Mademoiselle, is retained for one of the Stechlin house staff; it harkens back to an earlier Frenchified Prussia and brings with it a certain tone of comic striving for elegance that no English title such as Miss or Mrs. would provide.

Linguistic characterization, an art in which Fontane specialized, is the bane of translators. Fontane eschewed the proclivity of his younger contemporaries of the Naturalist generation to render every nuance of speech as a means of expressing the exigencies of the deterministic forces of heredity and environment. Nevertheless throughout his career as a novelist and especially in *Der Stechlin,* he occasionally employed his own phonetic renderings of the low German of the Brandenburg countryside, less for ideological reasons than to characterize the peasantry as an underclass. Even though he believed in the essential equality of men in a theoretical sense, one cannot overcome the feeling that his attitude towards the lower classes is always somewhat humorously condescending. But how is a subtlety of this sort to be rendered? The English language is rich enough in dialects, to be sure, but all are associated with English, Irish or American locales and have nothing to do with the swampy plains and woodlands of the Mark Brandenburg. I have resorted to the expedient of creating my own dialect, spoken nowhere on earth, I trust, but close enough to standard English, I hope, that the reader who phonetically works it out or pronounces it aloud will recognize that it is a substandard variant of the language and will have little difficulty in understanding what is said.

The same situation holds for the aristocrats of the novel. While not resorting to dialect for them, Fontane has some of his blue-bloods speak in what is essentially an easy-going variant of correct German, suggesting both their provinciality and a sense of confident superiority. Final consonants are frequently lost in words such as *nicht, ist, nun,* etc. These I have usually rendered with standard English contractions.

There remains, however, the matter of tone. While his narrative or descriptive passages sometimes bog down in a sort of teutonic journalese, Fontane is revered in German circles for the lightness and flow of his conversational exchanges. At the same time, however, German is a somewhat more restricted medium than English in this regard. Although not completely without such expressions, it lacks to a certain extent a variety of interjections such as, "I say," "dear me," "oh my," and the like, which subtly betray the speaker's attitude. Instead German relies quite effectively on a limited number of particles such as *ja*, *doch*, *nun*, *aber*, or else tone of voice to convey nuances of speech such as incredulity, curiosity or irritation or mild shock. In this regard I have not hesitated to take liberties in my translation. After all, the primary medium of Fontane's narrative prose is characterization through dialogue. Moreover, translation is of itself in part an act of interpretation; therefore, my renderings of the conversations in this text are a reflection of my understanding of what Fontane wished to portray in his characters. To present such an author as Fontane in gray but proper English would do him no real service and leave readers unfamiliar with his native idiom wondering just what is so special about a writer, so respected in his own land, whose characters speak in such a colorless and dispassionate manner. My versions of Fontane's highly idiomatic German are, therefore, my own and represent the closest I am able to get to the tone of the utterances given here, not their exact wording. For mistranslations, however, I take full responsibility.

Similarly, those for whom British English is the norm might also take umbrage here and there at Americanisms both in vocabulary and style which appear in the text. While it is certainly arguable that the more proper British tone might be more appropriate for rendering the speech of Prussian nobility, American English is my native idiom and not the language of the Thames and the Avon. Hence, avoiding anachronistic turns of phrase wherever possible, it is into the cultivated and sometimes uncultivated American English of Fontane's era that I have generally attempted to present my translation. I make no apologies for doing so.

The translated text is based upon the edition of *Der Stechlin* published as part of the complete edition of Fontane's works by the Hanser Verlag, Munich. Notes are drawn from this edition, that of the Aufbau Verlag, Berlin, the *Erläuterung und Dokumente* to *Der Stechlin* edited by Hugo Aust and published by the Philipp Reclam Jun. Verlag, Stuttgart, and my own research.

I am thankful to the College of the Holy Cross for partially supporting the publication of this work. For assistance in reading the manuscript and for many helpful suggestions in matters of style and translation, I am most grateful to my colleague Professor Eckhard Bernstein and to my wife, Marie, to whom I dedicate the work.

Castle Stechlin

1

I N THE NORTHERN part of the County of Ruppin, hard by the Mecklenburg border, through thinly settled woodlands, populated only here or there with a few old villages and otherwise nothing but foresters' lodges and glass or tar makers' kilns, runs a chain of lakes several miles long. These extend from the little town of Gransee as far as Rheinsberg and beyond. One of the lakes forming this chain bears the name "Stechlin." Bordered entirely by old beeches whose branches, drawn down by their own weight, touch its waters with their tips, it lies between flat banks which climb up steeply to provide a landing only at one spot. Here and there a few rushes and reeds may grow, but not a single boat leaves its wake and no bird may be heard to sing. Only rarely does a hawk pass overhead to leave its shadow on the surface. Everything is silence here.

Yet from time to time at this very spot things do get lively. That happens when far off in the outside world, perhaps on Iceland or in Java, a rumbling and thundering begins, or when the ash rain of the Hawaiian volcanoes is driven far out over the southern seas. Then things start to heaving at this spot too, and a waterspout erupts and then sinks down once more into the depths. All of those living around Lake Stechlin know of it and whenever they bring it up they're almost always likely to add, "That business about the water jet's hardly anything at all, practically an every day occurrence. But when something big's going on outside, like a hundred years ago in Lisbon,[1] then the water doesn't just seethe and bubble and swirl around. Instead, when the likes of that happens, a red rooster comes up in place of the geyser and crows so loudly it can be heard over the whole countryside."

That is the Stechlin, *Lake* Stechlin.

But it is not only the lake that bears this name, but the forest surrounding it as well. And Stechlin is also the name of the elongated village which curves around its southernmost point, following the bends of the lake. More or less a hundred houses and cottages make a long, narrow street which opens out to form something like a square only where the chestnut-lined road leading from the convent at Wutz intersects it. Thus it is at this very spot that the entire grandeur constituting the village of Stechlin comes together, the parsonage, the school, the village elder's office, and the inn, the latter, with a statue of a little moor and a garland of yellow sulfur ribbons in its show window, also acting at the same time as the local grocery and general store. Diagonally across from this corner, directly behind the parsonage, the churchyard ascends the hill. There just about exactly in the middle, stands the early medieval fieldstone church, with a small bell tower dating back to the last century and a wooden beam on which hangs a bell attached to one side of its rounded-arch portal. Next to churchyard and church, the chestnut-lined avenue from Wutz Convent continues on a bit until it ends at a plank bridge crossing a swampy moat, flanked by two gigantic glacial boulders. The bridge is extremely primitive. On its far side, however, the manor house rises, a yellow-tinted building with a tall roof and two lightning rods.

The manor house too bears the name Stechlin, Castle Stechlin.

A few centuries ago a real castle stood on this spot, a brick building with thick round towers. From those days too dates the moat that cuts through the little spit of land jutting out into the lake making it into a little island. So it remained until the days of the Reformation. But during the time of the Swedish invasion[2] the old castle was destroyed, and apparently willing to leave it to fall into ruin, no one sought to replace it with anything until shortly after the onset of the reign of Friedrich Wilhelm I, when the entire pile of rubble was carted off and a new building put up in its place.

The new building was the house still standing today. It possessed that same prosaic character as practically everything that had been erected under the Soldier King, being nothing more than a simple *corps de logis*[3] with two wings jutting to the edge of the moat, forming a horseshoe with a barren courtyard in between, in which, as the only item of decoration, a large and shiny glass sphere presented itself. Otherwise nothing could be seen except a ramp extending across the front of the house, from the front wall of which, on the side facing the courtyard, the mortar was beginning to fall.

And yet an effort had unmistakably been made to turn this very ramp into something out of the ordinary. This had been in fact achieved, with the aid of several large containers of exotic plants, among them two aloes, one of which was still in good condition. The other, however, was sickly. But precisely the ailing one was the favorite of the lord of the manor, because every summer it bloomed in an altogether inappropriate fashion. This came about in the following way: many years earlier the wind had carried a foreign seed from the swampy moat into the bucket of the sickly aloe. And so every year, right in the midst of its already yellowed leaves, the white and red umbels of the flowering rush or *butomus umbellatus* sprang up. Every stranger who passed by, if he did not by chance happen to be an authority, mistook these umbels to be genuine aloe blossoms, and the lord of the manor took good care not to destroy this belief which had become a source of great amusement for him.

And just as everything around here bore the name Stechlin, so too, of course, the lord of the manor himself. *He* too was a Stechlin.

Dubslav von Stechlin, Major, retired, and already a good bit over sixty, was the archetype of those Brandenburgers of the nobility, albeit of the gentler persuasion, one of those refreshing characters in whom even weaknesses were transformed into good qualities. He still possessed to the hilt that peculiarly attractive sense of self-esteem that characterized all of those who "were around these parts even before the Hohenzollerns." But he kept this self-esteem entirely to himself and if it nevertheless did come to the fore, it clothed itself in humor, sometimes even self-irony, for it was completely in keeping with his nature to place a question mark after everything in general. The most attractive of all his traits was a deeply felt warmth of character, which came directly from the heart. And while he was otherwise inclined to turn a blind eye, arrogance and conceit were more or less the only things which really ever outraged him. He derived pleasure from hearing any plain-spoken opinion, the more drastic and extreme, the better. That said opinion should concur with his own, was far from his desire. Indeed, almost the opposite. Paradoxes were his passion. "I'm really not clever enough to make them myself," he would always say, "but when others do, there's always something to'em. Absolutely incontestable truths simply don't exist, and if there are any, they're boring." He enjoyed listening to a good conversation and took great satisfaction in chatting himself.

The old squire's life had been typically in keeping with the traditions of the Brandenburg Mark. From boyhood days happier in the saddle than behind a book, not until twice failing at it had he victoriously steered his way through the cadet's examination. Immediately thereafter he had joined the Brandenburg Cuirassiers, with whom, of course, his father had also served. His entrance into the regiment more or less coincided with the beginning of the reign of Friedrich Wilhelm IV, and whenever he mentioned that fact, he took pleasure in poking a bit of fun at himself by stressing that "all great events have their accompanying secondary phenomena." The years spent in the cuirassiers had been by and large peaceful ones except for 1864 when he was in Schleswig, but here too without actually "seeing action."

"For a fellow from the Mark," he always held, "the main thing is just having been there at all. The rest is in the Good Lord's hands." And he grinned whenever he said something of that sort, leaving it up to his listeners as to whether he really meant it or was just having one of his little jokes.

Little more than a year before the outbreak of the 1864 war a son had been born to him and scarcely had he returned to duty at his garrison in Brandenburg than he applied for his discharge to withdraw to Castle Stechlin, which had been half-neglected since his father's death. Happy days awaited him there, the happiest of his life. But they were of brief duration; the very next year his wife died. Taking another was not for him, in part because of a sense of order and in part for aesthetic considerations. "After all," he maintained, "we all believe more or less in a resurrection (which is to say he personally really did not), and if I put in an appearance up there with one woman on my right and another on my left, well, that's always sort of an embarrassing business."

Comments like these — as is only too frequently the case when parental deeds encounter the disapproval of their children — were in reality directed at his thrice-married father, with whom he found fault in all sorts of things large and small. For example, the fact that he, the son, had been endowed with the Pomeranian[4] name "Dubslav." "Sure enough, my mother actually was a Pomeranian. And from the island of Usedom to boot. And her brother, well it's true, his name was Dubslav. And so just on account of my uncle there wasn't really that much to object to as far as the name goes, and all the less since he was a rich uncle. That when all's said and done he shamelessly left me in the lurch is something else again. But nevertheless, I'll stick to my guns, fooling around with names like that is just plain confusing. Anybody who comes from the Mark ought to have a name like Joachim or Woldemar. 'So shalt thou dwell in the land and be named in an honest fashion.' A fellow from Friesack better not have a name like Raoul."

Dubslav von Stechlin thus remained a widower. It had been almost thirty years now. In the beginning it had been difficult for him, but all that now lay behind him, and he lived '*comme philosophe*' in keeping with the words and ways of the great king, whom he at all times regarded with admiration. There was his man, more so than anyone else who had since made a name for himself. That became evident every time he was told he had a head like Bismarck's. "Well yes, yes, that I do. I'm even supposed to look like him. But people always say that as if I should be grateful for it. If only I knew to whom. Maybe to the Good Lord or when all's said and done, maybe even to Bismarck himself. But then we Stechlins don't come from such poor stock either. And besides, I for one served with the Sixth Cuirassiers and Bismarck only with the Seventh. And as everybody knows, the lower number always ranks higher here in Prussia — so that puts me one up on him. And Friedrichsruh, where everybody's making a pilgrimage these days, isn't supposed to be much more than just a cottage either. So we're even on that score too. And a lake like our Stechlin, well now, he doesn't have anything like that for sure. A thing like that is really rare."

Yes, Dubslav was proud of his lake. But all the less proud was he of his castle, which was why it irritated him whenever it was described as such. He put up with it from the poor folk, "For them it's a castle, but otherwise it's just an old barn and nothing else." And so he preferred to talk about his "house," and whenever he wrote a letter, at the top stood "Stechlin House." He was also aware that it was no castle life that he lived. In the old days, when the old brick structure still stood, with its thick towers and lookout platform, from which one could see far out over the countryside above the crowns of the trees, well, yes, in those days there had been a real castle way of life. The Stechlins of those times had participated in all the festivities that the counts of Ruppin or the Mecklenburg dukes had offered, and had been in-laws with the Boitzenburgs and the Bassewitzes.[5] But nowadays the Stechlins were folk of modest means, just able to hold their own and constantly seeking to pull themselves up a bit by means of "the right kind of marriage."

In fact, Dubslav's father had acquired his three wives in this very manner. To be sure, only the first had justified the confidence placed in her. For the present lord of the manor, however, who emanated from the second wife, there had unfortunately been no immediate advantages from that union, and Dubslav von Stechlin would never have been free and clear of worries and embarrassments great and small, had he not had his old friend Baruch Hirschfeld in neighboring Gransee.

This old-timer, who kept the large dry goods store on the marketplace and moreover carried the latest fashions including ladies' hats, in regard to which it was always said that Gerson[6] always delivered everything to him first, this old Baruch — without forgetting the business side of things in the process — had a soft spot in his heart for the old lord of Stechlin manor, which, whenever the matter of a new debenture was on the docket, led regularly to somewhat delicate disputations between Hirschfeld father and Hirschfeld son.

"Good God, Isadore, I know, you go in for whatever's new. But what is it, this new business? What's new is always holding meetings on our marketplace and one of these days it'll storm our shop and take our hats, one by one, and our egret feathers and the ostrich feathers. Me, I'm for the old things and for good old Herr von Stechlin. After all, his grandfather's father, he fell in that big battle at Prague and paid with his life."

"Sure, that one paid; at least he paid with his life. But this one we got today . . ."

"He pays too, when he can, and when he's got. And if he hasn't got, and I say 'Herr von Stechlin, I'll just put down seven and a half,' he doesn't haggle and doesn't start to dicker. And if he goes bottom up, well, then we got the property, middle quality ground and woods and game and good fishing. I can always see it real small in my telescope and I can even make out the church tower."

"But Poppa dear, what are we supposed to do wit' a church tower?"

Conversations between Hirschfeld father and son frequently took such a turn and what the elder Hirschfeld for the time being viewed "in the telescope" might indeed have by now become reality were it not for old Dubslav's ten-year-older sister Adelheid and the wealth she had inherited from her mother: Sister Adelheid, Domina of the convent at Wutz. It was she who helped out or made her endorsement whenever things were going poorly or even seemed to be coming to an end. But she did not help out of love for her brother — against whom, very much on the contrary, she had quite a few objections — but merely from a general sense of Stechlin family feeling. Prussia counted for something and the Mark Brandenburg as well, but most important of all were the Stechlins, and the thought of seeing the old castle pass into other hands, especially into such as those suggested above, was unbearable to her. And beyond all this there was, of course, her god-child, her nephew Woldemar, for whom she harbored all the love which she denied her brother.

Yes, the Domina lent her assistance, but such assistance notwithstanding, the feeling of estrangement between brother and sister continued to grow, and thus it came to pass that old Dubslav, who neither enjoyed visiting his sister in Wutz Convent nor being visited by her, had no one in the way of company except his Pastor Lorenzen (Woldemar's former teacher) and his sexton and village school teacher, Krippenstapel. To these at best could be added Chief Forester Katzler who had been a military courier and seen quite a bit of the world. But even these three put in an appearance only when called, and so there was really only one person who was always there to be held accountable at any and every moment. That was Engelke, his old servant who had gone through everything with his master for almost fifty years, his happy days as a lieutenant, his brief marriage, and his long loneliness. Engelke, older by a year than his master, had become his intimate, albeit without any intimacy. Dubslav knew how to draw the line between them. In any case it would have worked out even if he hadn't any such skill. For Engelke was one of those good souls who are devoted and humble not from calculation or cleverness, but by nature, and who find their complete fulfillment in loyal service. On regular days, winter or summer, he was clad in a linen outfit, and only when called on to serve at table did he wear real livery of sand-colored cloth with large buttons on it. Those were buttons which had seen the days of the Rheinsberg Prince Heinrich, for which reason Dubslav, when once again finding himself in an embarrassing situation, had remarked to the recently deceased old Herr von Kortschädel, "Yes sir, Kortschädel, if I could turn over that Engelke of mine to the Brandenburg Provincial Museum, just the way he walks and talks there, I'd get me a year's income and be clean out of it."

It was in May when old Stechlin made this remark to his friend Kort-schädel. Today, however, was the third of October and a wonderful autumn day besides. Dubslav, usually rather sensitive to drafts, had ordered all the doors opened and from the large entry portal came a refreshing current of air even out to the verandah with its white and black tile floor. A large, somewhat frayed awning had been let down here and provided protection against the sun, whose rays shone through its holes to play a shadow game on the tiles. Garden chairs stood all about, but in front of a bench, which leaned against the house wall, double straw mats had been laid. On this very bench, a picture of contentment, sat the old Stechlin squire himself in a casual jacket and broad-brimmed felt hat. Puffing numerous rings from his meerschaum, he looked out at a circular garden, in the middle of which gurgled a small fountain surrounded by flowers. Off to the right ran a so-called poet's walk, at the end of which a fairly high lookout tower arose, hammered together from all sorts of timbers. High atop was a platform with a flag pole from which flew, black and white, the Prussian flag, the whole thing rather tattered.

Just a short time ago Engelke had wanted to sew a red stripe on it,[7] but his suggestion had not carried the day. "Let it be. I'm not for it. That old black and white one is still barely holding together; but if you go sewing something red on it, it'll tear for sure."

7

His pipe had gone out and Dubslav was just about to get up from his seat and call for Engelke, when the latter stepped out on the verandah from the garden room.

"Good thing you've come Engelke . . . . But you've got what looks like a telegram there in your hand. I can't stand telegrams. Always somebody's croaked or there's somebody's coming who'd have better stayed home."

Engelke grinned. "The young master's coming."

"And you know that already?"

"Sure. Brose told me."

"Well, well. Official secrets. Well, let's have it."

And with these remarks he opened the telegram and read: "Dear Papa. With you by six. Rex and von Czako accompanying me. Your Woldemar."

Engelke stood by and waited.

"Well, what do we do now, Engelke?" said Dubslav, turning the telegram over and over. "And it's from Cremmen, and just this morning," he continued. "That means they must have spent the night in Cremmen. That's no joke either."

"But Cremmen isn't really all that bad."

"Oh, of course, of course. It's just that they have such short beds there . . . . But after all, when a fellow's a cavalry officer like Woldemar, he can do the forty miles from Berlin to Stechlin in one shot. Why the overnight stay? And Rex and von Czako accompanying him. I don't know anybody named Rex and don't know a von Czako either. Probably regimental comrades. Have we got anything in the house?"

"I think so, Master. And anyway, what do we have our Mamsell for? She'll be able to find something."

"Well then, fine. All right, we've got something. But who else should we invite? Just me alone won't do. I don't care to set the likes of me in front of anybody anymore. Czako, that might still do. But Rex. Even if I don't know him, for somebody as fine as Rex I just won't do anymore. I've gotten too old fashioned. What do you think? Will the Gundermanns be up to it?"

"Oh, they'll be up to it. He for sure and she never does anything but just sit around."

"Well then, Gundermanns. Fine. And then maybe the Chief Forester and his wife. Their oldest has the measles, true enough, and his wife, I mean his lady — and 'his lady' isn't the right word either — she's expecting again. You never know where you stand with her and what you're supposed to call her, Frau Chief Forester Katzler or Your Highness. But we can give it a try anyway. And then our pastor. At least he's cultured. Just Gundermann by himself isn't enough, really only a hayseed. And since he's got that mill at Siebenmühlen, he's even less."

Engelke nodded.

"Well then, better send Martin. But he's to dress properly. Or else maybe Brose is still here. He can stop in at Gundermanns on his way back. And have him tell them seven o'clock. But no earlier. Else they just sit around so long and nobody knows what to talk about. With him, I mean. She's always gabbing . . . And give Brose a schnapps and fifty pfennig."

"I'll give him thirty."

"No you don't. Fifty. First off he certainly has brought us something, and now he's taking something back with him. That's as good as double duty, for sure. Mind you, fifty. Don't skimp on him."

2

About the same time the telegraph messenger stopped by the Gundermanns to deliver old Herr von Stechlin's invitation, Woldemar, Rex, and Czako, who had announced their arrival for six o'clock, rode out of Cremmen abreast. Fritz, Woldemar's groom, followed the three of them. Their route passed through Wutz. As they neared the village and convent of this name, Woldemar carefully turned off towards the left because he wished to avoid the possibility of encountering his Aunt Adelheid, the Domina of the convent. Although he was on good terms with her, and, as was his custom, even intended to pay his respects on the return journey to Berlin, at this moment such an encounter, which would have prevented his punctual arrival in Stechlin, was the last thing he desired. For this reason he described a wide half circle and had the convent a quarter hour behind him before he turned back to the main road. The latter, running through moor and meadowlands, was a splendid path for riding, still showing a grassy line in many places, so that for six miles they were able to move on in a brisk trot until they reached an avenue which lead directly to Castle Stechlin. Here all three let their reins go slack and rode on in a walk. Above them splendid old chestnut trees arched, endowing their approach with a comfortable and homey atmosphere and at the same time an almost solemn one.

"Why it's almost like the nave of a church," remarked Rex, who rode on the left flank. "Don't you agree, Czako?"

"If you wish, I suppose. But begging your pardon, Rex, I find that turn of phrase almost trivial for a ministerial assessor."[8]

"Fine, see if you can come up with anything better."

9

"I wouldn't think of it. Under such circumstances whoever tries to come up with anything better, always says something worse."

As this conversation continued for a while they at last reached a point from which with complete clarity one could take in the whole of the picture spreading out at the end of the avenue. The view was not only clear but also so striking that Rex and Czako spontaneously came to a halt.

"Great guns, Stechlin, that really is charming," remarked Czako to Woldemar, riding on the other flank. "Strikes me as right out of a fairy tale, a regular *fata morgana* — although actually I've never really seen one up to now. That yellow wall over there just catching the last rays of daylight, that's your enchanted castle, is it? And that bit of gray off to the left there, I'd take it to be the corner of a church. Only thing left is the picket fence on the other side — the schoolmaster lives there, of course. I'll bet I've hit the nail right on the head. But those two black monsters right there in the middle standing out so against the yellow wall — 'standing out' is a bit trivial too by the way. Sorry, Rex. Why they're standing there like the very cherubim themselves. A bit too black, of course. What sort of chaps are they?"

"Those are erratics."

"Erratics?"

"Yes, erratics," repeated Woldemar. "But if that word bothers you, you can call them monoliths too. It's really remarkable, Czako, how extremely discriminating you get about phrases when you're not the one doing the talking at the moment . . . . But now, gentlemen, we've got to get going again at a trot. I'm convinced my papa is standing impatiently on his ramp by this time, and if he catches sight of us coming along at a pace like this, he'll either think we're bringing news of somebody's death or carrying somebody who's been wounded."

A few minutes later and all of them did in fact trot across the timbered bridge followed by Fritz, entering first the front courtyard, then passing the gleaming glass ball. The old man was already standing on the ramp, Engelke at his back, and behind him Martin, the old coachman. Quickly the three dismounted and Martin and Fritz took the horses. And so they stepped into the entrance hall.

"Permit me, dear Papa, to present to you two dear friends of mine: Assessor von Rex, Hauptmann von Czako."

The elder Stechlin shook each by the hand and expressed how happy he was at their visit. "You're most cordially welcome, gentlemen. You've no idea how much pleasure you're giving a cantanker-

10

ous old hermit like me. Don't get to see anything, don't hear anything. I'm hoping for a whole sack of the latest news."

"Dear me, Herr Major," replied Czako, "we've been away from things now for twenty-four hours, you know. And besides, who can still compete with the newspapers these days! Lucky thing some regularly come a day late in the mail. With the very latest news, I mean. Maybe otherwise too."

"Very true," laughed Dubslav. "They say anyway that conservatism is a retarding force by its very nature. You can excuse a lot just on that score. But here come your knapsacks, gentlemen. Engelke, take these gentlemen to their rooms. It's now six-fifteen. At seven, if you please."

Engelke had in the meantime picked up the two plaid bed rolls somewhat old-fashionedly designated as "knapsacks" by Dubslav, and preceding the two gentlemen, took them towards the double staircase which, at exactly the point where the two stairways crossed, formed a rather spacious landing with a gallery of small columns. Between these columns, however, and in fact facing the entry hall, a rococo clock with a figure of Chronos atop bearing a scythe had been installed. Czako pointed it out and said quietly to Rex, "A bit spooky."

It was a feeling which he found intensified when they reached the upper hallway which had been laid out with a tremendous waste of space. Over the doorway to a large room towards the rear hung a wooden plaque with the inscription: "Museum," while on both sides along the walls of the gallery to the right and left stood heavy cabinets of birch and oak, really splendid pieces with two large paintings between them, one a fortress with thick brick towers, the other a knight, larger than life, obviously from Frundsberg's day,[9] when the varied colors of the *Landsknecht* era began to cover armor.

"N' ancestor, right?" asked Czako.

"Yes, Herr Hauptmann. And he's down below in the church too."

"Same as here as well?"

"No, just a gravestone. Worn down a bit by now. But you can still see it's the same fellow."

Czako nodded. By now they had reached a corner room which bordered the hall on one side and a narrow corridor on the other. There too was the door. Engelke, going ahead, opened it and hung the two plaid bedrolls on the hooks of a clothes tree located right at the entrance. Immediately next to it was a bellpull with a green, somewhat worn tassel attached. Engelke indicated it saying, "If you gentlemen care for anything else . . . and at seven . . . the gong will be rung twice." And with that he left, leaving the two to make themselves comfortable.

11

Rex and Czako had been put up in two adjoining rooms; the first, larger and somewhat more luxuriously furnished, with a free-standing, full length mirror and dressing table. The mirror could even be tipped. The bed in this the front room even had a small canopy and next to it an *étagère*, on the topmost shelf of which stood a Meissen porcelain figurine raising her brief skirts, while on the lower shelf lay a New Testament, a chalice, cross and palm branch imprinted on its cover.

Czako took the petite Meissen doll and said, "Unless our friend Woldemar was involved in this arrangement, as far as props go, we've got a bit of prescience here that can't be beat. This little doll here *pour moi*, the New Testament *pour vous*."

"Czako, if only you could cut out that teasing of yours."

"Oh, don't say things like that, Rex. Why, you love me just because of my teasing."

And now they passed from the front room into the somewhat smaller living room, in which mirror and dressing table were missing. Making up for that, however, was a rococo sofa with bright blue satin on which were white flowers.

"Well now, Rex," said Czako, "how are we going to share this? I say you take the canopy next door and I'll take the rococo sofa, with its white flowers thrown in, could be they're lilies. I'll bet this little bit of a sofa here's got quite a story to tell."

"Rococo things always have a story to tell," said Rex by way of agreement. "But that's a hundred years back. The present inhabitant doesn't look like that sort to me, thank God. Of course I wouldn't put a bit of spooking past this old barn, but nothing in the way of rococo tales. Rococo is always immoral anyway. How do you like the old boy, by the way?"

"Top notch. I'd never have thought that our friend Woldemar could have had such a first rate old boy."

"I'd say," said Rex, "that almost sounds as if you've got something against our friend Stechlin."

"Which is by no means the case. Our Stechlin is the best chap in the world and if I didn't hate the damnable phrase, I'd even have to call him a 'perfect gentleman.' But . . . ."

"But . . . ?"

"But he just doesn't fit into the place he's in."

"Which place?"

"In his regiment."

"Come on now, Czako. I really don't understand you. He's stupendously well-liked. Everybody's favorite. The colonel puts great store by him and the princes are practically courting him . . . ."

"Right. That's just it. The princes, the princes."

"What's that supposed to mean? How do you mean that?"

"Oh, it's a long story. Much too long to drag it all up now before dinner. After all, it's already half past and we've got to get going. And anyway, it applies to quite a few, not just our Stechlin."

"Always more and more obscure. Constantly more enigmatic," said Rex.

"Well then, maybe I'll solve the enigma for you. After all, we can be pulling ourselves together and still have a little confabulation on the side.

"'The princes are courting him,' that's the way you deigned to put it, and I replied, 'That's just it.' And I can only repeat those remarks for you again. The princes — right, that's what the whole thing has to do with and even more with the fact that the finer regiments are constantly getting even finer. Just take a look at the old ranking lists, the really old ones, I mean, last century and then more or less up to 1806. When you get to the Regiment Garde du Corps or the Regiment Gensdarmes, you'll find those good old Prussian names of ours there, Marwitz, Wakenitz, Kracht, Löschebrand, Bredow, Rochow. Only now and then that some high-titled Silesian got himself mixed in. Naturally, there were princes in those days too, but it was the regular nobility that set the tone, and those few princes had to be pretty glad when they didn't bother anybody.

"But that sort of thing's all over now that we've become Kaiser and Reich. Completely done with. Of course, I'm not talking about the provinces, not Lithuania or Masuria, but about the Guard, the regiments that are right under the eyes of His Majesty. And then to top it all off, these Dragoon Guards! They always were posh, but since *pour combler le bonheur*[10] they've become 'Regiment of the Queen of Great Britain and Ireland'[11] they're getting even more so. And the more posh they get, the more princes come in, about whom I might add that there are more these days than meets the eye in any case, because there are some who really are and simply don't dare admit it. And then, if you add in the old timers, who are just '*à la suite*,'[12] but still always manage to be around when something's going on, well, when you put all that together, it may not be a parquet of kings[13] but it certainly is a circus of princes.

"And now our good friend Stechlin has been put into the midst of all that. He naturally does what he can and more or less goes along with certain kinds of extravagances, extravagances of feeling, extravagances of attitude, and if need be, extravagances of freedom too. More or less a little touch of socialism. But in the long run that's difficult to pull off. Real princes can afford things like that. They're not about to get 'bebelized' very easily. But Stechlin! Stechlin is a charming fellow, but, after all, he's only a human being."

"And you say that, Czako. You of all people, who always puts so much stress on the humanity factor?"

"Yes, Rex. I do indeed. Today as always. There are things that aren't fitting for everybody. One fellow can get away with it, the other can't. When our friend Stechlin withdraws into this old castle barn of his, he can be as much a regular fellow as he wants. But for a Dragoon Guardsman, it's not enough. I'll not mention that biblical business about casting-off-the-old-Adam-in-you and becoming a different person. But it's still got a sort of secondary meaning."

While Rex and Czako were dressing for dinner and alternately discussing the elder and younger Stechlin, those who were the object of this conversation, father and son, were pacing back and forth in the garden, holding a conversation of their own.

"I'm grateful to you that you've brought your friends along. I hope they enjoy themselves. My life is a bit too isolated, and besides it will be good to get used to having people around again. You've probably read that our good old Kortschädel has died and in about two weeks we'll be having an election here to replace him. That means I've got to step up and make myself popular. The Conservatives want me and nobody else. Actually, I don't want to, but I should. And so it's just the thing for me that you've brought some people with whom I can so to speak get in practice again for the outside world. Are they the kind of fellows who enjoy a good talk?"

"Oh very much so, Papa, maybe even too much. At least one of them."

"That'll be that Czako fellow for sure. Strange, those chaps from the Czar Alexander Regiment[14] all like to talk. But I'm really all for it; silence isn't the thing for everybody. And anyway, we're supposed to differentiate ourselves from the animals through speech as well, you know. Well then, whoever talks the most is the purest human being. And with this Czako, I could see that right away. But that Rex fellow. A ministerial assessor, you say. Does he come from that religious family?"

"No, Papa. You're making the same mistake that almost everybody does. That pious family, that's the Reckes, counts and very high up. The Rexes too, of course, but really not quite as high up as all that and not as pious, either. But you could say my friend the ministerial assessor has been getting a good start on possibly catching up with the Reckes."

14

"Well then, I was right about him too. He's sort of got the look that makes you suspect something like that, a bit lacking in flesh and so clean shaven. Did you find somebody right off in Cremmen for shaving?"

"He's always got his whole kit with him, nothing but English things. He won't hear a thing about Solingen or Suhl."[15]

"And do you have to be careful with him whenever the conversation turns to religious matters? Of course, I am actually religious, as you know, at least more religious than my good pastor. Things are going from bad to worse with him every day. But sometimes I am a bit more unrestrained in my way of expressing myself than a fellow maybe ought to be, and when it comes to 'descended into hell'[16] it can happen that *nolens volens* I talk a bit of crazy stuff. Well then, what's the story on him? Do I have to be careful? Or does he just go along?"

"I wouldn't exactly say that. It seems to me, he stands just about the way most people stand, which is to say, he doesn't rightly know."

"Right, right. Well-acquainted with that situation."

"And because be doesn't rightly know, he's got, so to speak, a choice, and so he chooses what's currently the accepted thing and what puts him in the good graces of the higher ups. I really can't find that so awful, either. Some call him a 'climber.' But if he is one, at least he's not one of the worst. He really does have a good character and in the *cercle intime* he can be quite charming. He doesn't so much make himself well liked by what he says, or at best only to a very small extent, but I could almost say, he makes himself liked by the way he listens. Czako says our friend Rex makes up with his ears for what he neglects with his mouth. Czako knows how to deal with him better than anyone else. He teases him constantly. And Rex, which I really do find charming, puts up with his teasing. So you can see he's someone you can get along with. His religiosity isn't a lie, just something inculcated into him. An acquired habit, and so it's finally become second nature with him."

"I'll put him next to Lorenzen at the dinner table. Then the two of them can see how they get along with one another. Maybe we'll get to see a conversion. I mean, Rex'll convert the pastor. But right now I hear a coach coming up the road from the village. That'll be the Gundermanns for sure. They always come too early. The poor fellow heard about the etiquette of kings somewhere and now he's making too much use of it. Self-taught persons always overdo it. I'm one myself, so I can say things like that.

"Well, we'll continue our talk tomorrow morning; can't do anymore today. You'll have to spruce yourself up a bit yet, and I want to put on m' black coat. That's the least I owe our dear Frau Gundermann, after all. She still always dolls herself up like a sled horse, by the way, just like she always did, and still wears that weird looking plume in her hair roll. That is, if it really is hers."

3

In the entrance hall below, Engelke twice struck an old shield functioning as a gong which was suspended from one of the two protruding pillars bearing the entire stairway. These same two pillars, along with the landing and the rococo clock placed before it, formed a rather picturesque portico leading to the garden salon, the main room of the ground floor. A visiting architect from the capital city had once remarked of the former that the entire litany of architectural misdeeds of Castle Stechlin was made up for by this bizarre but artistic stroke of inspiration.

The clock with the scythe bearer was just striking seven as Rex and Czako descended the steps, and making a turn, headed for the odd structure that had been the object of such professional leniency. As the two friends passed the latter — the large doors were already open — they could easily look into the salon and saw that several of the guests invited in their honor had by now appeared. Dubslav, in a dark frock coat with the ribboned rosettes of the Order of the Prussian as well as the Wendic Crown in his button hole,[17] approached them as they entered, welcoming them again with his usual warm cordiality. Immediately leading both into the circle of those already assembled, he said, "Please allow me to make introductions: Herr and Frau von Gundermann from Siebenmühlen, Pastor Lorenzen, Chief Forester Katzler." Then, turning to his left, "Ministerial Assessor von Rex, Hauptmann von Czako of the Regiment Czar Alexander."

All bowed, whereupon Dubslav sought to establish a link between Rex and Pastor Lorenzen, while Woldemar, as an Adlatus to his father, sought to do the same between Czako and Katzler. Both succeeded with ease, because on all sides neither social graces nor good will were lacking.

Yet at the same time Rex could not avoid closely studying the pair from Siebenmühlen, despite Herr von Gundermann's appearing in white tie and tails and Frau von Gundermann in a flower-covered satin dress with a fan of marabou feathers — he obviously a parvenu and she a Berliner from one of the northeastern suburbs.

Rex took it all in. He did not have the chance to think long about it, however, because at that very moment Dubslav took Frau Gundermann's arm and thus gave the sign that the party should make its way to the table set in the adjoining room. Everyone followed in the pairings they had previously established, but broke up once more in keeping with the table arrangement Dubslav had previously worked out. The two Stechlins, father and son, took places at the narrow ends of the table, across from one another. To Dubslav's right and left Herr and Frau Gundermann were seated, and to the right and left of Woldemar, Rex and Lorenzen. The center seats were occupied by Katzler and Czako. Next to a large and aged oaken buffet close to the door stood Engelke and Martin, Engelke in his sand-colored livery with its big buttons, and Martin, whose only task lay in keeping in touch with the kitchen, simply in a black frock coat and top boots.

Old Dubslav was in high good humor, and touching glasses confidentially with Frau von Gundermann after the first spoonfuls of soup, thanked her for putting in an appearance and apologized for the late invitation. "But Woldemar's telegram didn't come until twelve. That's how it is with this telegraphing business, some things are improved but some are made worse too, and more elegant manners suffer absolutely for sure. Just the form, the style. Brevity's supposed to be a virtue, but saying things briefly usually means saying them coarsely. Every trace of courtesy gets lost, and the word 'Herr' for example, is nowhere to be found. I had a friend once who quite seriously maintained, the ugliest mongrel was the best looking. So nowadays you could almost say, the coarsest telegram is the most elegant. At least the most perfect of its kind. Anybody who comes up with another five-pfennig saving is a genius."

Dubslav's comments were initially addressed to Frau von Gundermann, but were quite soon directed more at Gundermann himself, for which reason the latter responded. "Indeed, Herr von Stechlin. It's all a sign of the times. And quite indicative that precisely the word 'Herr', as you just had the kindness to point out, is as good as done away with. 'Herr' has become nonsense. 'Herr' won't do for those 'Herren' — I mean of course the ones who want to rule the world these days. But what can you expect? All these innovations, in which unfortunately the state too is taking part, what do they amount to? Aiding and abetting insubordination, nothing but water on the mills of the social democrats. Nothing more. And there isn't a soul around with the will or strength to shut this water off. But just the same, Herr von Stechlin — I wouldn't contradict you if the facts didn't force me — just the same, we can't get along without telegraphy. Especially way out here in our isolation. And with the constant fluctuation of the market. Particularly in the saw mill and lumber cutting business . . . ."

"Right as rain, my dear Gundermann. What I was just saying there . . . If I had said the opposite, it would have been just as right.

The devil isn't half as black as we paint'm. And telegraphy too. And we're not either.

"When you get right down to it though, it really is a marvelous thing, this science business, this electric current. Tap, tap, tap and if we had a mind to (even though we don't), why we could let the Emperor of China know we've gotten together here and were thinking about him. And then all these odd mix-ups in time and hours. Almost comical. When the September Revolution broke out back in seventy in Paris, they knew about it over there in America a couple of hours before there even was a revolution.

"The September Revolution, I said. Could've been another one though. They have so many over there that it's easy to get mixed up. One of'm was in June, another in July. Anybody who doesn't have a really knockout memory'll have a bad time for sure . . . .

"Engelke, offer the lady some fish again. And maybe Herr von Czako . . . ."

"Certainly, Herr von Stechlin," said Czako. "First off as a real gourmet but then out of the pure desire for knowledge or urge for progress. A fellow really wants to be part of whatever's going on at the moment, or what in some way counts towards the development of mankind, in whatever way one can, and these days fish nutrition is right up there at the top. And besides, fish are supposed to contain lots of phosphorus, and phosphorus, so they say, 'makes you bright.'"

"Sure," giggled Frau von Gundermann, who at the word "bright" felt herself personally singled out. "Why phosphorus was around even before the Swedish safety matches came in."

"Oh, a long time before that," concurred Czako. "But," he went on, turning to Dubslav, "what especially fascinates me about this carp — a really first rate specimen, by the way — is this, the fact that after all it most probably comes from your famous lake about which I've already been informed by your son, Woldemar.

"This remarkable lake, this Stechlin of yours! And then I involuntarily ask myself — because carp really do get old, which is why for example we have what they call mossback — what revolutions have passed by this splendid example of his kind? I don't know if I can peg him to be a hundred and fifty years old, but if so, he would have participated in the Lisbon affair as a youngster, and as a really old-timer, the recent eruption of Krakatoa. And taking all that into consideration, I can't suppress the question . . . ."

Dubslav smiled in agreement.

". . . And taking all that into consideration, I can't suppress the question, whenever things get to rumbling in that Lake Stechlin of yours, or that big funnel even begins to form — from which, if I've

18

heard correctly, now and then the crowing rooster emerges — how does this Stechlin carp, obviously the fellow who's most closely involved, how does he behave during all the announcing of that sort of world events? Does he envy the rooster, who gets to crow out across the Ruppin countryside, or is he instead a coward who heads for cover in the mud at the bottom, so to speak a bourgeois, who next morning asks, 'Are they still shooting up there?'"

"My dear Herr von Czako, answering your question has its difficulties, even for a resident of Stechlin. No mind in the whole of creation can penetrate the innermost things of nature. And the carp can surely be reckoned among the innermost and most secret of all. He is, in fact, extremely stupid. But according to the laws of probability, when the big eruption got going he probably headed for cover. The fact is, we all head for cover. Heroism is the exception and mostly the product of a desperate situation. You don't have to agree with me, by the way, after all you're still on active duty."

"Quite, quite." said Czako.

Much, much differently ran the conversation on the opposite side of the table. Rex, whenever he came to the country, either in official or unofficial capacity, felt the inclination to pursue questions of social import. Every time, for example, he could not resist making all sorts of observations concerning the numerical relationship of children born in and out of wedlock, partly for the benefit of the general welfare, or partly for the sake of morality. Again today he had turned to this favorite topic in a conversation begun with Pastor Lorenzen. But after Dubslav had cut the thread with an interjected question, instead of Lorenzen he now found himself temporarily occupied with Katzler, who by chance he learned had formerly been a military courier. That presented him with a good conversational topic and induced him to ask if the Herr Chief Forester did not sometimes painfully feel the difference between his past and his present. His former profession as a diplomatic military guard, he would have presumed, must have taken him out into the wide, wide world, whereas he was now "stabilized."

"Stabilization" was among Rex's favorite turns of phrase and derived from the carefully chosen vocabulary of foreign terms which he, having had to deal with them in an official capacity, had acquired from the decrees of Friedrich Wilhelm I and integrated into his own legal German. Katzler, a splendid fellow, but in the arena of conversation frequently possessing but a deficient orientational ability, did not immediately catch the drift of the ministerial assessor's somewhat elaborate line of thinking and was glad when the alert pastor, who in

19

the meantime had once more managed to liberate himself, came to his aid in the question posed by Rex.

"I do believe I hear in his question," commented Lorenzen, "that Herr von Rex is inclined to grant preference to life in the world outside over that in our peaceful county. I don't know, however, if we can agree with him in the matter. I, for one, most assuredly not. But our Herr Chief Forester too is presumably glad to have the days he used to spend as a courier gadding about in a railroad car behind him as well. Of course, as they say, 'Narrow grows the mind in a narrow sphere'[18] and in most cases that may be true. But then not always, and in any case unworldly things have certain great merits."

"Spoken right from my heart, Herr Pastor Lorenzen," said Rex. "If it sounded for a moment as if the 'globe-trotter' were my ideal, then I'm quite prepared to be gainsaid in the matter. But there's still something to be said for being-at-home-in-the-outside-world as well, and if you nevertheless make such a case for isolation and tranquillity, you're no doubt making a case for your own situation. For, after all, just as the Herr Chief Forester has withdrawn from the world, so too it would seem have you. In doing so, the two of you, quite individually of course, have followed your own hearts, and perhaps my personal inclinations might indeed take the same path. Nevertheless there must be others who are not at all interested in such a withdrawal from the world, who perhaps quite to the contrary find their destiny not in yielding to the needs of the individual but rather in dealing with the multitudes. I believe I know through friend Stechlin with what questions you've concerned yourself for quite some time, and I ask only that I might offer my congratulations to you on the matter. You've taken your stand in the Christian-Social movement. But take the man who created it, who is perhaps personally close to you, he and his activities really speak for me. His sphere is not the spiritual welfare of the individual, not some country parish, but instead a metropolis. Stöcker's activities and his mission are a repudiation of the idea that activity on a narrow and limited stage necessarily has to be the more beneficial."

Lorenzen was accustomed, whether in praise or criticism, to being placed in parallel with the equally celebrated as well as beleaguered court chaplain and always felt it to be a kind of homage. But no less did he regularly feel the deep difference which lay between the great agitator and his own quiet way.

"I believe, Herr von Rex," he continued, "that you have described the 'father of the Berlin movement,' quite correctly, perhaps even to the satisfaction of the personage described himself, which, as they say, is not supposed to be particularly easy. He has achieved a great deal and stands apparently under a triumphant sign. He has put down roots hither and yon and finds himself beloved and admired, and not only on the part of those for whom he charitably provides shoes, but perhaps almost more in the camp of those from whom he takes the leather for them. He has already acquired so many epithets, and that of St. Crispin[19] would not be the worst. There must be many who in the best sense envy his achievements. But I fear the day is nigh when this so calm and at the same time so courageous man, who has set such enormous goals for himself, will yearn to retire to a more secluded existence. He owns, if I am correctly informed, a modest farm somewhere in Franconia[20] and it's indeed possible, in fact, I personally think almost probable, that a more genuine happiness will sooner or later flower for him on that tranquil spot than he has now.

"True, the Bible says, 'Go hence and teach ye all the gentiles' but it's finer still if, seeking us out, the world comes to us. And the world will come when the right personality opens itself to it. Take that priest from Wörishofen[21] — he doesn't go looking for people, the people go looking for him. And when they come to him, he heals them, heals them with the simplest and most natural thing there is. Transfer that from the external to the inner being, and there you have my ideal. Digging your wellspring right at the spot where you stand. A Home Mission for the immediate vicinity, be it with the old, or be it with the new."

"Well then, with the new," said Woldemar, and extended his hand to his old teacher.

But the latter responded, "Not all that unconditionally with the new. Preferably with the old, as far as it's in any way possible. And with the new only as far as need be."

The meal had in the meantime progressed and reached a course which was a speciality of Castle Stechlin and always provoked the admiration of its guests: boneless thrush breasts, prepared with a dark consume sauce, which on those autumnal days when the berries of the mountain ash were ripe, customarily found its way to the table as a higher form of game ragout. Engelke poured a well-aged Burgundy to go with it, one from older, better days, and when everyone had partaken of it, Dubslav rose, first to briefly welcome his guests and then to toast the ladies. He needed to keep to this plural form, he said, despite the fact that the feminine world was represented only in the singular, but besides his dear friend and dinner companion (whose hand he proceeded to kiss in homage), he was also at the same time thinking of the "lady" of his friend Katzler, who unfortunately — even though from a familial point of view by reason of a most joyful occasion — had been prevented from appearing in their midst. "Meine Herren, Frau Chief Forester Katzler" — he interjected a brief pause here as if he had been seriously considering a loftier form of address — "Frau Chief Forester Katzler and Frau von Gundermann, to their health!"

Rex, Czako, Katzler rose to touch glasses with Frau von Gundermann. When each had returned to his place, however, they once again took up the private conversations which had been interrupted by the toast, while Dubslav, as a good host, limited himself to interjecting brief remarks left and right. This was not always easy, least of all for the chat going on between the captain and Frau von Gundermann, which was running on without pause, so that any intervention was scarcely possible. Czako was a good conversationalist but he paled next to his partner. The career of her father, originally a teacher of drawing and penmanship, who after a long period of service beginning way back in 1813 had succeeded in reaching the rank of captain in the government cartography department, endowed her in her own eyes with a certain military affiliation. Thus when after repeatedly straining, she finally recognized the insignia of the Alexander Regiment on Czako's epaulettes, she said, "Oh Lord, . . . Alexander. No, I really do say. But, you know, it brought it all back for me right away. Münzstraße. Why we lived on Linienstraße, corner of Weinmeister, I mean, when I met my husband. Before that way out, Schönhauser Allee.

"My goodness, when you meet somebody from your old neighborhood! I'm so happy, Herr Hauptmann. Oh, it's just too gloomy here. And if we didn't have our Herr von Stechlin, why, we practically wouldn't have anything at all. As for the Katzlers," this she whispered very softly, "as for the Katzlers, it's hopeless. They're too high and mighty. You've really got to bow and scrape there. And they're not so great either, when you get right down to it. They still fit in to a certain extent these days. But just you wait and see."

"Very true, very true," said Czako, who, without really understanding anything for certain, merely saw confirmed the feeling he had had during Dubslav's toast that there must be something special about the Katzlers. Frau von Gundermann though, giving up what was for her an uncomfortable whisper, continued in an increasingly louder voice, "we do have Herr von Stechlin, and that really is a lucky thing. And it's only just a good two miles. Most of the others live much too far away, and even if they did live closer, they're not really interested.

"The people around here, the ones we really ought to have to do with, are all so stuffy. And they weigh out everything on a gold balance. I mean, there's lots they don't weigh out on the gold balance, most of them don't have enough for that. Just always their ancestors. And sixteen's the least. I ask you, who's got sixteen right off like that? Gundermann's just been ennobled, and if he hadn't been lucky, he wouldn't have. He started small, you know, just only one mill. Now we have seven, of course, right down along the Rhin. All sawmills. Studs and boards, one by, two by and more. And the floorboards in Berlin, they're practically all from us."

"But my dearest lady, that must certainly give you a sense of accomplishment. All the floorboards in Berlin! And this river Rhin, you mentioned, it connects perhaps a whole chain of lakes and a charming villa probably lies on it! And from within you hear the saw running in the mill next door day and night. And all the trees around it gently swaying. Now and then there's a storm, of course. And you've got a pony cart for your children. I can assume, may I not, that you've got children? When one lives so cut off from everything and is so constantly dependent on one another . . . ."

"It's just like you say, Herr Hauptmann, I have children. But already grown, almost all of them. I got married young, you know. Yes indeed, Herr von Czako. We were all young once. And it's a good thing I've got my children. Otherwise there's not a soul around with whom a body could have a cultured conversation. My husband has his politics and wants to get himself elected. But nothing'll come of that. And whenever I bring home a few good magazines, he doesn't even look at the pictures. And the stories, he says, are just stuff and nonsense and nothing but water on the mills of the social democrats. He prefers his own mills, which, by the way, I find perfectly right and reasonable."

"But you must have lots of people around you, just in your household."

"Oh sure I do. And those mamsells you wind up with, sure, for a few weeks it's fine. But then right away they get to flirting around, preferably with one of the office boys. We have trainees in the sawmill business too, you know. And most of them come from very good families. But those young folks don't watch what they're doing and the next thing you know, you're in for it, and always right off out of the blue. It's all really sad, and now and then it even gets so awful you practically have to be embarrassed."

Czako sighed. "Really a horror to me, all that sort of thing. But I know from maneuvers what all goes on. And with such deviousness . . . nothing more devious than love-sick people. Dear me, there's a topic you could write volumes about. But you said Linienstraße, gracious lady. What number? I know practically every house

23

around there. Nice, charming little houses, always just two stories, at best now and then with an *oeil de bouef*."

"Huh? A what?"

"Big round window without glass. But I do love those houses."

"Right, I can say that about myself too. And it was in houses just like those I spent my best days. When I was still a little snip of a thing, fourteen at the most. And so awfully wild. In those days, you know, they still had stone gutters, and when it rained and everything got flooded, and the boards began to lift up and practically half-float away, then the rats hiding under there didn't know where to go. Then we'd jump on the boards and those little beasties would come out, left and right, and the boys right after them, pants rolled up and nearly always bare legged. And one time, when one of the boys didn't stop banging with his wooden shoe, the monster got tricky and bit the lad so hard that he screamed! No sir! I never did hear anybody ever scream like that since. And it really was horrible."

"Yes, there you have it. And in cases like that nothing but rat catchers can help."

"Right, rat catchers. I've heard of them too. The Pied Piper of Hameln. But they really don't have the likes of them anymore."

"No, gracious lady, those they don't have anymore. At least none of those sorcerers with magic incantations and a pipe to pipe tunes on. But it's not those who I mean, either. I don't at all mean people who do that sort of thing for a living and advertise themselves in the newspapers, weird looking fellows with fur caps. What I mean are simply terriers that are also called 'rat catchers' and really are. And going hunting with a rat catcher like that, why it's just about the most splendid thing you can do."

"But you can't go hunting with a terrier though!"

"Oh, but you can, you can, my dear lady. When I was in Paris, I was stationed there once, you know, I went along down into the so-called catacombs, high-vaulted sewers that run underground. And these sewers are the real rat El Dorado. They've got 'em by the millions. Up top, three million Frenchmen, down below, three million rats. And one time, as I was saying, I went down there and rode through this underworld in a boat, right through the middle of the rats."

"Horrible, horrible. And you got out unharmed?"

"By and large, yes. Because, gracious lady, it was actually a pleasure. We had two of those rat catchers in our boat, you know. One up front, the other in the back. And you should have seen how they went at it. 'Snap' and they had that animal around the ears and it was a goner. And so on and so forth, as fast as you could count, and now and then even faster. I can only compare it with Mr. Carver, that famous Mr. Carver fellow about whom you've read sometime for sure. The fellow who shot three glass balls in a second. And on and on like that. Hundreds of them.

"Yes indeed. A thing like that rat hunt down there, that's something you don't forget. And it was the best thing about the place too. Because whatever else they say about Paris, it's all an exaggeration. Mostly stupid nonsense. What do they have that's so grand? Operas and a circus and a museum. And in one room a Venus, you really can't rightly look at because it insults your sensibilities, especially when you're there in the company of ladies. And we have all that stuff too, when you get right down to it. And some of our things are even better. For example, Niemann and dell'Era.[22] But a battle of the rats like that, I've got to admit, we don't have anything like that. And why not? Because we don't have any catacombs."

Old Dubslav, who had heard the word "catacombs," turned across the table again and said, "Pardon, Herr von Czako, but you mustn't be telling my dear Frau von Gundermann such frightfully serious things, and especially here at table right after carp and horse radish. Catacombs! I beg of you. After all, they were really in Rome and always remind you of the gloomiest times, and that fiendish emperor Nero with those persecutions of his and his torches. And then there was another fellow with a bit longer name who was even more fiendish. And then those poor Christians slunk off into those very catacombs and some of them were betrayed and got killed. No indeed, Herr von Czako. Let's have something more cheerful than that. Right, my dear Frau von Gundermann?"

"Oh no, Herr von Stechlin. It's all so edifying. And when you so rarely get the chance . . . ."

"Well then, as you will. I meant well. Let's touch glasses. Here's to your Rudolph. After all, he's the favorite even if he is the oldest. How old is he now?"

"Twenty-four."

"Wonderful age. And from what I hear, a good fellow. Ought to get out more though. He'll stagnate a bit around here."

"That's what I tell'm too. But he doesn't want to leave. He says there's no place like home."

"Bravo. Then I take it all back. Just let him be. When you get right down to it there really is no place like home. And especially for us here, who've got the advantage of living in the Rheinsberg region. I ask you, where else is there anything like it? First off, the Great King and then Prince Heinrich, who never once lost a battle. And there's some say he was even smarter than his brother. But it wasn't me who said it."

4

Frau von Gundermann apparently wished to yield the right of being first to leave the table, to which she as the only, and therefore eldest lady was entitled, and waited until Dubslav, who for a quarter of an hour had been yearning for his meerschaum, gave the sign for all to rise. Everyone got up quickly to return from the dining room into the salon facing the garden, in which — was it by chance or intentional? — at this instant every form of illumination was lacking. Only in the fire place glimmered a few logs which had half burned during the meal. From the verandah, through the open high glass door, fell the light from the quarter moon standing over the trees in the park.

Everyone assembled directly around Frau von Gundermann to do her the required honors, while Martin brought in lamps and Engelke the coffee. The general conversation lasting a few minutes did not get beyond a restless back and forth throughout that time until the knot in which all were standing once again dispersed into smaller groups.

The first pair to separate were Rex and Katzler. Both were passionate billiard players and, with Katzler leading, they betook themselves first back to the dining room and from thence into the adjoining game room. The somewhat neglected billiard table standing here was almost fifty years old and dated back to the days of the father. Dubslav himself did not make much of this game, nor of games in general. As far as his billiards went, the only thing that interested him was a much darkened cue ball about which a Berlin visitor had once said, "Good grief, Stechlin, where did you ever get *that?* That's the yellowest cue ball I've seen in all my days." Those were remarks which at the time made such an impression on Dubslav that since that day he maintained a somewhat fonder relationship with his billiard table and not without pleasure, spoke of "his cue ball."

The second pair to separate from the company were Woldemar and Gundermann. Gundermann, like all of those who suffer from apoplexy, found it to be too warm everywhere, and after exchanging a few words with Woldemar, indicated the open door. "It's such a beautiful evening, Herr von Stechlin. Couldn't we step out onto the verandah?"

"Why of course, Herr von Gundermann. And since we're making ourselves scarce, we'll want to take all the good stuff along right from the start. Engelke, bring us that little box, you know which one."

"Ah, capital. A few good puffs, that hits the spot better than a soda water. And then it's undoubtedly more acceptable in the open air. My wife, when we're at home, has had to get used to it of course, and at the worst she complains now and then about my smoking like a chimney — well, that's the way it goes, that's what comes of being married — but when you're in somebody else's house, well then, you really do have to show some consideration. Our good old Kortschädel always talked about the '*dehors.*'"

As they were exchanging these remarks Woldemar and Gundermann left the salon and stepped out onto the verandah, to the edge of the steps, where they looked on at the thin column of water springing up in the rounded garden.

"Whenever I see that fountain there," continued Gundermann, "I always have to think of good old Kortschädel. Gone now too. Well, we all have to go sooner or later, and if anybody's sure of a place up there, it's him. Man of honor, through and through, loyal right down to the bone. No speech maker, that's actually always a virtue. Never cost the state any money with a lot of gab. But he knew what was what, and between the two of us, I've heard a thing or two from him, marvelous. And I tell myself, we won't get the likes of him again . . ."

"Ah, that's nothing but looking on the dark side of things, Herr von Gundermann. I think we've got quite a few who've got the same sort of attitudes. And I don't see why a man like you doesn't . . ."

"Can't be done."

"Why not?"

"Because your Herr Papa wants to run. And that means I've got to hold off. I'm a newcomer here. And the Stechlins were already here when . . . ."

"Well fine, I'll accept the last part. And as far as my father's running goes — it seems to me it's not come to that yet. There are plenty of things that can get in the way and in any case, he'll vacillate. But, let's assume things turn out as you suspect. In that case the very thing will occur that I just took the liberty of describing. In every respect my father shares exactly the same true blue views that Kortschädel did. And if he takes his place, what's to be lost by that? The situation will remain the same."

"No, Herr von Stechlin."

"Well, what will change?"

"A lot. Everything. Kortschädel was absolutely unyielding when it got down to the vital questions. But your father is willing to listen to other views."

"I'm not sure you're right about that. But if it were the case, it would be a good thing . . . ."

27

"A bad thing, Herr von Stechlin. Whoever listens to other views doesn't fight to the last and whoever doesn't fight to the last is weak. And when it comes to weakness, the destructive elements have a fine sensitivity for it, weakness is always water on the mills of the Social Democrats."

The four others of the small party had remained in the garden salon. But they too had arranged themselves two by two. In one of the window niches, positioned so they had a view of the moonlit garden as well as of the two gentlemen walking back and forth on the verandah, sat Lorenzen and Frau von Gundermann. The latter was happy about this *tete-a-tete* because all sorts of questions about her youngest son weighed on her heart, or at least she imagined they did. In fact, however, she really had no interest in anything at all. True Berliner that she was, she simply had to be able to talk.

"I'm so happy, Herr Pastor, that I've found the opportunity at last. My God, anybody who's got children has always got worries too. I really would like to have a chance to talk to you about my youngest, about my Arthur. Rudolph never caused me any worries. But Arthur! He's been confirmed now, and you gave him that beautiful saying from the Bible, Pastor, and right off the boy went and wrote it on a big white piece of paper, first all the letters between two lines next to one another and then filled in real thick. It looks just like a sign. And he pasted that big paper over his wash stand and there it stays always reminding him."

"Well, Frau von Gundermann. There's nothing to be said against that."

"No, I don't mean to either. Just the opposite. It's really sort of touching that somebody takes it so seriously. Because, you know, he was at it for two whole days. But when such a young person constantly reads something like that, he gets accustomed to it. But then right back comes temptation again. My God, that a person's always got to be talking about things like this. Not an hour ago I was talking with the captain about our office boy Vehmeyer, a nice fellow, and now here I am right off again talking with you, Herr Pastor, about the very same thing. But it can't be helped. But then when you think about it, it's you who's more or less responsible for his soul, so to speak."

Lorenzen smiled. "Of course, my dear Frau von Gundermann. But whatever is it? What's this really all about?"

"Oh, of itself it's not really much, but then when you think about it, it's really so irritating. We've gone and taken on Schoolmaster Brandt's youngest, you know. Pretty young thing, reddish brown hair, just as curly as can be. Well, Brandt wanted her to get some training

28

with us. Of course, we're not some fancy household, not at all, but helping guests with their coats and passing things around, and knowing if something goes on the left or right, my goodness, that much she ought to be able to learn by the time she's finished."

"Of course. And Frida Brandt, oh I know her quite well. Confirmed just a year ago she was. And she is, as you say, a sweet young thing, and clever and high spirited, perhaps a bit too much so. She wants to go to Berlin at Easter."

"If only she were there already. I'm almost sorry I didn't convince her to go there right off myself. But that's what always happens to you."

"Has something happened?"

"Happened? I wouldn't say that. After all, he's just sixteen and a regular Wandering Willie besides, just like his father. *He* just finally grew out of it since he's turned gray. Which isn't so good either, by the way. And I come up the steps yesterday morning wanting to tell the boy that he should go and check the traps and see if there are any thrushes in them, and the door is standing half open, which it turned out was the best thing, and there I catch sight of how she's thumbing her nose at him and sticking out her tongue. A pointy little tongue like that I never have seen in all my days. A regular Eve the seductress herself. She's still too young to be Potiphar's wife, as far as I go.[23] And then when I come in between'm, well, then the poor boy gets the shakes, and since I really didn't know what to say, I just went over and opened up the top of his wash stand, where that Bible verse was written, and gave him a good hard look. And he turned pale as could be right on the spot. But that little brat just laughed."

"But dear Frau von Gundermann, that's the way it is. Youth will have its fling."

"I'm not so sure about that. I was once young too . . . ."

"Yes, the ladies . . . ."

While Frau von Gundermann was coming up with intimacies of this sort during her conversation in the window niche, by turns embarrassing and then silently amusing the good Pastor Lorenzen, Dubslav and Hauptmann von Czako had withdrawn into a corner diagonally across the room where stood an old fashioned *causeuse*[24] with a marble table before it. On the table were two coffee cups along with an opened liqueur chest from which Dubslav took one bottle after another. "Nowadays, when you leave the table, it's always got to be cognac. But I'll confess to you, my dear Hauptmann, I don't go along with that fashion. Those of us from the old days, we were always a bit for something sweet. Creme de Cacao, well, of course, that's more for the ladies, that's out of the question, but bitter orange, or as they say nowadays, curaçao, there's the thing for me. May I pour you some? Or perhaps you'd rather have Danziger Goldwasser. Can recommend that too, by the way."

"Then I'll ask for the Goldwasser. It's got more bite to it, you know, and then, I'll openly admit it to you, Herr Major . . . You know how things are with us, a touch o' gold like that always has something about it that gets to you. You haven't any, and yet at the same time you've got the illusion that you can drink it — that's got something magnificent about it."

Dubslav nodded and poured a bit of the Goldwasser, first for Czako then for himself, saying, "Toasted the ladies at the table and especially Frau von Gundermann. Listen, Hauptmann, you understand these things. That story about the rats . . . ."

"Maybe it was a little too much."

"Oh, by no means. And anyway, you were completely innocent. After all, her graciousness started it. Remember, she plain fell in love with that story about the gutter boards and how she stomped on them, 'till the rats came out. I think she even said 'beasties.' But there's no harm in that. It's just the Berlin way. And our gracious lady here — née plain old Helfrich, by the way — she's a dyed in the wool Berlin gal."

"A term, though, which to a certain extent surprises me. "

"Ah," threatened Dubslav roguishly with his finger, "I understand what you mean. You noticed a certain insufficiency there and expect at least more square footage (not to mention cubic). But those of us from the nobility have to be somewhat lenient on this point too, you know, turn a blind eye, if that's the correct phrase. Our truest and bluest contingent extends to extremes as well, and has its left and right wings. The left approaches that of our née Helfrich. A very entertaining lady, by the way. And how blissfully happy she was when by luck she discovered that name on your epaulettes and in the process got her chance to go marching up the Münzstraße. The local patriotism you run across these days! "

"In which our regiment participates or joins in. After all, the world around Alexanderplatz[25] has its own charms, you know, merely by way of a certain lack of palace stuffiness. There's nothing I like to see better than the big market hall, when, for example, the fish barrels with five-hundred eels are poured into the nets. An unbelievable mass of wriggling."

"Right at home with what you're saying there, and I'm just as much for Alexanderplatz and the Alexander Barracks and everything that goes with them. And so I'll take the opportunity and ask about one of your previous regimental commanders, kindly old Colonel von Zeuner, whom I knew personally. Our Stechlin region here is a Zeuner region, you know. Not an hour from here is Köpernitz, charming estate, where the Zeuner family lived even in Friederician days. Been over there many a time. Of course that was twenty years ago now. And so I come back to my original question, did you ever get to know the Colonel?"

"No, Herr Major. He was gone by the time I entered the regiment. But I've heard a lot about him and about Köpernitz. Don't remember any more in what connection though."

"Too bad you've only set aside one day for Stechlin. Or else you'd have been able to take a look at the estate. All of it rather odd, especially a gravestone under which an almost ninety-year old lady lies buried, born von Zeuner she was. In her early days she'd married an emigrant at the Rheinsberg court, Count La Roche-Aymon. Remarkable woman. I'll tell you about her when I see you again one of these days. Just one thing you've got to hear today, because I think you've got the taste for it."

"For everything you tell."

"No flattery! But I'll leave you with this story nevertheless as a souvenir. Other folks give one another photographs, a thing I always find abominable, even if they're good looking people, which rarely happens to be the case, by the way."

"Never give out things like that."

"Which increases my feelings for you all the more. But to that story: Well, over there in Köpernitz, there was this La Roche-Aymon woman, and since she had even been around in the days of Prince Heinrich and played her part in them, she counted as one of the special favorites of Friedrich Wilhelm IV. And so — let's say it was around 1850 — as chance would have it, one time the king, who had come to the hunt, really enjoyed his breakfast at Köpernitz, especially their blood and tongue sausage. This was reason enough for the countess to have a whole case of sausages delivered to the royal kitchens in Potsdam on the following Christmas Eve. And so it went through the years. Finally the good old king decided to even things up for all those tasty gifts. So when Christmas came around again, along comes a package in the mail at Köpernitz. Contents: a single dainty little blood sausage. In fact it was a marvelous roundish blood red garnet with little golden knots at both ends, and these little knots themselves set with diamonds. And next to this present lay a note: 'One good sausage deserves another.'"

"Charming!"

"More than that. I personally prefer a good impulse like that over a good constitution any day.[26] And so did the king too, I reckon. And there's plenty who think so still today."

"Assuredly, Herr Major. There's plenty who still think so today, and considering the indecisive condition in which I unfortunately find myself, my personal sympathies are occasionally not far removed. But I fear nevertheless that when it comes to this view of ours we remain very much in the minority."

"So we will. But good sense is always only for the few. It would be best if one single Old Fritz mentality could take control of the whole business. Of course, such a supreme will would have need of its tools. But we've still got those in our nobility, in our army and especially in your regiment."

Just as the old fellow was playing this trump card, Engelke arrived to serve some new coffee.

"No, no, Engelke. We're past that stage. But just put it down there . . . . In your regiment, I say, Herr von Czako. Why even its name implies a program. And that program is: Russia. These days, of course, you can hardly even say a word about it. But that's all nonsense. I tell you, Hauptmann, those were Prussia's best days, when out there around Potsdam they built that Russian church and those Russian houses,[27] and there was a constant going and coming between Berlin and Petersburg. Your regiment, thank God, still upholds some of that old relationship, and I always get a lift when I read about it, especially when a Russian emperor comes calling and a double guard from the Alexander Regiment stands in front of his palace. And I get an even bigger lift when the regiment sends a deputation: Festival of St. George, Name Day of the Honorary Commander in Chief, or even if it's just a matter of uniform alterations, fold-down collars for example instead of stiff collars (damned stiff collars), and how then the emperor welcomes everybody, and wines and dines them and thinks to himself all the while, 'Yes sir, fine fellows those lads. I can really rely on them.'"

Czako nodded. He was, however, in visible embarrassment for despite previously assured "sympathies," he was a totally modern person, strongly infected by things political, one who, while possessed of the staunchest sense of service loyalty, took a rather dim view of every form of excess of that sort.

Old Dubslav in the meantime took no notice of all that and went on, "And so you see, my dear Hauptmann, that's how I still personally experienced things in my younger days and maybe it was even a little better than that. After all, begging your pardon, everybody considers his times the best. Maybe you'll even agree with me, when I've finally finished reciting my little piece.

"We had 'beyond the Njemen' as some of the cultured folks put it these days, the 'three Alexanders', the first, the second and the third. All three great men and all three real emperors and pious fellows, or at least relatively pious, and they meant well by their people and mankind in general too. And in the process, they were real human beings on their own.

"But right in the middle of all this Alexandereanism, that practically filled up the whole century, nevertheless another fellow pushes himself in, a non-Alexander, and without meaning to step on your toes, *he* was really the boss of'm all. And that was our Nicholas.[28] Some morons have made up satirical songs about him and sung about Old Black Nick the way people make children afraid of the bogeyman. But there was a man! And this very same Nicholas, just like the three Alexanders, he had his own regiment here too. And that was the Nicholas Cuirassiers, or I should say, is the Nicholas Cuirassiers, because, God be thanked, we've got them still. And, you see, my dear Czako, that was my regiment. That's where I served when I was still a young pup. And then I went and took my discharge. Much too early. Stupidity. Ought to have stayed with'm."

Czako nodded. Dubslav took another glass of Goldwasser. "To our Nicholas Cuirassiers. God keep them as they are! I could almost say in that regiment the Holy Alliance is still living on,[29] the brotherhood of arms of 1813. And those days of 1813, that we went through together with the Russians, always right next to one another in bivouac, in good times and bad, those were still our greatest times. Greater than the great ones now. Great times are only when things almost go wrong, when you've got to be worried every minute, 'It's all over with now.' That's when it shows. Courage is fine and dandy, but perseverance is better.

"Perseverance, there's what counts. Nothing in your belly, nothing on your back, freezing cold, rain and snow, so that you just lie there in the wet slush, and at best a corn schnapps — cognac, sure, if you had some, practically didn't exist in those days — like that the whole night through, that's when you could really get religion. I say so, even though I wasn't there. 1813, at Großgörschen,[30] that was the real brotherhood of arms for us. These days we've got the brotherhood of organ grinders and mouse trap peddlers.[31] I'm for Russia, for Nicholas and Alexander. Preobrashensk, Semenow, Kaluga — there's where the right support's to be found.[32] Everything else is revolutionary. And whatever's revolutionary, that's on shaky ground."

33

Shortly before eleven, the moon had set in the meantime, the affair came to an end and the carriages drove up, first Katzler's cabriolet then the Gundermanns' chaise. Martin, with a stable lantern, however, lit the way for the pastor across the front courtyard and timbered bridge as far as his parsonage, which lay completely in the dark. Immediately thereafter the three friends withdrew, and with Engelke leading the way, ascended the main staircase as far as the landing. Here Rex and Czako parted from Woldemar, whose room was located on the other side of the hallway. Czako, extremely weary, was ready for bed in an instant.

"We'll stick with it then, Rex. You'll take quarters in the rococo room — let's call it that without further ado — and I'll take this canopied bed here in room number one. Maybe the opposite would be more correct, but that's the way you wanted it." And as he spoke he pushed his boots out into the hall, locked the door and lay down.

In the meantime Rex was occupied with his bed roll, from which he took all sorts of toilet articles. "You'll have to excuse me, Czako, if I stay here in your room for another quarter hour. Got the habit of shaving at night, and the dressing table with the mirror, without which I can't do it too well, you know, well, it's standing here at your window instead of mine. Looks like I've got to disturb you."

"All right with me even though I'm really tuckered out. Nothing better than being able to have a little chat from your bed, especially when you're all bundled up nice and warm. Anyway, beds in the country are the best thing in the world."

"Well, Czako, glad that you're so ready to grant me quarters. But if you want a chat, you'll have to provide the main part yourself. Or else I'll cut myself, and that always looks really terrible afterwards. I've got to work up a lather first though, so I can hold my own for at least that long. It's a lucky thing by the way, that these two candlesticks are here besides this little lamp. If I don't have light from right and left I can't get on with it, although that one's flickering a lot — all of these skinny silver candlesticks flicker — but 'when goodly words the company be . . . .'[33] Well then, let's make an effort. What do you think of the Gundermanns? Strange couple. Ever hear the name Gundermann before?"

"Yes. But that was in *Waldmeister's Honeymoon*.[34]

"Right. That's the effect he makes too. And then that wife of his! The only one who fit in was that Katzler fellow. First rate billiard-player. Iron Cross by the way."

"And then the pastor."

"Oh yes, him too. A very sharp character. But at the same time a strange sort of saint, like the whole clan to which he belongs. He agrees with Stöcker, said so himself too, something not everybody is doing these days, but this 'new Luther,' who's become problematic enough these days — His Majesty was quite right in his condemnation of him,[35] — the fellow doesn't go far enough for him, that's for sure. Regardless of his years, this Lorenzen looks to me like one of the youngest of the young. And the only thing left to be astonished about is that old Stechlin is on such good terms with him. Our friend Woldemar told me about it. The old timer loves him and doesn't see that his beloved pastor is sawing off the branch he's sitting on.

"Yes sir, these fellows from the latest school of thought, they're the worst of the whole crowd. Always 'the people this, and the people that,' and now and then a bit of Christ thrown in for good measure. But they're not pulling the wool over my eyes so easily. The whole thing's aimed at getting rid of us and of old-fashioned Christianity as well. They've got a new brand, and they treat the traditional kind without any respect."

"Under certain circumstances, can't say I blame them. Just calm down, Rex, and let the synod and the party out of it for a second. The traditional kind — or at least what more or less comes our way in that regard these days, especially when you take a good look at mankind as it truly is — really could do with a good bit of repair work. And that sort of repair work is just what a fellow like this Lorenzen has in mind.

"Just make a little test. Lorenzen on one side, Gundermann on the other. With all due respect to your good faith, you certainly wouldn't want to place this Gundermann fellow higher than Lorenzen, or even take him at all seriously. And precisely the way this sawmill fellow is from the board-cutting line, is how most of them are. Twaddle, twaddle, and nothing but twaddle. Now and then a bit of business or even worse."

"I can't answer you right now, Czako. What you're saying there touches on an important question to which one's got to pay close attention. And right now, with a razor in my hand, it's too much to ask. And to top it off, this candle flickering here already has a dirty wick. Tell me something about Frau von Gundermann instead. I can't debate with you any more, but if you go on chatting, I'll only have to listen. I noticed, you made a long speech for her at dinner."

"I'll say. About rats to boot."

"Oh no, Czako. You can't go talking about things like that. If that's the case I'd prefer hearing about the old and the new faith.[36] Here of all places. In an old barn like this you're never safe from spooks or rats. If you can't come up with anything else then I'll ask for the story during which we were interrupted this morning in Cremmen. Seemed a bit spicy to me."

"Ah, the story about that little Stubbe woman.[37] Yes, well, now listen Rex, that one will get you exited for sure too. And if you can't get to sleep, in the end it doesn't make any difference whether it's on account of rats or the Stubbe woman."

5

Rex and Czako were so tired that if necessary they would have slept right through spooks or rats. But it was not necessary; there was nothing that could have disturbed them. Shortly after eight the old factotum appeared with a covered silver pitcher from which the steam of hot water ascended, one of the few showpieces which Castle Stechlin had at its disposal. In addition Engelke bid the gentlemen a good morning and provided them with his weather report. It would be a beautiful day for certain and the young master was already up, walking round the circular garden with the master.

And so in fact it was. Woldemar had appeared downstairs in the salon right after seven to have a family conversation about all sorts of delicate matters with his father, whom he knew to be an early riser. But he had decided not to be the one to begin, but instead to await everything from his father's curiosity and kind heart. And therein he was not disappointed.

"Ah, Woldemar. Good you're here this early. Never stay in bed too long. Most sleepy heads have a crack in'm. They can be otherwise quite good people. I'll bet your friend Rex sleeps till nine."

"No, Papa. Of all people, not he. Anybody who's like Rex can't allow himself that luxury. As a matter of fact, he's founded a club for sunrise services, alternately to be held in Schönhausen and Finkenkrug.[38] But it hasn't been all worked out yet."

"Glad to hear it's still not working out. I don't go for things like that. Of course, Old Wilhelm had wanted to revive religion among his people, which was a nice thing for him to say — everything he did and said was good — but religion and picnics, I'm against that, for sure. I'm completely against any sort of phony mix ups. Human beings included. The pure race, that's the really legitimate thing. That other business, whatever else they're calling legitimacy, that's all more or less artificial. Tell me, how do things stand? You know what I mean."

"Well, Papa . . . ."

"No, none of that. None of that constant 'well, Papa.' That's how you start every time I bring up this topic. I can hear a half refusal in it, or else a postponement, or a let's-wait-and-see attitude. And that's not the kind of thing I can accommodate myself to. You're thirty-two, or almost. That Hymen fellow with the torch has got to put in his appearance, but the only appearance you've been making is to shilly-shally around. Sorry about the pun; don't really go for them actually, more the thing for traveling salesmen. But you've been shilly-shallying, I say, and you're not getting serious about it. And this much I can say as well, your Aunt Sanctissima over there in the convent at Wutz, she's getting mighty impatient by now too. And that should give you something to think about. Me she's treated badly my whole life long; we've simply never agreed on anything and never could. Her being half Queen Elizabeth and half ladies' club member, that's a melange I've never been able to warm up to. Her every other word is always about that Financial Adviser Fix of hers, and if she weren't seventy-six, I'd cook me up a story about that whole thing as well."

"Be lenient, Papa. She really does mean well, you know. And she certainly does by me."

"Lenient? Fine, Woldemar. I'll give it a try. Except I'm afraid not much will come of it. They always say, one should have a sense of family, but things are always made too miserably hard for a fellow, and when it comes to me, I can't resist the temptation of practicing some real family criticism instead. Adelheid practically begs for it. On the other hand, of course, she's crazy about you. For you she's got money and love. Which of the two is more important, we'll leave open, but one thing is sure, without her none of it would ever have been possible, your life in your regiment, I mean.

"And so we're indebted to her. And since she knows that every bit as well as we do, or maybe even a little bit better, that's the very reason she's getting impatient. She wants to see some action, which from the female point of view always amounts to the same thing as marriage. And if you want to look at it that way, you can even call it that. Action, I mean. It is and remains sheer heroism. Anybody who'd have married Aunt Adelheid would have deserved a medal for bravery, and if I really wanted to be malicious, I'd even say the Iron Cross."

"Well Papa . . . ."

"Well Papa, again. All right, that's fine with me. After all, I'm not going to argue with you over your favorite turn of phrase. But just admit to me on the side — because when you get right down to it, that's what we're really talking about — have you got anything definite in your sights? Drawn a bead on anything?"

"Papa, these expressions of yours almost shock me. But if we have to use hunting terminology like that, yes; my wishes are aimed at a definite target, and I can say, these things are on my mind."

"These things are on my mind . . . . Don't take it amiss, Woldemar, but that doesn't mean a thing. On your mind! I'm not for poetry, that's for governesses and poor teachers who have to go off to Görbersdorf.[39] Except they usually don't have the money. But a turn of phrase like, 'it's on my mind,' is just a bit too prosaic even for me. When something like love is at stake — although I don't think much more of love than I do of poetry, except that love causes even more mischief because it appears more — when something like love is at stake, a fellow can't just say, 'it was on his mind.' After all, love is something high-spirited, or else it might as well be buried once and for all. And so, if it's all the same to you, I'd rather like to hear something from you that looks a little like passion. It doesn't have to be something overwhelming right off. But so completely without stimulus, as they're saying these days, I think, so completely without something like that just won't do. The whole of humanity's dependent on it, and wherever it goes slack, thing's are about over and done with.

"Of course, I know perfectly well, things can go on without the likes of our kind too. But yet that's just something imposed on you by force of reason. That egoistic feeling, that's always wrong and yet always right too, doesn't even care to trouble itself with anything of that sort at all and demands that the Stechlins go on living, *in aeternum* if can be. Living on eternally — granted there's something sort of comical about that. But there are very few serious things that don't have their comical side as well . . . . All right then, these things are 'on your mind.' Can you name any names? On whom has it pleased your highness to rest his eyes?"

"Papa, I can't name any names yet. I'm not yet certain enough where I stand. And that's also the reason why I've used expressions that seem dispassionate and prosaic to you. But I can tell you I would have rather expressed myself differently, only I can't just yet. And then I know too, that you yourself have a superstitious trait and believe with perfect sincerity that a person can frighten his good luck away by talking about it too much or too soon."

"Well said, well said. I like that. So it is. We're always surrounded by envious and malicious creatures with foxes' tails or bats' wings, and whenever we brag or get too sure of ourselves, they laugh at us. And as soon as they start laughing we're as good as goners. We can do nothing with our own strength. I'm not even certain of the blade of grass that I'm pulling up here. Humility, humility . . . . But just the same, I'll still put a naive question to you — we're continuously contradicting ourselves, you know — is she upper class, really posh? "

"Really posh, Papa? I won't say that. But upper class for sure."

38

"Well, that makes me feel good. Phony class is something I really loathe, but genuine class — *à la bonne heure*. Tell me, somebody from the court maybe?"

"No, Papa."

"Well that's all the better. But look there, here come the gentlemen. Rex really looks div'lishly good. Exactly like what we used to call a Guard-Assessor. And religious, you say. He'll probably make something of himself. Being religious is like havin' a hand up.'"

As Dubslav spoke, Rex and Czako descended the steps leading down to the garden and greeted the old man. He inquired about their nocturnal adventures and took pleasure in their having 'slept right through it all.' He then took Czako's arm to return from the garden to the verandah, where Engelke had in the meantime set up the breakfast table under the large awning.

"If I may, Herr von Rex." He indicated a garden chair directly across from him, while Woldemar and Czako took their seats to his left and right. "Lately I've introduced tea, not obligatory of course, on the contrary. Personally, I'd rather stick to coffee. 'Black as the devil, sweet as sin and hot as hell,' as Talleyrand's supposed to have said. But pardon my even bothering you with things like that at all. Why, even my father once said, 'Yes indeed, we folks out here in the country still hang on to our old Congress of Vienna jokes.' And that was a generation ago."

"Ah yes, those old congress jokes," said Rex cordially, "I should like to permit myself the comment, Herr Major, that those old jokes are better than the new ones. Can scarcely be otherwise. After all, who were the authors in those days? Talleyrand, whom you've already mentioned, and Wilhelm von Humboldt and Friedrich Gentz and the like. I believe the profession has gone downhill quite a bit since then."

"Right. Everything's gone downhill, and it keeps on going further downhill. That's what they call the new times, going right on down the hill. And my pastor, whom you met last evening, of course, he even holds that's where the truth is, that's what they call culture, that things just keep going right on downhill. The aristocratic world has run its course and now it's time for the democratic . . . ."

"Strange remarks coming from a cleric," said Rex, "for a man who after all ought to know the God-given order of things."

Dubslav laughed. "Yes sir, he'll dispute that one with you. And I've got to admit there's something to it even though it doesn't suit me particularly well. In any case, we'll see him, the pastor I mean, at our second breakfast quite probably. Then you'll be able to take the opportunity to have it out with him about it personally. He loves conversations like that, as you've probably noticed by now. And he's got a bit of the Luther tendency, to play the 'here I stand, I can do no other' bit that's around these days. Now and then it really looks as if a certain passion for martyrdom had overtaken humanity again. Just that somehow it all seems a bit fishy to me . . . ."

"To me too," commented Rex. "Mostly a lot of showing off."

"Now now," said Czako, "I've just heard the other day about a poor Russian teacher who got put in the army — they have something like compulsory military service there now too, you know — and this teacher fellow refused to fire a rifle, because it was nothing but preparation for murder and mayhem, therefore completely and absolutely against the Fifth Commandment. And they really tormented the poor fellow until he finally died. Are you calling that showing off?"

"Certainly I am."

"Herr von Rex," said Dubslav, "don't you think you're going too far there? When it comes down to dying, there's an end to showing off. But this incident, which by they way I heard about too, has another key altogether. It's not a matter of this showing off business that's become so general, it has to do with being a teacher. The whole lot of them are crazy as a matter of fact. I've got one here too, whom I've made a study of. Named Krippenstapel, which tells you something. He's exactly one year older than I, thus just about sixty-seven, and really a marvelous specimen, in any case a superb teacher. But crazy just the same."

"The whole lot of them are," said Rex. "All teachers are a horror. We in the Ministry of Culture can sing you a tune about that. These ABC drillers know everything, and since that ridiculous remark, 'The Austrians were defeated by the schoolmasters of Prussia,' that's been all the rage since '66 — if you ask me, I'd grant the prize instead to the firing-pin rifle or old Field Marshall Steinmetz, who was everything else but a schoolmaster — since then you can't put up with those people at all. Herr von Stechlin was just speaking about one of the Humboldts; well, as far as Wilhelm von Humboldt goes, they're still not quite so sure of themselves, but whatever Alexander von Humboldt could do, they've been able to do for years."

"You've hit it right there, Herr von Rex," said Dubslav. "Mine's exactly the same way. I can only say it again, a marvelous fellow, but he's got a case of priority madness. If Koch invents some antitoxin, or Edison plays you an opera from fifty miles away with foot stamping and applause in between, my Krippenstapel will go and prove to you that he was working on that idea already thirty years ago."

"Exactly, exactly. That's how they all are."

"By the way . . . . but can't I give you some of this baked ham? . . . By the way, mentioning Krippenstapel reminds me that it might well be time to set up a morning itinerary. Krippenstapel was born to be the local tour guide of this area, you know, and from Woldemar I've been made aware that you intend to give us the pleasure of informing yourselves a bit about Stechlin and surroundings. Village, church, forest and lake — the lake most of all, of course, because that's our *pièce de résistance*. The rest you can find in other places as well, but our lake . . . ."

"Lorenzen has proclaimed it a real revolutionary besides, one that starts rumbling along just as soon as anything's going on anywhere. And it's really true. But just in passing, that pastor of mine really ought not say things like that. Nothing but clever remarks that could easily be taken the wrong way. Personally, I let them pass. There's nothing I'd hate more than police measures or gagging some fellow who likes to say what's on his mind. I like to talk a bit myself and say whatever comes into my head."

"And lose track of time in the process," said Woldemar, "and for starts, you're forgetting our program. We've got to be on our way by two at the latest. That means we've only got four more hours. And Globsow, which can't be left out, is a good way off and will take at least half of that."

"Right, every word of it. Well then, the menu, gentlemen. In my opinion it ought to be as follows, first, right over there behind that boxwood path, a climb up the lookout tower — a structure still left over from my father's day. According to the view of folks about, it looked much better in the old days than it does now. Back then it only had all kinds of colored glass up top and every thing you saw looked red or blue or orange-colored. And the whole world hereabouts was unhappy when I had those colored panes taken out. Seemed to me sort of an insult to nature though. Green is green and woods are woods . . . ."

"Well then, number one, the lookout tower. Number two, Krippenstapel and the school. Number three, the church plus churchyard. We'll pass up the parsonage. Then the woods and the lake. And then Globsow, where there's a glass industry. Then we come back and to top things off, second breakfast. An old fashioned term that, but it still sounds better to me than 'lunch.' 'Second breakfast' has something particularly comfortable about it and lets everybody know you've already got the first under your belt . . . ."

"Woldemar, that's my program, herewith proposed to you by me as one of the initiate. Yes or no?"

"Naturally yes, Papa. You always hit that sort of thing best. For my part though, I'll only come along for the first half. When we're finished in the church, I've got to go see Lorenzen. Krippenstapel can easily more than replace me, and in Globsow he knows everything there is to know. He talks as if he had been a glass blower himself."

"Shouldn't surprise you. After all, he's a teacher in general and Krippenstapel in particular."

And so the program was set, and after Dubslav with Engelke's assistance exchanged his rather new white felt hat, which he carefully preserved, for a Wotanesque broad-brimmed black felt one and took a heavy oak walking stick, they started off to ascend the lookout tower established as the first local sight worthy of inspection. The path which led to it, not a hundred paces in length, passed along a so-called 'poet's walk.'

"I don't know," said Dubslav, "why my mother introduced that rather pretentious name here. As far as I know, nothing has ever befallen the place which could have brought about such an elevation in rank to what was formerly just a boxwood-hedged path. And it's just as well too."

"Why just as well, Papa?"

"Well now, don't take it amiss," laughed Dubslav. "You sound as if you were one yourself. Incidentally I admit that I have no real sense for that sort of thing. There weren't any in the cuirassiers and I've only seen one in my whole life. Had a little humpback and a gold pince-nez he always kept taking off and polishing. Naturally, nothing but a little peacock, small and vain. But very elegant."

"Elegant?" asked Czako. "Then it's not true. You've as good as never seen one."

As they conversed they reached the tower which extended skyward in several flights of stairs and finally nothing but ladders. One had to be without a fear of heights to make it to the top without problem. Once there, however, there was no longer any danger because a sturdy wooden enclosure surrounded the platform. Rex and Czako looked out over the countryside. To the south the land was open. On the three other sides, however, everything was covered by thick woodlands, through which here and there the chain of lakes, stretching for miles into the distance, was visible. The closest lake was the Stechlin.

"Well then, where's the spot?" asked Czako. "Naturally, the one where it bubbles and seethes."

"Do you see that little inlet there, with the white stone bench?"

"Yes indeed, clear as can be."

"Well, from that stone bench not two boat lengths out into the lake, there you've got the spot that if need be has a telephone line direct to Java."

"I'd give a lot," said Czako, "if that rooster would start crowing right now."

"Unfortunately I'll have to continue to owe you that little favor. In fact, I haven't anything else for you out there off to the right except those red tile roofs extending between the edge of the woods and the lake, as if they were on a quay. That's the Globsow colony. Where the glass blowers live. And behind it is the glass works. It got its start back in the days of Old Fritz. They call it the 'green glass works.'"

"Green? Why that almost sounds like a fairy tale."

"But in reality it's practically the opposite. It's called that because they make green glass there, the most common ordinary bottle glass there is. Don't even think of ruby glass with gold edging here. That's not the thing for our corner of the world."

With that they again clambered down, and after passing the fore-court of the manor, proceeded out to the village square where on one corner stood the school. It had to be the school; one could see that by the open windows and the hollyhocks in front. Even as the gentlemen reached the green picket fence, they were able to hear the precise educational process going on within, first the teacher's sharp, short questions followed instantly by a choral response. In the next instant, with Dubslav in the lead, they passed directly into the vestibule, where, because a little white mutt began yapping furiously, Krippenstapel appeared to see what was the matter.

"Good morning, Krippenstapel," said Dubslav. "I've brought you some visitors."

"Very flattering, Herr Baron."

"That's what you say. If only it were true. But under any circumstances you can drop the baron business . . . . You see, gentlemen, my friend Krippenstapel here is quite an independent old boy. Ordinarily he calls me Herr von Stechlin — the Major part he suppresses — and whenever he's angry about something, he calls me 'Your Lordship.' But the minute I show up with strangers, he bestows the title of Herr Baron on me. He wants to do his little bit for me."

Krippenstapel, quietly chuckling to himself, had in the meantime opened the door of his parlor, which was situated across from his classroom, and invited the gentlemen to enter. Each reached for a chair but supported himself merely on its back rest while the conversation between Dubslav and the teacher continued.

43

"Tell me, Krippenstapel, is it going to work out? You're naturally supposed to show us everything and school isn't out yet."

"Oh, certainly it will work out, Herr von Stechlin."

"Yes, but listen now, when the cat's away, the mice will play . . . ."

"Not a thing to worry about, Herr von Stechlin. There once was a Burgermeister, in the days around '48, rather not name names. He said, 'All I have to do is put one of my boots at the window and I can govern the whole town.' My kind of man."

"Right. I knew him too. Yes sir, he knew how things were done. And always in the fear of the Lord. That way everything works best of all. The rod's still the best ruler after all."

"The rod," confirmed Krippenstapel. "But then along with it, of course, the rewards."

"Rewards?" laughed Dubslav. "But Krippenstapel, wherever do you get those?"

"Oh I've got'em, Herr von Stechlin. But always with certain distinctions. If it's just a minor thing, then the lad just gets one less knock on the head, if it's something big then he gets a honeycomb."

"A honeycomb? Right. We were talking about them at breakfast when your honey came to the table. I informed these gentlemen you were the best beekeeper in the whole county."

"Too much honor, Herr von Stechlin. But this much I can say, I do understand how it's done. And if the gentlemen would care to follow me to see the community at work — right now happens to be the best time."

All agreed and thus passed through the vestibule and out into the courtyard and garden. There they took their places before an open shed with several levels in which the hives were located. They were not old-fashioned hives but regular bee houses according to Dzierzon's method,[40] whereby one could remove everything and comfortably peek right into the interior. Krippenstapel showed them everything and Rex and Czako were genuinely interested.

"Well now, Teacher Krippenstapel," said Czako. "Give us your commentary, if you please. What's the real story with bees? It's supposed to be something special, or so they say."

"So it is. Herr Hauptmann. The life of the bee is actually more refined and noble than that of humans."

"More refined I can well imagine. But more noble? Anything more noble than man doesn't exist. In any case, however that may be, 'yes' or 'no,' you excite a fellow's curiosity more and more. I once heard somewhere that bees are really supposed to understand the concept of the state, in an almost exemplary way."

"And so it is, Herr Hauptmann. And there's one thing, in fact, that perhaps really makes a topic of discussion. There are, you know, three groups or classes in every hive. In class one we've got the queen, in class two, the worker bees — who are sexless, probably always the best thing for all working peoples — and in class three we've got the drones. They're males, which at the same time happens to be their real profession, because except for that they don't do a single thing."

"Interesting state. I'm for it. But still not exemplary enough."

"And now just picture it, Herr Hauptmann. The whole winter long they've just been sitting there like that and working or even sleeping too. And then comes the spring and the new life awakening takes hold of the bees too, most powerfully though in class one, the queen. And then — with her whole population — she decides to take a spring ramble, which for her personally takes on the aspect of a sort of a wedding journey. That's what I'd have to call it. From among the crowd of drones, you know, the ones that follow on her heels, she picks a consort, a dance partner you might say, who is then also called upon quite soon to take up a more intimate position in regard to her. After about an hour or so the queen and her wedding party return to the narrow confines of her state. Her existence has thus been fulfilled. An entire generation of bees is born, but further relations with the aforementioned dance partner are over once and for all. That's the very thing that I previously characterized as refined and noble. Queen bees love only once. The queen bee loves and dies."

"And what happens to the preferred drone, the princess's dance partner, the Prince Consort, if that's a fitting title?"

"The dancer is murdered."

"No, Teacher Krippenstapel. That's not fair. With that last bit of information of yours my enthusiasm collapses altogether. Why that's even worse than Heine's Asra. He just dies.[41] But here we have murder. Tell us, Rex, how do you stand on the matter?"

"The monogamous principle on which, after all, our entire culture is based, could not be demonstrated in a more strict or convincing fashion. I find it magnificent."

Czako would have liked to respond but was unable to get that far, for in the same instant Dubslav called attention to the fact that they still had a great deal to do ahead of them. First off, the church. "The Reverend, who really ought to be there, won't take it amiss if we do without him. But you, Krippenstapel, can you come?"

Krippenstapel repeated that he had plenty of time. Moreover, the school clock struck and with the first stroke one could hear how things were getting lively in the classroom and how the boys rushed through the entry way and out into the street in their wooden shoes. Outside, however, they lined up in military formation, because they had heard in the meantime that His Lordship had come.

"Morning, lads," said Dubslav, stepping up to a young black-haired fellow. "You from Globsow?"

"No, Yer Lordship, from Dagow."

"Aha. Studying hard?"

The boy grinned.

"When was Fehrbellin?"

"Eighteenth of June."

"And Leipzig?"

"Eighteenth of October. Always the eighteenth fer us."

"That's the way, lad . . . Here."

And with that he reached in his pocket for a ten-pfennig piece. "You see, Herr Hauptmann, you're a bit of a cynic, I noticed as much. But there's how it's got to be done. The lad knows about Fehrbellin and about Leipzig, has an intelligent look and knows how to answer when he's asked. And he's got nice red cheeks too. Does he look like he's got a care in the world, or a worry about the Fatherland? Not a bit of it. Order and always keeping a firm hand. Well, as long as I'm still around, things will go on like that. But, of course, other days are coming."

Woldemar smiled.

"Well," continued the oldster, "By way of consoling myself, when Old Fritz came to die, he thought the world was coming to an end. But it's still here. And we Germans are on top again. A bit too much. But too much's always better than too little."

In the meantime Krippenstapel had pulled himself together properly in his room: black coat with the ribbon of the Hohenzollern eagle his gracious master had obtained for him. In place of the hat which in his haste he was unable to find, he wore a cap of extraordinary shape. In his right hand, however, he held a hollowed out church key which looked for all the world like a rusty old pistol.

The way to the church was short. In no time they stood before its portal.

Rex, whose department also was in charge of ecclesiastical structures, affixed his pince-nez and took measure. "Very interesting. I'd put that portal in the time of Bishop Luger. A Premonstratensian structure. If I'm not completely deceived, influenced by the crypt of the Brandenburg Cathedral. Let's say around 1200 then. If I might ask, Herr von Stechlin, is there any documentary evidence in existence? And has Herr von Quast been here perhaps, or Privy Councilor Adler, our top expert in such matters?"

Dubslav found himself a bit embarrassed, for he had not prepared himself for thoroughness of this sort. "Herr von Quast was here once, but it was in regard to electoral matters. And since Wrangel burned everything hereabouts, there's not a chance of any documentary evidence. When I say Wrangel naturally I don't mean our 'Father Wrangel,' who didn't go in for any fun and games either, by the way, but Schiller's Wrangel.[42] And anyway, Herr von Rex, it's all so complicated for a layman. But you, Krippenstapel, what's your opinion?"

Rex, suddenly overcome by a sense of official prestige, was taken aback. He had addressed Herr von Stechlin, if not as an authority, at least as someone equal, and that Krippenstapel was now being called upon to deliver the decisive comment in the matter did not seem quite appropriate to him. Anyway, what was he about, this character who came perilously close to being a caricature? Just that account concerning the bees, and especially what he had said about the relationship of the queen and prince-consort, had had such a strangely suggestive tone to it, and now this oddity of a schoolmaster was actually being called upon to offer his judgment about architectural questions and about from what century the church came as well. He had intentionally asked about Quast and Adler, and now came Krippenstapel! If one really wanted to, of course, one could consider it the whole thing had a patriarchal quality about it, but it displeased him nonetheless.

And unfortunately, Krippenstapel — who, in addition to his other eccentricities, also possessed the fulsome arrogance of those who are self-taught — was by no means the sort to smooth out the little bumps which had found their way into the conversation. On the contrary, he took the question 'Krippenstapel, what's your opinion,' perfectly seriously and replied: "Forgive me, Herr von Rex, if I venture to contradict you there on the basis of a recently published brochure by Chief Teacher Tucheband in Templin. Our little corner of the county has more the character of the Uckermark or Mecklenburg[43] than Brandenburg, and if we wish to look for models for this Stechlin church of ours here, we'd probably have to look for them in Cloister Himmelpfort or Gransee, but not in the Brandenburg Cathedral. If you'll permit me to add, Chief Teacher Tucheband's statements remain, as far as I know, uncontested."

Czako, who was following the controversy on the verge of flaring up between a ministerial assessor and a village schoolmaster with the greatest of pleasure, would have gladly thrown a bit more kindling on the fire. Woldemar found it was high time to intervene, however, and remarked that nothing was more difficult than to arrive at certainties in this area — a comment, incidentally which both Rex as well as

Krippenstapel seemed eager to deny — and he would like to suggest they enter the church itself instead, rather than continuing to debate about its pillars and capitals outside. The suggestion was accepted by everyone. Krippenstapel opened the church with his gigantic key and all stepped inside.

6

Right after twelve — Woldemar as planned had long since separated from the other gentlemen to stop in at Lorenzen's — Dubslav, Rex and Czako returned from their excursion to Globsow. As they passed through the forecourt, Rex, refined gentleman that he was, approached the polished glass sphere in its pewter setting to cordially grant it his ministerial attentiveness, presumably as a product of the recently inspected "green glassworks." He even went so far as to speak of an "industrial state." Czako, who along with Rex peeked into the sphere, fully agreed with everything, except, that is, his reflected image.

"If only a fellow were just a bit better looking . . . ."

Rex attempted to contradict him but Czako refused to give in, arguing, "Oh yes, Rex. You're a good looking fellow. You've simply got more to start with. And as a result there's always a bit more left over to work with."

On the ramp above stood Engelke.

"Well, Engelke, how are things? Woldemar and the Pastor here yet?"

"No, Master. But I can send Christel if you want . . . ."

"No, no. Don't do that. It'll only disturb them. But we won't wait either. It turned out it was further to Globsow than I thought, which is to say, it really wasn't any further, it's just that these legs of mine don't want to work right any more. And so the only thing good about such a strenuous effort is that you get hungry and thirsty. But here come the gentlemen now."

From the ramp he waved towards the timbered bridge as Woldemar and Lorenzen crossed to enter the courtyard. Rex walked out to meet them. Dubslav took Czako's arm, however, and said, "Well come along, Hauptmann, we'll go and do a bit of scouting out a good spot for us. It's no good on the verandah all the time. Beneath that awning the air stands like a wall, and I've got to have fresh air. Maybe it's the first symptom of hydropsy. Can't really stand foreign words like that. But some times they're really a blessing after all. If I've got to choose between hydropsy and water on the knees, I'll go for dropsy every time. Water on the knee has something so terrifically vivid about it."

As they spoke they had entered the garden, reaching a spot just directly opposite the poet's walk where grew a good deal of boxwood. "Look here, Hauptmann, this looks like something. Low wall of boxwood hedging. Here we've got air and yet no drafts. I've got to guard against drafts, you know, because of rheumatism, or may be it's gout too. And while we're here we can hear the splashing of my Sanssouci fountain. What do you think?"

"Capital, Herr Major."

"Ah, forget that Major business. Major always sounds so official . . . . Well then, right here, Engelke, set the table here and put a few fuchsia or whatever's in bloom in the middle. Only no asters. Asters are just fine, but they're lower class, so to speak. Always look like they just came from a peasant's garden. And then get down to the cellar and bring us up something decent. You know what I like best for breakfast. Maybe Hauptmann Czako has the very same taste."

"I don't yet know what it is, Herr von Stechlin, but I'm ready to vouch for my agreement already."

In the meantime Woldemar, Rex and the pastor had made their way from the garden salon onto the verandah and Dubslav walked toward them. "Good day, Pastor. Well that's fine. I had imagined that Woldemar would be annexed by you."

"Oh now, Herr von Stechlin . . . Your guests . . . And Woldemar's friends."

"Don't emphasize it that way, Lorenzen. There are manners and laws of etiquette. For sure. But all that doesn't go very far. The things people break before anything else are those very forms. And you can feel downright sorry for whoever doesn't break them. What happens in marriage for example? Did you ever know a man who observes the formalities when his wife gets him mad? Not me. Passion always carries the day."

"Yes, passion. But Woldemar and I . . . ."

"Share a passion too. You've got a passion for friendship, Orest and Pylades . . . that sort of thing's always existed. And then, what means even more, you've got the conspiratorial passion besides."

"Oh, but Herr von Stechlin."

"No, not the conspiratorial passion. I take that back. But in its place you've got something else, namely the world salvation passion. And that's one of the biggest there is. And when two of those world salvation types get together, Rex and Czako can wait, and even a warm breakfast can wait. Do they still use the term '*Dèjeuner à la fourchette*?'"

"Hardly, Papa. As you know, English is all the rage now."

"Of course. The French have been dismissed. And it's just as well too, even though our cousins over there are all the more worthless. Self reliance, that's what counts. But I do believe our breakfast is waiting."

In fact it was indeed. While the gentleman had been strolling back and forth in pairs along the boxwood hedge, Engelke had arranged the table which the host and his guests now approached.

It was a longish table. The side facing the circular garden had been left open permitting an overview of the charming garden scene. Dubslav, looking over the arrangement, nodded approvingly to Engelke as a sign that he had hit it just right. Then he took the central platter and said while passing it to Rex, *"Toujours perdrix."*[44] Which is to say, they're really thrush, as we had last evening. But who knows what thrush are in French. Not me in any case. And I don't think even Tucheband will be able to help us out."

A general embarrassed silence confirmed Dubslav's suspicions regarding knowledge of French vocabulary.

"Just before Globsow," he continued, "we came through a stretch full of traps. It struck me that there were quite a few thrushes hanging everywhere in the nettings, something I can ascribe, as so many good things, to my old friend Krippenstapel. It'd be nothing at all, you know, for the boys to steal everything from those nettings. But nothing of the sort happens. What do you think, Lorenzen?"

"I'm happy things are as they are and that the nets aren't plundered. But I do believe, Herr von Stechlin, you really shouldn't credit that to Krippenstapel."

Dubslav laughed heartily. "There we have the same old story again. Every schoolmaster schoolmasters his pastor and every pastor goes pastoring his schoolmaster. An eternal rivalry. But it's a natural trait, though, that the boys will take everything they can lay their hands on. People steal like crows. And if they refrain from it all of a sudden, there must be a reason for it somehow."

"There is indeed, Herr von Stechlin. Just a different one. What are they to do with a thrush? For us they're a delicacy. For a poor person they're nothing at all. Not much more than a sparrow."

"Oho, Lorenzen, I can see it coming. You're lying in wait there all set to pounce with that 'patrimony of the disinherited' business again. A sparrow — sounds just like it. But one thing is right for sure, Krippenstapel keeps those boys in order brilliantly. Just the way it went this morning. One thing right after another when I gave that short-haired black-topped little fellow an exam, and how straight those lads stood, and how well-behaved when we saw them an hour later in Globsow. The way they were all playing so cheerfully there and yet full of respect in everything. 'Free but not fresh,' that's more or less what I say."

Woldemar and Lorenzen who had not been present at the time were curious to know about the events that had induced old Dubslav's copious praise.

"Whatever was it," asked Woldemar, "that so suddenly earned the Globsow lads such a fine reputation?"

"Oh, it was really delightful," said Czako. "We were still hidden by the trees of the forest when we were able to hear voices sounding like commands. And hardly had we stepped out onto an open square bordered by chestnut trees — actually it was probably more a large factory yard — than we found ourselves as if right in the midst of a battle."

Rex nodded in agreement while Czako went on: "On our side stood what was apparently up until then the victorious party. But their further attacks came to a sudden halt because of the excellent cover the opponents had taken. Scarcely surprising. Because this very cover actually consisted of what was probably a thousand glass balloons in the form of a large square, behind which the defeated troop had withdrawn as if it were a barricade. There they stood then, and opened up a tremendous fire with the chestnuts lying *en masse* all over the place. Most of their shots dropped short and fell rattling like hail on the balloons. I could have watched the game for I don't know how long. But when they caught sight of us, they scattered every which way, cheering and waving their caps as they went. Photographers are everywhere you look. Only where they ought to be, never. Just like the police."

Dubslav had been chuckling to himself while listening to the description. "Let me tell you, Hauptmann, you really know how it's done. You could probably guild the Great Elector with a single gold ducat."[45]

"Yes," said Rex, suddenly leaving his partner in the lurch, "our friend Czako never does otherwise. Three quarters of what he says is always fiction."

"I've never pretended to be a historian, and least of all some kind of pedantic document person."

"And, my dear Czako," interjected Dubslav, "let's just leave it at that. To your special talent. In such an important matter you've got to raise your glass with me, but with my very own favorite. Not red wine, which my famous co-hermit has termed the 'natural beverage of the North German individual.'[46] One of his many errors, perhaps even his greatest. The natural beverage of the North German individual is to be found on the Rhine or the Main. And most superbly where, if I may use the term, the two of them join in wedlock. Not far from that wedlock spot comes this fellow here." As he spoke he pointed to a round bottle of green glass with a short neck[47] standing before him.

"You see, gentlemen, I hate all those long necks. Now this here, this is what I call a pleasing form. Doesn't it say somewhere 'Let me have fat fellows around me,' or something like that?[48] I agree completely. Fat bottles. They're for me." And as he spoke he again touched glasses with Czako. "Once again, to your health. And to yours, Herr von Rex. And then to my Globsowers, or at least those Globsow lads of mine, who don't just care about Fehrbellin and Leipzig, but, as we've seen, fight battles of their own as well. The only thing that gets me upset every time is when I see those huge balloons out there between my Globsowers. And behind that first factory yard, I just didn't want to bother you with any more of them, there's a second yard. That looks even worse. They've got regular glass monsters standing out there, you know. They're balloons too, but with long necks on'em and then they call them retorts."

"Now Papa," said Woldemar, "you just can't seem to calm down about those few retorts and glass balloons. As long as I can remember you've been fussing against them. It's really a stroke of good luck that so many of them get sent out into the world and guarantee those poor factory people a good salary. Why, anything like a strike doesn't ever even happen around here, and in this respect our Stechlin region is still really like a paradise."

Lorenzen laughed.

"Right, Lorenzen, you laugh," interjected Dubslav at this point. "But when you look at it in that light, Woldemar is right after all, which, and you know why too, actually doesn't happen too often. It's exactly as he says. Of course, we've still got Eve and the serpent; that's a legacy from as far back as things go. But as much of the good old days as can still be found in this world, can be found right here, right here in our dear old county. And as far as I go, into this picture of the right kind of organization, or if you like the right kind of subordination — I don't shy away from that sort of word either — into this picture of tranquillity, this whole Globsow retort-blowing factory doesn't fit. And if I didn't have to be afraid of being considered an old fogy, I'd have long since submitted my suggestions about these retorts and glass spheres to the higher authorities. And of course *against* them both. Why does it always have to be balloons? And if it does, well then, preferably the likes of these. These please me just fine." And with that he raised the stubby round wine bottle.

"Like these," said Czako in accord.

"Yes indeed, Czako. You're just the fellow to strengthen my papa in his idiosyncrasies."

"Idiosyncrasies," the old man repeated. "To hear the likes of that. Yes indeed, Woldemar, you really think you've come up with something sophisticated there. But it's nothing but a word, that's all. And when something's just another word, it's never really sophisticated, even if it looks like it. Obscure feelings, they're sophisticated. And as certainly as the concept that I associate with this wonderful bottle here has for me personally something celestial — can you say that, celestial?" — Lorenzen nodded approvingly — "so it's just as certain for me that associated with these gigantic Globsow wine bottles is something infernal."

"Now Papa."

"Quiet. Don't interrupt me, Woldemar. Because I'm just now getting to a calculation, and nobody should be disturbed when he's in the middle of a calculation. This glassworks exists for over a hundred years now. And so now, when I multiply their yearly production by a hundred, I calculate, all in all, a million. First off they send them to other factories and there they just go ahead as fast as they can distilling things right into these green balloons, all kinds of awful stuff as a matter of fact: hydrochloric acid, sulfuric acid, smoking nitric acid. That's the worst one of all. It always has a reddish yellow smoke that eats right into your lungs.

"But even if that smoke leaves you in peace, every drop of it burns a hole, in linen, in cloth, in leather, anything at all. Everything gets scorched or corroded. That's the sign of our times these days. Scorched or corroded. And so when I consider that my Globsowers are going along with it, and as cheerfully as can be, providing the tools for the great universal world scorching, well then, let me tell you, gentlemen, that gives me a stitch of pain right here in my heart. And I've got to say to you, I'd rather each one of'm got a half an acre of land from the state and bought himself a suckling pig at Easter time and at Martinmas they went and slaughtered that pig and had themselves two sides of bacon for the whole winter, a regular piece for every Sunday and potatoes and cracklings on weekdays."

"But Herr von Stechlin," laughed Lorenzen, "that's the 'New Land for All'[49] theory pure and simple. That's what the Social Democrats want too."

"Ach, nonsense, Lorenzen. Nobody can talk with you . . . . But here's to you anyway . . . even if you really don't deserve it."

Breakfast continued for a considerable while and the conversation turned toward politics several times but Lorenzen, who wished to avoid any little discordances, skillfully evaded them, preferring rather to bring the conversation around to the Stechlin church. Here too he proceeded with caution, and along with alluding to Tucheband, limited himself to architectural and historical questions until Dubslav somewhat abruptly asked him, "Do you know anything about the church attic, Lorenzen? Krippenstapel let me know just today that we've got two guilded bishops with crosiers up there. Or maybe they're just plain abbots." Lorenzen knew nothing about them whereupon Dubslav good-naturedly threatened him with his finger.

And so the conversation went on. But shortly before two an end had to be made to it all. Engelke came and reported that the horses were ready and the knapsacks already strapped in place. Dubslav raised his glass to toast their meeting again and with that everyone rose to leave.

Passing by the ramp, Rex once more walked up to the sickly aloe and let it be known that such blossoms really did have something peculiarly mysterious about them. Dubslav took care not to contradict him, pleased that the visit should conclude with such an amusing touch.

Shortly thereafter they rode off. As they passed the glass sphere all three turned once more and each raised his cap. Then their way continued past the boulders to the village lane on which a somewhat worse for wear looking buggy, its leather top laid back, passed them by. Its seats empty, everything about the vehicle showed a lack of care and maintenance. One horse was passably good, the other poor. And the coachman's old hat, resembling a piece of reddish brown peat, scarcely matched the new livery coat he was wearing.

"Why, that was Gundermann's buggy."

"Well, well," said Czako. "I almost could have guessed it."

"Yes indeed, this Gundermann fellow," laughed Woldemar. "My father really wanted to present you with a representative sample of our county folk yesterday. But he missed the mark. Gundermann from Siebenmühlen is pretty much our worst number. I see you didn't much care for him."

"Good God. Care for him, Stechlin? What does that mean — to care for him? As a matter of fact I like everybody — or nobody. A lady once told me when you get right down to it the boring people were just as good as the interesting ones. And there's something to it.

But this Gundermann! For exactly what reason is he letting his empty buggy ramble about like that?"

"I'm not sure of that either. Probably has to do with election matters. He's probably hanging around himself somewhere collecting a few votes. Our gallant old Kortschädel, you know, who was popular with everyone, died this summer and so Gundermann, who is trying to pass himself off as a conservative but really isn't one, is looking to fish in troubled waters. He's up to some tricks. I was able to make out that pretty clearly from a conversation I had with him, and Lorenzen has confirmed it."

"I can well imagine," responded Rex, "that Lorenzen of all people is against him. But this Gundermann, for whom I have nothing else positive to say, at least he's got the right principles."

"Oh Rex, come on now," said Czako. "The right principles! Tasteless phrases are what he's got and empty clichés. Three times I heard him say 'that would again be water on the mills of the Social Democrats.' No respectable person says a thing like that anymore, and in any case, he didn't add he was going 'to shut off their water.' Why that's a horrible turn of phrase."

As they continued to talk they reached the high-arched part of the chestnut-lined avenue. Engelke, who early that morning had prophesied fine weather, proved to be right; it was a real October day, clear, fresh and mild at the same time. The sun fell through the still rather thick foliage here and there and the riders enjoyed the play of light and shadows. But the scene became even more pleasant when soon afterwards they turned into an off-road which rambled through a flat meadow landscape, dotted here and there by small pools of water. The large heaths and forests, which are actually the most characteristic aspect of this northeastern part of the county, receded at this spot far into the distance, and only a few strips of forest, jutting forward like stage drops, became visible.

All three pulled up to let the scene have its effect on them. But they did not quite get around to it, for as they looked about, they caught sight of an old man who, separated from them merely by a shallow ditch, stood in the midst of a piece of meadowland mowing the high standing grass. Only then did he too look up from his work and lift his cap. The gentlemen did likewise and hesitated for a moment whether they should ride closer and have a chat with him. But he seemed neither to desire nor expect it and so they rode on.

"My God," said Rex, "why that was Krippenstapel. And way out here, so far from his school. If he hadn't had that sealskin cap that looks like it had been cut from a confiscated schoolbag, I'd never have recognized him."

"Yes, that was he. And what you said about the schoolbag might well be right," said Woldemar. "Krippenstapel can just about do anything. A regular Robinson Crusoe."

"Well now, Stechlin," interjected Czako, "You just say that in such a way as if you were looking to make fun of it. Actually it's really quite a great thing always to be able to help oneself. He's probably got a screw loose, I'll grant you that, but nevertheless he's got quite a bit on that much-praised Lorenzen of yours. If only because he's a real character and has a face like an owl. People with faces like an owl are almost always superior to other people."

"Good Lord, Czako, spare us. That's all nothing but sheer nonsense. And you know it. Just like Rex, even if for another reason, you simply want to carp about poor Lorenzen just because you have the feeling he's truly an altruistic personality."

"You're doing me wrong there, Stechlin. Completely. I'm for altruism, just as long as I'm not personally called upon."

"Well, you're safe on that point — you can't get wine from a bramble bush. In any case, I've got to break off at this point and beg you to excuse me for a while. I've got to make for the forester's house, that one over there next to the woods."

"But Stechlin, what in heaven's name do you want at the forester's?"

"Not a forester. It's a Chief Forester I want to visit, and in fact the same one you met last evening at my Papa's. Chief Forester Katzler. Bourgeois, but practically a historical name all the same."[50]

"Well, well. In any case from what Rex tells me he plays a brilliant game of billiards. And yet, unless you're really close friends with him, I find this little detour somewhat excessively courteous."

"You'd be right, Czako, if it were merely a matter of Katzler. But that's not the case. It's not him, but instead his young wife."

"*A la bonne heure.*"

"Ah yes. Well you're on the wrong track there too. That sort of thing can't happen, not even taking into account that it's never easy to get along with Chief Foresters. They can blow you away without you're ever knowing what happened . . . . It's merely a solicitous visit, if you will, something on the basis of pure humanity. As a matter of fact, Frau Katzler's expecting."

"Good Lord, Stechlin. You're talking more and more in riddles. You really don't intend to make a call on every Chief Forester's wife who's 'expecting,' do you? Why it would be a gigantic task, even if you intended to limit it just to this county of yours right here."

"It's all quite an exceptional situation. Anyway I'll make my visit short and if you ride on at a walk, if you don't mind, I'll catch up with you at Genshagen. From there it's scarcely an hour to Wutz, and if we want to push it, not even half an hour."

And as he spoke he turned off towards the right and rode toward the Forester's house.

Woldemar had occupied the middle between Rex and Czako. Now the two were riding next to one another. Czako was curious and would have liked to call Fritz up from the rear to hear a few tidbits about Katzler and his wife, but he realized that it was not the thing to do. Thus there was nothing left for him but to exchange views with Rex.

"Do you see," he began, "our friend Woldemar, isn't he trotting off there as if he were after happiness itself? Believe you me, there's a tale to be told behind all that. He had a love affair with that woman or he still loves her. And then this remarkable interest in the new citizen on the way. Maybe a girl, by the way. What do you think, Rex?"

"Ah, Czako, you only want to hear what fits that frivolous nature of yours. You don't believe in pure relationships. Very unjust. I can assure you, there really are things like that."

"Oh certainly, you, Rex, you who arrange sunrise services. But Stechlin . . . ."

"Stechlin is a moral individual too. Morality is inborn to him. And what he has by nature his regiment has developed even further in him."

Czako laughed. "Now listen, Rex, I'm familiar with regiments too, you know. There's all kinds of them. But morality regiments are something I haven't run across yet."

"But they exist just the same. Or at least there have always been some. Even a few with ascetic traits."

"Well yes, Cromwell and the Puritans. But that was 'long, long ago,' as the English say. Forgive me for that played-out turn of phrase. But when you're talking about something as fancy as asceticism, a fellow has to throw in an English crumb or two. In reality everything remains just as it's always been. You're a poor judge of human nature, Rex, just like all religious fundamentalists. They always believe what they want to. And I imagine you'll find out when it comes to our Stechlin as well, just how badly you've calculated. In any case there's a road sign just at the right time. Let's see where we really are. We've just been riding along here and don't have the faintest idea whether we're supposed to go left or right."

Rex, who was not interested in the road sign, was in favor of just riding on, which was, in fact, the right thing to do, for not even half an hour had passed before Stechlin caught up with them. "I knew I would meet you before Genshagen. The Frau Chief Forester sends you her greetings, by the way. He wasn't there, which was all the better."

"I can well imagine," said Czako.

"And what was even better, she looked marvelous. She's no beauty actually. A blond with great big forget-me-not eyes and rather phlegmatic disposition. Probably not quite healthy either. But it's strange though, such women always look better when they're expecting than they do in their natural condition; a situation, to be sure, which in the case of Frau Katzler hardly ever occurs. She's not yet been married for a full six years and she's expecting her seventh."

"Why that's absolutely unheard of. Why, I think something like that's grounds for divorce."

"Never heard of it as that, and anyway I'd have to admit, not too probable. In any case though, the princess won't use it as grounds for divorce."

"The princess?" blurted Rex and Czako a tempo.

"Yes, the princess," Woldemar repeated. "I was really on tenterhooks the whole time, to find out what sort of an impression that would make on you. That's why I was careful to avoid giving you any hints in advance. And it worked out well that my father merely passed it over very lightly last evening, I would almost even say discreetly, which usually isn't his way."

"Princess," repeated Rex, for whom the matter was almost breathtaking. "And from a reigning family?"

"Well, what do you mean by reigning family? They all reigned at one time or another. And as far as I know, this 'having reigned at one time or another' is always still taken into account when it comes to them, at least when it comes to concluding marriages. That makes it all the more magnificent when a few of the ladies in question give up all those privileges and without consideration of equality of birth enter the state of matrimony out of pure love. I use the term 'enter the state of matrimony' because 'get married' sounds somewhat plebeian. Frau Katzler is an Ippe-Büchsenstein."

"An Ippe!" said Rex. "Incredible. And expecting again. I confess, that's what shocks me the most. This extravagance, I can't find another word for it, or really, I even don't want to find another. I mean, it's really the most bourgeois thing there is."

"Admittedly so. And that's exactly the way the princess herself probably looks at it. But that's exactly the wonderful thing about it. Yes indeed, as strange as it may sound, what makes it ideal."

"Stechlin, it's asking too much for a fellow to comprehend that sort of thing just like that. Half a dozen brats, where's the ideal there?"

"On the contrary, Rex, on the contrary. The princess herself, and this is what's the most touching thing about it all, has been perfectly frank in discussing the whole thing. To my father, as a matter of fact. She sees him quite frequently and I believe she'd like to convert him. She hews to the strictly orthodox line, you know, and stands behind Superintendent Koseleger too, our local pope. To make a long story short, she's practically courting my papa and calls him a perfect cavalier, to which Katzler always makes a sort of sweet-sour face, but naturally doesn't do anything to contradict."

"And how did she ever come to make confessions to your father in of all things such a delicate matter?"

"It was last year, just about this time, when she was expecting again. My father was over at their place and as the topic engendered by that circumstance came up, he started half humorously, half diplomatically talking about Queen Luise, and how old Doctor Heim, when the queen was supposed to bear number six or number seven, rather straight out mentioned the need for a fallow period."

"Rather strong stuff," said Rex. "Right in the old Heim style. But of course, queens put up with all sorts of things. And how did the princess take it?"

"Oh, she was charming. She laughed and was neither embarrassed nor put out. Instead she took my father's hand just as warmly as if she had been his daughter. 'Yes indeed, my dear Herr von Stechlin,' she said, 'whoever starts something, has got to see it through. If I hadn't wanted a blessing of this sort, I would have had to marry just an average prince. Then maybe I would have had what old Heim felt necessary to recommend. Instead though I took my dear, good Katzler. A wonderful man. You know him and understand he has that beautiful simplicity of all handsomely-built men and his capabilities, insofar as one can really talk about them at all, have something one-sided about them. For that reason, when I married him, I was completely filled with the idea of shedding anything about myself that had to do with being a princess and to let nothing be left about me that detractors could have used to infer, 'Ah, she still wants to be a princess.' And so I decided for what was bourgeois and as a matter of fact, went 'the complete route,' as they say nowadays, I think. And what followed then, well, those were simply the natural consequences.'"

"Magnificent," said Rex. "On hearing that sort of information I relinquish all further opposition. What a measure of resignation! Because even in not renouncing something, there can be a kind of resignation. Continuing sacrifice of one's innermost and highest values."

"Incredible," laughed Czako. "Rex, Rex. A while ago, I denied you had the slightest knowledge of human nature. But here you're even outdoing yourself. Anybody who's involved with leading a religious group ought at least to know something about women. Remember, Stechlin said she was phlegmatic and had forget-me-not eyes. Now take a look at Katzler. Nearly six foot, reddish blond and the Iron Cross."

"Czako, you're getting frivolous again. But one shouldn't take you quite so seriously. It's that Slavic blood that bubbles up in you, latent sensuality."

"Oh yes, very latent, a treasure that's been completely buried. If it were up to me, I wouldn't mind getting into a situation where I could really make the most of it. But . . . ."

The conversation went on like this for a good while.

The main road into which their path had turned in the meanwhile gradually began to ascend. When they had reached the highest point of the grade, the convent, along with its little town of the same name, lay before them in relative proximity. On their first ride through this area, Rex and Czako had gotten to see so little of it, that a certain amazement at the beauty of the landscape as well as the architectural picture now spread out before them could not be suppressed. Czako especially was completely carried away, but Rex too chimed in.

"That huge gabled wall of field stone," he said, "as chancy as definite time references in this area in general are, I'd be for setting it at 1375, in the days of the 'Landbook' of Emperor Karl IV."[51]

"Could well be," Woldemar responded laughing. "There are numbers that can't be easily contradicted, you know. And 'Landbook' of Emperor Karl IV fits almost everything."

Rex chose not to hear that, for in his mind he was once again striving toward a more general and at the same time loftier point of view.

"Yes, gentlemen," he began, "the much-scorned Middle Ages. They knew how to do it in those days. I'll venture the claim, which by the way I haven't lifted from some handbook on art but which has slowly ripened in my own mind, 'The question of location supersedes the question of style.' These days they always pick the ugliest spot. They didn't have glasses back there in the Middle Ages, but they could see better."

"Of course," said Czako. "But this attack on glasses isn't for you, Rex. Anybody who depends so much on a pince-nez or a monocle . . . ."

Their conversation got no further, for just at this instant the powerful strokes of the bell tower clock from the little town of Wutz re-

sounded across to them. They pulled up and each counted. "Four."
Scarcely had the clock stopped ringing, however than a second began
and contributed its four strokes.

"That's the convent clock," said Czako.

"How do you know?"

"Because it's striking late. All convent clocks are slow. Naturally.
But however that may be, friend Woldemar, I do believe, announced
us for four o'clock and so we'll have to hurry."

Wutz Convent

7

THUS THEY ALL set off again at a trot, including Fritz, who closed up on the gentlemen riding ahead. The conversation came to a complete halt, because each was full of expectation of things to come.

The broad avenue ran on for a goodly distance between poplars. Once one was in the immediate proximity of Wutz Convent, however, the poplars ceased, and the increasingly narrowing road was bordered on both sides by fieldstone walls, beyond which various garden plots with all sorts of vegetable and flower beds and many fruit trees could soon be seen. All three let their horses slow to a walk.

"That garden on the left here," said Woldemar, "is the Domina's garden, my Aunt Adelheid's. A bit primitive but wonderful fruit. And over here on the right is where the canonesses plant their dill and marjoram. There's only four of them, and if any have died — although they only rarely do — there are even less."

As they listened to this orientating information from Woldemar, who since his boyhood days had known the area like the back of his hand, they all rode through an opening in the wall into a large farmyard. Structurally it more or less contained everything that had ever been Wutz Convent, right up to the days of the Thirty Years War, which, of course, had then destroyed everything. From the saddle everything could be comfortably taken in. For the most part what they saw were masses of jumbled rubble overgrown by trees and bushes.

"Reminds me of the Palatine Hill," said Rex, "only transposed into the Christian-Gothic mode."

"For sure," Czako confirmed with a laugh. "As far as I can judge, quite similar. Too bad Krippenstapel isn't here. Or Tucheband."

With that the conversation broke off once more.

In fact, wherever one looked lay the remains of walls into which, strangely enough, the dwellings of the ladies of the convent had been built. First off, the larger one of the Domina, next to it the smaller ones of the four canonesses, all on the longer side at the front. Across from this ran a second line of rubble, parallel to the first, in which were housed the stable buildings, the carriage and tool-shed, and the laundry and ironing room. That left only the two narrow sides, of which one was nothing but a wall overgrown by elder bushes. The second, on the other hand, was a massive gabled end wall, looming high over everything, the very one they had seen from a distance as they rode up. It stood there as if ready to bury everything by its constant threat of collapse. One thing alone was able to countervail this, however, a pair of storks, who always have a highly developed sense whether something is going to stand or fall, had made their nests at its highest point.

From the opening in the wall through which they had ridden it was only a few paces to the living quarters built into the fieldstone rubble. As they halted before them, the Domina herself soon appeared to welcome her nephew and his two friends. Fritz, who here as everywhere else knew what to do, led the horses over to one of the stable buildings on the other side while Rex and Czako, after brief introductions, made their way into the entry where cabinets stood on all sides.

"I didn't receive your telegram until one o'clock," said the Domina. "It goes by way of Gransee and the messenger has a long way to walk. But they want to get him one of those wheel things, the kind that's the rage everywhere these days. I say a wheel thing, because I can't stand that foreign word they pronounce every which way.[1] Some say 'ci' and some say 'shi'. I don't have any pretensions of fancy culture myself, but after all a person doesn't want to make a fool of herself either."

A flight of stairs led up to the second floor, in fact it was practically not much more than a ladder. The Domina, after she had accompanied the gentlemen to the lowest step, left them for a while. "You will be so good, Woldemar, as to take things in hand. Take the gentlemen upstairs. I've arranged our modest convent meal for five o'clock. Still a good half an hour yet. Until then, gentlemen."

Upstairs a large ironing chamber had been transformed into a guest room. A wash table with finger bowls and miniature cruets had been set up, which would have been completely appropriate considering the Lilliputian spatial circumstances, had not six gigantic towels hanging on the same number of door hooks once more thrown the ensemble out of balance. Rex, who yearned for a short respite of ten minutes — his boots were pinching — made use of an iron boot-jack, while Czako buried his face in one of the small wash bowls, and while drying himself, praised the firm weave of the towels.

"Their own weaving, for sure. All things considered, Stechlin, one thing's certain, your aunt's got something about her. You really get the impression, if you know what I mean, that she's the boss around here. And has been for quite a while too, I'll bet. If I heard rightly, she's older than your papa."

"Oh, quite a bit. Practically by ten years. She's going to be seventy-six."

"Respectable age. And I've got to admit, well-preserved."

"Yes, one can almost say that. That's just the advantage of those types people call 'slim.' A euphemism, I'd say in passing. Where there's nothing, even the Kaiser himself can't get much, and time can't either. It can't take anything away where there's nothing to start with. However — I feel sorry for Rex, by the way, he's going to have to get into his boots again — I think we should be making our way downstairs now and do our very best to be charming for my aunt. She's probably waiting by now to introduce her favorite to us."

"Who's that?"

"Well, that varies. But since there are only four possibilities, each one gets a chance at it sooner or later. When I was here last it was a certain Fräulein von Schmargendorf. Quite possibly it's her turn again right now."

"A nice lady?"

"Oh yes. A veritable dumpling."

And as suggested, after briefly "pulling themselves together" in the improvised guest room, the three gentlemen returned to Aunt Adelheid's salon, which was low, smoke-stained and somewhat old-fashioned. The furniture, nothing but heirlooms, had an almost grotesque effect in the low-ceilinged room and the heavy table cloth, with a massive, somewhat modern circular oil lamp atop, fit poorly with the bird cage at the window and even worse with the battle picture hanging over the small piano: King Wilhelm on the Heights of Lipa.[2] Nevertheless this unstylish mishmash had something homey about it. In the primitive hearth — merely a flat stone with a chimney — a wood fire had been started. Both windows stood open, but were as much as closed again by heavy draperies, and from the square mirror, hanging somewhat askew over the sofa, projected three peacock feathers.

Aunt Adelheid had clad herself in all her finery, even pinning on her Karlsbad garnet brooch, which because of the seven mid-sized stones surrounding a larger one leaping out in humped-back prominence, old Dubslav called "The Seven Electoral Prince Brooch."[3] Her long thin neck made the Domina look even taller and more imperious than she was, and completely justified her brother's malicious comment to the effect that, "when they set eyes on her, little babies begin squirming, and when she gets affectionate, they start screaming." One could see by looking at her that she had lived in higher social spheres only at times, but that throughout her life she had always remained aware of her inborn membership in these very circles. It was only reasonable that they had made her Domina. She knew how to keep accounts and organize affairs and was not simply possessed of considerable plain common sense, but under certain conditions was filled with interest for certain specific persons and things. What made dealing with her so difficult, however, such qualities notwithstanding, was her profoundly prosaic nature, that Brandenburgian narrowness, the distrust of everything that so much as touched upon the world of beauty or even that of freedom.

She arose as the three gentlemen entered and again displayed the utmost courtesy towards Rex and Czako. "Once again, gentlemen, I must express my deepest regret at being able to see you under my roof for only so short a time."

"You're forgetting *me*, dear Aunt," said Woldemar. "I'll be staying with you for a good while yet. I do believe my train doesn't leave till nine. And until then I'll tell you a world of news and — confess everything."

"No, no, Woldemar. None of that, none of that. There's a great deal I want to hear from you, a great deal. And I've even got some important questions on my own mind. You probably know what they are. But let's not have any of that confession talk. Just the very word makes me uncomfortable every time I hear it. It's got such a downright Catholic ring to it. Our Pension Director Fix is right when he says, 'Confession has no value because it's always insincere. And in Berlin — although it was a long time ago, of course, a long, long time ago — there was a clergyman who called the confessional box a veritable box of Satan.' I obviously find that overdone and I let Fix know about it in no uncertain terms. But on the other hand, I really do enjoy coming across such a forthright Protestant remark like that. We need courage like that. A good strong Protestant, even when he comes across a bit brusquely, is a real tonic for me every time, and I presume I might expect the same sort of reaction from you as well, Herr von Rex?"

Rex bowed.

"Yes indeed, Czako," remarked Woldemar, however, "there you have it. Your name wasn't even mentioned. A Domina — you'll pardon me, Aunt — simply develops a highly refined sense of discrimination."

His aunt smiled politely and said, "Herr von Czako is an officer. There are many mansions in my father's house. But one thing I must say, lack of faith is spreading, and Catholicism is too. And Catholicism, that is the worst of the two. Idolatry is worse than no faith at all."

"Aren't you going a bit too far there, dear Aunt?"

"No, Woldemar. You see, lack of faith, which is really nothingness, that can't offend the dear Lord. But idolatry does offend Him. Thou shalt have no strange gods before me. There you have it. And now this pope in Rome, who wants to be a god above all and infallible."[4]

While Rex was keeping his silence and merely repeating his bow, Czako got the foolhardy idea of breaking a lance for pope and papacy. He quickly relinquished this intention, however, as he realized that the old lady had put on her Domina look. It was, however, merely a quickly passing cloud. Changing the subject, her good humor speedily recovered, Aunt Adelheid continued, "I've had the windows opened. But right now it's still a bit stuffy here, gentlemen. Comes from the low ceiling. Might I perhaps invite you to a promenade through our garden? Our convent garden is actually the nicest thing we've got here. Only the one belonging to our Pension Director is better tended and larger, and lies on the lake as well.

"Pension Director Fix, who keeps everything going here, is a real model for us, just as in economic matters, so too especially when it comes to his garden plots. A man of estimable character in every way, and when it comes to loyalty, good as gold, despite the fact that his salary is insignificant and his other income sources float about in the air quite insecurely. I did have Fix invited to join us at dinner; he really does know how to chat so well and easily. You could almost say with total frankness, yet always completely discreet. But professional obligations prevent him. You gentlemen will just have to be satisfied with me and one of the members of our convent, a sister quite dear to me, who is always cheerful and high-spirited, but yet at the same time firm in her spiritual conviction, a person with that wonderful cheerfulness you find only in those whose faith has taken strong root. A good conscience, as they say, makes the best pillow for sleeping well. That explains it, no doubt."

Rex, to whom these remarks had been mainly addressed, expressed his agreement repeatedly, while Czako lamented the fact that Fix had been prevented from coming. "Hearing men like that who are in touch with the common folk and know just how things are in the castles on one hand and in the huts of the poor on the other, that's something that's always extremely helpful and instructive, and it's a thing that I never like to pass up."

Immediately thereafter everyone arose and went outside.

The garden was a real country garden. Along its entire length ran a path bounded by boxwood hedging, next to which on the left and right delphiniums and marigolds were blooming in well-kept beds. Exactly at the mid-point the otherwise narrow path widened to a rounded space on which stood a large glass sphere, very much like the one at Stechlin except that the inlaid polished pewter was missing. Both spheres came, of course, from the "Green Glassworks" at Globsow. Further down, all the way at the end of the garden, one could make out a somewhat crooked wooden fence with a plum tree behind it, one of whose main branches reached over from the neighboring garden into that of the Domina.

Rex walked with the aunt on his arm. Then followed Woldemar with Captain von Czako, far enough behind the leading pair to be able to speak openly with one another."

"Now then, Czako," said Woldemar, "let's stay a bit further back if we can. I can't begin to tell you how much I enjoy being in this garden. In all seriousness. As a boy I played here, you know, and sat up in those pear trees a hundred times; there were quite a few standing here in those days, over here on the left, where the carrots are growing now. I don't care for carrots, from which, by the way, I conclude that we'll get some for dinner today. How do you like the garden?"

"Splendid. Why, it really is a farmer's garden, but yet there are quite a few delphiniums. And for every delphinium there's a canoness."

"No, Czako. It's not like that. Now tell me quite seriously, whether you're particularly fond of gardens like this."

"Actually I can put up with gardens like this only when they have a bowling green. And this one here is practically made for one, long and narrow. All our modern nine-pin alleys are too short, just the way all the beds used to be too short. The ball scarcely hits the ground than it's got there and the pin boy at the other end is shouting his 'eight down around the kingpin' at you. For me the fun only just begins when the alley is long and you can feel how the ball wants to wander to the right or to the left but the innate force of the throw keeps holding it straight, staying on the right path. There's something symbolic or pedagogical about it, or if you want, something political as well."

As they conversed they had come to the far end, the place where the neighboring plum tree stretched its branch over the fence. Next to the fence, however, although in line with it, stood a green-painted bench on which, sheltered by the branches, sat a lady wearing a small round hat with an eagle's feather. As the group approached, she arose and walked towards the Domina to kiss her hand. At the same time she bowed in the direction of the three gentlemen.

"Permit me, "said Adelheid, "to acquaint you with my dear friend Fräulein von Schmargendorf. Hauptmann von Czako, Ministerial Assessor von Rex . . . . Of course, you already know my nephew, my dear Schmargendorf."

Adelheid, having thus made the introductions, drew her little watch from her belt and said, "We still have ten minutes. If it's all right with you, we'll stay out here in God's fresh air. Woldemar, take my dear friend's arm, or rather, you, Herr Hauptmann — Fräulein von Schmargendorf is to be your table partner anyway."

Fräulein von Schmargendorf was small and plumpish, somewhere in her forties, possessed of a short neck and little in the way of a waist. Of the seven beauties every one of the daughters of Eve are supposed to have at their disposal, she possessed, as far as the credit side could be established, only the bust. But then she was fully conscious of this fact and always wore dark dresses with velvet trimming above the waist. Said trimming consisted of three triangles pointing downwards. She was always cheerful, to begin with as a result of a naturally cheerful disposition, but then also because she had heard somewhere that cheerfulness preserved youth. It was important to her to stay young, although she could no longer really gain much by it. Neighboring nobility were not to be found, the pastor was, of course, already married, and Fix was too. And lower down the scale was out of the question.

Adelheid and Rex were so far ahead most of the time that they usually met only at the glass sphere when the leading pair was making its way back. Each time Czako then saluted the Domina in a military fashion.

The latter was deeply involved in a conversation with Rex and was arguing with him about the ominous growth of sectarianism. Rex felt himself personally touched, since he himself was on the point of becoming an Irvingite.[5] He was, however, man of the world enough to quickly cope with the matter and above all to abstain from any sustained opposition to the views expressed by Adelheid. He skillfully steered the discussion to the realm of the general decline in faith, thereby immediately encountering complete agreement. Indeed, the Domina went even further and alternately alluding first to the Apocalypse and then to Fix, she emphasized that we were facing the beginning of the end. Fix, she said, went a bit far, no doubt, when he practically didn't believe things could go on for one single day more. Those were useless concerns, for which reason she had urged him to dispense with such worries or at least to reexamine them all once more.

"No doubt about it," she concluded, "Fix is decisively talented when it comes to matters involving bookkeeping, but nevertheless I've had to tell him there's still always a difference when it comes to calculations of one sort and calculations of another."

Czako had proffered his arm to Fräulein von Schmargendorf. Because the path was so narrow, Woldemar followed a few steps behind the two of them, temporarily stepping up to their side only where the path widened.

"How fortunate I am, Herr Hauptmann," said Fräulein von Schmargendorf, "to be your partner. Here right now and then later at table."

Czako bowed.

"And it's remarkable," she continued, "that it's specifically the Alexander Regiment which has always has such cheerful gentlemen. A cousin of yours with the same name, or perhaps it was even your elder brother, I remember him perfectly well from when he was posted to the Priegnitz area, despite its being twenty years ago or more. Because, you know, in those days I was just a young snip of a thing and danced a first rate radowa with your cousin — that's a dance that was in style in those days, but not so much anymore. And I've still got his signature and a little verse he wrote in my album. 'Jegor von Baczko, Second Lieutenant, Alexander Regiment.' Well there you are, Herr von Baczko, and so now we've come together again. Or at least with a gentleman of the same name."

Czako remained silent and merely nodded. Correcting people was something he detested in general. Woldemar, however, who had heard every word and with regard to things of that sort was somewhat more punctilious than his friend the captain, sought by all means to remedy the situation, and begged to call the lady's attention to the fact that the gentleman presently enjoying the honor of walking arm in arm with her was not a Herr von Baczko but rather, a Herr von Czako.

The plump little woman was momentarily embarrassed. Czako himself chivalrously came to her aid. "My dear Stechlin," he began, "By sixty-six stacks of Saxon shoe tacks, I beg you, don't bring up such trivialities, called *velleités* nowadays, I think. Anyway, that's how I've always translated the word. . Czako, Baczko, Baczko, Czako — how can anybody make so much out of that anyway? 'Names,' as you know, 'are naught but sound and smoke,' look it up in Goethe; you don't really want to go contradicting the likes of *him*, do you? Because when you get right down to it you don't have enough going for your side of things."

"Tee hee."

"And besides, a fellow like you, who, his liberalism notwithstanding, can still manage to trace his nobility back at least as far as the Third Crusade, a fellow like you should at least be generous enough not to begrudge me a little mix-up like this. I mean, this 'Baczko' that's just fallen right into my lap . . . . Thank God that anything at all can still fall into the lap of the likes of me."

"Tee hee."

"Because this Baczko that's just come falling into my lap is, after all, nothing less than an step up in rank and standing, a regular first class advancement. The Baczkos go back at least as far as Hus or Ziska[6] and if it turns out they're Hungarians, as far back as the Hunyadis,[7] while the first of the real Czakos hasn't even made it to being two hundred years old yet. And of course, all of us naturally come from that first genuine Czako.

"Just think about it, before there were any real shakos, in other words those stiff gray felt hats trimmed with leather or metal, there can't have been any *von* Czakos either. Nobility is always traced back to things such as the region it comes from, or its profession, or whatever it was involved with. If I were ever really to get the urge again to get married in keeping with my station, maybe I'll come to grief on the youthfulness of my noble name, and then I'll think back mournfully to this very hour, which for a brief instant, even if it was just on the basis of a mix-up in names, endeavored to raise me up a bit higher."

Woldemar, growing aware of his Philistine pedantry, once more withdrew, while Fräulein von Schmargendorf artlessly remarked, "Then you really do believe Herr von . . . Herr Hauptmann . . . , that you're descended from one of those shako hats?"

"As far as such remarkable whims of nature are at all possible, I am thoroughly convinced of it."

At this moment, having once again passed the place with the glass sphere, the pair reached the bench under the plum tree. Fräulein von Schmargendorf had long since been eyeing two large plums hanging close together. Now, as she stretched her hand towards them, she said "Well then, it's time we eat a 'sweetheart's snack,' Herr Hauptmann, because wherever, as here, two persons are together there's always a sweetheart"[8]

"A definition which I totally endorse. But, my dear lady, if I might be so bold as to suggest we rather wait with this glorious gift of God until dessert. After all, that really is the proper time for a 'sweetheart's snack.'"

"Well, as you wish, Herr Hauptmann. And I'll save these two until then for us. But this third one here, that doesn't quite fit in so much, I'll eat this one right now. I really do love plums. And you'll let me have it, won't you?"

"Everything, everything. The whole world."

It almost seemed as if Czako had the urge to expand on the topic of plums, especially with regard to the hazards lurking therein. He never got that far, however, for just then a servant in white cotton gloves, apparently an inspiration of the moment, became visible in the courtyard door. This was the sign agreed to by the Domina that the table had been set. Fräulein von Schmargendorf, equally initiated into the meaning of this sort of sign language, which meant that speedy decisions had to be taken, therefore bent down to break off hastily a large cabbage leaf from one of the vegetable beds into which she carefully placed the two red-spotted plums. Immediately thereafter, once more taking the captain's arm, she proceeded, the Domina in the lead, through the courtyard and entry hall and finally to the salon.

The latter had been altered in a number of ways, above all, however, by the presence of a second lady of the convent, standing next to the fireplace in dark silk with a beribboned head and deeply-set fixed cockatoo eyes which seemed to penetrate through to the essence of all things.

"Ah my dearest," said the Domina, striding towards this second convent member, "I'm truly glad to see that despite your headache you've come out. Otherwise we would have been left without a third lady at table. Allow me to make the introductions: Herr von Rex, Herr von Czako . . . Fräulein von Triglaff from the House of Triglaff."

Rex and Czako bowed, while Woldemar, to whom she was no stranger, approached the canoness to offer a word of greeting. Czako, who was unable to refrain from peering closely at the Triglaff woman, was instantly touched by a striking similarity, and immediately whispered softly to Rex who was repeatedly resorting to his monocle, "Krippenstapel, female line." Rex nodded.

While this scene was taking place, the servant in the background had with a certain ostentatiousness drawn back the upper and lower bolts on the door; a brief instant later both wings leading into the dining room next to the salon opened with quiet solemnity.

"Herr von Rex," said the Domina, "may I take your arm."

In a flash Rex was at her side and immediately thereafter all three pairs entered the adjoining room. On its inviting table, arranged not without a certain skill, stood two vases full of flowers and two silver candelabra. The servant too was in action by now; he had taken his stand at the buffet before a Meissen soup tureen, and as he removed the lid topped by a somewhat chipped angel, the steam rose upward like incense.

Aunt Adelheid, when nothing occurred to put her out of sorts, was an excellent hostess in the old style, and possessed among other things those directorial eyes which mean so much at table. But there was one gift she did *not* possess, that of holding the conversation together as in an intimate circle it ought to be. Thus right from the start the little party fell into three groups, of which one, if not absolutely taciturn, nevertheless functioned primarily as a table decoration. This was the pairing of Woldemar-Triglaff. And no doubt it could not have been otherwise. The Triglaff woman, as so often is the case with cockatoo-faced types, combined an expression of the most grand profundity with one of an utterly extraordinary vacuity, and the last shred of intelligence that might have been left remaining to her had at last become lost through a stupendous sense of Triglaffian vanity.

A direct line of descent from the Wendic divinity[9] of the same name, somewhat in the manner of Czako from shako, was, it must be admitted, not provable. At the same time it also could not be ruled out. And if things of that sort actually do occur, or by tacit agreement could merely be generally accepted, well then, it was not easy to see why she of all people should come up empty-handed or have to do without such a possibility. This extreme sense of aristocratic superiority also went hand in hand, of course, with the sense of pique she maintained against that particular branch of the House of Thadden which had endowed itself with the sobriquet Thadden-Triglaff after its Pomeranian estate Triglaff. That was an augmentation which seemed to *her*, the only genuine Triglaff, to be an encroachment plain and simple, or at the very least, a diminution of her good name.

Woldemar, who was well aware of all of this, was immune to it and had known for a long time how he ought to behave when it fell to him to have Fräulein Triglaff as a table partner. For such a contingency, which incidentally befell him more frequently than he cared to see, he had memorized the names of all the canonesses who had lived at Wutz Convent throughout his childhood, and who he knew quite well were long since dead. Nevertheless he regularly began to ask questions in such a manner as if the existence of these long since dearly departed was still a possibility.

"There used to be a Drachenhausen here, dearest Fräulein. Aurelia von Drachenhausen, and if I'm not mistaken she then moved over to the convent at Zehdenick. It would really interest me to find out whether she's still alive or if she's perhaps dead by now."

Fräulein Triglaff nodded.

Czako, taking note of her nod, later observed to Rex that it all fit in quite naturally with the Triglaff woman's lineage. "All idols ever do is nod."

Considerably more lively was the exchange between Aunt Adelheid and the Ministerial Assessor. Their conversation, which touched only upon morally uplifting topics, would have completely possessed the character of a pleasantly comfortable, albeit by virtue of its seriousness, spiritual synodic chat, had not the figure of Pension Director Fix kept on intruding itself, that protégé of the Domina of whom Rex, while suppressing his true opinion, time and again asserted, "that this official of the convent seemed to represent a unique blending of sternly-held principles with a genius for business."

Those were the two couples who formed the left flank and middle of the table respectively. The two chief figures, however, were Czako and Fräulein von Schmargendorf, who sat all the way over to the right in the vicinity of the thick woolen curtains in whose folds a great deal fortunately got absorbed. Following the soup came a fish course, after which a lentil puree with baked ham appeared. Then larded partridge wings in spice sauce, which at the same time was the Domina's culinary secret, were also passed around. Czako, despite having partaken considerably of the baked ham, took a second helping of the partridge, and felt the need to justify his action.

"A richly endowed region, your county here," he began. "But of course it's also a richly endowed autumn we're having this year. Last evening, breasts of thrush at Dubslav von Stechlin's, this evening at Adelheid von Stechlin's, partridge wings."

"And which do you prefer?" asked Fräulein von Schmargendorf.

"In general, gracious lady, that question would be probably decided in favor of the former. But here and especially for me, I would think we have the exception."

"Why an exception?"

"You're quite right in asking that very question. And I'll respond as well as I can. Well then, when we consider breasts and wings . . . ."

"Tee hee."

"In breasts and wings reposes, so it seems to me, the magnificent antitheses of the earthly and the celestial. There is nothing more earthly than the breast and nothing more celestial than wings. Wings carry us aloft, bear us upward. And for that very reason, despite all enticements of the other side, I would prefer to place everything that has to do with wings nevertheless on a higher plane."

He had said this in as low a tone as possible. But it wasn't really necessary, for on one hand Fräulein Triglaff, sitting next to him on his left, closed her ears to everything being said out of a sense of sheer superiority, while at the same time, once the servant had passed around a number of small stemmed glasses, the Domina was quite visibly occupied with preparing a speech.

"Permit me to express once more," she said, half rising from her seat, "how happy it makes me to be able to welcome you here in my convent. Herr von Rex, Herr von Czako, your health."

Everyone touched glasses. Rex immediately expressed thanks and once everyone was seated again also, gave vent to his admiration for the excellent wine. "A Montefiascone, I suspect ."

"More distinguished, Herr von Rex," responded Adelheid cheerfully, "a step higher than that. It's not a Montefiascone, which by the way we did indeed lay in here in our cellars under my predecessor in office. Instead it's Lacrimae Christi. When I offered it to him some time ago, my brother, who finds fault with everything, said of course, it wasn't at all appropriate. Called it funeral wine, a wine for confirmations at best, but not at all the thing for cheerful get-togethers."

"A remark with an idiosyncratic meaning, wherein I fully recognize your distinguished brother."

"To be sure, Herr von Rex. And I am fully aware that the name of this particular wine imposes all sorts of considerations upon us. But if one would only keep in mind, that we are in a priory, a convent . . . and so, you see, in my opinion, the place in which we live really does grant us a right and a certain dignified solemnity."

"No doubt about it. And I must belatedly acknowledge your brother's reservations to be erroneous. But, if I may put it in such a way, a charming error . . . . To your brother's health."

And with that the somewhat awkward conversation, which all had followed with a certain embarrassment, came to an end. For all except Fräulein von Schmargendorf. "Dear me," she said, while half hiding herself in the curtains, "whenever we drink any of this wine, we always hear the same story along with it . . . . The Domina certainly must have been angry at old Herr von Stechlin that time. And yet he really is right, you know. Just the mere name puts you in a serious and solemn mood. And there's something about it that really does give a true Christian person something to think about, after all. And just when one is feeling so downright cheery."

"And let's drink to that too," said Czako, leaving totally unclear as to whether he meant the Christian person, the serious and solemn mood, or being cheery.

And in general," continued Fräulein von Schmargendorf, "wines really ought to have other names. Or at least an awful lot of them."

"My opinion exactly, gracious lady," said Czako. "There really are some . . . . But then one really shouldn't overextend one's sense of delicacy. If we try doing that, why we'll simply deny ourselves the richest sources of true poetry. We've got for example, speaking merely in general and simply as a generic term, the 'old man's milk'.[10] At first blush a totally unobjectionable phrase. But quite soon — our language loves tricks like this, you know — there appears a variety of extensions and new formulations, even leaps from one gender to another, and before we know it, 'old man's milk' has turned into *Liebfrauenmilch*, 'The Blessed Mother's Milk'."[11]

"Tee, hee. Oh yes, *Liebfrauenmilch*, we drink that too. But only rarely. And that isn't *the* name, I was actually thinking about either."

"Most certainly not, dear lady. Because the fact is, there are still others, more definite than that, for which the only thing left for us is the refuge offered by using the French pronunciation."

"Tee, hee . . . You're right. French. That works. But then again not always, and every time Pension Director Fix is our guest and Triglaff there starts turning the bottle around and around — and I've seen her turn it around three times — then Fix starts to laugh . . . . Well, anyway, it looks as if the Domina has something on her mind, she's got such a solemn look on her face. Or maybe she just wants to bring the festivities to an end."

And it indeed was as Fräulein Schmargendorf suspected. "Gentlemen," said the Domina, "since to my chagrin you must be on your way so soon — we've got just a bit more than a quarter hour left — I'll leave it up to you whether we prefer to have our coffee in my room or outside beneath the elder tree."

A general answer was not to be heard but while all were rising immediately thereafter, Czako kissed Fräulein Schmargendorf's hand and remarked with a certain eagerness, "Beneath the elder tree then."

Fräulein Schmargendorf did not have the faintest idea to what he was referring. But it meant nothing to Czako. The only thing that mattered to him was being able to imagine Fräulein Schmargendorf just for himself, privatim so to speak, for a brief but magnificent moment as Kätchen von Heilbronn.[12]

As for the rest, it turned out that not only Czako but Rex and Woldemar too were also in favor of the elder tree, and so they made their way toward it.

It was the very same tree which the gentlemen had caught sight of as they rode into the convent yard. At that moment, however, they had taken little notice of it. Only now did they realize what they really had before them. The tree, which was probably ancient, stood outside the farmyard. Like the plum tree in the garden, however, its branches had continued to grow over the crumbling walls. Simply in and of itself it was a splendor. What imparted an especial beauty to it, however, was that its leafy canopy had become intertwined with several mountain ashes standing behind it, so that everywhere next to the blackish umbels of the elder, one could see the glowing reddish berry clusters of the ash trees. The differing leaves also imparted shadings among the foliage.

Rex and Czako were truly delighted, almost more than the situation allowed. For as charming as the arbor was, all the more questionable was the sight of the courtyard, spreading itself out immediately before them in its disorder and lack of cleanliness. But picturesque it was, that much had to be admitted. Clumps of mortared fieldstone lay in high grass, between them wheel barrows and manure carts along with duck and chicken cages, all the while a gobbling turkey from time to time approached close by the arbor, be it out of curiosity or to compete with Fräulein Triglaff.

At six Fritz appeared leading the horses. Czako called attention to it. But before he was able to approach the Domina and express a few words of thanks, Fräulein Schmargendorf returned. She had left her place a few minutes before and now she was carrying the large cabbage leaf on which the two intergrown plums were lying.

"You're trying to escape me, Herr von Czako. But you won't get away with it. I want to win my 'sweetheart's snack.' And you'll see, I'll win."

"You always win, gracious lady."

9

Rex and Czako rode off. Fritz led Woldemar's horse by the reins. But neither Fräulein Schmargendorf nor Fräulein Triglaff showed any inclination to leave after the two gentlemen had departed and the three ladies, in the company of Woldemar, had retired to the living quarters. This was something that annoyed the Domina considerably, for she wished to be alone with her nephew because of the delicate matters she had to discuss with him. She made it quite clear as well, remaining stiff and taciturn and not brightening up until Fräulein Schmargendorf radiantly declared all of a sudden that she now knew exactly what she would do. She still had a picture which she would send right off to Herr von Czako and when he arrived tomorrow in Berlin from Cremmen, he'd find a picture and a letter waiting for him and, on the back of the picture the lines "Good morning, Sweetheart."

The Domina found it all as ridiculous and inappropriate as could be. Since, however, her chief desire was to be rid of Fräulein Schmargendorf, she kept her true opinion to herself and responded, "Oh my, yes indeed, my dear Schmargendorf. If you intend to do something like that, it's high time you got busy. The mailman could be here any minute."

And sure enough Fräulein Schmargendorf went on her way, leaving only Fräulein Triglaff, whose glance flitted from the Domina to Woldemar and then back again from Woldemar to the Domina. In the process she was completely ingenuous about it all. The desire to overhear something or to pry into family matters never even occurred to her. All that nevertheless made her linger on was simply the wish to endow such an historic get-together with a heightened sanctity by means of her Triglaffian presence.

Finally, however, she too left. No one had taken much notice of her and now that they were alone aunt and nephew settled into two brown plush easy chairs — heirlooms from Stechlin Castle. Woldemar, it must be conceded, did so with the greatest of care because the springs had by then reached an age when not only did they emit a dull sound, but they had begun to stick as well.

His aunt took not the slightest note of that sort of thing. Instead she was happy to have her nephew all to herself. Her contentment quickly regained, she said, "I'd have been happy to have given you someone better as your table partner, but as you know, we've only got our four canonesses here, and of the four of them, the Schmargendorf woman and Triglaff are still the best. Dear old Schimonski, who turns eighty-one tomorrow, really is a treasure, but sad to say, she's deaf as a post. As for Teschendorf, who used to be the Governess for the Esterhazys and even knew Prince Schwarzenberg — the one whose wife burned up in Paris — [13] well, you can imagine, naturally I'd have been happy to present her to as fine a gentleman as Herr von Rex, but it's a sad thing that the poor soul, Teschendorf I mean, is so terribly shaky she can't even hold a spoon right any more. So I decided on Triglaff instead. She is rather stupid, but at least she's got some manners, that much you can say about her. And as far as Schmargendorf . . . ."

Woldemar laughed.

"Oh yes, you can laugh, Woldemar. And I won't even argue with you that anybody can laugh about that dear, sweet soul. But she's got something substantial in her nature that just manifested itself again the other evening in intimate conversation with our Fix, who despite the strictness of his religious convictions — which even Koseleger admits are strict — said a few things at our last whist party that we all had to deplore deeply, those of us who were playing whist for certain, of course, but also good old, deaf Schimonski, for whom we had to write it all down on a piece of paper because she saw us get so upset about it."

"And whatever was it all about?"

"Dear me. It had to do with something that as you can well imagine is the dearest thing to all of us these days, the wording of the scriptural text. And just imagine, Fix was against it. He must have read something that very day that made him heretical. People like Fix are very easily influenced. Well, to make a long story short, he said that business about the wording just wouldn't do any more. 'Values' had now become totally different, and since values weren't the same any more, the wording would have to change too and get revalued. That's what he said, 'revalued.' But what he emphasized most of all was the values and the need for a 'revaluation.'"[14]

"And what did Fräulein Schmargendorf say to that?"

"Quite right of you to remind me of Fräulein Schmargendorf again. Well then, she was beside herself and couldn't sleep the following night. It wasn't until towards morning that she finally fell into a deep sleep and then — at least so she's assured me and the Superintendent — she saw an angel who kept on pointing to a book with a finger of fire and to one and the same passage over and over in the book."

"What passage?"

"Well, in fact we argued about that. Schmargendorf had read it exactly and wanted to recite it to us. But she got it wrong because she never actually pays attention in church on Sundays. And we told her so right then and there. And just imagine, she didn't contradict us at all but stayed as calm as could be and said, Yes, she knew quite well that she had recited the passage wrong. She never could recite anything correctly. But one thing she knew absolutely for sure, that passage with the finger of fire, that had been the scriptural Word.'"

"And you really believed all of that, my dear Aunt? Good old Schmargendorf! I'll gladly stick by her, but as far as that dream of hers goes, I can't go along there even with the best of good intentions. It was probably a magistrate who appeared to her, or some pastor. Thirty years back and it would have been a student."

"Now Woldemar. Don't say things like that! Why that's nothing but the new way Berliners are talking these days. And in that regard one's just the same as another. Your friend Czako talks that way too. Now you're sniggering at our dear good Schmargendorf and your friend the captain, I could see as much quite clearly, he did it too, and at table he was even twitting her."

"Twitting her?"

"The word surprises you, I see. Well, it surprises me too. But our good Herr Fix is the one to blame for it. He goes off to Berlin every month or so and when he comes back he brings things like that along with him. And even though I consider it rather inappropriate, I pick it up and so does Schmargendorf too. Only Triglaff doesn't and of course dear good Schimonski doesn't either on account of her deafness. Yes indeed, Woldemar, I say 'twitting her' and your friend Czako ought rather not to have done it. But it is true nevertheless, he is an amusing fellow even if he's a bit on the see-saw. Do you see much of him?"

"No, dear Aunt. Not often. Just remember the distances involved. Why, from our barracks to his or back it's practically a small safari. And then there's the fact that those of us out at the Halle Gate[15] really haven't got anything at all, just the cemeteries, the Tempelhof practice field and Rother's home for unmarried officers' daughters."

"But you do have horse-drawn street cars if you want to go somewhere. I've almost got to say, unfortunately, because it really does give me a twinge whenever I get to Berlin, to see the officers, how they stand there at the back of the car and make room when some '*Madamm*' or other climbs on, sometimes carrying a basket and sometimes even with a wet nurse from the Spreewald. That's always a real *horreur* for me."

"Yes, the horse car, dear Aunt. True enough, we do have it and with it you can be at Czako's barracks in a half hour. The fact is, though, it's not really the long distance, or at least that's not the only thing that keeps me from seeing Czako very frequently. When I think about it, the chief reason is probably that he doesn't quite fit in with us. As a matter of fact, he scarcely fits in with his regiment. Oh, he's a good fellow all right, but he goes in for too many equivocations and is always telling tales about the sort of things that go on after midnight. When you're alone with him, things are fine. But give him an audience and he really gets the itch. The more elegant his audience, the worse he gets. He's embarrassed me quite a few times. I must admit, I really do like him a lot, but socially you've got to concede, Rex is very much his superior."

"Oh yes, Rex. Certainly. Of course, I could see that right away without even trying to figure out exactly why. But I'm sure you must know what it is about him that makes him the superior of the two."

"Quite a few things. First off, when you weigh the families against one another, a Rex is more than a Czako. And then Rex is a cavalryman."

"But I thought he's a Ministerial Assessor."

"Oh, he's that too. But along with that, or perhaps even beyond that, he's an officer. And in our dragoons brigade besides."

"That's nice to hear. Why then he's as much as one of your very special comrades."

"I can admit to that, but then on the other hand, I can't either. Because first of all he's in the reserves and secondly, he's serving in the Second Dragoons."

"Does that make a difference?"

"Good Lord, Aunt, it all depends on how you look at it, whether it does or not. At Mars-la-Tour we all rode to the same attack."[16]

"And yet . . . ."

"And yet, there's still that certain '*Je-ne-sais-quoi*.'"

"Don't talk French. That always irritates me. Some people are even saying things in English these days, which pleases me even less. But never mind that. It seems to me it would be awful if you only went just by the number alone. After all, what's the regiment in which our dear, good Schmargendorf's brother's serving supposed to do? I do believe it's the 145th."

"Right, well, when you get that high, it doesn't make a difference any more. But when it comes to the Guard . . . ."

The Domina shook her head. "When it gets to that sort of thing, my dear Woldemar, I can scarcely follow you. Our Herr Fix now and again says I'm too exclusive. But I'm a far cry from being that exclusive. And such a reasonable person like you, so objective and so 'above such things,' as some people are saying these days, besides. And God forgive me the sin, so liberal too, something even your father laments. And now you come to me with a prejudice like that? Yes indeed, if you'll forgive me for saying it, such superior airs. I don't recognize you at all anymore in that sort of talk. And even if I take the First Guards Regiment,[17] when you get right down to it, it's only the first. Does that make it more than the second? Of course, one can say, that much I'll admit, they've got those fancy brass helmets of theirs, and all look as if they wanted to marry nothing but girls from Holland . . . . Which ought to please them no end."

"The girls from Holland?"

"Well, them too," laughed his aunt. "But it's our boys I meant just now. Now don't misunderstand me. I know perfectly well all about that extra tall grenadier business. But the others are just as fine. And Potsdam is, after all, just Potsdam."

"Yes, Aunt. That's exactly the point. That they're still in Potsdam, that's what makes the difference. That's why today as always it's the 'Potsdam Changing of the Guard.' And for sure, that word 'first' also has to do with it as well. An old Roman, whose name I won't burden you with, said he'd rather be first in his Potsdam than second in his Berlin. Whoever's the first, well, he's the first, plain and simple. And when the others got out of bed, this 'first' fellow had already taken his morning stroll. And now and then what a stroll it was! Just imagine, when the second regiment was born, those fellows with the brass helmets had the whole Seven Years War behind them. It's like the eldest son. Under certain conditions the eldest can be dumber and worse than his brother, but he's still the eldest. Nobody can take that away from him. And that gives him a certain pride of place, even if he has no superior qualities. It's all a gift from God. Why is one fellow handsome and another ugly? And then, what about the ladies? The whole world falls in love with one little lady and the other one winds up being nothing but the wall flower. Everyone's given a place. And so it is with our regiment too. We may not be better than the others, but we are the first. We wear number one."

"I can't agree with you there, Woldemar, even with the best of intentions. In our army the most decisive factor really is its dash."

"Oh my dear Aunt, talk about whatever you want. Only just not that. That's a phrase for insignificant garrisons. We know, what our job is. Duty is everything, and dash is nothing but braggadocio. And that's what stands lowest with us."

"Splendid, Woldemar. What you just said there really pleases me. And on this point I've got to praise your father as well. There's a lot about him which doesn't suit me, but when it comes to something like that, he's still a true Stechlin. And you are too. And one thing I've always found to be true, anyone who's that sort of person always stands head and shoulders above the rest, especially when it comes to the ladies."

This 'when it comes to the ladies,' was by no means said without purpose and seemed intended to lead to the main topic of discussion, which until now had been carefully avoided. But before Woldemar's aunt could ask a direct question, the Pension Director was announced. It was a highly inconvenient moment. Visibly irritated, the Domina turned to Woldemar. "Should I send him away?"

"It would scarcely do, dear Aunt."

"Well then."

And immediately thereafter Fix entered the room.

10

While Woldemar and the Domina were chatting, first alone and then in the company of Pension Director Fix, Czako and Rex rode on towards Cremmen, with Fritz bringing up the rear leading the extra horse by a line. That was still a good distance away, easily fifteen miles. Nevertheless the two riders had agreed not to hurry and as far as possible to take things at a comfortable pace.

"In the end it doesn't really make the slightest difference whether we cross the Cremmen Pike at eight or at nine. That bit of twilight glow still behind the church tower over there . . . Fritz, what's its name? What church tower is that? . . ."

"That's the Wulkow Church, Herr Hauptmann."

"Well, that bit of twilight glow still behind the Wulkow Church won't last much longer, that's for sure. So it's going to be dark anyway. And we won't get any of the Hohenlohe monument in our sights during daylight anymore. The monument stands a distance off to the side of the road. Incidentally, I really would have liked to get a closer look at it, you know. One should always take in something like that when you're passing through."

"Too bad," said Rex.

"Yes, you can almost say that. Personally I can get over it, but a fellow like you, Rex, should view that sort of thing much more from the perspective of a pilgrimage."

"Good grief, Czako. There you go talking nonsense again. This time with a touch of the ridiculous thrown in. What does a pilgrimage have to do with it at all? And then, what have you got against pilgrimages anyway? And what is it you've got against the Hohenlohes?"

"Good Lord, Rex. How wrong you are again. I've got nothing against either the one nor the other. Everything I've read about pilgrimages has always made me wish to take part in one some day. And *ad vocem* the Hohenlohes, the only thing I can tell you there, is that for the likes of them I've even got a soft spot in my heart. Much, much more than for our home grown varieties. Or, if you want to put it that way, our autochthones."

"And you really mean that seriously?"

"Completely. And let's just take five minutes to talk about it like rational people. When I say 'us' I really mean me, of course. After all, you always talk like a rational fellow. Perhaps a bit too much."

Rex smiled. "Well, all right. I'll believe you on that score."

"Well then, the Hohenlohes," continued Czako. "Let's see now, what about them? Just what is the truth of the matter? There comes one *anno domini* a burgrave ariding into the region, and the place doesn't want him. And so for starters he's got to conquer everything, almost all the towns roundabout and all the castles for sure. And then, of course, especially everybody's heart. And the emperor as usual is sitting way far away and can't help him out at all. And so this Nuremberg burgrave has half dozen men around him at the most, Swabian fellows, who clamber down into this murderers' den with him. Because to an extent that's what it was, you know. And right off they all go at it, and the Quitzows and those who want to be like'em, call in their friends from Pomerania, and right here on this old Cremmen Pike they all run into one another.

"And the few that fall in the battle, why it turns out they're the Swabians, the ones who'd taken the risk and climbed into the boat along with the burgrave. And at their head was this count, a fellow more or less in his middle years. He was the first to go down and sank right here in the marsh. And there he lies. That is, they did pull him out and now he's buried in the Cloister Church in Berlin. And that particular fellow, who was the first to fall, was named Hohenlohe."

"Of course, Czako. For heaven's sake, I know all that. Why, it says all that in the Brandenburg Primer. Why, you always think you alone had a monopoly on things like that."

"Careful there, Rex. Yes, it's all in the primer. Quite right. But what all doesn't it say — not even mentioning the primer — in the Bible and Catechism that people still don't know anyway. Me for example. And whether it's in there or it isn't in there, the only thing I'm saying is: that's how it all began, and that's the way things are still running today. Or do you really think the old prince whose turn it is right now,[18] do you think he's moved into our so-called Reich's Chancellor's Palace for his own special pleasure, where Bismark's successors, who, God knows, certainly didn't fall over one another trying to get in, have been moping away their days? It's a sacrifice, no more and no less. And making a sacrifice is just what the old prince is doing too, just like that fellow who was the first to fall that time at the Cremmen Pike. And I'll tell you, Rex, that's what really impresses me, always being right on hand when the danger's greatest. The petty people from here, despite their talk of 'loyalty right down to their bones,' they don't do anything but grumble. But the truly noble people, they obey, and not just a power figure, but rather their sense of duty."

Rex agreed and merely repeated, "Too bad we'll be passing the monument so late."

"Yes, too bad," said Czako. "We'll have to pass it up. As for the rest, I think we can leave the Hohenlohes out of what we've still got to talk about. There are other things a bit more immediate for us today. How did you like Fräulein von Schmargendorf, by the way?"

Answering that, Czako, will be the last thing I do. In any case, it was you who took her strolling through the garden, not I. And the whole time it seemed as if I were watching Faust and Gretchen."

Czako laughed. "Of course it's the other couple you're really imagining. And it doesn't bother me. The role that falls to me in the process — the fellow with the rooster's feather in his cap is quite a different number from that sentimental 'I've studied, alas, . . . fellow,' when you get right down to it. This Mephisto role, I can tell you, suits me better, and as far as the Schmargendorf woman goes, the only thing I can say is, 'From my Martha I'll not turn.'"

"Czako, you're getting frivolous again."

"All right, all right, Rex. You're getting irritated, and you've a right to be. Let's drop the Schmargendorf woman along with the Hohenlohes. But there certainly is something to talk about when you get to the Domina, and once we've gotten to the aunt, it won't be long before we get to the nephew as well. Our friend Woldemar, I fear, is in a rather nasty spot just now. The Domina has been harping at him for years with all sorts of marriage schemes. He's even hinted to me about it himself. I suspect it's because the idea of a world without Stechlins is simply a horror for her. Old maids like that with garnet brooches always have an oddly high opinion of their families. Of course, others who ought to know better do too. People of our sort just seem to take to the idea that they are intimately connected with the continued existence of the divine world order. The truth of the matter is that they could do without the whole lot of us. Things will keep going on without the Czakos for certain, for which, so to speak, proof has already been historically-symbolically presented."

"And the Rexes?"

"At this name I draw the line."

"As if anyone believes you. But let's forget the Rexes and the Czakos and stick to the Stechlins, in other words, to our friend Woldemar. His aunt wants to marry him off, you're right there."

"And I think I'm right too when I call that a delicate situation. Because I do believe that he wants to keep his freedom and is consciously steering towards the harbor of celibacy."

"A belief, my dear Czako, in which — as is always the case when you start believing things — you find yourself in complete error."

"Can't be."

"Not only can it be, it is. And I'm only surprised that you, who usually keeps tabs on everything that's going on, and knows every bit of local gossip like nobody else, that you of all people, ought not to have heard a peep about it. After all, you socialize at the Xylanders too. In fact, I do believe I saw you there one time last winter fighting your way to the buffet."

"Certainly."

"And the Berchtesgadens were there on that evening too, the baron and his wife. And in a lively discussion with this Bavarian baron there was a distinguished elderly gentleman and two ladies. And the three of them, those were the Barbys."

"The Barbys," Czako repeated. "Senior diplomatic official or something like that. Yes, of course, I have heard of them, but I can't in any case recollect ever having seen him with the ladies. And not on that evening for sure. Why, you couldn't even think of making introductions that time. A regular Battle of the Nations. But you were, I believe, just about to tell me something about these Barbys."

"Yes, that I was. I wanted in fact to let you know that your celibate has been visiting this very house regularly since the end of the winter."

"Well, he probably visits a lot of houses."

"Possibly, but not very likely, since that one house takes up his time completely."

"Well then, fine. So he visits the Barbys. We'll let him. But what's that supposed to mean?"

"It means that visiting a house like that and getting engaged to one of the daughters of the house is more or less one and the same thing. Just a question of time. And his aunt will have to reconcile herself to it, even if, as is most likely to be the case, she will have made other plans for the apple of her eye. Things of that sort square themselves out almost always in time. But our Woldemar finds himself in the meantime face to face with quite different difficulties."

"Which are . . . ? Not good enough? His love not requited perhaps?"

"No, Czako. As far as 'unrequited love,' as you prefer to put it, goes, there's no question of that. His difficulties lie somewhere else. There are, in fact, as I took the liberty of suggesting, two countesses in the house. Well, it will probably be the younger of the two, I suppose, just because, well, just because she's the younger one. But it's by no means all that certain, either. Because the elder one, even though she's over thirty, is tremendously charming and to top it off, she's a widow besides. The fact is, not actually a widow, but to put it more accurately, a woman who got divorced right after marriage. She was only married for half a year — or maybe not so married either."

"Married or maybe not so married either," repeated Czako while impulsively pulling up his horse. "I say, Rex. That's really quite spicy, you know. And that I should just be learning about it today and, moreover, from you, who would far rather turn away from that sort of thing with horror. But that's just the way you fundamentalist fellows are. When you get right down to it everything like that is really your favorite field of action. But for now, keep going on with your story. I'm as curious as a schoolgirl. Who was the unlucky lucky fellow anyhow?"

"You mean, if I understand you aright, who was it who married the elder comtesse. Well then, this lucky unlucky fellow — or maybe the reverse — was also a count, an Italian one even, presuming you consider that higher yet, and naturally had a genuine Italian name: Conte Ghiberti, the very same name as that of the Italian sculptor from whom the famous doors come."

"What doors?"

"Why, those famous baptistery doors in Florence. The ones about which Michelangelo is supposed to have said were worthy of being the entrance to Paradise. And these doors are called the Ghiberti doors too, in honor of their great artist. Something, by the by, a fellow like you ought to know."

"Of course, Rex. It's easy for you to talk about having to know this and that. You come from a rich family and probably had some theology student as your tutor, and then went off traveling besides, where a body can pick up fancy things like that. But me, I'm from Ostrowo."

"That doesn't make any difference."

"Oh it does. It does, Rex. Italian art! I ask you, from where are the likes of me supposed to have gotten something of that sort? What Johnny doesn't learn — well, that's just how it stays once and for all. I remember as clear as can be an auction in Ostrowo, it was in the house of a merchant, at which finally a red box came up to be auctioned off, a box with double pictures and an opera glass too, which actually wasn't one. Well, my mother bought the whole thing. And it was through this stereoscope, a word, by the way, I didn't know in those days, that I learned my Italian art. Those doors though weren't included. So what sort of thing can you expect? If you'll allow me to put it that way, I've got a panopticum education."

Rex laughed. "Well, never mind . . . . Now then, the count who married the elder Countess Barby was named Ghiberti. In his marriage, however, the doors of paradise were definitely missing. That much can be said with absolute certainty. And for that reason it came to a divorce. In fact, beyond that, the charming lady — charming by the way is far too trivial and inferior a word — the charming lady in her indignation, did away with the name Ghiberti and the entire world knows her today just by her first name."

"Which is?"

"Melusine."

"Melusine? Say there, Rex, that really lets you look down deep."[19]

86

Engrossed in this conversation they had approached the Cremmen Pike. It had become very dark by now and the clouds passing overhead hid the crescent moon. A few times in fact it showed through and then they saw in the half light the Hohenlohe monument shimmering below in the marsh. To ride down to it, which they briefly considered, was impossible and so they set off in a cheerful trot and did not stop again until pulling up before the little inn called *The Margrave Otto* in Cremmen. From the tower of St. Nicholas' Church it was just striking nine.

Once inside they were soon engaged in a lively conversation through which Rex sought to inform himself of the patriotic attitudes and religiosity prevailing in the town. The innkeeper presented an equally good grade for both and had the satisfaction of receiving a friendly nod from Rex. Czako, however, remarked. "Say there, innkeeper. You've got a dandy billiard table there. Just the other day somebody was telling me, if thing's really get moving, a body could pull in nearly three thousand marks a year. Naturally, working at it twelve hours a day. What's the story on that? I think it's possible."

To the Egg Cottage

11

THE BARBYS, THE old count and his two daughters, had been living in Berlin for a number of years, on the Kronprinzenufer[1] in fact, between the Alsen and Moltke bridges. The house in which they occupied the second floor, without otherwise standing out in any manner — Berlin is not rich in private homes which combine beauty with character — differed advantageously from its neighbors from which it was separated by two strips of ground. The first of these was a small orchard with all kinds of hedges and bushes in between, the other a courtyard space, with a delicate and picturesque-looking stable building. Its upper windows, behind which the coachman's dwelling was located, were overgrown with wild grape vines.

Merely the location of this house would have assured a certain measure of attention, but the facade too, with its two loggia to the left and right, made any passerby involuntarily cast an eye upon it. Here, in these selfsame loggia the family liked to spend the morning and afternoon hours, and depending on the season, allotting preference on some occasions to the pompean red one belonging to the room of the old count and on others to the identical loggia belonging to the room of the two young ladies. In between lay a third large room which served both for representational purposes and at the same time as the dining room. That was, with the exception of the bedrooms and those for household facilities, the whole over which they held sway.

They lived somewhat restrictedly as a consequence but were so attached to the house that a change of quarters or even the thought of such a thing was as good as out of the question. On one occasion the amiable Baroness Berchtesgaden, an especially close friend of Countess Melusine, had suggested such a change, but only immediately to encounter lively resistance. "I see, Baroness, you're bringing up the whole of your Lennéstraße pride into the line. That Lennéstraße of yours! Well it's all right enough, I suppose. But what is it that's so grand about it? You've got one whole Lessing monument and half a Goethe. I'm willing to be envious of you for both of those, and take the nursemaids from the Spreewald into account as well. But the Lennéstraße world is closed, shut in. It hasn't any open vistas, no flowing water, no traffic streaming past. When I sit in our niche, with the long rows of approaching Stadtbahn² cars before me, not too close, but not too far either, and when I see how the evening twilight glows through the smoke of the locomotives and shimmers in the filigree trim of the little exhibition park tower, what can that wall of Tiergarten greenery of yours offer to match that?" And as she spoke, the countess pointed to a locomotive just steaming past and the baroness gave in.

Today brought just such an evening. The balcony door stood open and a small fire in the hearth threw its glow onto the heavy carpet covering the entire room. It was almost six o'clock and the windows in the houses on the other side of the Spree were bathed in a reddish glow. Close by the fireplace sat Armgard, the younger daughter, leaning back into her chair, the toe of her left foot lightly propped up against the frame of the fireplace screen. The embroidery she had been working on had been laid aside since it had begun to get dark; instead she was playing with a ball and cup, to which she regularly had recourse whenever she needed to fill empty minutes. She played the game with considerable skill and there always came a bright little sound when the ball fell into the cup. Melusine stood outside on the balcony, her hand at her brow to screen out the rays of the sinking sun.

"Armgard," she called into the room, "come out. The sun's just going down."

"Never mind. I'd rather look into the fireplace. And I've made twelve catches already."

"Whom?"

"The ball, of course."

"I think you'd rather be catching someone else. And whenever I see you sitting there like that, it almost seems to me as if you were thinking the same thing yourself. You're sitting there just like in a fairy tale."

"Oh, you never think of anything but fairy tales and just because your name is Melusine you think you've got sort of an obligation to do so."

"That could well be. But above all, I think I've hit the mark. Do you know what?"

"Well?"

"I can't say it so easily. You're sitting too far away."

"Well then come here and whisper it into my ear."

"That's asking too much. First off, because I'm the elder here and secondly it's you who wants something from me. But I won't be so difficult."

And with that Melusine left the balcony and went to her sister, took the ball and cup game from her and said, as she placed her hand on her brow, "You're in love."

. "Oh now, Melusine. What's that supposed to mean this time! And from someone as clever as you . . . . In love. Why, that's nothing at all. One's always a little bit in love."

"Of course. But with whom? That's where the questions and the stratagems begin."

At that instant the bell outside rang and Armgard strained to listen.

"Oh, how you give yourself away," laughed Melusine. "You're listening because you want to know who's coming."

Melusine was on the point of continuing but the door opened and Lizzi, the two sisters' chambermaid, entered, immediately behind her a delivery man in the livery of Gerson's department store with a box held closed with a strap. "He's bringing the hats," said the maid.

"Ah, the hats. Well then, Armgard, it looks like we'll have to put that question off for a bit. That's your opinion too, I imagine. Please, put them down there. But you, Lizzi, you're to stay and help us out. You've got a good sense of taste. By the way, isn't there a standing mirror around?"

"Should I get it?"

"No, no. Let it be. We'll be able to see our heads — which after all are all that counts — in this mirror here just as well . . . . I presume, Armgard, you'll let me take the lead. This one here with the heliotrope and pansies, is the one for me, of course. It's got a real lady-like character, practically widowish."

As she spoke she placed the hat on her head and strode over to the mirror. "Well, Lizzi, what have you got to say?"

"I'm really not so sure, Your Ladyship. It doesn't seem modern enough to me. That one there, the one Comtesse Armgard is putting on just now, I think that'd probably be more the thing for Your Lady-ship — those tall ostrich feathers like the plume on a knight's helmet and the shape of the hat itself. Here's another one, practically the same, but almost even prettier."

Both ladies now took their place before the mirror; Armgard, standing behind her sister and taller than she, looked over her left shoulder. The two of them took uncommon pleasure in what they saw and finally began to laugh, for each noticed about the other how pretty she found herself.

"You know, I could almost believe . . . ," said Melusine. She got no further, however, for just at that moment an old servant dressed in black tails and buckled slippers entered the room and announced, "Rittmeister von Stechlin."[3]

Immediately thereafter Woldemar himself appeared and bowed to the ladies. "I fear I've come at a highly inconvenient time."

"Quite the opposite, my dear Stechlin. For whose sake do we torture ourselves with things like this anyway? For nobody else but our lords and masters, whom one, of course, still has, unfortunately perhaps, even when one doesn't have them any longer."

"Always the charming lady."

"No flattery, if you please. And anyhow, these hats are important. I take it as a stroke of fortune that you've come just at this moment. You'll be the one to decide. Of course, we've called on Lizzi's opinion, but Lizzi's too diplomatic. You are a soldier and have to have more courage. Armgard, do say something too. You're not young enough anymore to go on playing the embarrassed little thing for ever and ever.

"I'm generally against all depositions, especially in legal matters, I can tell you a thing or two when it comes to them, but a deposition from you, in that case I'll drop all my reservations. And besides, I'm all for experts and if ever there were experts in matters of taste and fashion, where would they be better found than in the Regiment of her Imperial and Royal Majesty of Great Britain and India? I've left Ireland out on purpose and prefer to take India instead, from where every bit of good taste emanates, all that old culture, all those shawls and carpets, and Buddha and those white elephants.

"All right then, Armgard, fall in. Naturally you go on the right flank because you're taller. And now, my dear Stechlin, how do you think we look?"

"But ladies . . . ."

"No cowardice. How do we look?"

"Marvelously nice."

"Nice? You'll pardon me, Stechlin, but nice is hardly the word. At least it's not a very nice word. Or at the very least, insufficient."

"Well then, simply delightful."

"That's fine. And as your reward for that, now comes this question: which of us is more delightful?"

"Oh, but your Ladyship, why that's nothing but the old story of poor old Paris. Except that he had it much easier because there were three. But two. And sisters in the bargain."

"Out with it. Come on, out with it!"

"Well, if there's no other way out, you, your Ladyship."

"Shameless liar! But we'll keep these two hats. Lizzi, send the rest of them back. And have Jeserich bring in the lamps. A touch of twilight outside and a dying fire in here — I'd say that's really too little light, or if you will, a bit too comfy."

The lamps had already been burning outside so that they were brought in immediately.

"And now close the balcony door, Jeserich, and tell Papa the Herr Rittmeister has come. Papa really isn't feeling very well. His neuralgic pains again. But when he hears that you're here, he'll put in a bit of extra effort. You're his favorite, you know. One always knows when one is somebody's favorite. I always have at least."

"I can believe you there."

"I can believe you there. How do you explain that?"

"Simple enough, you Ladyship. Everything must be learned. It's all a matter of experience when you get right down to it. And I believe that you were given ample opportunity to deal practically with the question of being or not being the favorite."

"You wriggled out of that one nicely. But now, Armgard, tell Herr von Stechlin — I personally wouldn't venture to do so — that in half an hour we've got to be on our way. Off to the opera house. *Tristan und Isolde*. What do you say to that? Not to *Tristan und Isolde*, no indeed, but to the more delicate question that we're just going out the same moment you arrive. Because I can see by the look of you that you just didn't come for, as the English say, 'five o'clock tea'. You had something better in mind for us. You intended to stay."

"I confess . . . ."

"That's it then. And as a sign that you'll be merciful and grant us forgiveness, promise us we'll see you soon again, very, very soon again. You word on it. And to Papa, who's perhaps expecting you, if Jeserich found it appropriate to announce you, I'll tell Papa you weren't able to stay. An appointment, your club or something like that."

While Woldemar descended the stairs following this farewell conversation with Melusine and walked towards the closest cab stand, the old count sat in his room. His right foot propped on a chair, he looked out through the balcony window at the evening sky. He loved these twilight hours and did not care to be disturbed during them, least of all when a light was brought in too soon. Thus, as Jeserich, who was well aware all of that, now entered, it was not to bring the old gentleman a lamp but merely to add a few coals to the fire.

"Who was it that was here, Jeserich?"

"The Herr Rittmeister."

"I see, I see. Too bad he didn't stay. But then, of course, what would he want with me? And this foot and the pains, they don't make one any more interesting either. Armgard, and of course, especially

Melusine, to be sure, with them things go better, a body can have a better chat with them. And the Herr Rittmeister no doubt finds that so too. But one thing is certain, I do enjoy talking with him. There's something calm and sensible about him, always straight-forward and natural. Don't you think so too?"

Jeserich nodded.

"And don't you also think — otherwise why would he come here so often — that he's got something in mind?"

"I think so too, your Lordship."

"Well then, what do you think it is?"

"Oh Lord, your Lordship . . . ."

"I see, Jeserich, you don't want to come out with it. You can't get out of it that easily though. What do you think about the matter?"

Jeserich grinned but continued his silence, for which reason the old count had no other recourse than to continue. "Naturally Armgard is more suitable because she's young. It's more or less the right relationship. And anyway, Armgard is, so to speak, up next. But the devil knows, Melusine . . . ."

"Of course, your Lordship."

"Well then, you've seen what's going on too. Everything always revolves around her. Well, what's your opinion of the Rittmeister? And what do you think about the ladies? And where do things stand in general? Is it the one or the other?"

"Well, your Lordship, what should I think about it all? With the ladies, of course, one never knows. High class or low class, tall or short, rich or poor, they're all the same. With our Lizzi it's just the same as with Countess Melusine. When y' think it's one way then it turns out it's another, and when y' think it's the other, then it's the other way again. When my wife was still alive, God bless her soul, she always used to say, 'Yes sir, Jeserich, no matter what you think, we're nothin' but a riddle.' Good God, she was simple t' figure out, but one thing you can take my word on, your Lordship, they're all the same."

"You're absolutely right there, Jeserich. And that's why there's really nothing we can do about it. And I'm glad to see that you see it all so clearly too. You're a first rate judge of human nature. Wherever did you come by it? You've got a bit o' the philosopher in you. Have you ever seen one of those fellows?"

"No, your Lordship. When you've got so much to do and always have to polish the silver."

"True, Jeserich. No way of getting out of that. Can't free you from all that."

"No, that's not what I mean anyways, your Lordship. Me, I'm for the old ways too. Good employers and always thinking, 'a body sort of half ways fits in with'm too.' I'm for that. And they say there's some actually do half way fit in too . . . . But it does get a bit hard sometimes, and when you get right down to it, we're all human too."

"Now wait a minute, Jeserich, I haven't declared you aren't yet."

"No, no, your Lordship. Good Lord, it's just a way of talkin'. But there's a bit to it all the same . . . ."

12

Woldemar, as Rex quite correctly had informed his friend Czako as they rode across the Cremmen Pike, had been a regular visitor at the Barby's house since the end of the winter and very soon preferred it to all others which belonged to his circle of acquaintances. A great deal captivated him there, above all the two ladies, but the old count as well. He found similarities even in external appearance between the count and his father, and in the journal, which despite other modern traits he had continued to keep in an old-fashioned way since his youth, he had expressed a certain kinship between the two of them already on the very first evening. Thus under the eighteenth of April was written the following:

"I can not be grateful enough to Wedel for having introduced me at the Barbys. Everything he said of the house I've found confirmed. This countess, how charming she is! And the same for her sister, despite the fact that greater opposites can scarcely be imagined. In the former, everything is vivacity and charm and in the latter all character, or if that's going too far, simplicity, firmness. There really is something special about names after all. Her Ladyship, the countess, is Melusine to the core and the comtesse just as much Armgard. I've actually come across only one person of that name so far, and she was merely as a stage character.[4] I constantly had to think of her — it was Fräulein Stolberg, I think, she's the right size for the role — and the way she so courageously took the reins from the hands of the Governor in that play. That's just the effect that Comtesse Armgard has on me! I could almost say that you can actually tell by looking at her that her mother was a real Swiss woman.

"And then there's the old count! Like a twin brother to Papa, the same Bismarck head, the same humane nature, the same kindness, the same good humor. Papa is a bit more expansive and doubtless more of an original character as well. Perhaps it was only their different life paths that created these differences. Papa's been sitting in his little corner out there in Ruppin for a good thirty years now, and the count was abroad for the same amount of time! An ambassadorial councilor is simply quite a different thing than a provincial estate's councilor, and one evolves into something quite different on the Thames than on our Stechlin — with all due respect to our Stechlin, naturally.

"Nevertheless, the kinship holds. And that old servant, the one they call Jeserich, no question about it, he's our Engelke completely from top to toe. But the thing that's most closely related is the whole atmosphere in the house, the liberal feeling. Papa would laugh about it himself, of course. He never laughs at anything as much as he does about liberalism. And yet, I don't know a single soul who's inwardly as free as that dear old boy of mine. He'd never admit it, of course, and he'll die absolutely convinced that they'll all say, 'Tomorrow they're carrying a genuine old Junker to his grave.' And that he is too, but at the same time, he's just the complete opposite of it as well. There's not a selfish bone in his body.

"And this same splendid trait — alas, something you find so rarely — the old count has it too. At the same time, of course, he's a man of the world and that's what makes the difference and tips the balance. He knows something they either don't know or don't want to know in this country, that there are people out there beyond the mountains too. And now and then quite different ones at that."

Those were the remarks Woldemar entered in his journal. He had been pleasantly touched by everything he had seen, including the house and its interior. And there was good reason for that, more than he could know after his first visit. The house in which the count's family resided, with its loggias and diminutive yard and garden, was divided into two halves, each of which in turn had its own special annexes. To the upper floor belonged the picturesque courtyard and stable building situated on the side in which resided the count's coachman, Herr Imme, whereas as a part of the mezzanine floor forming the second half it was rather to be taken for granted that the small low basement area was to be reckoned, in which, besides concierge Hartwig himself and his wife, also lived his son Rudolph and his niece Hedwig. The latter, it must be said, only occasionally, in fact only at those times when she was once more without a position — which, admittedly, was a rather frequent occurrence. The landlady of the house, the widow Schickedanz, her full title was Frau Hail Insurance Secretary Schickedanz, ought really to have objected to the occasional presence of Hartwig's niece. But she let things ride because Hedwig was a cheerful, vivacious and clever young thing and possessed certain talents which reconciled Frau Schickedanz to the impropriety of her perpetual changes of position.

Frau Schickedanz, a woman of sixty, was already a widow when the Barbys moved in during the autumn of 1885. Comtesse Armgard was only ten years old at the time. Frau Schickedanz herself was still in mourning in those days, for her spouse, the hail insurance secretary, had passed away only in December of the previous year.

"Three days before Christmas," it was, a circumstance to which the assistant preacher, a young theology student, constantly referred in his funeral sermon, and which had also achieved the desired effect. If the truth be told, only with Frau Schickedanz herself and to a certain extent with Frau Hartwig, who had nodded her head continuously throughout the entire sermon and afterwards remarked to her husband, "Yes sir, Hartwig, you got to admit, there's something to what he says."

Hartwig himself, however, who contrary to most of his class had a touch of humor about him, displayed not the slightest trace of comprehension for the remarkable stroke of fate of "three days before Christmas." Indeed, the only comment he had on the point was, "Beats me, what you actually mean by that, Mother. One day's the same as the other. Sooner or later, we all gotta go." To which his wife had nevertheless responded, "Oh sure, Hartwig. That's what you always say. But when your number comes up, you'll talk different."

The late Herr Schickedanz, when death overcame him, had had a life behind him divided into two very different halves, a completely insignificant and petty one and a very great one. The insignificant half had lasted a long time, the great one was but very brief. He was a brick-maker's son from the village of Caput near Potsdam, something that, once out of the condition corresponding to the meaning of the village name, he enjoyed pointing out in the society of good friends. It was more or less the only joke of his entire life, to which, however, he firmly held, because he noticed it always hit the mark. There were some who even went so far as to give him moral credit for it, maintaining that Schickedanz was not only a character but a modest fellow as well.

Whether this was actually the case, who's to say! But one thing was certain, from the beginning he had shown himself to be a sharp young fellow. When only sixteen he had begun as assistant clerk in the German-English hail insurance firm of Pluvius, and at sixty-six had celebrated his fiftieth anniversary in the very same company.

That had been a great day for various reasons. For when Schickedanz reached it, he still bore the title "Herr Insurance Secretary," though more or less only superficially In point of truth he had grown far beyond this his title and by then owned the splendid house on the Kronprinzenufer. He had been able to afford that because in the course of the last five years he had twice in a row won a quarter share of the grand lottery. This was regarded from all quarters as his personal merit, and no doubt rightly so, for anybody can work, but winning the grand lottery was not something that just anybody can do. And thus he stayed on at the insurance company, now merely in the capacity of a pampered piece of ornamentation, because then as now it made a good impression to have persons of that sort on the staff or even as partners. One always has to have a prince at the top. And Schickedanz was now a prince. Not only did everybody throng to him, but his old cronies at the pub, who had unconditional faith in his twice proven lucky touch, for a time even made him draw lots from the lottery for them too. But nobody won a thing, which finally brought about a change of opinion and even led some to talk about an "evil eye," and even, quite absurdly, dirty dealings. Most, however, considered it prudent to keep their ill will to themselves, after all, he was still a man who, whenever he wished, could give each and every one cover or support.

Yes indeed, Schickedanz's fortune and fame were great, greatest of all, naturally, on his anniversary day. It was not to be believed who all came. The only thing that did not come was a medal, a thing which was noted with great displeasure on the part of certain Schickedanz fanatics. It was his wife who felt it especially painfully. "My God, after all, he always voted so loyally," said she. She was never to be in the position of learning to live with this sorrow, however, for the next days were fated to bring her much worse. The anniversary had been on the twenty-first of September, on the twenty-first of October he took ill, and on the twenty-first of December he died. This thrice-repeated twenty-first had been omitted from the piece of paper presented to the theology candidate at the time, something that all in all could probably be viewed as a stroke of good fortune, since had it been mentioned, the "three days before Christmas" would either have never come into being or else would have been weakened in their effect by having to share their dominance.

Schickedanz had been fully conscious when he died. Shortly before his end, he called his wife to his bed and said, "Riekchen, keep calm. We all got to go. I didn't make a will. That never leads to anything but squabbles and quarrels. On my desk there's a piece of paper. I've written everything you need on that. For me much more important is the business about the house. You've got to keep it, so people can say, 'That's where Frau Schickedanz lives. House names, street names, they're what really count most of all. A street name'll last you longer than a monument."

"Oh good God, Schickedanz, don't talk so much. It takes too much out of you. You know I'll keep it all sacred, just for love's sake . . . ."

"That's right, Riekchen. It's true. You always were a good wife even if we didn't have any children. And that's why I ask you, never forget, it was my pride and joy. Make sure you take only first class people. Rich folks who're just rich, don't take them, because they just grumble and put big hooks into the door panels and hang swings on them. And whatever happens, if you can, no children. Hartwig downstairs you got to keep. He's actually a smart-aleck, but his wife's a good person. And little Rudolph, my god child, when he's a year old, he's to get a hundred talers. Talers, I said, not marks.[5] And the school teacher in Caput's to get a hundred talers too. That'll be a surprise to him. But it makes me happy just to think of it even now. And I want to be buried in the disabled veteran's cemetery, if that's any way possible. Every one of us is actually a disabled veteran, when you think about it. And back there in '70, I was right up there on top of the enemy bringing donations, even if Luchterhand always kept saying, 'Don't get too close.' Be nice to people and not too frugal, you do get a bit too frugal. And keep a place for me in your heart. I know you were always faithful to me, a voice inside tells me so."

Riekchen had lived according to every one of these precepts since that day. The upstairs apartment, which was empty when Schickedanz died, remained uninhabited for another three quarters of a year, despite the fact that a goodly number showed interest in it. But they did not meet the standards that Schickedanz had set before his passing. Then in the autumn of '85 came the Barbys. The little widow immediately realized, "Yes sir, those are the ones my dear departed husband had in mind." And in fact, she had chosen rightly. In the nearly ten years that had passed since then, there had not been a single instance of disagreement, with the count's family certainly none at all, and hardly ever with the staff either. A personal communication between downstairs and upstairs naturally could not take place; Hartwig was simply the alter ego who had the task of discussing all necessary details with Jeserich.   If by chance, however, it came to some sort of encounter between landlady and tenant, the tiny little woman, who had never been particularly large, and since her husband's demise had become even smaller, maintained a remarkably dignified demeanor which would have called forth the astonishment of anyone not familiar with Berlin ways. Riekchen in fact felt herself in such instances to be very much "one power against another."

As is the case with practically everyone born in these parts, the talent for actually being able to make real comparisons was totally lacking in her. This was because all real Berliners, baptized with the waters of the Spree, be they male or female, measure their situation only against their own minuscule past, never against the world outside, of which, if they are the genuine article, they possess neither the slightest concept nor the slightest desire to possess one. The indigenous "cellar worm," on fifty years later moving into a villa in Steglitz, develops in himself — even if by nature he is really the most modest of persons — a certain naive Croesus complex and believes quite seriously that he belongs to those gold and silver royalties who rule the world.

So too Madame Schickedanz. Born behind a garret window on the Georgenkirchstraße, at which garret window she had later done sewing for a linen shop, her life seemed to her, when she looked back on it, like a fairy tale in which she had played the role of the princess. In keeping therewith, she tacitly but tenaciously infused herself with a sense of superiority which steered entirely in the direction of complete equality with grandees of finance as much as with those of birth. She classified herself in such an order and, insofar as her historical knowledge permitted, endowed herself with a definite place in that order: Prince Dolgorucki, the Duke of Devonshire, Schickedanz.

That faithfulness for which in his last moments the dearly departed had praised her, intensified more and more to a cult. The morning hours of every day belonged to the rosewood cabinet in which neatly arranged stood the anniversary presents: a large silver cup with St. George slaying the dragon on its lid, an album of photographs of all the sights of Caput, a large homage address surrounded by watercolored arabesques, several songs in deluxe editions including a skittles song with the refrain, "Got all nine," gigantic bouquets of sun flowers, a fancy pillow with an Iron Cross and a poem stitched into it emanating from a ladies committee in whose name he, Schickedanz, had brought charitable donations from the home front practically to the outskirts of Paris. Next to the cabinet, on an ebony column, reposed a plaster bust, the gift of a sculptor who was also a fellow regular at the pub, and who had thereupon expected but unfortunately never received a commission for its duplicate in marble. Chairs and armchairs were encased in slip covers decorated with large flowers, the same held for the candelabra in a gauze dust cover, and in the front windows throughout the winter stood lilies of the valley.

Riekchen also wore lilies of the valley on every one of her bonnets and, since the end of her year of mourning, dressed brightly in general, by means of which her form acquired an even more ethereal effect. Every first Monday of the month was given over to a general cleaning, wind or cold notwithstanding. This was always a day of greatest excitement because invariably something would be broken or upset. Things went on this way for several years until the advent of Hedwig — who was happily possessed of an extremely skillful hand — brought about a change in this particular point. Knickknacks were now no longer broken, and Riekchen was all the happier at the fact that Hartwig's pretty niece, whenever she had once again given notice from service, regularly had all sorts of things to recount on that particular topic and knew how to command the field with ever new and often quite intricate yarns.

The Barbys had every reason to be pleased with the Schickedanz residence. Only one thing was disturbing. That was that every Wednesday and Saturday carpets were beaten at exactly the same hour in which the old count wished to take his afternoon nap. That irritated him for a while until he came to the conclusion, "The fact is, I'm to blame myself. Why do I always sit down in the back room instead of not simply up front at the window? Every time I gamble and think, maybe today it will stay quiet, let's give it another try."

Yes indeed, the old count was not only happy to have the apartment, he almost superstitiously held on to it. As long as he lived there things had gone well for him, not more splendidly than earlier, but with fewer worries. And he told himself so with every passing day. His life, as colorful as it had been, had nevertheless passed to a certain degree in an average manner, exactly as that of a Prussian 'magnate' was wont to run — by which, as a rule, Silesians are meant, although in fact there are others.

In July of 1830, just as the French were bombarding Algiers, and at the same time tangentially disposing with the House of Bourbon once and for all, the count had been born on one of the Barby estates located on the middle Elbe. On this very same estate, which was agriculturally under the administrative hand of strangers, was spent his childhood. At twelve he entered the Ritterakademie, a school for young aristocrats, and at eighteen the Regiment Garde-du-Corps[6] in which the Barbys had served as long as there had been a Regiment Garde-du-Corps.

By thirty he had become Rittmeister, commanding a squadron. But not for much longer. During cavalry maneuvers in the vicinity of Potsdam, he had taken a serious fall and broken his upper thigh directly below the hip. Passably healed, he repaired to the waters at Ragaz in Switzerland to seek complete recovery and there made the acquaintance of an elderly Freiherr[7] von Planta, who soon invited him to his estates. Since these lay quite close by, he accepted the invitation to Schuder Castle. Here he stayed longer than expected and by the time he left the picturesquely situated mountain castle he was engaged to the daughter and heir of the family.

It had been a deeply felt affection which brought the pair together. The young baroness soon urged him to retire from the service, and he acquiesced all the more readily since he himself was not sure of his complete recovery. He thus took his leave from the military and transferred to the diplomatic service for which his education, wealth and social standing made him seem equally suitable. The very same year he went to London, first as an attaché then becoming ambassadorial councilor, a post in which he remained to begin with right up to the days of the establishment of the German Reich. His relations, both with the local English as well as with the foreign aristocracy, were always of the best, and his friendship with the Baron and Baroness Berchtesgaden stemmed from this period. He was greatly devoted to London. The English way of life, with which he took issue on a number of things, above all its pretentious religiosity, was nevertheless extraordinarily agreeable to him and he grew accustomed to viewing himself as having become wholly integrated into it. His family too, his wife and two daughters, both of whom, even if many years apart, had been born during the London days, shared their father's fondness for England and English life.

But a bitter stroke of fate turned everything upside down that the baron had planned; his wife suddenly died, and further residence in the place grown so dear to him was spoiled forever. He submitted his resignation in the first half of the eighties and initially went to the Planta estates in Graubünden and then further south to settle in Florence. The air, the art, the cheerful good humor of the natives, all of these things did him good there and he felt that he was recovering, in so far as he could ever again recover.

Happy days ensued for him, and his happiness seemed on the point of intensifying even more, when his elder daughter became engaged to the Italian Count Ghiberti. The wedding followed almost immediately. But the continuation of this marriage soon proved an impossibility, and before a year had passed, the divorce had been decreed. Shortly thereafter the count returned to Germany, which he had seen only fleetingly in the last quarter century while on visits. The idea of retirement to one or the other of his estates on the Elbe was still repugnant to him even now, and thus it came that he decided on Berlin.

He took the apartment on the Kronprinzenufer and lived here entirely for himself, his house and his daughters. He refrained from intercourse with the great outside world as far as possible and only a small circle of friends, among whom were the Berchtesgadens, whom a lucky chance had also brought to Berlin, assembled around him. Besides these old friends it was preferably Court Chaplain Frommel, Doctor Wrschowitz and since the previous spring, also Rittmeister von Stechlin, who formed the Barby circle. Everyone had quickly become attached to Woldemar and the friendly feelings he encountered both from the old count and his daughters were shared by all the inhabitants of the house as well. Even the Hartwigs were interested in the Rittmeister, and when he passed by the concierge's lodging in the evening, Hedwig would peek out nosily through the little window and say, "A fellow like him — yes sir, I wouldn't mind the likes of that at all."

13

Woldemar, when taking leave of the young ladies of the Barby household, had been compelled to promise to repeat his visit very soon. But what was "very soon"? He turned it over back and forth and came to the conclusion that the third day would more or less proper. That was "very soon," but at the same time, not too soon. And so when the evening of the third day arrived, he strolled towards the Halle Bridge, waited for the city tram, and rode past the Potsdam and Brandenburg gates as far as that peculiar Reichtagsufer spot, where from a sturdy gabled wall, a gigantic coffee girl some twenty feet tall, a tiny bonnet on her head, cheerfully looks down on the world of those passing by to present them with a packet of Kneipp's malt coffee. At this genuinely Berlin-picturesque corner Woldemar got off, to cover the remaining short stretch from here to the Kronprinzenufer on foot.

It was going on eight as he ascended the carpet-covered marble steps of the Barby residence and rang the bell. At the same instant in which Jeserich opened the door, Woldemar saw in the old man's embarrassed look that in all probability the ladies were once more not at home. But displeasure in that regard could not be displayed, and thus he permitted Jeserich to announce him to the old count.

"His Lordship, the count, asks that you enter."

And now Woldemar entered the room of the old man, who was once more in the throes of being plagued by neuralgia. Leaning on a heavy cane, he approached his guest with a welcoming gesture.

"But Your Lordship," said Woldemar, taking the old man's left arm to lead him back to his easy-chair with its support for the ailing foot, "I fear, I'm disturbing you."

"Quite the contrary, my dear Stechlin. Very welcome indeed. Besides, I've got strict orders to hold on to you *coûte que coûte*. You know, women are great when it comes to their intuitions and with Melusine it's practically a prophetic quality."

Woldemar smiled.

"You're smiling, my dear Stechlin. You're quite right. After all, the fact that she nevertheless did go out, to the Berchtesgadens, of course, is proof that to a certain extent she distrusted both herself and her prophecy. But one is always clever and wise when it comes to others. The doctors do the very same thing. When it comes to treating themselves they push the responsibility away and prefer to die at the hands of a stranger.

"But why I am just talking about Melusine? Of course, it's perfectly true that anyone who is as familiar with our house as you will find nothing surprising in that. And at the same time you know how to take it. Armgard is in sight too, by the way. In less than ten minutes we'll have her here with us."

"Did she go along to the baroness?"

"No. you needn't look so far afield. Armgard is in her room and Doctor Wrschowitz is with her. They won't be much longer."

"But I beg you, your Lordship, is the comtesse ill?"

"Thank God, no. And Wrschowitz isn't a medical man either, but a music doctor instead. You haven't heard of him yet merely by chance because it was only last week that the music lessons were started again after a long, long pause. But he's been Armgard's music teacher for years."

"Music doctor? Do such things exist?"

"My dear Stechlin, everything exists. Therefore that too, of course. And as much as I'm in general against all this doctor-grabbing nonsense, the way things lie in this case, I'm willing to let poor Wrschowitz have his music doctorship or at least have to forgive him for it. He doesn't have the title all that long yet."

"That almost sounds like there's a story behind it."

"Right on the mark. Can you imagine that Wrschowitz has become a doctor of music on the basis of a sort of despair?"

"Hardly. And if it's not a secret . . . ."

"Not at all. Merely a curiosity. As a matter of fact, Wrschowitz, when he first came to our house two years ago as a piano teacher — but a high-class one, by the way, he's written an opera, you know —

used to be named plain Niels Wrschowitz. And he's only become a doctor to get rid of the Niels on his calling card."

"And he's pulled it off?"

"I imagine so, although it still does happen that some people call him Niels just as before, either by chance or maybe even out of malice. In the latter case it's always colleagues. Musicians are the nastiest people, you know. Usually people think preachers and the theater folk are the worst. Far from it. Musicians top them all. And the ones who are especially nasty are the ones who make that so-called sacred music."

"I've heard something like that too," said Woldemar. "But whatever is this business with Niels? When you think about it, of itself Niels is an attractive and completely harmless name. Nothing suggestive about it."

"Of course not. But Wrschowitz and Niels! He suffered, I would imagine, from the disparity."

Woldemar laughed. "That's something I'm familiar with. I know it from my father, whose name is Dubslav; that's always been extremely uncomfortable for him. And it can't be less than a hundred times that I've heard him complain about his father because of this name."

"Exactly the case here," remarked the count, continuing his story. "Wrschowitz's father, an insignificant Kapellmeister on the Czech-Polish border, was a Niels Gade[8] fanatic, whereupon he simply baptized his boy Niels. That was problematic enough because of the contrast. But the really problematic thing didn't come about until the slowly but surely developing passionate Wagner fanatic Wrschowitz turned into a regular Niels Gade hater. Niels Gade became for him the epitome of everything trivial and insignificant, and on top of that, as sure as night follows day, it turned out that every time our young friend was introduced as Niels Wrschowitz, he would be sure to encounter some remark like, 'Niels? I say, Niels. A splendid name in our musical world. And highly pleasing to see it represented here a second time.' The poor fellow couldn't put up with the likes of all that in the long run, and so he got the idea of conjuring it right out of existence with a doctor's title."

Woldemar nodded.

"In any case, my dear Stechlin, you can sufficiently perceive from all this that our Wrschowitz, as a true artist, belongs to the classification *gens irritablis*, and if Armgard has perhaps invited him to stay to tea, I beg you most avidly to keep this irritability in mind. If any way possible stay away from references to the entire Scandinavian world, but especially directly to Denmark. He smells treachery everywhere. Otherwise, if one is on one's guard, he is a cultured and sophisticated gentleman. In fact, I like him very much because he's different from others."

The old count turned out to be right in his assumption; Armgard had asked Doctor Wrschowitz to stay. Thus when Jeserich shortly thereafter entered to call the count and Woldemar to tea, on entering the middle room they found not only Armgard but Wrschowitz, as well, who stood in the center of the salon with fingers interlocked, taking stock of the pictures hanging on the wall over the sideboard with a peculiarly mixed expression of genuine boredom and artificially induced interest.

The Rittmeister had once again offered his arm to the count. Armgard approached Woldemar and expressed her pleasure at his coming. Melusine too would surely soon be there, she told him, the last thing she had said was, "You'll see, Stechlin's coming today." Thereupon the young countess turned again to Wrschowitz, who seemed to have just engrossed himself in the portrait of the late countess by Hubert Herkomer, and introducing them said, "Doctor Wrschowitz, Rittmeister von Stechlin."

Woldemar, remembering his instructions, bowed courteously, while Wrschowitz, in a rather peremptory fashion, endowed his countenance with the haughty double expression of artist and Hussite.

In the meantime the old count had taken a seat, excusing himself that with his unfortunate foot support he made so much trouble, and invited the two gentlemen to sit down next to him. Armgard, at the other narrow end of the table, sat directly opposite her father. The old count took his cup of tea and with a humorous sigh pushed the cognac, "the better part of any cup of tea," aside and said while turning to Wrschowitz on his left, "If I heard aright — a bit of my musical ear is still with me — that was Chopin Armgard was playing at the beginning of the lesson."

Wrschowitz bowed.

"Chopin, for whom I've always had a predilection as for all Poles, presuming they're musicians or poets or else men of science. As politicians I can't warm to them. But perhaps that merely comes from my being a German and a Prussian at that."

"Varry true. Varry true," responded Wrschowitz, more candidly than courteously.

"I may say I've always had an enthusiastic leaning for Polish musicians since my earliest days as a lieutenant. Among other things there was a Polonaise by Oginski which in those days used to be played as regularly and with as much passion as later the *Erlkönig* or

The Bells of Speyer. It was also the days of the *Old General* and *Do you remember, my gallant Lagienka*."[9]

"Yas indeed, Your Lordship, a bad time. And alvays a special pleasure for me to see how sentimental tings fall away. Alvays, alvays. I hate sentimental tings *de tout mon coeur*."

"A point," said Woldemar, "in which I fully agree with Herr Doctor Wrschowitz. In poetry we have exactly the same phenomenon. There too we had that sort of thing and I confess how as a boy I was completely carried away by such sentimental trash. My special passion was *King René's Daughter* by Henrik Hertz, a young fellow from Copenhagen, if I'm not mistaken . . . ."

Wrschowitz changed color, which induced Woldemar, as soon as he perceived it, to a speedy change of course. ". . . *King René's Daughter*, a lyrical drama. But long since forgotten. Nowadays we stand under the sign of Tolstoy and *The Kreutzer Sonata*."

"Varry true, varry true," responded Wrschowitz, who quickly calmed down once more, merely taking the opportunity to protest energetically against any mixture of art and sectarianism.

Woldemar, a great admirer of Tolstoy, wished to break a lance for the Russian count, but Armgard, who, when such topics were touched upon, strongly mistrusted the social presentability of her friend Wrschowitz, immediately endeavored ardently to direct the conversation into more harmless realms. The County of Ruppin, from the most remote northeastern corner of which Woldemar had only recently arrived, appeared quite eminently to her at this instant as such a realm, redolent with the promise of peace. Thus she expressed to the latter her desire to see him present a brief report regarding his most recent excursion.

"I well know that I'm doing a poor service to my sister Melusine — who is brimming with curiosity and the desire to hear all about it too — but Herr von Stechlin won't disdain coming back to the topic once my sister is finally here again. As we all know, everything doesn't have to be absolutely new when one is just chatting. One may repeat oneself now and then. Papa too has a few things he tells us about more than once."

"A few things?" laughed the count. "My daughter Armgard means 'quite a few things'."

"No indeed, Papa, I mean a few things. There are others who are quite different, our good baron for example. And the baroness always looks the other way when he starts up. But let's forget the baron and his stories and hear instead about Herr von Stechlin's trip. Doctor Wrschowitz surely shares my taste."

"Share completely."

106

"Well then, Herr von Stechlin," continued Armgard, "with our friend Wrschowitz's declaration, you've got one friendly listener more, perhaps even an enthusiastic one. And I'll vouch for Papa too. We're actually from the Mark ourselves, or at least almost, and yet we know so little about it because we were always abroad. I know Saatwinkel and the Grunewald area,[10] but the real Brandenburg countryside, that's something else again. It's all supposed to be so romantic and so melancholy, sand and swamps and a few rushes in the water or a birch tree with trembling leaves. Is your Ruppin area like that?"

"No, Comtesse, we've got quite a bit of forested land and lakes. The so-called Mecklenburg lake plain."

"Well, that's beautiful too. Mecklenburg has its Romanticism too, as the Berchtesgadens just recently assured me."

"Varry true. I have read *Stromtid* and have read *Franzosentid* . . . ."[11]

"And then I believe," continued Armgard, "you've got Rheinsberg right in the vicinity. Is that right? And are you familiar with it? They say it's got so much that's interesting. I remember about it from my childhood, even though we lived in London at the time. Or perhaps for that very reason. Because it was the time when Carlyle's book about Frederick the Great was still the rage, and when it was still considered the thing not only to concern yourself with the terraces of Sanssouci, but with Rheinsberg too and the order '*de la générosité.* Is all that still alive today? Do the country folk still talk about it?"

"No, Comtesse, that's all gone now. And no one even speaks about the great king in the Rheinsberg area any more. And it can hardly be otherwise. The great king was there only for a brief period as crown prince, but his brother Heinrich was there for fifty years. And so the Prince Heinrich era has lamentably suppressed the era of the crown prince altogether. But it's not lamentable in every regard. After all, Prince Heinrich was important too and above all very critical. Something that's always an advantage."

"Varry true, varry true," interrupted Wrschowitz at this point.

"He was very critical," repeated Woldemar, "especially of his brother, the king. And the malcontents, of whom there were an abundance even in those days, were always around him. And something always comes of situations like that."

"Varry true, varry true . . . ."

"Because contented courtiers are always sterile and boring, but factionalists, *frondeurs* as they were called back then, when the likes of them speak up, then there's something worth hearing, and one gets a different perspective."

"I suppose so," said Armgard. "But nevertheless, Herr von Stechlin, I can't abide factionalism. A factionalist is always simply the habitually dissatisfied type, and anybody who's continuously dissatisfied simply isn't good for anything. Perpetually disgruntled individuals are arrogant and often malicious besides, and while they're making fun of others, they themselves often leave quite a lot to be desired."

"Varry true, varry true, Your Ladysheep," bowed Wrschowitz. "But you forgive me, Comtesse, if I neverdeless am for *frondeur*. *Frondeur* is critizzizm, and vare good tings desired, must be critizzizm. German art — much critizzizm. First must be art, certainly, certainly, but right after must be critizzizm. Critizzizm is like great revolution. Off wid d'head on principle. Art must have principle. And vare is principle, is off wid d'head."

Everyone was silent. Thus there was nothing for the count to do but somewhat tardily express his lukewarm agreement. For her part, Armgard hastened to return to Rheinsberg, which seemed to her, despite the awkward "off with their head" incident, still a safe haven compared to any music discussions which might perhaps occur.

"I do believe," she began anew, "among other things to have also heard of the Prince's antipathy towards women. They say — if I'm wrong, I'm sure you'll set me straight — he was a so-called misogynist. Something utterly abnormal in my eyes or at least something rather strange."

"Varry strange," said Wrschowitz, while at the same time his visage, under the effect of an admiring glance at Armgard, practically glowed.

"How good, my dear Wrschowitz," continued Armgard, "that in confirming my remarks you take a stand for us poor women and girls. There still are men of chivalry, and we do need the likes of them so very much. Because, as Melusine told me, women haters are even proud of being women haters and treat their way of thinking and acting as some sort of higher way of life. Are you acquainted with any such people, Herr von Stechlin? And if you do know such people, what do you think of them?"

"I view them first off as unfortunate souls."

"I'll agree with that."

"And secondly as sick people. The Prince, as Your Ladyship has quite rightly expressed, was also such a sick person."

"And how did it manifest itself? Or is it perhaps not at all possible to talk about such a topic."

"Not very easily, Your Ladyship. But in the presence of His Lordship the Count and, not to be forgotten, in the presence of Doctor Wrschowitz, who has already taken a stand against misogyny in such a splendid and chivalrous fashion, with this sort of support, I'll take a stab at it anyway."

"Well, that's good. I'm burning with curiosity, you know."

"Therefore we won't timidly tip-toe around the matter any longer. Our Rheinsberg prince was a real prince in the sense of the previous century. The ones we have now are human beings, the ones in those days were nothing if not princes. One of the passions of our Rheinsberg prince — if you will, in a sort of contrast to what has been said up to now — was a mysterious predilection for dead maidens, especially those who were engaged to be married. Whenever such a young girl had died in the Rheinsberg area, preferably one from the country, he invited himself as a guest at the funeral. And before the clergyman could get there — he always avoided him — he would make his appearance and stand at the foot of the coffin and stare at the dead girl. But she always had to be made up to look as if she were alive."

"Why that's downright horrible," cried Armgard almost passionately. "I don't care for this prince at all, nor his whole band of factionalists either. Because they must have been exactly the same. Why it's nothing but blasphemy, grave-robbing, that's what. That's the only word I can use, because I'm so horrified about it. I just can't do otherwise."

The old count looked at his daughter and a halo of joy illuminated his good old face. Wrschowitz too felt something akin to absolute adoration, but restrained himself and instead of at Armgard, peered at the portrait of her countess mother which looked down from the wall.

Only Woldemar remained calm and said, "Comtesse, perhaps you're going too far. Do you know what went on in the prince's soul? It may well have been something infernal, but it can also have been something entirely different. We simply don't know. And because at the same time he also possessed absolutely great traits, I'm for including those in our overall picture of him as well."

"Bravo, Stechlin," said the old count. "At first I was of Armgard's opinion. But you are right, we don't know. And one thing I still remember from the realm of jurisprudence, in which for better or worse I put in a stint as a guest artist, in doubtful cases you've got to decide *in favorem.* Anyway, there goes the doorbell. Conversations are always getting interrupted just in their best moments. That's probably Melusine. And as much as I'd have wished she had been here from the start, if she joins in all of a sudden right now in the middle of things, even Melusine is a disturbance."

It was indeed Melusine. She entered the room, and not having removed it outside, threw the Scottish cape she was wearing into a corner of the sofa. Still loosening her hat from her hair, she strode to the table to greet her father first and then the two other gentlemen. "You're all looking so embarrassed, from which I conclude that something dangerous has just been said. Concerning me without a doubt."

"Why Melusine, how vain."

"Well then, not about me. But about whom then? That much at least I want to know. Who was it you were you talking about?"

"About Prince Heinrich. But about the old, old one, the one who's been dead nearly a hundred years already."[12]

"You could have been doing something better than that."

"If you knew what Stechlin's been telling us about him and that he — not Stechlin but the prince — was a misogynist, you might perhaps talk differently."

"A misogynist. Well, that does change things, I'll admit. Yes indeed, my dear Stechlin, I can't help you there. I've got to hear all about it too. And if you refuse me, you've got to come up with something that's at least every bit as interesting."

"Countess Melusine, there isn't anything as interesting as this."

"That's good, very good indeed, because it's so true. Well then, I'll request something second class from you. I see you've told about your trip, and about your Papa and Castle Stechlin itself or about your village and the region. Well then, I'd like to hear about all that too, even if it doesn't come close to the other business, I'm sure."

"Dear me, Countess, you've no idea how modest things are in our little Stechlin corner of the world. Apart from a pastor who's practically a Social Democrat, and for another thing a chief forester who's married to a princess, an Ippe-Büchsenstein, we've got . . . ."

"Oh, but that's all absolutely marvelous . . . ."

"Apart from these two marvels, the only other thing we've got there is actually the Stechlin itself. That might do, I suppose. One could perhaps say a thing or two about it."

"The Stechlin? What's that? I'm fortunate enough to be aware," as she spoke she made a courteous gesture with her hand toward Woldemar, "I'm fortunate enough to be aware that there are Stechlins. But *the* Stechlin. Whatever is *the* Stechlin?"

"It's a lake."

"A lake. That doesn't tell me much. Lakes, unless it happens to be Lake Lucerne,[13] only turn out to be interesting because of their fish, like sturgeon or whitefish. I won't bore you with the rest of the list. But what does the Stechlin have? Stechlin — Sticklin, I'd say stickleback."

"No, Countess, that's one kind of fish it doesn't have. It's got exactly the one thing you're least inclined to suspect. Connections with the world are what it has, high-placed, mysterious connections. And the only thing it doesn't have is anything that's commonplace, such as stickleback for example. You won't find any stickleback there."

"Now Stechlin, you're not going to play the oversensitive type, are you? You, a Rittmeister in the Guard?"

"Not at all, Countess. And in any case, I'd just like to see the fellow who'd get away with it with you."

"Well then, let's have it. Of what do these high class connections consist?"

"It is on a close personal basis with the highest and most exclusive circles, those whose genealogical pedigree far exceeds anything you'll find in the *Almanac de Gotha*. Because when things start rumbling out in Java or in Iceland, or some geyser starts steaming and shoots up twice its normal height, then a jet of water shoots up in our Stechlin as well, and there are some — even if no one has ever seen it yet — some even say that in really important cases a red cockerel appears amidst the waves and crows clear and far to awaken the whole of Ruppin County. I call those high-placed connections."

"And so do I," said Melusine.

Wrschowitz, however, whose eyes had grown larger and larger, murmured, "Varry true, varry true"

14

It was at the beginning of the week when Woldemar had visited the Barbys. By Wednesday morning he received a billet from Melusine.

"Dear Friend. Permit me again to express my belated regrets that day before yesterday I was able to be present only for the last scene of the last act — the tale of Lake Stechlin. But I've got a lively interest in knowing more about it. In this so called 'great' world of ours there is so little worth hearing or seeing. Almost everything has withdrawn to the quiet corners of the earth. Above all, it seems to me, to your Lake Stechlin area. I'll bet you still have a lot to tell us about, and I can only repeat I'd like to hear it. Our dear baroness, whom I've told about it, shares my views. She's got the trait of all naive and kindly people, that of being inquisitive.

"I, without meeting the above-mentioned preconditions, am nevertheless every bit her equal when it comes to curiosity. And so we've arranged an afternoon excursion, during which you are to be the great teller of tales. As a rule, of course, things work out other than planned and one does not get to hear what one wanted to hear. But

111

that should not discourage us in our good intentions. The baroness has gone into raptures with me about an area she calls the 'Upper Spree.' Perhaps that really is its name, for all I know. It's supposed to be so beautiful there that even the glories of the banks of the Havel are no match. I'll give her the benefit of the doubt, and in any case will later assure her of the fact even if I should not find it so.

"The goal of our journey, a spot by the way with which the Berchtesgadens are not yet familiar because they have always gone considerably further up river, the goal of our excursion bears a rather strange name. It's called 'Egg Cottage.' For my part I haven't been able to get the idea of something oval out of my head ever since, and probably won't be cured of it until I'm personally introduced to this so strangely named wonderment of the River Spree.

"Tomorrow then, Thursday: Egg Cottage. A 'no' is out of the question. Departure, 4 PM, Jannowitz Bridge. Papa will be accompanying us. He feels considerably better today, and says he feels up to it. Perhaps four may be a little late but, as Lizzi tells me, that way we have the advantage of seeing the lights playing on the water during the return journey. And maybe there will be fireworks somewhere and we can watch rockets going up. Armgard is excited. I am too, almost.

"*Au revoir.* A certain Herr Rittmeister's most affectionate,

Melusine."

And now the next afternoon had arrived and shortly before four o'clock the Berchtesgadens, and immediately after them, the Barbys pulled up at the Jannowitz Bridge. Woldemar was already waiting. All were in that sort of cheerful mood which makes one ready to find everything charming and delightful, a mood that immediately came in handy at the steamer landing. Laughingly admiring the timbered architecture which presented itself, they descended a tangled maze of wooden stairs. Arriving at the bottom and passing an "establishment" located there, whose tables at this hour of the day were still empty, they made their way directly to the boat. Its bell had just rung for the first time.

The weather was splendid. Upstream all was clear and sunlit, while a thin haze lay over the city. They seated themselves on chairs and benches at both sides of the stern deck and from there looked back on the veiled outline of the city.

"People always say Berlin has so few churches," said Melusine. "But we'll soon be driving Cologne and Mainz from the field. I see St. Nicholas, St. Peter's, the Orphans' Church, and the dome of the palace church. And that roof over there with a kind of Chinese roof cap, I do

112

believe that's the tower of the city hall. But, I admit I'm not sure you can count something like that."

"A tower's a tower," said the baroness. "That's all we'd need if someone were to deny poor old Berlin its city hall tower as a tower. People are jealous enough as it is."

Just then four o'clock rang out. From the Parochial Church the glockenspiel could be heard and mingling with it sounded the ship's bell. As the latter ceased, the gangway was hauled up, and with a shrill whistle, the steamer got under way, heading towards the central arch of the bridge.

Above, in the vicinity of the Jannowitz Bridge, the group's two coaches still remained, presumably considering it proper to await the departure of the ship before they themselves went on their way. Not until the former had disappeared beneath the bridge did the coachman of the Count of Barby drive up alongside that of the baronial house of Berchtesgaden for the purpose of exchanging greetings.

Both coachmen had known one another a long time, as far back as London, in fact, where they had been in the service of their respective families. In this regard they were much the same. Otherwise, however, they were as different as could possibly be, even in their external appearance. Imme, the Barbys' coachman, a Mecklenburger, equally as good natured as he was martial looking, could, with his gray-tinged sappeur's beard, have stepped up without further ado before a troop of guards and opened the parade as the drum major. At the same time the Berchtesgadens' coachman, who had spent his youth as a trainer and semi-sportsman, not only possessed an English name, but was, in fact, a typical Englishman, gaunt and wiry, with short cropped hair and clean-shaven countenance. His goggle eyes had something doltish about them, yet he was clever enough nevertheless, and knew how to pursue his own advantage when it counted. German still gave him problems, despite sincere efforts to master it, even to the point of avoiding the comfortable assistance of using English words, most of all when he saw the Berlin ladies of his acquaintance torturing themselves by coming to his aid with a "well, well, Mr. Robinson," or even a mysterious "indeed." With one thing alone he was completely in agreement, however. Being called "Mr. Robinson." That was something that pleased him.

"Now, Mr. Robinson," said Imme in English, as they rode along next to one another, "How are you? I hope quite well."

"Danke, Mr. Imme, danke! How's your wife?"

"Well now, Robinson, I think you ought to see for yourself, this very day, in fact, while our people are off and won't be back until late. And they're taking the Stadtbahn back besides. At least from here, Jannowitz Bridge Station. Let's say about nine. They won't be back before that. And until then we can have a fine game of skat. Hartwig will show up for sure as a third. Concierges always have time. His wife can open the door just as well as he and he doesn't have anything else to do. Well then, five o'clock it'll be, and I'll not take no for an answer. As you Englishmen say, 'Where there's a will, there is a way.' As you can see, a little bit of 'dear old England' has stuck."

"Danke, Mr. Imme," said Robinson, "danke. Ja, Skat ist das Beste von all Germany. Glad to. Skat is even better than Bavarian brew."

"Now just a minute, Robinson. I'm not so sure about that. The way I see it, it's more or less both together, there's where the truth lies. That's the thing."

Robinson agreed, and since neither had anything else on his mind, they broke off the conversation at this point and prepared to set out for home at a moderately fast trot, the Berchtesgaden coachman taking the route across the Molkenmarkt and Schloßplatz, the Barbys' heading up the Neue Friedrichstraße. Once over the Friedrichsbrücke, he stayed close to the water and thus took the most comfortable way back to his Kronprinzenufer.

The steamer, immediately after it had passed under the bridge arch, set off at a more rapid pace, holding to the left side of the river so as to keep only a slight distance between the boat and the bricked arches of the elevated tramway, the Stadtbahn, running close to the edge of the bank. Every arch created a frame to the picture of what lay behind it, naturally in the form of a lunette. Masonry of every sort, along with sheds and fences, passed by in colorful variety. But in front of all these objects meant to serve the realms of the commonplace and labor, again and again could be seen bits of garden ground in which a few belated hollyhocks or sun flowers bloomed. Only after they had passed the second bridge did the Stadtbahn arches fall back, so that it was no longer possible to speak of the bank as having some sort of bordering. In its place, meadows and poplar-lined paths now appeared, and where the banks fell off as if to form a quay, sand-filled boats lay, heavy barges, from the innards of which a shovel-like machine dumped gravel and sand into the lime pits close to the edge of the bank. It was the Berlin Mortar Works which held sway here, determining the look of the river's edge.

114

Our travelers said little, for with the rapid variety of images passing by one question suppressed the next. Not until beyond Treptow, as the steamer passed between the small islands emerging numerously from the river at this spot, did Melusine turn to Woldemar and say, "Lizzi's told me that here between Treptow and Stralau lies 'Lovers' Isle.' That's where lovers always die, usually with a note in their hands explaining everything. Is that right?"

"Yes, Countess, as far as I know, that's right. The fact is, there are quite a few 'Lovers' Isles' like that in our area, which can serve as proof of just how wide-spread the condition in need of remedy is, even if it has to be by way of dying."

"I'll hold it against you for making fun of something like that. And Armgard will too, even more than I, because she's more emotional than I. And besides, as well you ought to know, things like that come back to haunt you."

"I know. But you're reading my soul completely wrong. I'm sure you've heard that when somebody's afraid, he starts to sing. And whoever can't sing, well, he just does the best he can and makes jokes. And incidentally, as beautiful as 'Lovers' Isle' may sound, the magic disappears right out of it when you think of the name of this entire area. This section of the Spree spreading out so broadly around us here is actually called 'Rummelsburger Lake.'"

"Not particularly pretty, I'll admit. But the spot itself is beautiful and names don't mean anything."

"Anyone named Melusine ought to know what names mean."

"I do know, alas. Because there are people who are afraid of 'Melusine.'"

"Which is really a rather stupid mistake, but at the same time it's even more a kind of homage."

As they continued this conversation they had passed beyond the area where the Spree broadened and once more entered the narrower river bed. Here the rows of houses lining both banks ceased running on in thin lines. In their place groups of trees now closed upon the shore, and further inland raised railway embankments became visible, above which the telegraph poles rose, their wires spanned from pole to pole. Here and there, extending quite far out into the water, large patches of reeds stood, and from their thickets a river duck flew up now and then.

"It's actually further than I thought," said Melusine. "Why, we're already in a sort of semi-isolation. And it's getting chilly too. A good thing we've brought blankets along. After all, we will be staying outside, won't we? Or are there rooms there too? The truth of the matter is, I can scarcely imagine all six of us fitting into an egg cottage."

115

"Dear me, Countess, I see you're counting on something idyllic in the extreme and expecting something between a kiosk and a cottage when we get there. You're in for an awful disappointment. The Egg Cottage is one of those things they call a 'pub.' And if we have a mind to, we can even dance there or hold a public gathering. There's plenty of room there. Do you see, the boat's already turning and that red building over there with the tower and the bay window coming into view between those willows, that's the Egg Cottage."

"Oh dear! A *pallazo*," said the baroness, who was on the point of expressing further displeasure. But before she was able to do so, the boat made fast to the projecting landing platform, from which they strolled along a river path to the Egg Cottage. This path, once it finally reached the garden restaurant, continued on for a goodly distance beyond the place. Since the wonderful fresh air was so inviting, it was decided that before settling in at the Egg Cottage itself, all would stroll along the bank together farther up the river.

Because of the narrowness of the path, they walked in pairs, Woldemar with Melusine in front, then the baroness with Armgard. Considerably farther behind followed the two elderly gentlemen, who had begun a political conversation even while still aboard the steamer. Both were liberally inclined, but the circumstance that the baron was a Bavarian and had grown up amidst Catholic attitudes, nevertheless constantly induced differences between them to come to the fore.

"I can't agree with you, my dear Count. All the trump cards today, in fact more than ever, are in the hands of the Pope. Rome is eternal, and Italy is not at all as firmly built as it would like the world to imagine. The Quirinal will be moving out again and the Vatican will move back in. And then what?"[14]

"Nothing at all, my dear Baron. Not even if it should actually come to that, which, I personally believe, is out of the question."

"You say that with such composure. And one is composed only when one is sure of himself. Are you that sure? And if you are, can you afford to be? I'll say it again, the ultimate decisions still lie with this question of the Pope and Rome."

"They used to. But that's all completely over with now, even in Italy itself. The ultimate decisions you're talking about lie in totally different places today, and it's only a few of those newspapers of yours that never weary of assuring the world to the contrary. All nothing but dying echoes. Our modern age is mercilessly ridding itself of all that's been handed down. Whether they succeed in erecting an empire on the Nile, whether Japan becomes the England of the Pacific, whether China with its four hundred million souls wakes up from its slumbers and raises its hand to call out to us and the rest of the world, 'Here I am,' but above everything else, the question whether the lower classes can establish themselves or even become a stable force — because when you get right down to it, in its logical essence that's what the whole thing really boils down to — all of that is of far greater weight than the question whether it's to be the Vatican or the Quirinal. That's outlived itself. And the only amazing thing about it, is that it still keeps going on the way it has at all. That's the miracle of miracles."

"And you say that, you, who's been so close to these things?"

"Precisely *because* I've been so close to them."

The two couples strolling ahead were also engaged in lively conversation. On the eastern horizon, already filled with a twilight glow, the factory chimneys of Spindlersfelde rose up before them and long banners of smoke moved in slow puffs across the sky.

"What's that?" asked the baroness, turning to Woldemar.

"That's Spindlersfelde."

"Don't know the place."

"Perhaps you do after all, dear lady, especially when you hear that in this very Spindlersfelde, none other than that most important gentleman of the world of ladies' fashions, Herr Spindler[15] himself, conjures his mysterious arts. Or better yet, his secret arts. Because our lady friends don't care to admit their dependence on them."

"Aha, that fellow! Why yes, of course, that benefactor of ours, whom we — you're quite right about it — in our ingratitude we're pleased to keep quiet about. But this business of keeping quiet has something forgivable about it too, you know. These days, unfortunately, we do so many things which according to an older point of view we really ought not do. It's not proper, I think, to stand on the platform of a horse car between the conductor and some delivery woman with baskets on her back, and it's even less fitting to make all sorts of purchases in a fifty-pfennig bazaar and silently pass over the question that keeps forcing itself upon one, 'What is it that makes prices like this possible?' Our friend over there in Spindlersfelde also degrades us, perhaps, even by what he does for us in such a helpful way. Armgard, what do you think about the matter?"

"Completely in agreement with you, Baroness."

"And Melusine?"

With a shake of her head the latter passed the question by, urging that the two elderly gentlemen, who in the meantime had now approached, should give the deciding vote on the matter. But the old

117

count would not hear of it. "Those are questions for specialists. I don't get involved with things of that sort. I suggest instead we all turn around and look for a pleasant spot in the Egg Cottage from where we can watch what's happening on the river and hopefully get a nice view of the sunset as well."

At about the same hour in which the Barby and Berchtesgaden group began their stroll in the direction of Spindlersfelde, our friend Mr. Robinson, coming from the stable, appeared at the front of the Lennéstraße house, first taking note of the weather as usual, and then striding diagonally through the Tiergarten towards the Kronprinzenufer, where the Immes already awaited him.

Frau Imme, who like most childless women — and women with husbands sporting a sappeur's beard are almost always childless — had a real disposition for household matters and sense of cleanliness, and had put everything into truly splendid order to receive Mr. Robinson. She had done so all the more, since she knew that her guest as a rather fastidious Englishman always succumbed to the inclination of finding fault with everything German, if only by allusion. Thus it was a matter of pride for her to let him feel that people knew how things should be done here too. And so she had set out not only a splendid coffee service, but also a silver sugar bowl along with plates of streusel cake both to its left and right. Frau Imme could do all this and more as a result of the preferential position she had long occupied with the Barbys, into whose service she had come as a young thing of fifteen, remaining with them until her marriage. Even now both ladies were still warmly attached to her, and with the aid of Lizzi, who as discreet as she was, nevertheless enjoyed gossiping, Frau Imme was at all times very well-informed of what transpired in the front part of the house. That the Rittmeister was taking an interest in the ladies she knew, of course, like everyone else, but here too, like everyone else, she did not know in which one.

Ah, yes, which one?

That was the great question, even for Mr. Robinson, who regularly asked about it whenever he saw the Immes. And of course, the topic came up again today, in fact, immediately after his arrival.

A family-sized cup with a picture of Cupid drawing his bow before a temple facade had been placed before him. After having lovingly, and yet at the same time also with moderation, dispatched the streusel cake — for which he harbored such a tremendous preference as to regularly declare that its like was not to be found in the three united kingdoms of England, Scotland and Wales — he inspected the picture

118

embellishing the sizable cup. With a roguish smile, which considering the nature of his eyes, had something comical about it, he pointed to the Cupid drawing his bow and said, "Back here a temple and up front a laurel bush. And right here," this he expressed in English, "this little fellow with his arrow." Reverting once more to German, he continued, "If I might permit myself the question — you're such a clever woman, Frau Imme — will he be letting that arrow fly, or won't he? And if he does let it fly, is it this priestess standing next to the laurel bush here or is it some other?"

"Well now, Mr. Robinson," said Frau Imme, "it's difficult to give you an answer to that. Because first off, we don't know what's on his mind at all, and then we don't know who the priestess is, either. Is it the comtesse who's the priestess or is it the countess? If you ask me, anybody who's already been married can't really be a priestess."

"Ach," said Imme, in whom the down-to-earth native Mecklenburger was making itself felt, "Anything is possible. The grass'll grow right over it. I say it's the countess."

Robinson nodded. "Me too." Slipping again into his native language, he went on, "And what's the reason, dear Mistress Imme?" Once again he reverted to German, reserving English only for key words, "Because a *widow* takes precedence over a *virgin*. Oh, I know perfectly well, people are constantly talking about *virginity* all the time, but widow is more than *virgin*."

Frau Imme, who only partially comprehended all that, comprehended enough to giggle, which, however, she demurely accompanied with the remark that she never would have believed anything like that of Mr. Robinson.

Robinson accepted this comment as a form of homage and, after with the "lady's" permission lighting a short pipe filled with Turkish tobacco, strode over to a small window where red verbena bloomed in a hand-sawed flower box. As he looked out over the courtyard with its three acacia trees, he asked, "Who's that good-looking youngster down there playing with a hoop, or as they call it here, a *Reifen?*"

"Why that's Hartwig's boy, Rudolph," replied Frau Imme. "Yes sir, that lad's really a charmer. And the way he plays out there with that hoop of his and that girl Hedwig always chasing right after him, even though she could almost be his mother. Well, I always enjoy seeing folks being happy, and when Hartwig gets here — I just wonder where he can be keeping himself — you can tell him yourself, just how cute you think that spoiled little rascal is. He'll get a kick out of it. He's awful vain. All concierge people are. But one thing's true for sure, he is a cute lad."

119

While they were still chatting this way, Hartwig, for whom the skat-thirsty Imme had already been waiting a quarter hour, put in his appearance. It was not even three minutes later and Hedwig too arrived, she who but shortly before had been knocking herself out dashing about with her little cousin Rudolph in the courtyard below. Both were received with equal cordial warmth, Hartwig because with his arrival the skat game could at last get under way, and Hedwig because Frau Imme now had good company.

Hedwig, be it known, was a wonderful story teller and always had something new and exciting to relate. She was about twenty-four, was always extremely tidily dressed and possessed of a cheerful, saucy countenance. Added to these was curly, chestnut brown hair. And, as it happened, she was also once again out of a job.

"Well that's real nice, Hedwig, that you've come over," commented Frau Imme. "I was just askin' Rudolph where you might be keepin' yourself, 'cause I certainly did see you playing with him. But a lad like that never knows anything. Always just thinks about himself and if he'll be gettin' his piece of cake. Oh well, when he shows up, he'll get it. Robinson always eats so little, even though he's just crazy about the streusel. But that's those Englishmen for you, they're not as ready to dive right in. And then my Imme gets bashful too and half of it is left over. Well, anyways, it's nice you're here again. I haven't really seen you since your last job. That was with some Privy Councilor's wife, wasn't it? Well, those Privy Councilor's wives, I know them for sure. But there's good ones too. Tell me now, how was *he*?"

"Well, with *him* it wasn't so bad."

"Probably your curly hair was to blame again. Lot's of 'em don't go for it. And once the wife get's to noticing anything, it's all over with then."

"No, it wasn't that way at all. He was a very respectable gentleman. Almost too much."

"But child, how can you say a thing like that? How can somebody be *too* respectable?"

"Well, Frau Imme, when somebody doesn't even look at a body at all, that isn't so nice either."

"My goodness, Hedwig, the things you say! And if I didn't know myself that you're not that sort at all . . . . But whatever went on then?"

"Well, Frau Imme, what can I say about what went on? It's always the same old thing. You know. Those kind of people can't ever put a body up right. Else they don't want to. It's always the place you get to sleep, or the way some call it around here, the sleeping accommodations."

"But child, what's that supposed to mean? You got to have some sort o' accommodation for sleepin'?"

"Oh sure, Frau Imme. An' any old accommodation, at least that's what some think, is an accommodation. But that's just what you don't get. You're so tired you're ready to drop, but still you can't get no sleep just the same."

"I don't understand."

"Naturally, Frau Imme, that's because from the time you were a child you were always with such nice people, and the same holds for Lizzi too. She's got it good, just like she was one of the family. My Aunt Hartwig is always telling me about that. And there was one time I had it that good too. But it was just that once. All the other times it's always the sleeping accommodation that's missing."

Frau Imme laughed.

"You laugh about it, Frau Imme. But it's not right, your laughing. Just you believe me, it makes you want to cry. An' now an' then I even did cry. When I first came to Berlin, they still had those servants lofts, y'know."

"Know what you mean. Know what you mean. I mean, I heard about'm."

"Yeah. When somebody's just heard about'm, that doesn't mean much. You gotta really know what they're like. They're always right in the kitchen, now an' then up real close to the stove or even straight across from it. And then you gotta climb up a ladder. And you can fall off, if you're tired. But most of the time you can make it. An' then you open up the door an' push yourself into that hole up there, just like into a bake oven. That's what they call a sleepin' accommodation. An' the only thing I can say is, it's better in a hay loft, even when they got mice there. An' it's worst of all in summer. Outside it's ninety degrees, an' all day long there's been a fire on the stove. Why it's like somebody put you on a grill. That's how it was when I came to Berlin. But I don't think they're allowed to build anything like that any more. Police regulations. Oh, Frau Imme, the police is really a regular blessing. If we didn't have the police — an' they're always so nice to you too — we wouldn't have nothing. My Uncle Hartwig, whenever I tell him how you can't sleep, he always says, 'Know exactly what you're talkin' about. Those bourgeois don't do a thing for mankind. And them that don't do nothing for mankind got to be done away with.'"

"Yep, that's what your uncle says. And is that how it was with that Court Councilor's family of your's, who you were last with?"

"No, at their place it wasn't that way at all. They live in a brand new house, you know. The Court Councilor's family were damp-wallers.[16] And in those new houses these days, I don't think they've

121

even got lofts any more at all, they've just got those bath rooms instead."

"Well, that's some kind of progress, after all."

"Well, I suppose you can say that. A bath room that's a bath room is progress, or the way Uncle Hartwig always puts it, cultural progress. He's always using terms like that. But a bathroom as a sleeping accommodation ain't no progress at all."

"Good God, child, you don't mean to tell me they packed you into a bath tub?"

"Lord a' mercy. They wouldn't do that — just for sake o' the bathtub. That's the last thing they'd do. But, . . . Oh my, Frau Imme, the only thing I can say is, you've just got no idea at all. You had it good even when you weren't married and now you've really got it good. You live here like in a nice little summer cottage, an' the fact that it smells a little like horses doesn't hurt a thing. Horses are fine animals, an' nice n'clean too, an everything they do's got something real noble about it. Why people even call it the noble steed, you know. And besides, it's supposed to be real healthy too, practically as good as a dairy barn where they cure TB, you know. And then here you've got this view of the acacia bushes and of the navy panorama over there across the way, where you can see how they do things like that, and behind that you've got a view of the art exhibit, where they always have such an awful draft just so they can say they got fresh air. But at the Court Councilor's place, . . . no sir, that bathroom!"

"Good God, Hedwig," said Frau Imme, "you act as if it was a den a' murderers or a hang-out for nothin' but criminals."

"A hang out for criminals? Glory, Frau Imme, that's nothin'. I've seen hang outs. Just by chance, of course. They just drink weissbier an play cards, an' in one corner they're plannin' somethin'. But you never even notice what's really goin' on."

"But the bath room. What's so awful about that, that it makes you actually shudder so? After all, a body's got to be able to take a bath."

"Oh sure, take a bath! You bet. But a bath room isn't ever a bath room. Least of all, not there. A bath room's a junk closet, where they throw everything, anything they haven't got a place for somewhere else. An' that includes a serving girl. The iron cot I had, which got set up at night, always stood right next to the bathtub where all the old beer and wine bottles wound up. An' then with the dregs drippin' out besides. And in the corner was a mattress cover that the missies used to stuff their wash into, and in the other corner there was one o' them little doors. But I don't even want go into that with you, because I've got an aversion towards unmentionable things like that. That's why my mother always said, 'The day'll come Hedwig, when you'll get to

122

know our Lord an' Savior Jesus Christ.' And I gotta' say, those words were fulfilled at the Councilors' place for sure. But otherwise they weren't the least bit pious."

While Hedwig continued to complain, the doorbell outside could be heard to ring and as Frau Imme opened it, there stood Rudolph in the tiny hallway to explain that he had to get father and Hedwig too because mother had to go out."

"Well then," said Frau Imme, "you just come on in here, Rudolph, and eat a piece of streusel cake and then you can tell your father."

Soon thereafter she took the boy by the hand and led him into the adjoining room where the three men were cheerfully sitting at their skat table. A crucial hand had just been concluded; everything still in great excitement. Robinson, as he caught sight of Rudolph, nodded to him and said, "That's the good looking lad I saw in the courtyard before with his 'hoop.' 'Nice boy.'"

"Aye," said Imme. "That's our friend Hartwig's lad."

Hartwig himself called his boy to him and said, "Well now, Rudolph, what's up? You came to get me. But you deserve a bit of fun too. Take a look at that fellow there who's looking at you so friendly like. That's Robinson."

"Ha ha."

"Now then, laddy, why are you laughing? Don't you believe me when I tell you that's Robinson?"

"Lord a' mercy, father. Robinson, I know all about him. He's got an umbrella and a lama. An' anyway, he's long since dead n' gone."

15

In sight of Spindlersfelde our excursionists had turned back to the Egg Cottage, and there taken their places at two tables which had been pushed together close to the river's bank, an umbrella of foliage spreading above them. Sparrows hopped about awaiting their chance. Soon a waiter put in his appearance to take their orders and the traditional embarrassing pause ensued. No one knew what to say until the baroness pointed to the trunk of an elm across from her on which it said 'Wiener Wurstel' and next to it, in even larger letters, the helpful word 'Löwenbräu.' In a short time the waiter appeared anew and the baroness raised her stein to both the Egg Cottage and the River Spree, adding at the same time that these days one could drink a really genuine Munich beer only in Berlin. For his part old Baron Berchtesgaden wished to hear none of that sort of thing and urged his wife instead to slide a bit more to the left in order to get a better look at the sunset, which he had to admit, was just as good in Berlin as anywhere else. The baroness held out, however, and did not make a move.

"Who cares about the sunset? I get to see that every evening. I'm perfectly comfortable right where I am and I'm looking forward to the lights."

And it was not much longer and the lights actually did put in their appearance. Not only did the entire establishment become illuminated, but on the opposite side of the river along the railroad embankment, varicolored signals gradually began to appear, while in the middle of the Spree, where tugboats were pulling barges, a sooty reddish glow emanated from their cabin windows. Gradually too it became cool and the ladies wrapped themselves in blankets and shawls.

The gentlemen too felt the chill a bit as well. Thus Woldemar, obviously planning something or other, after briefly striding back and forth, made his way to the nearby buffet and arranged for what was needed to produce a better internal temperature. And lo and behold it was not long before a large tray with glasses and bottles stood before them, in the midst of which was a covered pitcher, from which, when the top was opened, hot steam arose.

The baroness, who was the most astute in such matters, was immediately in the picture and said, "Congratulations, my dear Stechlin. A magnificent idea."

"Yes, ladies. I felt that something had to be done or else every single one of us would wake up tomorrow with an acute case of rheumatism. And we've still got the return journey ahead of us. And on the ship, where any such preventative measures, I do believe, are lacking, we're exposed to every tribulation of the elements."

"And you really couldn't have made a better choice," interrupted Melusine. "Swedish Punch, just what I've a 'liking' for. As for the Swedes in general. Since Dr. Wrschowitz isn't with us, we can abandon ourselves to a moderate amount of Scandinavianism with impunity."

"Preferably without any moderation whatsoever," said Woldemar, "that's how pro-Scandinavian I am. I favor the Scandinavians over all the otherwise most-favored nations of the world. All countries are expanding their specialty areas these days, by the way. It used to be that Sweden just had two things, iron and courage, of which it must be said, they go well together. Then along came the 'Säkerhets Tänd-stickors'[17] and now we've got Swedish Punch, which, at this very moment, I place at the top of the list. To your health, ladies."

"And to yours," responded Melusine. "After all, it's you who are the person responsible for this happy moment. But, do you know, my dear Stechlin, that in your enumeration of Swedish glories I noticed something missing? The Swedes have something else again — or at least they did have. And that was the Swedish Nightingale."[18]

"Right. I did forget her. That was before my time."

"I'd perhaps have to say it was before *my* time," laughed the countess. "But on the other hand I can't deny actually having known Lind in person. Of course, not quite actually as the Swedish Nightingale anymore. And in any case, under a different name."

"Yes, I recall," said Woldemar. "She got married. Whatever was her name?"

"Goldschmidt — a name we can accept if only for Uhland's poem about Goldschmied's Little Daughter. But when you get right down to it, it doesn't quite come up to Jenny Lind."

"Indeed it doesn't. But you were saying, Countess, that you actually knew her personally?"

"Yes, I knew her and heard her sing. She was still singing back then, although no longer in public, but still in her salon at home. My acquaintance with her counts even yet among my dearest and proudest recollections. I was still only half a child, but was invited to attend nevertheless, something that in itself meant a great deal to me. And then the ride from Hyde Park out to her villa. I still remember clearly, I wore a white dress with a light blue cashmere shawl and had my hair loose. Jenny Lind looked me over and I could see that I pleased her. When one makes a good impression, one remembers it. Especially at fourteen!"

"They say Lind is supposed to have been rather ugly as a child," interjected the baroness somewhat prosaically.

"I'd have thought just the opposite," remarked Woldemar.

"And on what basis, my dear Stechlin?"

"Because I'm acquainted with a picture of her. We've had one, as you know, in our national gallery for some time now. By one of our best painters. But long before I ever saw it there, I knew it *en miniature*. As a matter of fact from a water color belonging to my friend Lorenzen. The copy hangs over his sofa, right under a *Descent from the Cross* by Rubens. If you will, a rather strange combination."

"And the likes of all that in your Stechlin parsonage!" exclaimed Melusine. "Do you know, Rittmeister, that I place the fact that something of that sort can actually exist in a little village almost on a par with that famous lake of yours? Our Swedish Nightingale in that little 'Ruppin corner of the world' as you love to put it all the time. Jenny Lind! And how did your pastor ever come by it?"

"Lind was his first love, I believe. In all probability his last too. Lorenzen was still on the school bench in those days, making ends meet by doing tutoring. But he heard the diva every evening nonetheless, and also managed to acquire that picture, despite really modest means. It practically touches on the miraculous. Of course things usually go that way. If he'd been rich, he'd probably have thrown his money away on other things and maybe never gotten to see or hear Lind. Only the poor manage to pull together what it takes for something that lies beyond the range of the commonplace. From enthusiasm and love flows everything. And it's something truly beautiful, that it is that way in our life. Perhaps the most beautiful thing of all."

"I really think so too," said the countess. "And I'm grateful to you, my dear Stechlin, that you said so. That was a good thing you said, and I won't forget it. And this Lorenzen was your teacher and mentor?"

"Yes, my teacher and mentor. At the same time, my friend and advisor. The person whom I love above everything else."

"Aren't you going a bit far there?" laughed Melusine.

"Perhaps I am, Countess, or let's rather say, for certain. And I ought to have kept that in mind, particularly today, and particularly here. But one thing remains, I love him very much because I owe everything I am to him, and because he's pure of heart."

"Pure of heart," said Melusine. "That's saying a lot. And you're sure of it?"

"Absolutely sure."

"And you're only telling us about this unique individual for the first time today! Just recently you were visiting us along with good old Wrschowitz and let us know all sorts of horrible things about that misogynistic prince of yours. And while you were putting the likes of him in the front line, as comfortably as you please you were holding this Pastor Lorenzen in reserve. How can a body be so cruel and put his rhetorical talents and information to such capricious use? But at least make up for what you've neglected. Why there's just one question after another. How did your father ever get the idea of giving you such an extraordinary mentor? And how did a man like this Lorenzen ever wind up around here? And however did he wind up in this world? It's so rare, so rare."

Armgard and the baroness nodded.

"I confess I'm tortured by curiosity to hear more about him," continued Melusine. "Is he unmarried? Just that alone is always a good sign. Your average fellow always believes he's got to perpetuate himself just as fast as possible, merely so the glory of him doesn't become extinct. But this Lorenzen of yours is an exceptional human being, it appears to me, in just about everything. Well then, let's hear it."

126

"I'm quite willing to do so, Countess. But it's too late for it. That bright light you see over there is our steamer already. We haven't any choice, we've got to break up unless we want to spend the night at Egg Cottage. But on the way, though, Lorenzen will be a marvelous topic, presuming that the sight of Lovers' Isle doesn't divert us to other things. But just listen, the steamer's already blowing its whistle, . . we've got to hurry. It will take us at least three minutes to get to the dock!"

And now everyone was safely aboard ship, where Woldemar and the ladies immediately took the seats they had occupied on the trip out. Only the two elder gentlemen, wrapped in their plaid shawls, strode back and forth on deck, looking, whenever they paused for a brief rest up forward at the bowsprit, at the many hundreds of lights reflecting in the river from both banks. Below deck in the engine room a rattle and banging could be heard, while the ship's screws pushed the water to the rear so that a wake of white foam pursued it. Otherwise everything was still, so still, in fact, that the ladies interrupted their conversation.

"Armgard, you're so silent," said Melusine. "Don't you think so too, my dear Stechlin? My sister hasn't even said ten words."

"I think, Countess, we'll do well to let the comtesse be. It suits some people to talk and others to be silent. Every get-together needs its silent person."

"I'll know how to profit from that lesson."

"I don't believe it, Countess, and above all, I don't wish it. Who could wish something like that?"

She threatened him with her finger. Then everyone became silent again and gazed once more out at the landscape, which lay in deep darkness where the road along the bank showed broad gaps. Suddenly and unexpectedly, however, a streak of light rose directly out of the darkness high into the sky, scattering there, as red and blue glowing balls fell slowly back to earth.

"How beautiful," said Melusine. "That's more than we had a right to expect. All's well that ends well. Now we've even got fireworks. Where can they be? What villages lie over there? You're practically a member of the General Staff, my dear Stechlin, you must know that. I suspect it's Friedrichsfelde. Charming village and a charming castle. I was there once; the lady of the house is a sister of Frau von Hülsen. Is it Friedrichsfelde?"

"It might be, your Ladyship. But I don't think it's particularly probable. Friedrichsfelde doesn't fit on the list of suburbs where fireworks

127

are, so to speak, the order of the day. I think we'll leave it in the realm of the unknown and just enjoy the thing itself. Do you see there, things are really getting going now. That rocket we just saw a few minutes ago was just the overture. Only now are we getting to the piece itself. It's too far off or else we could hear the chatter of the musketry and the canon shots. It's probably the Battle of Sedan they're doing, or Düppel, or the Crossing to Alsen.[19] In any case, pyrotechnics has become a profound science."

"And there are supposed to be people who live entirely for it and spend their entire fortune on it just like the Dutch used to for tulips. Tulips certainly wouldn't be to my taste. But fireworks!"

"You're absolutely right there. But it's a shame though, that anybody who's got anything to do with them sooner or later gets blown sky high."

"That is a bit awkward. But on the other hand it increases the fascination. It's strange, but professions that don't have anything dangerous about them, the sort that come with a tassel-cap, so to speak, have always been a horror to me. It's only gambling with everything at stake that is interesting, torpedo boats, tunnels under the sea, airships. I think the next thing we're going to be seeing is airship battles. When one of those gondola things attacks and boards the other more or less. I could practically fall in love with fantasies like that."

"Yes indeed, Melusine dear, I well see that," interrupted the baroness. "You fall in love with those sort of fantasies and in the process forget the realties and even our program. With regard to these airship battles that are after all yet to come, I'm compelled with all due respect to remind you that for today someone else is floating in the air, none other than Pastor Lorenzen. *He's* the one we were supposed to be talking about. Of course, he's no fireworks expert."

"No," laughed Woldemar, "that he isn't. But I can practically introduce him to you as an aeronaut. He's so truly a real 'Excelsior' type, a man of the clouds, someone from the genuine realm of higher things, exactly from where everything that's high-minded has its place — hope and even love."

"Oho," laughed the baroness, "hope and even love! Where's the third, I'd like to ask? There you've got to come to us. We still have the third, which is to say, we know too, what we ought to *believe*."

"Exactly, *ought to*."

"Ought to, of course. Ought to, that's the main thing. When one know's what one ought to do, the rest will come of its own. But where a sense of what one ought to do is missing, the will to do it is certain to be missing as well. It's sure 'nuff a good thing that we've got Rome and the Holy Father."

"Ah," said Melusine. "Whoever believes you on the point, Baroness. But let's put such delicate questions aside and hear about the person, whom — I really am ashamed of myself — I could forget in such an offhand way. Let's hear about our man of miracles with his love of students, this anchorite on his pillar, who is so pure of heart and above all, let's hear about the creator and spiritual provider of our friend Stechlin. *Eh bien*, what about him? 'By their fruits shall ye know them' — that could practically satisfy us. But I'm still for more details. And so then, *attention au jeu*. Our friend Stechlin has the floor."

"Yes indeed, our friend Stechlin has the floor," repeated Woldemar. "That's easy enough to say, Your Ladyship. But following up isn't so easy. A while ago I was in full swing; starting over again now has its problems. And then the ladies always expect a love story, even when we're dealing with a man whom I've already introduced with so little promise as far as things of that sort tend to go. Just as you've already done several times today — I need only remind you of the Egg Cottage — your heading for a terrible disappointment."

"No excuses!"

"Well then, so be it. I'll have to attempt it in a roundabout way though, by first describing to you on this occasion how my last encounter with Lorenzen went. As I entered his room he was visibly in tremendous excitement, as a matter of fact over a little book he had in his hands."

"And I'll take a guess at what it was," interrupted Melusine.

"Well?"

"A book by Tolstoy. Something with a lot of sacrifice and resignation in it. You know, the glorification of asceticism."

"You're on the right track there, Countess, just not geographically. As a matter of fact, it wasn't anything eastern, something Russian or other, but western, a Portuguese."

"A Portuguese," laughed the baroness. "Oh I know a few of those. They're all so small and yellowish. And one of them found some sea route or another. Of course, that was way back when. Isn't that so?"

"Certainly, Baroness, indeed it is. Except that the fellow we're dealing with here isn't anybody who discovered a sea route, but rather just a poet."

"Oh, I remember him too. Of course, I've even got his name right on the tip of my tongue. It starts with a capital C. But Calderon it isn't."

"No, Calderon it isn't. Some similarities, even on a purely cartographic basis, don't quite fit with the fellow we're discussing here. And he's by no means one of the older poets either, but a modern one. His name's Joao de Deus."[20]

"Joao de Deus," the countess repeated. "Just the very name. Strange. And what about him?"

"Yes indeed, what about him? I asked the very same question. And I haven't forgotten how Lorenzen answered me. 'This Joao de Deus,' these were more or less his words, 'was exactly what I would dearly like to be, just what I've been searching for since I've begun to live, I mean, *really* live, the sort they always say in the world outside doesn't exist anymore. But they still do exist, they've got to exist or else they've got to exist *again*. Our whole society — and especially that particular class which specifically uses that word to designate itself — is built around the ego. Therein lies its curse and that is what's going to destroy it. The Ten Commandments, they were the Old Covenant. But the New Covenant has just one single commandment, and that ends with the words, 'And if there be not love . . . . '

"Yes, that's what Lorenzen said," continued Woldemar after a pause, "and he said other things too until I interrupted him and cried, 'Wait a minute, Lorenzen, those are all nothing but generalities. You were going to tell me some personal details about Joao de Deus. What about him? Who was he? Is he alive? Or is he dead?'"

"'He's dead, but only recently, and this little booklet here tells all about his death. Listen.' And then he began to read. And what he read went more or less like this: 'And after he had died, this Joao de Deus, there was a national mourning, and all the schools in the capital were closed, and the ministers and the people from the palace, the scholars and the craftsmen, everybody, all followed crowding around the coffin. And sobbing factory workers raised up their children and pointed to the dead man and said, *un santo, un santo*. And they did this and said these things because he had lived for the poor and *not for himself*.'"

"That's beautiful," said Melusine.

"Yes, it is beautiful," repeated Woldemar, "and I believe I can add that in this story you not only have Joao de Deus, but my friend Lorenzen too. Perhaps he's not exactly like his ideal. But love puts them both on the same level."

"And so I therefore suggest," said the baroness, "that for the time being we drop that fellow with the C, whose name will occur to me yet, and in his place we raise our glasses to the new one with a D. And naturally our Lorenzen as well."

"Yes, raise our glasses," laughed Woldemar. "But with what? How? *Le jours de féte* . . . ," and he pointed back toward the Egg Cottage.

"In a dire situation of this sort we'll have to help ourselves out as best we can, and instead of some other ceremony, simply shake hands on it, crosswise, of course. Here, first Stechlin and Armgard, and then Melusine and I."

And thus with cheerful solemnity they did in fact extend hands to each other. Just as they had done so, however, the two elderly gentlemen approached the group and the baron exclaimed, "Why this's just like the Swiss oath at the Rütli."

"More, much more. Bah, freedom. What's freedom compared to love!"

"Well then, did we just have an engagement?"

"No, . . . not yet," laughed Melusine.

Election in Rheinsberg-Wutz

16

THE NEXT MORNING called Woldemar to duty at an early hour. When he returned to his room at nine he found the newspapers and several letters on his breakfast table. Among the latter was one with a rather large seal. The sealing wax was of poor quality and the letter itself, quite unfashionable in appearance, was really nothing but a piece of quarto-sized paper folded over on itself. Knowing full well from its postmark and handwriting, from whom and whence it came, Woldemar pushed it aside as Fritz brought in his tea. Not until he had taken a cup and lingered longer than necessary over it, did he again reach for the letter, turning it between his thumb and index finger.

"After last evening, I'd have wished for something better this morning than this particular letter."

As he spoke to himself, whether he wished it or not, the final moments of his visit to Wutz came to his mind once more. Shortly before he had left the convent his aunt had warmly taken his hand to tell him in passing what had long been on her mind.

"This bachelor's life, Woldemar, it's no good. Your father was already too old when he got married. I don't want to mix into your personal secrets, but just the same I would like to ask you how you stand on it?"

"Well, a beginning's been made. But so far only superficially."

"Berlin girl?"

"Yes and no. The young lady in question has been living in Berlin for a number of years now, and she loves our city more than one has a right to expect. To that extent you could say she's a Berliner. But actually she isn't. She was born over in London and her mother was Swiss."

"Oh, for heaven's sake!"

"I do believe, dear Aunt, you've got the wrong idea of a Swiss woman. You're picturing her up on an alpine meadow with a milk bucket."

"I'm not doing any such thing, Woldemar. I just know that it's a wild country."

"A free country, dear Aunt."

"Oh yes, we all know about that sort of thing. But if you've still got the cards more or less in your hand, well, then I implore you . . . ."

At this point, as previously with Fix, once again the discussion was interrupted because of an intrusion. The conversation with his aunt had then turned to other things. Now, however, he held her letter in his hand and hesitated to break its seal. "I'm well aware of what's in it and almost afraid to open it. Even if there are no arguments, at the best it will lead to nothing but tensions and ill-will. And they're possibly even more disconcerting . . . . But what good will it do!"

Then he opened the letter and read: "I presume, my dear Woldemar, that you have not forgotten my last remarks. They boiled down to the advice and plea that you not forget your homeland in this matter and, if possible, keep to the things that are closest to you. Even our provinces are so diverse. I can see you smiling over these remarks, but I'm sticking to what I say. What I call aristocracy is left nowhere but in our own Mark Brandenburg and in our old neighboring sister province. There, in fact, perhaps with an even greater purity than with us.

"I won't go into detail about how things stand upon close inspection with the entire class of the nobility as a whole, but at least I will give you a few hints. I've seen them in every shape and form. There are, for example, the young ladies from the Rhineland. The ones from Cologne and Aachen. They may be all right, but they're Catholic. And if they aren't Catholic, they're something else again, where their father's just been ennobled. Next to the Rhinelanders we've got the ones from Westphalia. I suppose one could say a few good things about them. But Silesia. Those Silesian people, Magnates they call themselves sometimes, the whole lot are practically nothing but Polish and live off gambling, while managing to keep the cutest young governesses; makes things much easier that way. And furthermore, there are the Prussians, which is to say the East Prussians, from so far out that the whole world comes to a end. Let me tell you, I'm well acquainted with their sort too. They're all exactly like those Lithuanian foals of theirs, they kick out and nibble at everything. And the richer they are, the worse."

"By now, I'm sure you're asking why I'm so hard on the others and so much for our Mark Brandenburg, especially for our Middlemark. Because, my dear Woldemar, we here in the Middlemark aren't just geographically located in the middle, but because we have and hold the true middle way in everything as well. I once heard it said our Mark Brandenburg is the land where there never were any saints, but where they never burned any heretics either. So you see, that's what really matters, the middle of the road — there's the foundation for all happiness and good fortune.

"And besides that, we have two more things here: among our folk the one true faith, and in our aristocracy pure blood. And we're well-acquainted with the sort where something like that is not the case. There are some who say, of course, what are called 'intellectual and spiritual matters' suffer because of this. Nothing but poppycock. And if they did suffer — although I say they don't — it doesn't make any difference anyway. Where the heart is healthy, the head can never be very bad. There's a precept you can depend on.

"And so, stay in our Mark while you're looking. And don't ever forget that it is we who are what is generally known as 'Brandenburg History.' And let me recommend our Rheinsberg area to you above all. Koseleger himself, despite the fact that his enemies say he's really yearning to get away to a post in the Berlin cathedral and considers himself practically in exile out here, Koseleger himself has told me, 'When you take a close look at Prussian history, you always find that everything can be traced back to this dear, old county of ours. *Here* lie the roots of our strength.' And so I close with this request, marry locally and marry Lutheran. And not for money — money's degrading — and be assured of the affection of your loving aunt and god-mother, Adelheid von St."

Woldemar laughed. "Marry locally and marry Lutheran — I've been hearing that one for years now. And I always get to hear the third too — money's degrading. But I'm well-acquainted with that. If it turns out to be a large enough amount she could even be Chinese. In the Mark everything's money. Money, simply because there's none to be had out there — money is enough to canonize anybody or anything, and what's more, in the end it will even overcome the stubbornness of an old aunt."

As he laughingly said these things to himself, he again scanned the letter and this time noticed a postscript had been scribbled in the margin of the fourth page. "Katzler was just here to tell me about the special election which is to take place in our district on Saturday. Your father has been nominated and has accepted. He's just the same as ever. Naturally he'll believe he's making·a sacrifice. He's been suffering from such delusions since he was a boy. But the things which seemed to him like sacrifices always turned out by the light of day to be nothing but vanity. Your A. von St."

17

It was just as his aunt had written: Dubslav had allowed his name to be entered as a conservative candidate and if there had still been any doubts on the matter for Woldemar, a few lines arriving from Lorenzen the next day sufficed to put them aside. It said in Lorenzen's letter:

"All sorts of grand and glorious things have transpired since your last visit. On the very same evening both Gundermann and Koseleger appeared and urged your father to run for office. Of course he refused at first. Said he was unfamiliar with the ways of the world and had no understanding for that sort of thing. But that didn't get him very far. Koseleger, who always has a few good stories up his sleeve — which is sure to stand him in good stead someday — immediately told him how years ago some fellow picked by Bismarck to be Minister of Finance who tried to extricate himself from the affair in the same manner with an 'I don't know anything about that sort of thing,' had run straight into the prompt Bismarckian reply, 'But that's exactly the reason I'm picking you, my dear fellow.' That was a tale which your father naturally couldn't resist.

"To make a long story short, he agreed. Traveling around to electioneer has naturally been ruled out; the same applies for speechmaking. The election is already next Saturday. As always, the die will be cast in Rheinsberg. I think he'll win. Only the Progressives might come into consideration or, at the very outside, the Social Democrats, if — which is easily possible — a few were to fall away from the Progressives. Under any circumstances, do write your Papa that you are glad about his decision. You can do so with a good conscience. If we get him through, I know for certain that no better man will be sitting in the Reichstag, and that we will all be able to congratulate ourselves on his election.

"And he too, of course. His life here is too lonely, you know, so much so that now and then even he complains about it, a thing that has never been his style. That's what I had to let you know about. 'Otherwise,' as they used to say during the war, 'All's quiet in the lines before Paris.' Krippenstapel is gadding about in great excitement. I think it's because of the pre-election meeting set for Thursday in Stechlin itself, where I suspect he will give his usual speech on the bee state. My regards to your two kind friends, especially Czako. As always, your old friend, Lorenzen."

After reading this, Woldemar was not quite certain how he should react. What Lorenzen had written, that no better man would be sitting in the Parliament, was quite right. Yet he nevertheless had reservations and concerns as well. The old fellow was by no means a politician. He could easily get himself deeply into nettles, perhaps even make a fool of himself in fact. And this thought was extremely painful to a son who ardently loved his father. Moreover, there was always the possibility he might be defeated in the campaign.

Woldemar's concerns were only too well-founded. It was by no means certain that old Dubslav, as popular as he was even with the opposition, would necessarily emerge as victor in the electoral contest. The Conservatives, of course, had grown accustomed to viewing Rheinsberg-Wutz as a citadel which could not be lost to their party. This belief was an error, however, and whatever previous reverence had existed toward old Kortschädel had its roots solely in the personal element. True enough, old Dubslav was his equal in esteem and popularity, but the whole business of perpetual personal favoritism had to come to an end sometime and the claim old Kortschädel had gained by serving so long, simply had to be over and done with, if for no other reason than at last there was someone new. No doubt about it, the opposition parties were springing into action and the situation was exactly as Lorenzen had written Woldemar, a Progressive, in fact, even a Social Democrat, could be elected.

What the mood of the district really was would have been best learned by anyone listening in passing at the office door of old Baruch Hirschfeld.

"Let me tell you, Isadore, you should be electing our good old Herr von Stechlin for sure."

"No, father, I *won't* be electing our good old Herr von Stechlin."

"So why not? After all, he's a nice gentleman, and he's got his heart in the right place."

"That he does. But his principles is wrong."

"Isadore, don't give me that principles business. I seen you fooling around with that little Marie from next door, and the way you undid her apron, and she was giving you a slap in the face. You made eyes at a gentile girl. And with the election coming now it's public opinion you're making eyes at. For that business with the girl, I've forgiven you. But that public opinion business, for that I ain't forgiven you."

"You will, Papa, dear. These is the new times, you know. And when I vote, it's humanity I'm voting for."

"Don't give me that, Isadore. I know about that business. Humanity. All it wants is to do is to have, but never to give. And now they want to share everything besides."

"So let them share, Papa."

"God in heaven above, what do you think you'll get? Not a tenth of it."

And so it went in the other localities as well. In Wutz, Fix spoke for the convent and the Conservatives in general, without recommending Dubslav specifically, because he knew how the Domina stood with regard to her brother. Then too, a leftist candidate from Cremmen looked as if he wanted to gain the upper hand in the Wutz area. More perilous for the entire county, however, was an itinerant speechifier from Berlin, who tramped about from village to village instructing the poorer folk that it was nonsense to expect anything from either the aristocracy or the church. They were always content to let heaven take care of things. But an eight-hour workday, an increase in wages and a Sunday outing to Finkenkrug — now there you had the one true gospel.

And thus things fell apart everywhere. But at least in the Stechlin area itself they hoped to keep matters under control and to swing all votes to Dubslav. For this purpose it was decided that all should get together in the village inn; Thursday at seven was set as the time.

The Stechlin inn lay on the square formed by the intersection of the chestnut-lined road from Wutz with the actual village road, and was the most imposing of its four corner houses. In front stood a few age-old linden trees. Three, four feeding troughs were pushed close to the building's walls, but off towards the left where the corner shop and the inn's pub-room were located. Towards the right lay the large assembly room in which Dubslav was today to be acclaimed — if not for the world then at least for Rheinsberg-Wutz, and if not for Rheinsberg-Wutz, at least for Stechlin and its surroundings. The aforementioned main assembly room was a long hall with five windows that had seen many a schottische, something its appearance today by no means attempted to deny. Not only were all the polished sconces still in place, but the prodigious double bass, which would have been far too much trouble to be removed every time, also peeked over the railing of the music loft, its long neck set at an angle.

Beneath this loft, across the room, stood a longish table covered with a table cloth, intended for the committee. On benches to the right and left sat about twenty party deputies, whose duty it was to carry out the decisions of the committee. These party representatives were for the most part well-to-do Stechlin farmers, intermingled with official and half official personages from the neighborhood, foresters, rangers and foremen at the various glass and tar works. Also joining them were a peat inspector, an official from the surveyor's office, a

137

tax official and finally an unsuccessful merchant, now an agent running the post office. Of course, rural postman Brose was in attendance, along with the entire constabulary, made up of foot patrolman Uncke and constable Pyterke of the mounted police. Pyterke only half belonged to the district, something that had long been a point of contention, but he particularly enjoyed appearing at assemblies like this nonetheless. Nothing was more pleasurable for him, in fact, than to observe his comrade and official colleague Uncke on occasions of this sort, and in the process to fully realize his own tremendous but actually quite justified superiority over the latter as a handsome fellow and former cuirassier-guard. Uncke was to him the absolute epitome of the comical and if his bronzed-reddish countenance in and of itself amused him to begin with, far, far more did his dyed shoe-brush side whiskers, and above all the way he tended to roll his eyes as he followed negotiations. Pyterke was right; Uncke really was a comical figure. His expression constantly said, "It all depends on me." At the same time he was a truly good-natured man who never wrote down more than was necessary in the line of duty and also only rarely broke things up.

The hall had three doors opening to the vestibule. At the middle door stood the two gendarmes who straightened to attention as the chairman of the committee rose from his seat at the stroke of seven and declared the meeting open. The afore-mentioned chairman was, of course, Chief Forester Katzler, who today, instead of merely a black and white ribbon, had pinned on the actual Iron Cross he had won at St. Marie-aux-Chênes. Next to him sat Superintendent Koseleger and Pastor Lorenzen. On the narrow side of the table to the left was Krippenstapel, on the right, Mayor Kluckhuhn, the latter also wearing a medal, the Düppel Medal, even though he had only served in the reserve at Düppel. He enjoyed joking about it and said, while revealing his enviable teeth, "Yes sir, boys. That's how it goes. At Alsen I was, but at Düppel I wasn't. And so now I've got the Düppel medal."

Mayor Kluckhuhn was all in all a personality touched with a good sense of humor. He was a favorite of old Dubslav's and whenever the old veterans of sixty-six and seventy began getting on their high horse, he stepped in for the fellows of sixty-four. "Let me tell you, boys, sixty-four, that's where it all began. And beginnings are always the hardest. A good beginning's always the main thing. After that everything else just follows on its own." An old Globsower, who had participated in the storming of Spichern and distinguished himself by special bravery, was also an object of his particular fault finding, simply because he was one of those fellows from the year seventy. "Course, I don't mean to say that that business at Spichern was nothing at all, Tübbecke. But compared with Düppel — even if I wasn't involved — compared with Düppel it doesn't even count. What went on there at Spichern anyway, that you're always talking about it so much, that sixty-four's supposed to take second place? At Spichern there were men up top there, but at Düppel it was entrenchments. And entrenchments with a tower in the middle, I'll tell you. Things whistle a differ'nt tune altogether in places like that. I mean, actually nobody was even talking about whistling any more."

One consequence of this attitude was that Sapper Klinke, who at the cost of his life had blown up the palisade support of Bastion Three of the Düppel fortifications, was the genuine hero of all three wars in Kluckhuhn's eyes, and when all was said and done, had but one single rival. This one single rival, however, had been on the side of the Danes and was, in fact, not a person at all, but a ship instead named *Rolf Krake*. "Yes sir, boys, while we were floatin' across there like that, there lay that black beast staying right up close to us, lookin' just like a coffin. And if it had wanted to, it would have been all over with us and plop, down we'd have gone right into Flensburg Bay. And since we all knew that, we just kept on blasting away at her, because when a fellow feels like that, he just keeps on shooting."[1]

Ah yes, *Rolf Krake* had been a dire and fateful thing for Kluckhuhn. But the very same black ship that had once given him such fear and anxiety was nonetheless a blessing for him too. One could say that his life now stood under the sign of *Rolf Krake*. In the same way that Gundermann was always wanting to "turn off the water" on the Social Democrats, so too Kluckhuhn compared everything having to do with the Social Democrats with that black monster in the Flensburg Bay. "I tell you, what they call the social revolution these days is lying right up next to us just like *Rolf Krake* did back then. Bebel's just waiting and just like that he'll sweep right in."

Mayor Kluckhuhn was highly regarded in the entire Stechlin region and as he sat there now close to Koseleger, his medal resplendent on his chest, he was also well aware of it. But compared to Krippenstapel, whom as a classroom pedant and beekeeper he did not really consider fully acceptable, on this particular occasion he really did not measure up. Today was Krippenstapel's great day, so much so that even Kluckhuhn had to lower his tone.

Katzler, who was definitely no orator, rising with a note paper which contained various sentence beginnings, started by assuring all in attendance, among whom, perhaps, there were even a few dissenters, of his gratitude for their coming. They all knew why they were there. Old Kortschädel was dead, "passed on after a long and honorable life," and the matter at hand today was to give old Herr von

Kortschädel a successor in the Reichstag. The county had always gone Conservative and it was a matter of honor to go Conservative again, as Luther had said, "Even if the world were full of a thousand devils." It was incumbent upon the county to show this decadent world that there were still "sanctuaries" and here was such a sanctuary. "We have, I believe," he concluded, "no one at this table who is completely at home in parliamentary matters, for which reason I have endeavored to set down in written form that which brings us here tonight. It is but a feeble attempt. Each of us does what he can and the bramble bush can offer nothing but its own berries. But even they can refresh the thirsty wanderer. And therefore I ask our political colleague, to whom by the way, we owe so much for the study and research of this area, I ask Schoolmaster Krippenstapel to be so kind as to read what I have set down. A *pro memoria*. One can perhaps call it that."

With a bow Katzler again took his seat while Krippenstapel arose. Like a lawyer, he paged through a number of papers and then said, "I defer to the request of the Chairman, and am pleased to be called upon to present the reading of a document that aids in bringing — of this point I am quite sure, we can, I believe, disregard those limitations expressed by the Chairman — the most powerful expression of the feelings of *every one of us*."

And now Krippenstapel put on his horn-rimmed glasses and read. It was a very brief piece and actually contained the same thing Katzler had just been saying. Krippenstapel's way of emphasizing things, however, made sure that there was considerably more applause and that the final peroration, "and thus we unite in the declaration, 'whoever lives in and around Stechlin, is *for* Stechlin,'" unleashed a tremendous uproar of approbation. Pyterke raised his helmet and pushed down on his sword, while Uncke looked around to see if there might perhaps be a single ill-disposed personage worthy of being noted down. Not to directly report him, but to take note of him, just in case. Brose, who — no doubt as a consequence of his profession — had been suffering because of the extended period of standing still, quickly started up with a sort of speed stride in the front hall, as if to control the nervousness in his legs, while Kluckhuhn rose up from his chair to greet Katzler, first with a military salute and then with the usual bow, whereby his Düppel medal dangled towards the Katzlerean Iron Cross. Only Koseleger and Lorenzen remained calm. Around the Superintendent's mouth played a faintly ironical smile.

Then the Chairman declared the meeting adjourned. Everyone broke up and Uncke alone said to Brose, "we'll stick around a while, Brose. Tomorrow there'll be running around aplenty."

"I think so too. But it's better running around than standing still here like this."

18

Outside, under the branches of the old linden tree, stood several barouches. The Superintendent's, however, had not yet arrived because Koseleger had expected a much longer meeting and therefore not ordered his until ten. There was still quite a bit of time until then, but the Superintendent did not seem dissatisfied. Taking his fellow clergyman's arm, he said, "My dear Lorenzen, as you see, it looks like I will have to invite myself as your guest. As a bachelor you will, I hope, easily deal with the intrusion. Marriage, as a rule, means a blessing, at least as far as children go, but the unmarried state has its blessings too. Our dear ladies do not take advantage of this insight and this unconditional faith in themselves and their importance often has something touching about it."

Lorenzen, although fully aware of the talents of his fellow clergyman, who was both his superior and at the same time enjoyed employing a mocking tone, did not care much for Koseleger in general. This time, however, he was completely in agreement and nodded as they strode diagonally across the square towards the parsonage.

"Ah yes, these illusions!" went on Koseleger, for whom this was a favorite conversational topic. "Of course, it's quite right that the whole lot of us live on nothing but illusions, but for women it's their daily bread. They mistreat their husbands and talk about love in the process. *They* themselves are mistreated and then they really go on about love. They see everything the way they want to and above all have a talent to deck themselves out with virtues — excuse my not enumerating them — that they don't possess in the slightest. Amongst these virtues existing mostly only in the realm of the illusory, is that of hospitality, at least in this country.

"And then those parsons' wives of ours! Each one of them takes herself for St. Elizabeth, with the well-known loaves of bread in her basket. Have you ever seen that picture at the Wartburg by the way? Of all of the paintings by Schwind it's more or less my favorite. And in truth — to get back to our parson's spouses — the fact of the matter is, I've always felt most at home with pastoral bachelors."[2]

Lorenzen laughed. "Let's hope you're not proven wrong today, Herr Superintendent."

"Absolutely unthinkable, my dear Lorenzen. I haven't yet been in this region for very long, in my beloved Quaden-Hennersdorf over there. But if not for long, at least long enough to know how things are around here. And your reputation . . . I've heard you've got a bit of the gourmet about you. I can well imagine it, by the way. You're an aesthete and one doesn't get away with that without paying the price, especially when it comes to matters pertaining to the palate. Yes indeed, the aesthetic factor. For some it's a misfortune. I know about that. This building here in front of us, your schoolhouse, no doubt? Painted solid white and not a shred of curtain. There's a Prussian school for you. That's how we educate our national soul when it comes to things that are beautiful. But there's something good come of it too. Sometimes I ask myself, though, why they don't conserve the buildings from the days of Friedrich Wilhelm I better. Actually, that really was the ideal. A gray wall, a hundred holes in it and down below a big main entrance hole. And a little guard house next to it, of course. That last touch the most important. Too bad things like that are being lost. This green picket fence here saves the whole thing, by the way . . . . What did you say was the teacher's name?"

"Krippenstapel."

"Right, Krippenstapel. Katzler used it during the meeting with a sort of aplomb. I still remember how good that name sounded to me when I first heard it. Not everybody has a name like that. How do you get along with the fellow?"

"Very well, Herr Superintendent."

"Pleases me, truly. But it must be quite a trick. Got a face like an owl, he does. And something about him that's so stiff and at the same time self-assured. A regular teacher. The one I had in Quaden-Hennersdorf was just the same. But he's losing it a bit now."

With that they reached the parsonage where, without any messenger having been sent ahead, it was already known that the Herr Superintendent was to appear. And now there he was. Only a few minutes had passed since their departure from the inn, yet despite their brevity they had sufficed for Frau Kulicke, a teacher's widow who ran the house for Lorenzen, to make everything spic-and-span. Immediately upon entering one beheld the sparkling kitchen at the farthest end of a longish corridor in which a few bright paraffin candles were burning. At the same time in the open study on the right a large lamp with a green shade gave off a subdued glow. Lorenzen pushed the sofa table, on which newspapers were piled high, back a bit and invited Koseleger to seat himself. But the latter, catching sight of the large picture which hung over the sofa in an almost luxurious frame, did not immediately take the proffered seat. Bending over the table, he remarked instead, "Ah, congratulations, Lorenzen, *Descent from the Cross*; Rubens. Why that's a wonderful engraving. Or actually sepia-print. You probably won't find the likes of that very often in a twenty-mile circle around here, not even in the somewhat over-puffed Rheinsberg. In Rheinsberg they were more inclined to hoop-skirted Watteauean ladies on a swing, but not for descents from the cross or that sort of thing. And for sure it doesn't come from what passes for a castle of that dear old Lord and Master of yours over there, a huge cottage with a glass ball out front. Lord, when I see those glass balls. And right next door something like this here. You know, Lorenzen, this picture brings back for me a wonderful hour of my life, a day in my travels, when I was in Antwerp with Grand Princess Vera from the Hague. That's when I saw that picture in the cathedral. Were you ever there?"

Lorenzen indicated he had not been.

"That would be the thing for you. This Rubens here in the original, in all the power of its color. They always say he was only capable of painting Flemish women. Well, that wouldn't have been the worst thing in the world, either, I imagine. But he could do more. Just look at that Christ. Happy the man who's been out in the world and to whom it occasionally spoke in other tongues! What flourishes around here is cheap illustrated news portfolios.[3] Turks on one page, Russkies on the other. Ach, Lorenzen, it's a sad thing to have to rot in a place like this."

Having said this, he sat down in the corner of the sofa, staring into space as if he were completely lost in other times and did not look up again until a pretty young thing, tall, slim, and blond, entered the room and, embarrassed and blushing, whispered something to the pastor.

"My good Frau Kulicke," said Lorenzen, "is just asking if we would like to have our snack in the adjoining room. I'd almost think it's best we stay here. Of course, they always say a dining room ought to be cold. Well, we'd have that next door. Personally though I find a touch of warmth better. But I leave it to you to decide, Herr Superintendent."

"A touch of warmth. Spoken right from the bottom of my soul. Well then, we'll stay where we are . . . . But tell me, Lorenzen, who was that enchanting creature? Like a picture by Knaus. Half princess, half Red-Riding-Hood. How old is she then?"

"Seventeen. A niece of my good Frau Kulicke."

"Seventeen. Ach, Lorenzen, how you're to be envied. To see such blossoming perfection all the time. And seventeen, you say? Yes, that's the real thing. Sixteen still has a touch of the egg shell about it, still a touch of just-having-been-confirmed, and eighteen is already commonplace. Anybody can be eighteen. But seventeen. A wonderful intermediate condition. And what's her name?"

"Elfriede"

"And *that* too on top of it all."

Lorenzen rocked his head and smiled.

"Yes, you're smiling, Lorenzen, and you don't know how good you've got it in this woodland parsonage of yours. What I see here makes me feel warm all over, the whole village, everything. When, for example, I picture that table to myself again, where we were sitting over there in the inn half an hour ago, on my left that Krippenstapel fellow — be he what he may — and on the right, that Rolf Krake. They're all nothing but magnificent personalities. Because the grotesque has its own greats too, you know, and by no means the worst. And then there's this Katzler fellow with his Ermyntrud. You've got all of that right here around you and this child, this Elfriede besides — who, I hope, isn't named Kulicke or else, I've got to admit, the whole structure of my enthusiasm comes tumbling down again.

"And now, take *me*, your Superintendent, the great ecclesiastical light of the neighborhood. Nothing but naked prose, uncooperative colleagues and fellow clergymen, who can't forgive me for having been to The Hague, or that I had the chance to travel around with a Grand Princess. Believe you me, Grand Princesses, even when they have their defects — and they do have their defects — are still far more preferable to me than the local ilk of Quaden-Hennersdorf, and sometimes I feel as if there's no order left in the world anymore."

"But Herr Superintendent . . . ."

"Yes indeed, Lorenzen, you put on an astonished face and are amazed that somebody for whom the high clergy has done so much, even made him Superintendent in this blessed Middlemark, and this even more blessed Ruppin County, you're amazed that such a ten-times happier fellow is talking such high treason. But am I a happy man? I'm an unhappy man . . . ."

"But Herr Superintendent . . . ."

". . . And wish that I had a congregation of a hundred-and-fifty souls, let's say at some off-the-beaten-path place like Dead Man's Village or the Tuchler Heath. You see, then it would be all over and done with, then I'd know for sure, 'you've been trumped and thrown on the discard pile.' And that can be a consolation under certain circumstances. People who have gone off the deep end and who've wound up sitting in an isolation cell gluing bags or pulling wool, they're not the worst off. The worst off are the ones who are only the half-wayers. And I have the honor to present myself to you as one of those. I'm a half-wayer, perhaps even in the one thing that's most important of all, but we'll let that pass. I'm speaking only about what it means to be a human being in general. And that when it comes to being a true human being, I'm a half-wayer, torments me. As for the rest, I suppose I might get over that."

Lorenzen's eyes continued to grow larger.

"You see, there I was then — forgive me for harping on it — there I was at twenty-seven in The Hague, and came in contact with the upper class world that's at home there. And so today I'd be in Amsterdam and tomorrow in Scheveningen and on the third in Ghent or Bruges. Bruges, the reliquary there, the Hans Memling paintings — you really ought to see something like that. What are all these eternally boring Brandenburg Margraves or even the 'Lazy Grete' to us?[4] There are some, I know full well, who were born for a hair shirt or to become hermits. Not me. I'm from the other side, my soul yearns for life and beauty. And then all those things out there say something to you, and you soak them up and you have ambition, not the childish kind, but genuine, the kind that wants to move up the ladder because you can work and do things, for yourself, of course, but for others too. That's what you thirst after.

"And then comes the cup that's supposed to still this thirst. And the name of that cup is Quaden-Hennersdorf. The village that surrounds me is nothing but an overgrown peasants' village, stuffed-up people, pompous and hard-hearted, and naturally as dry and petty as they all are around here. And proud of it, besides. Ach Lorenzen, again and again, how I envy you!"

While Koseleger was still going on in this fashion, Frau Kulicke appeared. She pushed the newspapers aside to enable her to lay out two place mats and then brought the red wine and a plate of rolls. Lorenzen poured the wine into large delicately cut glasses and the two clergymen raised them "to better times." But they had very different things in mind as they did, for the one was occupied solely with himself, the other only with others.

"We can toast a few other things, I think, along with our 'better times,'" said Lorenzen. "First off, to *your* health, Herr Superintendent. And secondly, to the health of our good old Stechlin, who, after all, brought us together this evening. Will we get him through, do you think? Katzler acted so certain about it and Kluckhuhn and Krippenstapel seem absolutely convinced. But I've got my doubts nevertheless. The Conservatives, I can scarcely say 'our party comrades,' or else only in an extremely limited sense, the Conservatives are divided among themselves. There are many of them for whom our old Stechlin is a good bit too wishy-washy. *'Fortiter in re, suaviter in modo,'*[5] one of those who likes to display his schooling recently said of the old fellow. But as far as *'suaviter'* goes, even if only *'in modo,'* the whole pack of those gentlemen don't care to hear a thing about it.

145

Also among these ultras is, of course, Gundermann from Siebenmühlen, who perhaps is known to you . . . ."

"Of course. At my place just recently. A man of three turns of
phrase, of which the best two are drawn from the water mill sphere."

"Well then, this Gundermann, as stupid fellows always are, is at
the same time the conspiratorial type, and while he's pretending to
beat the drum for our good, old Stechlin, he's dripping poison in
people's ears and telling them the old fellow's senile and doesn't have
any dash any more. But old Stechlin's got more dash than seven Gundermanns. Gundermann is a bourgeois and a parvenu, therefore more
or less the worst thing one can be. It will be enough for me if that
miserable wretch loses out. But it's the old fellow that I'm concerned
for. I can only repeat, things don't stand as favorably for him as this
area around here imagines. Because you can't depend on the poor
folk. A promise and a whiskey and they all jump ship."

"I will do my part," said Koseleger, with a mixture of pomposity
and benevolence. But Lorenzen had the impression that his Quaden-
Hennersdorf Superintendent had already abandoned himself to other
fantasies. And so indeed it was. What mattered this shabby present to
Koseleger? He was occupied with the future alone and when he
looked into it, he saw a long, long corridor with light radiating from
above, and at its end a door bell with a sign above it that read, "Dr.
Koseleger, General Superintendent."

More or less at the same hour in which the two clergymen touched
glasses "to better times," Katzler's hunting chaise — the stars were already shining — came to a halt before his chief forester's house. The
bellowing of the dogs, which had echoed unceasingly over the forest
meadow as long as the chaise was still far away, was suddenly transformed into whimpering howls and strange sounds of joy. Katzler
sprang from his chaise, hung his hat on a stand in the entrance — as
a person of discrimination he wished to have nothing to do with
those perpetual stag horn coat stands — and immediately thereupon
entered the dimly illuminated parlor of his wife, which lay to the left
side of the vestibule.

The soft light made her appear even more pale than she was. As
the wagon halted, she had arisen from her place on the sofa, and, as
she was regularly in the habit of doing whenever he returned from
the forest, approached her husband in friendly greeting. Before rising
from the sofa, she had put aside a piece of batiste intended for a
younger sister as a Christmas gift, into which she had just embroi-
dered the last point of the Ippe-Büchsenstein crown. She was not

beautiful, possessing, moreover, a lymphatically sentimental expression, yet her imposing manner, and even more, the way in which she was dressed, made her seem distinctly striking and almost foreign. She wore a smoothly hanging, lightly yellow-toned woolen dress, somewhat like a housecoat and as the most peculiar element, a headdress fashioned of the same yellowish woolen material. Of this it was uncertain whether it was supposed to represent a crown or a turban. The whole of her appearance had something intentionally eye-catching about it, yet along with its striking quality it was nevertheless also somewhat flattering. It expressed a talent for doing the best with what one has.

"How happy I am you're back," said Ermyntrud. "I was truly anxious, this time not for you, but for myself. I must be egoist and confess it. These were truly difficult hours for me, this entire time you've been away."

He kissed her hand and led her back to her seat. "You mustn't stand, Ermyntrud. And now you're back at that embroidering again. That tires you out and, as you well know, has an effect on *everything*. Our good doctor was just saying yesterday that everything is connected together. And I can see too, how pale you are."

"Oh, that's just the lampshade."

"You don't want to admit it and don't want to say anything to me that might perhaps sound like a reproach. But it's I who reproaches myself. I ought to have stayed here and not gone off to that Stechlin election meeting."

"You *had to go*, Vladimir."

"I think all the more highly of you, Ermyntrud, for saying something like that. But in the end they could have done without me just as well. Koseleger was there, he could take the chair just as easily as I. And if he hadn't wanted to, well then, Peat Inspector Etzlius could have jumped in. Or perhaps even Krippenstapel. When you get right down to it, it's Krippenstapel who does everything. In any case that's how it is, if it's not one person, it's another."

"I can admit that. How else could the world go on? There's nothing that so preaches humility to us as the realization of how dispensable each of us is. But that's not the important thing here. What is important — is the fulfillment of our duty."

Katzler, on hearing this word, looked about for something that might have put him into the position of giving the conversation another turn. But, as is always the case in such moments, whatever might save us was not to be found. Thus he saw himself clearly doomed to a lecture by the princess on her favorite topic, duty. And the whole time he was actually hungry.

147

Ermyntrud pointed to a footstool that she had pushed next to her place on the sofa in the meantime and said, "It's something I've always got to remind you about, Vladimir. We don't merely live in the world for our own sake, but for the sake of others. I shan't say for the sake of all mankind, that sounds vain, even though it should really be so. Our true obligation is not the joy of living, and not even love either — genuine love, I mean — but rather, it's nothing but duty . . . ."

"Certainly, Ermyntrud. We're in complete agreement there. And besides it's something so especially Prussian. It's a thing that distinguishes us from all other nations and even for those who don't understand us, or who don't really wish us well, there glimmers the idea of the superiority we possess that comes from it. But, after all, there are differences, degrees. If instead of going to the Stechlin election meeting, I'd have gone to Doctor Sponholz, or to old Frau Stinten in Wutz Convent, who, of course, was there long ago, perhaps that might well have been the better thing. It's a lucky thing we've made it through once again. But you can't count on it in every case."

"No, you can't count on it in every case. But you can count on the fact that whenever one acts in accordance with his duty, one is at the same time also doing the right thing. So much depends on the election of our splendid old Stechlin. And he stands, moreover, morally much higher than Kortschädel, about whom, despite his seventy years, all sorts of things could be said. Stechlin is completely inviolate. A real rarity. And to smooth the way to victory for the moral principle, why, that's actually the very reason we live. At least that's why *I* live."

"Certainly, Ermyntrud, certainly."

"To be aware of my higher obligations at every moment without first taking inclination or mood into consideration, *that* was something I vowed to myself in a solemn hour, you know in which one, and you can be my witness that I have fulfilled this vow . . . ."

"Certainly, Ermyntrud, certainly. It was our foundation . . . . "

"And when it is a matter of moral duty, as it obviously was today, how could I have ever even thought of saying, stay home. I would have felt petty — petty and disloyal."

"Not disloyal, Ermyntrud."

"Oh yes, oh yes. There are many forms of disloyalty. Personal desires have got to accommodate themselves and yield to the needs of the family and the family for its part to society. That's the way I was brought up and that's what made me take this step. Don't ask me to take it back in anything."

"Never."

At this instant the little servant girl, the daughter of one of the heath dwellers, whose unmanageable hair, untamed by any brush, constantly stuck out, appeared to inform them that she had brought the tea. Katzler took his wife's arm to lead her into the adjoining room which faced towards the courtyard. But as he realized how difficult walking was for her, he said, "It really pleases me to hear you talk like that. It's just like you. But nevertheless I am a bit concerned and want to send for the midwife tomorrow."

She nodded in agreement. At the same time a half loving glance passed over the good Katzler who, as long as that conversation concerning duty endured, only too well known to him, had from minute to minute grown more and more embarrassed.

19

And now it was election morning. Shortly before eight Lorenzen appeared at the castle to climb into Dubslav's barouche, already waiting on the ramp, to ride to Rheinsberg with him. The old gentleman, ready in boots and spurs, met him with his usual warmth and good spirits. "That's the thing, Lorenzen. And now we can get right in. But why didn't you wait for me at your parsonage garden? Have to pass it anyway, you know."

With great solicitude he handed a blanket to him as he spoke, just as the horses started to move. "By the way, it does please me, nonetheless — one is always contradicting oneself — that you weren't so practical after all and preferred to come over here. A nice touch of courtesy. And people are so frightfully discourteous these days, and practically ill-mannered . . . . But let's forget that business. I can't do anything to change it and it doesn't bother me that much either."

"Because you're so kind and have the sort of cheerfulness about you that from the point of view of human nature is more or less the best thing we've got."

Dubslav laughed. "Yes, that much is true. Hanging my head was never my sort of thing and if it weren't for that damned money business . . . . You know, Lorenzen, that business with mammon and the golden calf, those are really all very fine and dandy things."

"Of course, Herr von Stechlin."

". . . And if it weren't for that damned money business I'd have had to hang my head even less than I have. But money. Back in the days under Friedrich Wilhelm III there was that old General von der Marwitz from Friedersdorf. You must have heard of him one time or another. Somewhere in his memoirs he said, he'd have gladly retired from active service earlier than he did and had stayed in only for the sake of the worst thing there is in the world, money. And back then when I read that, it really made a tremendous impression on me. Because it really takes something to say a thing like that so calmly. People are so hypocritical and dishonorable in everything, in financial affairs too, almost more so than when it comes to virtue. And that tells you something. Yes sir, Lorenzen, that's true . . . . Well, let's forget it. After all, you know what's what too. And anyhow, those aren't the sort of ideas for a day like today, when I'm supposed to be elected and play the triumphant hero. By the way, I'm heading for a total smash. I'm not going to be elected."

Lorenzen was embarrassed, for what Dubslav was saying agreed only too well with his own opinion. But, for better or for worse, and as difficult as it was for him, he had to assure him of the opposite. "Herr von Stechlin, your election is, I think, certain. In our district at least. The Globsowers and Dagowers are leading the way with their good example. Good people, every one of them."

"Maybe. But rotten fiddlers. People are all weather vanes, a bit more, a bit less. And we do the same. Whoosh, and we're on the other side."

"Yes, everybody's weak and I wouldn't care to vouch for each and every one. But in this particular case . . . . Even Koseleger seemed full of confidence and trust when he was chatting with me just last Thursday."

"Koseleger full of confidence. Well then, things are sure to fall apart . . . . Wherever he says 'Amen,' it's every bit as good as the last rites. He doesn't have the lucky touch, that fellow clergyman and superior of yours."

"Unfortunately, I share your reservations toward him to a certain extent. But as for something that can perhaps reconcile one to him, he does have pleasant manners and a certain courteousness about him."

"That he has. And yet, as much as I'm usually for manners and civility, not for his sort. We shouldn't hold a person's name against him. But Koseleger! I still don't know whether he's more for cozying up or trying to get a leg up on everybody.[6] Maybe he's both at the same time. He's like an eclair, sweet but unhealthy. No, Lorenzen. When it comes to that I'm more for you. You're not worth much either, but at least one can say you're honest."

"Perhaps," said Lorenzen. "But in the midst of all his civilities and pretty words, Koseleger still has something free about him too, something almost daring, and as a result made some admissions to me just recently almost like a man of character."

Dubslav laughed out loud. "Character. Come on now, Lorenzen. How can you let yourself be led down the primrose path like that? I'll lay odds he told you something about your 'gifts'. That's the faddish word you pastors are all using with one another these days. It's supposed to sound modest and impersonal and to lead everything back to inspiration, so to speak, for which, of course, in the end no one can do anything about as with everything that comes from on high. But for that very reason it's really the most arrogant thing there is . . . . Was it anything like that? Did he manage to take in my clever friend Lorenzen with such flattery before pawning himself off as a 'man of character?'"

"That was not the case, Herr von Stechlin. For this once you do him an injustice here. He did not say a word about me but rather about himself and in the process he made certain confessions to me. For example he admitted to me that he felt unhappy."

"Why?"

"Because he considered himself 'ill-placed' in Quaden-Hennersdorf."

"'Ill-placed.' That's another one of those fancy turns of phrase. I'm familiar with that. If one simply wanted to look at it that way, everybody is 'ill-placed,' I, you, Krippenstapel, Engelke. I ought to be the chairman of a barroom regulars crew or maybe the director of a spa, you, missionary in the Congo, Krippenstapel, the curator of a Brandenburg museum and Engelke, well, he'd have to go right into it himself. Number one-hundred-thirteen. 'Ill-placed!' Nothing but vanity and megalomania. And this Koseleger fellow, with that consistorial councilor's chin of his. He was an orderly to a Grand Princess, that's something he can't forget, he thinks he can push his way around with that and in his frustration and pique pawns himself off as a man of character and has the presumption, as you say, to make confessions and rash statements. And now if he ever succeeds — may God prevent it — then you've got the burn-'em-at the stake-type *comme il faut* on your hands. And the first one who'll be put up there to burn is you. Because he'll immediately feel the need of making up for today's rash remarks with some incinerated sacrificial victim or other."

As they continued this conversation, they finally reached the end of the woods and approached a piece of marshland several miles long which extended to the horizon. Across it several roads lined with willows and silver poplars ran like the spokes of a wheel towards Rheinsberg. All of these byways were filled, chiefly with people on foot, but also with vehicles. One of them, of yellowish wood which gleamed brightly in the sun, was easy to identify.

"Why, there goes Katzler," said Dubslav. "Could almost say it surprises me. Something has, in fact, come up again, which you perhaps don't know about yet. He sent me a messenger with the news of it early this morning, and from it I concluded that he *wouldn't* be coming to the election. But Ermyntrud with her grandiose ideas about duty probably packed him off on his way again."

"Is it another girl?" asked Lorenzen.

"Of course. The seventh in fact. At seven, I think — of course, it's got to be laddies — you're allowed to invite the Kaiser as godfather. Anyway, several of them have died and taking everything into account, it's probable that Ermyntrud is getting herself all sorts of ideas and worries about this constant 'nothing-but-girls' business."

Lorenzen nodded. "I can imagine that the princess views it as a form of atonement, atonement for the step she's taken. Everything about her is a bit extravagant. And yet she's a very amiable lady."

"Of which nobody is more convinced than I," said Dubslav. "Of course I've been bought off. Because she always says the most flattering things to me, you know. That she likes to chat with me so much, which in the end is probably true. And in the process she's really gets quite cheerful and playful every time, despite the fact that she's really sentimental to the nth degree. Sentimental, which isn't all that surprising. Because, after all, sentimentality is at the bottom of the whole Katzler business.

"By the way, I'm seriously concerned where her Highness will dig up the right baptismal name for her latest-born. In this particular matter, the only one perhaps, she's remained one hundred percent the princess. And you, my dear Lorenzen, are sure to be called in for advice on the matter."

"Something I don't imagine to be particularly difficult."

"Don't say that. In a case like this there are far fewer useful items than you can imagine. Princesses names, in and of themselves, without any further additions, sure, there are plenty of those. But Ermyntrud isn't satisfied with that. In keeping with her nature, along with the dynastic-genealogical element, she demands something poetical and fairy-tale-like. And that complicates the matter tremendously. You can see that when you run through the Katzlerean nursery or call to mind the names of the ones who were baptized before. Naturally, the Katzlerean crown princess is also named Ermyntrud. And then, as a matter of course, come Dagmar and Thyra. After that we run into an Inez and a Maud and finally an Arabella. But when you get to Arabella you can clearly sense a certain dilemma. If she were to turn to me on account of her latest born, I would suggest something ancient-Judaic. In the end that's always the best. What do you think of Rebecca?"

Lorenzen did not get to answer this question for Dubslav, because at this very moment they had crossed through the marshland and were already rattling over a stone-surfaced road directly toward Rheinsberg, making further conversation impossible,

Dubslav was in a splendid good humor. The glorious autumn weather, and in addition, the lively scene, had all raised his mood. Most uplifting of all, however, was that on the way and while passing down the main street, he had had occasion to greet various good friends. It was sounding ten from the church as he stopped before the Prince Regent's Inn, which had been set up as the polling place. Already standing before its front facade were several more or less dubious looking electoral delegates, all endeavoring to pass out their handbills to supposed party comrades.

Within the hall, the election was underway. Behind the urn presided old Herr von Zühlen, who, well into his seventies, knew how to combine the most grotesque feudalistic views with equally great charm, a talent which assured him of great popularity even with his political opponents. Next to him, on his left and right, sat Herr von Storbeck and Herr van dem Peerenboom. The latter was a Dutchman from the region of Delft, who but a few years earlier had bought a large estate in the Ruppin area and since that time had turned himself into a Prussian, and what was even more, into a "county man." They did not view him as being completely legitimate, however, for all sorts of reasons, even starting with his "van." None of this was shown, however, because he was not without the primary characteristic, which made a profound impression on most of the local county folk, of being a Dutch-Javanese coffee dealer, born so and so many years ago in Batavia. His neighbor von Storbeck's life history was more prosaic.

Among the others who also usually sat at the committee table was Katzler, whom Ermyntrud, as Dubslav had quite correctly surmised, had sent from her childbed with the comment, that in the modern bourgeois state voting was every bit as valuable as taking up arms. "The child will be my angel in the meanwhile," she added, "and the feeling of fulfilled duty will keep up my strength." Gundermann too, who always had to be in the middle of things, was also sitting at the committee table. His behavior had something excited about it because, as Lorenzen had hinted, he really had secretly conspired against Dubslav. That he would be defeated was obvious and scarcely concerned him any more. Filling him with dread, however, was the concern that his earlier duplicity might be revealed.

Dubslav dearly wished the whole affair were behind him. Thus after greeting several acquaintances outside and exchanging a few words with each, he proceeded from the vestibule into the polling room to place his ballot in the urn as quickly as possible. In the process his glance encountered that of old Zühlen. With a mixture of solemnity and whimsicality it seemed to say, "Yes sir, Stechlin, nothing much'll help either, one's just got to go along with the whole silly affair." Dubslav, it must be said, scarcely came to take note of this look because he caught sight of Katzler and advanced toward him immediately to congratulate him with a handshake on the birth of his seventh daughter. The old man passed Gundermann without taking notice. This was just by chance, of course; he knew nothing of the Siebenmühlener's duplicity. But the latter himself, having a bad conscience, became embarrassed and felt the oldster's bearing to be a rejection.

Once Dubslav was again outside, the great question naturally became, "Well, what now?" It was only now going on eleven and the whole business would not be over before six, if it wasn't drawn out even longer. He expressed these sentiments to a number of the gentlemen seated on one of the benches in front of the inn who had somewhat prematurely helped themselves to the Prince Regent's liqueur cabinet, which under normal circumstances did not put in an appearance until after dinner.

There were five of them in all, every one a fellow comrade from county and party, not actually friends, however, for old Dubslav was not much for friendships. He saw too clearly what each one of them lacked. Those who were sitting there, arguing the merits of Caraway and Chartreuse, were Herr von Molchow, Herr von Krangen and Herr von Gnewkow along with Baron Beetz and a Freiherr von der Nonne, whom nature apparently formed while taking particular consideration of his name. He wore a high black cravat on which sat a puny little head and when he spoke it was as if mice were peeping. As the comical figure of the group, he was constantly the butt of teasing. Yet he took no offense, because his mother had been a Silesian countess whose name ended in -inski, a fact which in his eyes assured him of such superiority that like Frederick the Great, he was at every moment prepared "to hang any pasquil that might present itself even lower."[7]

"I think, gentlemen," said Dubslav, "we'll go into the park. There's always something there. At one spot rests the heart of the prince and at another spot, he himself's resting. He's even got a pyramid at his head as if he'd been Sesostris himself. I'd be glad to mention another Egyptian king, but I only know that one."

"Certainly we'll go into the park," said von Gnewkow. "After all, it's a lucky thing we've still got the likes of it . . . ."

"And a lucky thing too," added von Molchow, "that we've got an election day like today, which downright forces you to concern yourself with historical and cultural things now and then. Happened to Bismarck too one time, with a rich American woman in fact, and right off — actually a long time later, that is — he came up with the right thing to say."

"He always came up with the right thing to say."

"Always. But go on there, Molchow."

". . . Well then, when this rich American woman saw him some forty years later and tried to thank him on account of the picture gallery he'd half out of embarrassment and half out of chivalry accompanied her to, and apparently explained all the pictures wrong to her, he just refused all her thanks. I can actually see and hear him as if he were right here. And just as cheerfully as could be, he told her she shouldn't thank him, but instead he had to thank her, because if it hadn't been for that day he'd probably never have had a chance to see that whole gallery. Yes sir, he always had the luck. Big things or small. What would have been the last straw is his later becoming the general director of the royal museums as well, which, when you get right down to it, he could have done too. The fact is he could do everything and has practically been everything besides."

"Yes," said Gnewkow, who out of boredom had done a considerable bit of travel, taking up anew his original thought that such a park was actually a lucky thing. "I think what Molchow was saying there is absolutely correct. It all depends on one's being forced into it. Otherwise you don't know a thing. When I just think back about Italy. You see, you run around there all over the place like that, which finally tires you out, and then there's this eternally blazing sunshine. You can last a few hours, but then by the time you've stopped for coffee twice and eaten a *granito* besides, and it's still not even noon yet, well then, I ask you, what have you got to show for it? What are you supposed to do then? Downright frightful. And I can only say, that's when I became a church-going person. And when you quietly step in from the side door, and all of a sudden that coolness surrounds you, well, of course, a fellow doesn't ever want to go outside again, and more or less takes in his fifty pictures without even noticing how. Always better than outside, y'know. And time passes and the hour when you can get a real meal again creeps right up on you."

"I do believe," said Baron Beetz, a great admirer of ecclesiastical art, "that our friend Gnewkow underestimates the effect that, perhaps even against his will, the artists of the Quattrocento have had on him. He's felt their impact on himself, but he chooses not to admit that this

155

freshness emanated from them. Anybody who knows anything about it . . . ."

"Of course, Baron, that's it exactly. Whoever knows anything about it! But who knows anything about it? Not me, in any case."

As this conversation continued, they had made their way from the Prince Regent, down the main street and across a little bridge, entering first the courtyard of the castle and then its park. The lake gently splashed. Small boats lay about, several at a dock which led from the pebbled beach out into the lake. A few of the gentlemen, among them Dubslav, strolled to the end of the rather rickety boarded structure and, having reached it, looked back at the two wings of the castle and their short, stumpy towers. The tower on the right was the one in which Crown Prince Fritz had had his study.

"That's where he lived," said von der Nonne. "How limited our abilities really are. The sight of such Fredericean places always awakens a feeling of pain in me about the insufficiencies of human nature in general and, of course a feeling of pride as well, that we're capable of mastering these insufficiencies and weaknesses. Death, where is thy sting, hell, where is thy victory? This king. He was a great personality, for certain, but yet a personality gone astray as well. And the more patriotic we feel, the more painfully we're touched by the question of the salvation of his soul. Masses for the souls of the departed — in moments like this I actually do feel they're a truly consoling side of Catholicism. And that it's given to the power of those who live on afterwards — naturally with the guarantee of the Will of the Most High — to release a soul through prayer, that is and always will be a truly magnificent thing."

"Nonne," said Molchow, "don't make yourself ridiculous. What sort of an idea have you got o' the Good Lord? If you showed up wanting to pray for Old Fritz's release, they'd throw you out."

Baron Beetz — also a doubter of the Philosopher of Sanssouci — wished to come to the aid of his friend Nonne and for an instant seriously deliberated as to whether or not he should not launch into his lecture known far and wide throughout the entire county on 'Leaving the Straight and Narrow', or 'c'est le premier pas qui coute.' Wisely, however, he let it pass and was in agreement when Dubslav announced, "Gentlemen, I personally suggest that we finally give up our lookout post here on this rickety jetty we're all standing on — any minute now one of us can fall into the water — and instead have ourselves rowed across the lake in one of these boats lying around here. On the way we can pick a few water lilies, if there are any left, and over there on the other bank we can have a look at the Prince Heinrich obelisk with its French inscriptions. Recapitulations of that sort always fortify one both historically and patriotically, and our elementary French will also be refreshed in the process."

All were in accord, even Nonne.

Around four everyone had returned from the excursion and again stopped in front of the Prince Regent on a plaza occupied by old trees, which since time immemorial had born the name 'The Triangle' because of its shape. The election results were by no means yet certain. By now it could be seen rather clearly, however, that many Progressive votes would pass to the candidate of the Social Democrats, to file maker Torgelow, who, although not personally present, had the simple folk behind him. Hundreds of his party comrades stood around in groups on the Triangle, conversing laughingly about the election speeches that had been presented by speakers of the opposing parties, partly in Rheinsberg and Wutz, and partly out in the flat countryside. One of those standing under the trees, an intimate of Torgelow, was the wood turner's journeyman Söderkopp, who simply in his capacity as wood turner's journeyman enjoyed considerable standing. Everyone thought, "that fellow can turn out to be a Bebel someday. Why not? Bebel is old and then we'll have this fellow." But Söderkopp also knew how to really enthrall the people. He went after Gundermann the hardest. "Yes sir, this Gundermann, I know the likes o' him. A board-cutter and stock-market swindler. Scrounges every penny that comes his way. Got seven mills, he does, but only two turns of phrase, and progress is alternately the 'precursor' or else it's the 'father' of socialism. Maybe we all come from the likes of him. That sort's capable of anything."

Uncke, as Söderkopp was going on in this way, edged closer and closer from tree to tree, taking his notes. At a further distance stood Pyterke, smiling to himself, visibly surprised that Uncke found so much worthy of copying down.

Pyterke's astonishment regarding Uncke's "note taking" was only too justified, but it would have been a good bit less so if Uncke's auditory zeal had been directed, instead of at the Social Democrat Söderkopp, toward a group standing off to the side. Here, in fact, several of those considered stalwarts of the state were chatting about the presumable outcome of the election and that the chances for old Stechlin's victory were getting worse from minute to minute. Especially the Rheinsbergers were said to have turned the outcome to his disadvantage.

"Devil take the whole of Rheinsberg," swore an elderly Herr von Kraatz, whose red face as he spoke became all the redder. "Miserable

157

hole this. As truly as I'm standing here, we're not going to get him in, our good, old Stechlin. And what that means, we all know. Anybody who votes against *us*, votes against the king. It's all one and the same. That's what they call 'solidarity' these days."

"Yes sir, Kraatz," began Molchow, towards whom this tirade had been primarily directed, "You can call it whatever you want, solidarity or not, the one doesn't say anything and the other doesn't either. But what you said there about Rheinsberg, that hits the nail right on the head, for sure. Dissension was always right at home here from the beginning. First off, Fritz dissented against his father, then Heinrich dissented against his brother, and finally August, our good old gallant Prince August, whom a few of us still even knew quite well, I tell you, our old August dissented against morality itself.[8] And, of course, that was worst of all. (Agreement and laughing.) And that always winds up providing its own punishment besides. Because do you know, gentlemen, what finally happened with August when he really wanted to get into heaven?"

"No. Tell us. What went on, Molchow?"

"Well, he had to wait outside for practically half an hour. And so then when he was about ready to yell at St. Peter about it, the Rock of the Church says to him, 'With all due respect, Royal Highness, nothing else we could do.' And why not? Because he had to get the eleven thousand virgins to safety first."

"Righto, righto," said Kraatz. "Just like the old boy. A regular devil of a fellow. But dashing. And a real prince, he was. And when you think about it, gentlemen — well, good God in heaven above, if somebody's a prince, well then, you've got to get something out of it . . . . And one thing I know, if I were a prince . . . ."

20

By six the outcome was as good as certain. A few reports were still outstanding but those were localities whose few votes could no longer change anything. It was clear that the Social Democrats had pulled off an almost stunning victory. Old Stechlin was far behind. Progressive candidate Katzenstein from Gransee even farther. By and large both defeated parties calmly accepted events; among the Free Thinkers little disappointment could be noticed, and as for the Con-servatives, none at all. Dubslav dealt with it completely from the cheerful perspective, his party comrades even more so. Each of them thought, "Winning is a fine thing, but sitting down to dinner even better."

And, as a matter of fact, it was time to eat. Everyone longed to forget the whole boring process over a trout and a good bottle of Chablis. And once the trout was dispatched, and the saddle of venison began to beckon on the horizon, why, then the champagne was in sight as well. And the Prince Regent prided itself on the best of labels.

The table ran the length of the upstairs dining room. The majority of its occupants were manored lords or estate tenants, but also court councilors, fortunate enough to have "Captain of the Reserve" appended to their calling cards. To this *gros d'armee* were added forestry and tax officials, pension officials, preachers and high school teachers. At the head of the latter stood School Rector Thormeyer from Rheinsberg. He possessed large protruding eyes, a massive double chin — more massive even than Koseleger's — and besides that a reputation for his stories. That in addition he was a dyed-in-the-wool conservative was, of course, obvious. He had — it was decades in the past, however — conceived and carried out the magnificent idea of leading the strayed east-Elbian provinces back to the straight and narrow through Gustav Kühn's illustrated portfolios[9] and had been decorated for doing so. As a result they said of him that he counted for something up above. That was, however, not quite correct. They knew him "above" only too well.

At six thirty — sconces and chandeliers were already burning — they ascended the steps, here and there a bit worn down, to the strains of the *Tannhäuser March*. Immediately before, some vacillation as to who would preside at table had still occurred. A few had been for Dubslav, expecting something stimulating from him, especially considering the situation. But the majority in the end rejected Dubslav's chairmanship as absolutely unthinkable since the noble Lord of Alten-Friesack, despite his advanced years, had also appeared at the election. The noble Lord of Alten-Friesack, it was said, was simply — and from a certain standpoint rightfully and fittingly so — the pride of the county, a unique personage in every way. Whether he could speak or not was, in a case like this where it was a matter of principle, utterly unimportant. In any case, the entire business of "being able to give a speech" was nothing but modern nonsense. The simple fact that the old man from Alten-Friesack would be sitting there was far, far more important than a speech, and his imposing cathedral chapter cross did not merely adorn him but rather the entire table. A few might make remarks about his petrified countenance or his ugliness, but even that did no harm. These days, when most people had heads trimmed into shape by a barber, it was downright refreshing to encounter a face which in its uniqueness resisted any and all classification.

This tirade, forcibly delivered by old Zühlen, despite his preference for Dubslav, had generally been agreed to, and Baron Beetz led the petrified old Alten-Friesacker to his place of honor. Naturally there were those with malicious tongues. At their head was Molchow who whispered to Katzler seated next to him, "A real bit of luck, Katzler, that the old boy over there has that big flower vase in front of him, or else right in the middle of my *veau en tortue*,[10] presuming of course something as good as that's in sight, I'd have never been up to the whole thing."

And now the *Tannhäuser March,* performed by one of Thormeyer's teachers, was brought to a conclusion, and when after a certain time the moment for the first toast had arrived, Baron Beetz arose and announced, "Gentlemen. Our noble Lord of Alten-Friesack is filled with the duty and desire to propose a toast to His Majesty our King and Kaiser." And while the oldster in confirmation of this announcement raised his glass, Baron Beetz, continuing in the role of his alter ego added, "His Majesty, the King and Kaiser, long life to him!" The Alten-Friesacker affirmed his accordance with a nod, and as the young teacher hastened again to the old grand piano obtained at a Rheinsberg Castle auction, the entire length of the table struck up *Heil dir im Siegerkranz,*[11] the first verse of which was sung standing.

Formalities had hereby been concluded and a certain cheerfulness, of which by the way there had been no dearth from the beginning, could now more sustainedly assume its rightful place. To be sure there was still an important and at the same time difficult toast in sight, the one which had to deal with Dubslav and the unfortunate outcome of the election. Who should propose that? All preoccupied themselves with a certain amount of concern with this question and were actually relieved when all at once it was said that Gundermann would speak. Of course, everybody knew that the fellow from Siebenmühlen was not to be taken seriously, indeed that grotesqueries and perhaps even botchery were in sight. All, however, consoled themselves; the more he botched, the better. The majority were by now in a considerable uproar, in other words quite uncritical. A little while was allowed to pass, after which Baron Beetz, upon whom the role of master of ceremonies had fallen, asked Herr von Gundermann of Siebenmühlen to address them. A few went on chatting undisturbed. "Quiet, quiet!" called others interrupting them, and after Baron Beetz once again tapped on his glass and himself asked anew for quiet, a relative silence was gained.

Gundermann now stepped behind his chair and began, while sticking his left hand in his pants pocket with affected nonchalance, "Gentlemen. When I was studying in Berlin so and so many years ago

160

("well, well"), "when I was studying in Berlin some years ago, one day there was 'n execution . . . ."

"Damnation, *he* sure knows how to start off well."

". . . . one day there was 'n execution, because a fat plumber's *madamm*, after she fell in love with her apprentice, went and poisoned her husband, a respectable master plumber. And the lad himself was only seventeen. Yes sir, gentlemen, one thing I've got to say, even in those days some pretty wild things happened. And I, because I knew the prison director, I got admitted to the execution. And around me were standing nothing but assistant judges and civil service clerks, real young fellows, most of'm with a pince-nez. They had pince-nez back then already, y'know. And then came the widow, if that's what you could call her. And she looked downright stout and almost portly because, everybody talked about it at the time, she had a goiter, so that the block had to be especially prepared. With a *decolleté*, so to speak."

"With a *decolleté* . . . . Pretty good, Gundermann."

"And when she, the criminal, I mean, saw all those young clerks, her apprentice probably crossed her mind . . ."

"Lets have no making fun of our clerks . . . "

". . . her apprentice probably crossed her mind, and she walked right over next to the edge of the scaffold and nodded to us — I'm saying 'us' because she was looking at me too — and said, 'Yes sir, you young gents, *dat's* wot comes of it . . . . ' And you see, gentlemen, this very remark, even if emanating from a criminal, I've never ever forgotten since that day. And whenever I go through something like today, then such a remark absolutely *has* to occur to you, and so I say, just like that old girl did back then, 'Yes sir, gentlemen, dat's wot comes of it.' And what does it come of? From the Social Democrats. And what do the Social Democrats come from?"

"From progress. Old story. We know that. Give us something new!"

"Nothing new in it. All I can do is agree. From progress. And where does *that* come from? That comes from our having this system for voting for everything and that huge building with four towers.[12] And as far as I go, if they can't get along without that huge building, because in the end money for the state does have to be approved — and without money, gentlemen, nothing's going to work" (Agreement: "Without money the good times stop") — "well then, if it absolutely has to be, which I admit it does, what are we supposed to do, even with the concessions we've gladly made — with an election law, where it's Herr von Stechlin who's supposed to be elected and where it's his coachman Martin, who's driven him to the election, who actually gets elected, or at least might be able to get himself elected? And our Herr von Stechlin's coachman Martin is still far more preferable to me than this Torgelow fellow. And all of this is what they call freedom. Nonsense's what I call it. And a lot of others do too. But I imagine that this very election, in a county where the old Prussia is still alive, this election in particular, will do its part to open the eyes of those up above. I won't say whose eyes."

"Finish, finish!"

"I'm coming to the finish. They say back in seventy the French called themselves 'the gloriously vanquished.' A proud remark, a remark worthy of emulation. And for us too, gentlemen. And just as we, without having to excuse ourselves for doing so, accept this champagne from France, so too, I believe, can we also adopt that just-quoted proud phrase of grieving from France. We have been vanquished, but we are the gloriously vanquished. We will have our *revanche*. We will take it. And until that day, in every way, To Herr von Stechlin of Castle Stechlin, long life to him!"

All rose and touched glasses with Dubslav. A few, it must be admitted, laughed and von Molchow, as he was ordering a new wine bucket said to Katzler who was sitting beside him, "Heaven knows, this Gundermann always was and still is a jackass. What are we supposed to do with people like that? First off he describes that woman with a goiter for us, then he wants to get rid of the Reichstag. Monstrous stupidity. If we don't have that huge building, we won't have anything; it's still our salvation, practically the only place where we can, to a certain extent, open our mouth (mouth, I say) and get something through. We've got to come to some sort of an agreement with the Center Party. Then we're in the clear. And now comes this Gundermann and wants to take that from us too. It's really true, y'know, that the parties and the upper class ruin themselves every time. Which is to say, you really can't talk about upper class in this case. This Gundermann fellow doesn't belong to it. His mother was a midwife in Wrietzen. That's why he's always so pushy."

Soon after Gundermann's speech, which had been sort of an epilogue, Baron Beetz whispered to the old Alten-Friesacker that it was time to bring the meal to its conclusion. The old fellow, however, did not yet really want to do so, for once they got him sitting, he was sitting. But since immediately thereafter several chairs were pushed back, he had no other recourse but to join in. Thus with the tones of the *Hohenfriedberger March* resounding — considering the overall situation, the *Prague March*, in which it says, "Schwerin has fallen" might have been more appropriate — they returned to the ground floor rooms where most of them wished to have at the coffee. At the same time a small party of the most courageous stepped out to the street, there, under the trees of the Triangle, to continue enjoying themselves with champagne and cognac.

At the top of this list was von Molchow, next to him von Kraatz and van Peerenboom, across from von Molchow, Director Thormeyer and the teacher to whom till then the festive music had been entrusted, and who on such occasions was generally Thormeyer's Adlatus. Strangely enough, Katzler had settled here as well. No doubt he yearned for impressions which lay beyond anything having to do with "duty." And next to him, perhaps even more surprisingly, sat von der Nonne. Molchow and Thormeyer led the discussion. The election and politics had long ceased to be topics of conversation; only with regard to Gundermann did a mocking remark occasionally fall. Instead, it was the latest tales of gossip from the county to which they zealously devoted themselves.

"Is it really true," said Kraatz, "that that fair Miss Lily really is going to marry her cousin after all, or rather, the cousin, the fair Lily?"

"Cousin?" asked Peerenboom.

"Ach, Peerenboom, you don't know a thing. You're still sitting in the middle of those Delft tiles of yours even though you'd been here a long time when the whole Lily business took place."

Peerenboom accepted such comments and resisted any further questions, a thing he was able to do without damaging himself in any way, since there was not the slightest doubt that he who had brought up the topic of Lily would sooner or later make everything clear anyway. As indeed happened.

"Yes, these damned rascals," continued von Kraatz, "these teachers! Excuse me, Luckhardt, but you're at the gymnasium, of course. Things are different there. The fellow who's involved here, of course, was naturally nothing but a home tutor. Tutor for Lily's youngest brother. And one fine day the two of them were off and away, Lily and the tutor. Naturally to England. Anybody can be as stupid as he wants to be, but they've all heard or read about Gretna Green one time or another.[13] And so that's where they both wanted to head for. And away they went. But I do believe the Gretna Greeners aren't allowed to marry anyone anymore. And so they took 'lodgings' in London, without even getting married. And they went along like that until their money ran out."

"Of course. The old story."

"And so, back they came again. That is, Lily came back again. And she had been as good as engaged to her cousin beforehand as well."

"And so then he got out of it?"

163

"Not quite that. Or actually not at all. After all, Lily is really a cute little thing and very rich to boot. And so the cousin is supposed to have said that he really did love her, and if you love, you can forgive too. And he considered something like exculpation to be completely possible. In fact, he's even supposed to have mentioned purgatory."

"Don't like it, sounds bad," said Molchow. "But what he said earlier, 'exculpation' that's a beautiful word and a beautiful thing too. But the 'how' — ach, we always know so little about these things — that's what just isn't clear to me. As a Christian I naturally know — things aren't that bad with a fellow after all — as a Christian I know that there is atonement. But in a case like this? Thormeyer, what's your opinion? What do you say about it? You're a specialist, you've read all the church fathers and a few more as well."

Thormeyer became radiant. Here was a topic that was truly to his taste. His eyes became even larger and his smooth face even smoother.

"Yes," he said, as he bowed across the table to Molchow. "Something of that sort does exist. And it's a good thing that it does. Because, you know, poor mankind stands in need of it. I prefer to avoid the word purgatory, for one thing because my Protestant conscience resists it, for another because of the associations. But there is a purification. And that's precisely the thing, on which everything really depends, you know. The restoration of purity. A rather awkward turn of phrase. But nevertheless the very thing that's at stake here, very well does exist. You encounter this tendency towards restitution everywhere, and especially in the orient — from which, of course, our entire culture emanates — especially there do you find this theory, this dogma, this fact."

"Really, is it a fact?"

"Hard to say. But it is taken to be fact. And that's just as good. *Blood atones.*"

"Blood atones," repeated Molchow. "Certainly. That's the source of our own institution of the duel too, of course. But where is this blood atonement supposed to come from? In this particular case it's absolutely impossible. The tutor stayed over there in England, if he hasn't even gone off to America. And if he were to come back anyway, he's not at all acceptable to give satisfaction. If he were a reserve officer I'd have long since heard about it . . . ."

"Yes, Herr von Molchow, that is the local view of things. Somewhat primitive, aboriginal, the so-called principle of blood vengeance. But it doesn't always have to be the blood of the transgressor. Among the orientals . . . "

"Good grief, the orientals . . . crazy bunch . . . ."

164

"Well, however you care to have it, among almost all the peoples of the East, blood atones of itself. Yes, even more. According to the oriental view, I can't avoid using the word, Herr von Molchow, I've got to keep coming back to the same thing time and again, according to the oriental view, blood restores innocence as such."

"Now just a minute, Rector."

"Yes, so it is, gentlemen. And I may say, that counts among the most refined and profound things there are. And I only recently read a story that more or less confirms it not just superficially, but practically magnificently. And moreover, from Siam."

"From Siam?"

"Yes, from Siam. And I'd trouble you with it, if the business weren't a bit too long. You gentlemen from the country get impatient so easily and I've often been amazed that you even stay to hear the end of the sermon. Compared to that, to be sure, my story from Siam is . . . ."

"Tell it, old boy, tell it."

"Well then, at your peril. To be sure, at mine too . . . . Well then, there was, and it's not so long ago either, there was this king of Siam. The Siamese have kings too, you know."

"Well naturally. After all, they're not that far down the ladder."

"Well, there was a king of Siam and this king had a daughter."

"Sounds like it's straight out of a fairy tale."

"It is too, gentlemen. A daughter, a regular princess. And a neighboring prince, but of a lower class, so that even here one is reminded of the tutor, this neighboring prince stole the princess, and took her off to his homeland and his harem, despite all her resistance."

"My, my."

"At least so the story goes. But the king of Siam was not the man to accept the likes of that very calmly. Instead, he undertook a holy war against this neighboring prince, defeated him and brought the princess back again in triumph. And all the people were carried away with their victory and happiness. But the princess herself was melancholy."

"So I can imagine. Wanted to get away again."

"No indeed, gentlemen. She *did not* want to go back. After all, she was a very fine lady who had suffered . . . ."

"Righto. But how . . . ."

". . . Who had suffered and who from that time on lived only with the single thought of 'exculpation,' with the idea of how this unholy thing, this having been violated, could again be taken from her."

"Can't be done. Taken is taken."

"By no means, Herr von Molchow. The high priests were called in and held, as we might say here, a synod, in which they dealt with the question of exculpation or, what more or less amounts to the same thing, with the question of the restoration of virginity. They came to the conclusion, or perhaps they discovered it in ancient books, that she had to be bathed in blood."

"Brr."

"And to this end she was soon taken into the hall of one of their temples in which stood two huge tubs, one of red porphyry and one of white marble. And between these tubs, on a kind of stairway, stood the princess herself. And then three white buffalo were brought into the temple hall, and with one stroke the high priest severed the head of each from its body and let the blood flow into the porphyry tub standing nearby. And so the bath was prepared and the princess, after Siamese virgins had disrobed her, climbed into the bath of buffalo blood. And the high priest took a holy vessel and dipped it into it and poured it out over the princess."

"A strong story. At table I'd probably have left several courses go by. I find it definitely too much."

"I don't," said old Zühlen, who had in the meantime joined them and had been listening with them for several minutes. "What does that mean, too much or too strong? Strong it is, that much I'll admit, but not *too* strong. That it is strong, why of course, that's exactly the point of the whole business. If this princess had just had a liver spot, of course I'd find it too strong right off the bat. There always has to be the right relationship between the means and the end. A liver spot is nothing at all. But just think about it, a regular princess as a slave in a harem. You've got to deal with that in a totally different way. We're as much as talking here about 'extraordinary means.' Yes indeed, gentlemen, in this particular case only extraordinary means could do the trick."

"*Igni et ferro*," said the rector by way of confirmation.

"And," continued old Zühlen, "this much ought to be clear to anybody, to drive out the devil — which is how I see this neighboring prince and his deed — to do something like that, something special had to take place, something Beelzebubean. And that was exactly the blood of these three buffaloes. *I* don't find it too much at all."

Thormeyer raised his glass to touch it with old Zühlen's. "It's exactly as Herr von Zühlen says. And fortunately as the last step something took place which could satisfy those of our desires which are more inclined towards beauty — because, after all, we do live in a world of beauty. Directly from the porphyry tub the princess stepped into the marble tub, in which all the perfumes of Arabia had found a home. And all the priests approached her once more with their ladles, and they poured them over the princess in cascades. And everyone could actually see how the melancholy fell away from her and how everything that that thieving neighbor prince had taken from her bloomed again. And finally the servant girls wrapped their mistress in snow-white garments and led her to a resting place and fanned her with peacock feathers until she turned her head and gently fell into a sleep. And not a thing remained. And later she became the bride of the King of Annam. He's supposed to have been a man of great enlightenment by the way, because France had been dominating his country for some time by then."

"Let's hope Lilly's cousin sees some reason too."

"He will. He will."

They all raised their glasses to that and then broke up. Their carriages had long since pulled up and stood in a long row between the *Prince Regent* and the Triangle. The Stechlin carriage too was waiting and Martin, to pass the time, had been snapping the whip. Dubslav looked about for his pastor and was beginning to get impatient as Lorenzen finally approached to excuse himself for having made him wait. But it had been the Chief Forester's fault. The latter had involved him in a conversation that was still not concluded, for which reason he planned making the return trip in the company of Katzler.

Dubslav laughed. "Well then, God be with you. But don't let him tell you too many stories. Ermyntrud will probably play the chief part or what's even more likely, the new name that's supposed to be found. I'll bet I'm right too . . . . Well then, let's be off, Martin."

And thus off they went over the bumpy cobblestones.

In the city everything had by then become quiet, but out in the countryside they passed by large or small groups of cottagers, tar burners and glass factory folk, who had made a day of it for themselves and now were wending their way home, howling and singing as they went. Women too were among them, adding a certain flavor to it all.

Thus Dubslav trotted on towards Lake Nehmitz, which was considered the half-way point. Not far from it a charcoal kiln, Dietrichsofen, was to be found, and as Martin was making his way around the southerly protruding lake point, he saw someone lying on the road, his torso hidden by grass and reeds, but his feet directly across the roadway.

Martin pulled up. "Master, there be somebody lying there. I think it's old Tuxen."

"Tuxen, the old souse from Dietrichsofen?"

167

"Aye, Master. I'll take a look an' see what's wrong with'm."

He gave Dubslav the reins and climbed down and shoved and shook the old fellow lying on the road. "Aye then, Tuxen, what be ya doin' here? If there waren't no moon, man, you'd be a ded'n."

"Oiye, oiye," said the old timer. But one could see that his head was not clear.

And now Dubslav climbed down as well to help Martin lay the totally helpless old timer on the back seat. In the process the drunkard regained his senses to a certain extent and said, "Noi, noi, Martin, not thar. A'druther yer put mey op on the front sate."

And in fact they pulled him up and there he sat then, not saying a word. He was ashamed of himself in front of the master.

Finally, however, the latter spoke up and said, "Well say now, Tuxen, can't you leave off wi' the brandy then? Laying down in a place like that. 'Tis nightfrost already. 'Nother hour, an you'd be a ded'n. Were they all like that?"

"Mosht o'em."

"And so you all voted for Katzenstein."

"Noi, Master, not fer Katzenstein."

And now he became silent again as he reeled back and forth uncertainly on the coachman's box.

"Well let's hear it then. You know perfectly well, I'll not take anybody's noggin off. It's all the same anyway. Well then, not fer Katzenstein. Well, fer who then?"

"Fer that Torgelow feller."

Dubslav laughed. "For Torgelow, the one the Berliners sent you. Has he ever done anything for you yet?"

"Noi, not yet."

"Well, why then?"

"Oiye, they be tellin' us, e *wants* ta do somethin' fer us, an e's really fer us poor folk. An' we'll all get a piece o' p'tater land. An' they be sayin' too, e's smarter than th'others."

"Might well be. But he's a long way from bein' as smart as you're all dumb. Have any of you ever gone hungry?"

"Noi, not zactly."

"Well, that can still come too, y'know."

"Ach, Master, that prob'ly won't be aither."

"Well, who knows, Tuxen. But here's Dietrichsofen. Now climb down there and be careful you don't fall when the horses start up. And here's something for you. But no more for today. You've had enough for today. An' now see that you get t'bed and dream about that p'tater land."

On Mission to England

21

ON THE NEXT morning Woldemar learned from last minute newspaper reports that the Social Democratic candidate, the filemaker Torgelow, had been the victor in the Rheinsberg-Wutz electoral district. Soon thereafter arrived a letter from Lorenzen, who initially confirmed the reports and at the conclusion added that Dubslav was actually heartily pleased about the outcome. Woldemar was as well. He believed that at Dressel's or Borchardt's his father quite probably had the stuff in him to hold forth with a good deal of common sense on every sort of political topic and what was more, with the roguish wit worthy of an Eulenspiegel. But to speak objectively and knowledgeably in the Reichstag on such matters was something he neither could nor wished to do. Woldemar was so convinced of this that he was able to come to terms with the idea of a defeat relatively quickly, even though as the old man's son he nevertheless also felt a certain involvement. At the same time, however, he was thankful that just at this moment he had been entrusted with a command to East Prussia which would keep him away from Berlin for a few weeks. By the time he would return, inquiries about the whole election business would no longer need be of concern, least of all in his regiment, in which, apart from a few intimate friends, everyone had actually kept a stony silence about the whole unpleasant incident.

Everyone at the Kronprinzenufer also cloaked themselves in silence when Woldemar stopped by to take leave of the count's family on the eve of his departure. The latest victory of the Social Democrats was only superficially touched upon, an intentionally fleeting allusion which did not stand out because the conversation quite soon began to turn to Rex and Czako. The latter, although having been invited to do so for some time, had made their first visit to the Barby house only the day before, finding considerable kindness, especially from the old count. Melusine too was completely satisfied by their visit, notwithstanding the fact that the weaknesses of both, in opposite directions to be sure, had not escaped her.

"What the one has too little of," she said, "the other has too much."

169

"And how did that manifest itself, Your Ladyship?"

"Oh, you can't miss it. By chance it turned out that in the same instant the gentlemen sat down, the bells were rung in Grace Church. Of course — one is always grateful during first visits like that to be able to pick up on something — that steered our conversation immediately to ecclesiastical matters. The two of them gave themselves away right off. Probably because he had a suspicion of what his friend was going to say next, Captain von Czako displayed visible signs of impatience from the outset while Herr von Rex, in fact, not only began talking about the 'seriousness of the times,' but also how as a result of the construction of new churches he anticipated a general change of things to be just before the door. Which, of course, amused me."

Woldemar's orders to East Prussia would keep him there until the beginning of November. More than once in the course of this period Rex and Czako put in an appearance at the Barbys. Separately, to be sure. Arrangements for a visit together had indeed been initiated on several occasions but every time without success. Not until two days before Woldemar's return did it happen that the two friends met at the Barbys. It was an especially successful evening, for along with Baroness Berchtesgaden and Doctor Wrschowitz, an old professor of painting, a new acquaintance of the house, was also in attendance. All of this made for a lively conversation. Especially the old professor, who along with his other idiosyncrasies, stood out because of his long white hair and great glowing eyes, had been able to enrapture everyone on the basis of an unremitting enthusiasm for Peter Cornelius.

"I'm fortunate to have still seen the days of that magnificent and unique artist. You are all, of course, familiar with his sketches, which seem to me to be the most significant things of that sort we possess in general. In the foreground of one of these sketches stands a tuba player setting his instrument to his mouth to sound the Last Judgment. This single figure is worth five art exhibits, in other words, a net of 15,000 pictures. And these very sketches, including this Last Judgment trumpeter, it's these they want to get rid of, and with naive impudence say such black stuff with nothing but charcoal strokes shouldn't take up so much space in general. But I tell you, my friends, one charcoal stroke of Cornelius is worth more than all their modern palettes altogether. And the tuba that this tuba player is setting to his mouth — you'll forgive an old fellow like me such an awful pun, this tuba outweighs all the tubes they squeeze their paint from these days. Another miserable innovation, by the way. In my day we still had paint bags, and those pig's bladder paint bags were much better. A lucky thing that King Friedrich Wilhelm IV didn't live to see the epoch of decline that's taken hold right now, this epoch of decadence, a truly genuine era of apocalyptic horsemen. Except that along with the three our great master created for us, there comes a fourth horseman nowadays, a half-caste of envy and tastelessness. And when it comes to laying waste to things, this fourth one is worst of all."

Everyone nodded, even those who did not quite agree, for the old man with the head of an apostle had spoken just like a prophet. Melusine alone remained in silent opposition, whispering to the baroness, "Tuba player. As far as I go, Böcklin's mermaid with a fish body is more my style. Of course, I'm biased."

The evenings at the Barbys always concluded at an early hour. So it was again today. It was just striking ten as Rex and Czako walked out to the street. Thousands of lights could be seen along the river bank extending distantly before them, the foremost shimmering in the water.

"I think I'd like to take a walk just now," said Czako. "What do you think, Rex? Are you with me? We'll stroll along the bank here, past the Zelten[1] as far as Bellevue and there we'll get on the Stadtbahn and ride back, you to Friedrichstraße and me as far as Alexanderplatz. Then both of us are only three minutes from home."

Rex agreed. "Really a lucky thing," he said, "that we finally got together for a change. Been acquainted with that house for three weeks now and haven't had a discussion about it yet. And that's always the main thing, you know. For you especially."

"Yes indeed, Rex, that 'for you especially;' you say it so mockingly and with such a superior tone because you think gossip is something inferior, and just the very thing for a fellow like me. But in my opinion there's where you make a double error. Because in the first place gossip is by no means inferior, and in the second, you like to gossip just as much as I do, and maybe even a bit more. You just always manage to stay a bit more stiff and formal in the process and you reject my little frivolities at first, but in point of fact, you wait for them. Anyway, I think we'll put all that to rest and talk about the main thing instead.

"Seems to me we can't be grateful enough to our friend Stechlin for having acquainted us with such a delightful house. That Wrschowitz fellow and the old art professor, the one who couldn't leave off about the Judgment angel — well, you can have the two of them. I imagine the painter is probably pretty much to your taste

171

anyway. But the others you run into there, how charming they all are. So natural. Top of the list, this Frommel fellow, the Court Chaplain. I like him almost more at the tea table than in the pulpit. And then that Bavarian baroness. It really is remarkable that the south Germans are always a full step ahead of us when it comes to social graces. It's not the cultural background, but on account of their cheerful natures. And a cheerful nature like that, that's really true culture, you know."

"Good grief, Czako, you're overestimating that. It's true, of course, when they fish out the sausage from some huge kettle, and along comes some Loni or Toni balancing one of those beer steins of theirs, that it really does look like something, and we get the idea we come off like nothing but half-starved schoolmasters next to all of it. But when you get right down to it, what we have is still on a higher plane, you know."

"Heaven save us! Everything connected to grammar and examinations is never a higher plane. Did they give examinations to the patriarchs, or to Moses, or Christ? It was the Pharisees who got the examinations. And there you see what comes of that sort of thing. But to stay closer to home, just take the old count. He was an ambassadorial councilor, of course, and that does have a certain ring to it, but actually he's really just a natural type who's never been put through any examinations either, and that's the very thing that gives him his charm. By the way, don't you think too he looks a lot like old Stechlin?"

"Yes, outwardly."

"Inwardly too. Naturally, a diff'rent number, but spun from the same yarn. Sorry about that rather worn-out Berlin cliché. And if maybe you were thinking about politics, there too there's hardly a difference. The old count is a long way from being as liberal, but old Dubslav's a long way from being as much a Junker as it looks. This Barby, whose family, I believe, used to belong to the preferred nobility in the days of the First Reich, he's still got a touch of that 'by the grace of God-attitude' left in his bones. And that results in that sort of aristocratic bearing we're all familiar with, the sort that imagines it can allow itself to indulge in a little liberalism. And old Dubslav, well, for his part, beneath that skin of his he's got just what all the genuine Junkers have, a touch of the Social Democrat. When they get riled up they even admit it themselves."

"You're misjudging that, Czako. All of that's nothing but playing around."

"Yes, but what's that supposed to mean, playing around? Playing around. We've got fine old verses in our primers that warn about the dangers of playing around with fire. But let's forget about Dubslav

172

and old Barby. After all, in the end it's always the ladies who are more important, the countess and the comtesse. Which one will it be? I think we've talked about this once before. That time we were coming from Wutz Convent and riding over the Cremmen Pike. I can't say I've really got much confidence in friend Woldemar's true understanding of women, but nevertheless I say Melusine."

"And I say Armgard. And you say it too when you're alone."

It was two days before Woldemar's return from East Prussia that Rex and Czako had this conversation in the Tiergarten. A half hour later they rode, as agreed, from Bellevue station back into the city. Everywhere there was still a hustle and bustle, and bustle there was too in the Dragoon Guard's officer's club, which consisted of but three rooms of various sizes. In the large dining room closest to the entry hall, from whose walls previous commandants of the regiment, princes and non-princes alike, stared down, few guests could be seen. Adjoining it, however, was a corner room having more occupants and leisurely activity. Here since but recently, above the diagonally-placed fireplace in which a small fire flickered, hung the portrait of the "Commander in Chief" of the regiment, the Queen of England. Close to this very picture also hung a glorious memento from the wars of '66 and '70: the bugle on which the same man, Staff Bugler Wollhaupt, had signaled the regiment to charge, first on the Heights of Lipa on the 3rd of July, and then at Mars-la-Tour on the 16th of August, until he fell at the side of his colonel, and his colonel with him.

This small corner room was, as always, today again the preferred spot in which younger and older officers had assembled to gamble and to chat. Among them were Herr von Wolfshagen, von Herbstfelde, von Wohlgemuth, von Grumbach, and von Raspe.

"Heaven knows," said Raspe, "we'll never be finished with all of these deputations. I admit we've got three fellows named Sender in the regiment ourselves, but all this sending of emissarial deputations is almost too much. And now this time our Stechlin's among them to boot. What's he going to say up there in East Prussia when he hears about the honor they've got in store for him? He'll probably be having rather mixed feelings about it. Day after tomorrow he gets back from Trakehnen, presumably pretty much out of sorts from all that bad weather, and then head over heels with a terrific rat-ta-ta-ta off to London. And London, that alone would be enough. But to Windsor as well. When it comes to style, everything really does need its own good time, you know, and particularly those cousins of ours over there really do keep a close eye on you when it comes to that sort of thing."

"Let them look," said Herbstfelde. "We'll do our own looking. And Stechlin isn't the fellow to get gray hair over things like that. I'd imagine it's something else entirely that's bothering him. One way or the other, it's quite the thing his having to go along over there to England. And being singled out like that naturally corresponds to someone else's not being picked. That's not the thing for everybody, and the way I see Stechlin, he's one of the latter. Doesn't care to do his fighting with 'over their dead bodies' as his battle cry. He's got the tendency of putting himself in the second line instead. And now it looks as if he were one of those pushy types."

"Not true," said Raspe. "I can't consider any of us getting that carried away. Stechlin's sitting up there in East Prussia, and it's impossible that in his leisure time he could have been cooking something up back here to pitch some rival or other out of the saddle. And then the colonel! He's certainly not the man to let himself be talked into just anybody either, you know. Knows his troopers, he does. And when he picks out Stechlin for himself, he knows why. Anyway, orders are orders. One doesn't go because one wants to but because one must. Does he speak English, by the way?"

"Don't think so," said von Grumbach. "as far as I know he started with it just recently. But not on account of this mission, of course — which as we all know has just fallen on him right out of the blue — but because of the Barbys, who were in England for practically twenty years and are half English themselves. Anyway, I've been told you can make it over there without the language. Herbstfelde, that's right, you were over there last year. With good German and bad French you can get by anywhere."

"True," said Herbstfelde. "It's just that a bit of the local language really does have to be included. But then, of course, there are those little all purpose dictionaries. And then you've just got to look it up. Otherwise a hundred words are plenty. When I was still at home we had a crazy old fellow in our neighborhood, who had more or less kicked around quite a bit in the world before the gout got to him. Always a hundred new words per country. Among other spots he was in southern Russia one time, from which point on — as a matter of fact, after striking up a friendship with a teriffically old orthodox priest in front of a gigantic liqueur cabinet — he always added the amendment, 'A hundred words, but when it comes to an old priest only fifty.' And one thing I do have to say, I found that business with a hundred words pretty much confirmed in England. 'Mary, please, a jug of hot water,' that much you've got to have ready, otherwise you'll just sit there empty-handed. Because your native Englishman doesn't know anything at all."

"How long were you actually over there, Herbstfelde?"

"Three weeks. But that includes travel days."

"And did you pretty much get something out of it? Insight into everyday life, Parliament, Oxford, Cambridge, Gladstone?"

Herbstfelde nodded.

"And when you sort of add it all up, what was it that made the greatest impression on you? Architecture, art, life, the ships, those tremendous bridges of theirs? I hear the street urchins always run next to you doing cartwheels when you pass by them in a cab, and what's even more important, the serving girls are supposed to be rather cute — little white caps and aprons."

"Yes indeed, Raspe. You've hit it there. And that's actually what's most interesting. After all, we've got so-called masterworks just about everywhere these days, not even mentioning churches and things of that sort. And, of course, we've got ships now too and a Parliament as well. And some even say ours is better. But the common people. There's where you really find it, you see. The common people are everything."

"Exactly, the common people. Upper class, one and the same everywhere. We know what the story is there."

"I actually sat on'n omnibus for the entire three weeks, y'know, and evenings I went to the sailors' dens on the Thames. A bit dangerous. You'll get a knife in the ribs before you know it, same as in Italy. Except that in Italy there's always some sort of love affair beforehand, which isn't even needed in Old-Wapping — that's what they call that part of the city on the Thames, by the way. And then when I got home, naturally I had a little conversation with Mary. Not much, it's true. The fact is, at the time I didn't quite completely have the entire hundred words you need for that."

"Well, did it work out anyway?"

"More or less passably. And in the process I had one thing happen that really was the neatest thing of all. My living quarters were actually one flight up in a small, quiet cross-street off Oxford Street. And Mary was with me just at that very time. Well then, just at the moment I'm trying to get through to the pretty young thing . . ."

"About what?"

"In the very same moment a Chinaman looks into my window, grinning so that he actually deserved a box on the ears."

"How in heaven's name was that ever possible?"

"Well, that's the very thing I call London street life. All sorts of things we haven't got the slightest idea about take place there right in the middle of the street. It turned out that on that day two Chinese fellows, acrobats by trade, had come into this cross street off Oxford Street. And one of them, a big strong fellow, had a belt around his waist and stuck a pole in a loop of this belt on which the second Chinaman climbed up. And when he got to the top, he was right at the level of my second floor room and looked in just as I was doing my best to make myself clear to Mary."

"Well, I say, Herbstfelde, that certainly was a bit of bad luck, for sure. And when you get over there again you'll have to live in the back or else a bit higher up. But it is interesting, I've got to admit that. Although I do doubt that Stechlin will get himself into the same situation."

"Certainly not. His morals will prevent that."

"And the Barbys even more."

22

Woldemar, informed of the distinction awaiting him, cut short his stay in East Prussia by twenty-four hours. Nevertheless, after his return to Berlin he still had only two days at his disposal. That was very little. For besides all sorts of travel preparations, it was also still incumbent upon him to undertake various visits such as to the Barbys, to whom he had already sent a note announcing himself for his last evening.

That evening had now come. His bags stood packed around him. He himself leaned back rather wearily in his rocking chair, once more taking stock that nothing might be forgotten. At last he said to himself, "Whatever's still missing, is missing. I can't do any more." As he spoke, he looked at the clock. Until his announced visit at the Kronprinzenufer there was still almost an hour. He wanted to put it to use and if possible take a slight rest beforehand. But he did not get to do so. His orderly entered and announced, "Captain von Czako."

"Ah, glad to see him."

And Woldemar, as inconvenient as Czako's visit actually was, nevertheless leaped up and extended his hand to his friend. "You've come to congratulate me on my English journey. And even though it's only a so-so affair, you, I believe, mean it honestly. You're among the few people who aren't acquainted with envy."

"Now, now. let's drop that topic. I'm not so terribly sure as all that. There's many a fellow looks better than he is. But, of course, I have come for better or for worse to bring you my best wishes and to throw in my travel blessing as well.

"Great guns, Stechlin! Where is all this leading to with you? Of course you'll become London Military Attaché, in six months let's say,

176

and in the very same amount of time you'll get to be at home in the sporting circles over there and make your name as the winner in a steeple chase, presuming they still have something like that. In fact, I do believe they're calling it something else these days. And then two weeks after your first great victories, you'll be getting engaged to Ruth Russel or Geraldine Cavendish, with the Duke of Bedford or Devonshire as your rear guard, and you'll be off as Governor General to Central Africa, pygmies on your left and cannibals on your right. After all, they say Emin actually got eaten up, you know."[2]

"Czako, you're taking advantage of the fact that noon is well past by now, otherwise you'd scarcely be able to take responsibility for all this. But pull up an arm chair. Here are some cigarettes. Or would you rather a cigar?"

"No, cigarettes . . . . Well, you see, Stechlin. A mission like this, or even if only a fraction thereof . . ."

"Let's say an appendage."

". . . Such a mission is the very thing I've been wishing for my whole life long. It's just that 'my plea hath ne'er been heard.' And yet precisely in our regiment there's always something going on. Somebody or other's always on the way to Petersburg. But devil take it, regardless of all this hither and thither, yours truly hasn't gotten the nod to this day. I think it's got something to do with my name. Around here 'Czako' has of course an after taste, a touch of the comical, but the Slavic note in it gives it something unusual in Berlin, while in Petersburg they'd probably say, 'Czako, what's that supposed to mean? What's Czako supposed to be? We've got the likes of that here finer and dandier.' Yes sir, I'll go even further and say I'm not even sure if they might not take it into their heads to suspect a joke or a hidden affront in the choice of 'Czako' over there. But whatever the case may be, the Winter Palace and the Kremlin are closed to me. And now you're off to London and even to Windsor. And Windsor is after all the finest thing you can think of. Russia, if you'll allow me such breakfast time comparisons, always has that certain touch of Astrakhan, England always smacks of Colchester. And I do believe Colchester stands higher. In my eyes for sure.[3] Ah, Stechlin, you're a lucky toad, a phrase you've got to make allowances for on account of my excitement. I'm sure to get hung up on the Major's rung of the ladder because of various shortcomings. But y'see, the fact that I realize it, that could still reconcile me to my fate, you know."

"Czako, you're the best fellow in the world. It's really a shame we don't have people like you in our regiment. Or at least, not enough. 'Fine' is of course perfectly good. But now and then there's got to be some kind of a bomb blast, a cynicism, a malicious word, it doesn't have to have a poisoned fang in it right off. By the way, as far as the blue-blooded qualifications go, I feel clearly that I too only just barely make the grade. Just take the language question for example. Anybody these days who doesn't speak three languages belongs in a corner . . . ."

"That's what I tell myself too. And that's why I've started with Russian. And when I'm really going at it and get almost amazed at my progress, I pull myself together for a moment or so and tell myself, 'Courage won, everything won.' And then for my further edification I have all our Prussian heroes, on foot and in the saddle, pass by in my mind's eye, always with the feeling of a certain scientific superiority and now and then even moral superiority besides. First comes Derfflinger. Well, he's supposed to have been a tailor. Then came Blücher — he was simply just a gambler. And then came Wrangel and played his crazy game with the rules of the German language. Couldn't tell the difference between me and I."[4]

"Bravo, Czako. That's the way you've got to talk. And you won't get stuck on the Major's rung either. Actually, it all boils down to how one looks at one's self. That's an art, I admit, that not everybody understands. Those lines of Old Fritz, 'Just always imagine you've got a hundred thousand men behind you,' some of us have lost that encouraging phrase a bit, our victories notwithstanding. Or maybe just because of them. Under certain conditions victories can produce modesty too."

"In any case, my dear Stechlin, you've got too much of it. But once you've got that Ruth of yours . . . ."

"Good grief, Czako, don't keep bring up Ruth. Or rather, I'm grateful to you for doing it nevertheless. Because that feminine name reminds me I've announced myself for this evening at the Kronprinzenufer, at the Barbys where, as you know, they certainly don't have any Ruths, but in their place there's a Melusine, and that's almost more."

"Why, of course, Melusine's more. Everything that comes out of the water is more. Venus came out of the water, and so did Hero . . . . No, no, excuse me, it was Leander."

"Doesn't matter. Just leave it as it is. A mixed up Schiller line like that always does a body some good. In any case you can accompany me in my coupe. From the Kronprinzenufer you'll have just about half the distance back to your barracks."

The coupe did its part and it was just striking eight as Woldemar pulled up before the Barby house and, taking leave of Czako, ascended the steps. He found only the family present, which was much to his liking, because he did not wish to indulge in a general conversation, but merely to acquire advice for his journey. The old count knew London better than Berlin and Melusine too had been past seventeen, when soon after their mother's death, they had left England and withdrawn to their estates in Graubünden. Nearly a decade and a half had now passed since that time, yet father and daughters were still as attached as ever to Hyde Park and the beautiful house they had lived in there, and gratefully remembered the days they had spent in London. Even Armgard enjoyed talking about the little she still recollected from her early childhood.

"How lucky I am to find you alone," said Woldemar. "That sounds quite selfish, I admit, but perhaps I may be excused. If you had guests, Wrschowitz, for example, and I were to let myself be carried away to speak of the Princess of Wales, and as a natural result, of her two sisters Dagmar and Thyra,[5] then perhaps out of sheer Danophilism I might even have to fight a duel this evening. Which would have been somewhat inconvenient for me. Better to be on the safe side."

Old Barby nodded with amusement.

"Yes, Your Lordship," Woldemar continued, "I've come to say good-bye to you and the ladies, but above all as well, I've come to inform myself as best as I can at the very last minute. Just at the moment when the hopelessly ignorant candidate goes off in his dress coat, he takes a peek for one last time in the *corpus juris* — things like that do happen, they say — and reads, let's say, ten lines. And it's exactly these lines that he then gets asked about and so he sees himself saved. Something like that could be in store for me too. You were over there for a long time and the ladies as well. What should I be on the lookout for? What should I avoid? What should I do? Above all, what have I got to see? And what must I not? It may be the latter is the most important of all."

"Certainly, my dear Stechlin. But before we get started, take up your position here and allow yourself a cup of tea. Of course, that you'll be able to appreciate the tea is practically impossible, you're much too excited for anything like that. Why, you're just like a waterfall. I scarcely recognize you."

Woldemar attempted to apologize.

"No apologies. Least of all about that. Everything is so earnest-minded these days that I'm always glad to run across a bit of excitement now and then. Excitement is more becoming than indifference, and in any case more interesting. What's your opinion on that, Melusine?"

"Papa's teasing me. But I'll be careful not to answer that one."

"Well then, back to the matter at hand. Yes indeed, my dear Stechlin. What to do? What to see? Or, as you quite correctly note, what not to see? A difficult thing, no matter where you look. In Italy one wastes one's time with pictures, in England it's executioners' blocks. They've got entire collections of them over there. Well then, as little historical stuff as possible. And then, of course, no churches — Westminster excepted, as always. I believe that what they trivially call 'people and places' is and always will be the best. Up the Thames and down again. Richmond Hill — still, even though it's already November — and the hucksters' booths and the bagpipers. And if, as you're traversing some quiet square, you run into one of those so-called 'Sidewalk Raphaels', by all means do stop and take a look at what that peculiar genius might be painting on the broad sidewalk there with his left hand, which is often crippled. Those Sidewalk Raphaels always have only a left hand, you know."

"And what is it he'll be painting?"

"What is it they paint? It varies. The fellow's capable of conjuring up a regular Sistine Madonna for you on the sidewalk in ten minutes. But as a rule he's more a Ruysdael or Hobbema. Landscapes are his forte, seascapes too. I've probably seen the cliffs of Dover twenty times over with moonlight rippling on the water.

"There, now you've got a whole list of choices. But now put the question to Melusine. She's seen much more of London and its surroundings than I, I think, and knows her way around Hampton Court and Waltham Abbey better than the Upper Spree — the Egg Cottage excepted, of course. And if Melusine were to fail, well then, we still have our Cordelia here. True enough, Cordelia was only six or else not much more at the time. But 'out of the mouths of babes,' as they say. Armgard, how would it be if you were to see to our friend here."

"I don't know, Papa, if Herr von Stechlin will agree to it or can even do so. Perhaps it would be all right if only you hadn't spoken about my just being six. But as it is now. At six one hasn't experienced anything that would be worth telling in the eyes of others."

"Comtesse, if you'll permit me . . . things in themselves are unimportant. Every experience becomes something only through the eyes of the individual who experiences it."

"Dear me," said Melusine, "I've never been asked to tell anything like that my whole life long. Now you'll have to speak, Armgard."

"And I will too, even at the risk of not measuring up."

"No prefaces, Armgard. Least of all when they sound like self praise."

"Well, back then we had an old woman in our house who had been our nurse, even for Melusine. Her name was Susan. I really did love her, because like most Irish, she had something uncommonly cheerful and endearing about her. I often went on walks with her in Hyde Park. After all, we lived right on the big street which runs along its northern side. Hyde Park always seemed really beautiful to me. But because day in, day out it was always the same, I wanted to see something different for a change and Susan agreed right off, even though it was actually forbidden to her. 'Why certainly, Comtesse,' she said, 'we'll go to Martins le Grand.'

"'What's that?' I asked, but instead of any sort of answer, she just gave me my little cloak to put on, since it was already late autumn, more or less like now, and getting dark by then too. From what happened afterwards, I have to assume it was around five o'clock. And so off we went down our street. Since there were all kinds of large pipes lying along the park fence for putting in new sewers, I jumped up on them and Susan held me by my left index finger.

"And so we went along, with me walking up there on the pipes, until we got to a place where the park came to an end. There was a hackney stand there and oats and chaff lying about and a lot of sparrows all around. And there in the middle of it all stood an iron fountain. Susan pointed it out to me and said, 'Look at it, Armgard dear. There stood Tyburn-Gallows. And whoever stole as much as a noose was worth, was hanged there.'"

"A strange children's nurse," said Stechlin. "Weren't you frightened, Comtesse?"

"No. There was never any question of being frightened when Susan was with me. She would have protected me against the whole world."

"That makes up for it."

"And to make a long story short, we kept on our way and pretty soon climbed into a two-wheeled cab, from which we could easily look out. And down Oxford Street we flew into the City, in a tangle of traffic that kept getting thicker and thicker. I'd never been in anything like it before and haven't been since either. Except two years ago when we were over there on a visit and I looked up the old places again."

"I think," said Melusine, "you're borrowing quite a bit from that second visit, since by now you probably don't have much of what you saw with Susan at your disposal anymore."

"Oh, but I do, I do. And then our Hansom cab stopped in front of a big building that looked half like a palace and half like a Greek temple, and through the entrance columns we entered a huge hall filled with hundreds and hundreds of people. And above their heads lay what seemed to be a stream of light, and towards the back, where the light seemed brightest, two officials wearing red jackets were standing on a platform with several large containers at their right and left, which looked like feed boxes with wide opened lids."

"And now let Stechlin guess what it was."

"He doesn't have to guess," continued Armgard, "naturally, he knows already. But he's got to hold out all the same. Because he wanted it this way himself. Well then, a platform and red-coats along with open boxes right and left. And the brightly-lit clock above them showed it was only one minute till six. You couldn't even think of pushing your way up to the front and so the letter packets and news-papers that were supposed to leave with the next mail trains flew in a wide arc over the heads of those standing in front. And anything that just landed on the platform instead of in the containers was more or less raked up by the red-coats with a deft sweep of the foot right into the feed boxes. And then the clock started to strike and the flying packets increased until exactly on the sixth stroke the cover of both boxes came down."

"Charming, Comtesse. Naturally I'll have a look at that, even if I might have to miss an appointment with the queen."

"No anti-monarchical remarks," laughed the old count. "And so Susan's misdeeds are finally coming to light."

"And my own as well. Fortunately through myself."

The conversation continued for a while and a variety of descriptions of commonplace and everyday life held sway. A few times, well-noting that Woldemar would have preferred to hear about something else, the old count attempted to change the topic. But both ladies stuck to 'shopping' and 'five o'clock tea,' until Melusine, who had also not failed to notice Woldemar's impatience, suddenly asked, "Have you ever heard of Traitors Gate?"

"No," said Woldemar, "but I can translate it for myself and draw my own conclusions from that."

"That suffices. Well then, of course, the Tower. Well now, you see, Traitors Gate, that was my domain whenever visitors came from Germany and for better or for worse I had to be their guide. There were lots of things in the Tower that bored me, but Traitors Gate never. Perhaps it was because it more or less stands at the beginning, so that by the time we reached it I was still fresh and hadn't been worn down by all the horrors which followed."

"Well then, Traitors Gate's a thing to see?"

"Absolutely. Of course, when I take into consideration that nothing particularly dramatic's to be seen at this famous spot, when it comes to my suggestions I've got to be able to rely on your imagination. And

I'm not so sure that will work. Anybody who comes from the Mark usually doesn't have much imagination."

The old count and Armgard remained silent and Melusine also saw quite well that she had gone somewhat too far with her remark. Some sort of redress seemed necessary. "I'll take a chance with you nevertheless," she continued with a laugh, "Traitors Gate. Well then, you see, you walk along this narrow passage way from the entrance and all of a sudden, instead of the gray stone wall, you've got a wooden gate with heavy iron fittings next to you. Behind this gate though, way down below there, lies a little boat landing, from which a stairway with a number of steps leads up right to the spot on which you're standing. And now just go back three-hundred years. Anybody for whom that gate opened back then, to close again behind him, was somebody who'd taken leave of life . . . . If you'll forgive the word — they're nothing but slimy steps, but *who* all it was that climbed up those steps: Essex, Sir Walter Raleigh, Thomas Moore and last of all as well, those clan chieftains who'd fought for Bonney Prince Charlie, and whose heads looked down on the City from the Temple Bar just a few days later."

"That was a long time ago, thank God."

"Yes, a long time ago. But it can happen again. And it was just *that*, that always made such an impression on me when I stood there. This possibility that it might come again. Because I still recollect very well — yes, it was you yourself who told me about it, Papa — that Lord Palmerston, put out one time about Coburgean political meddling — I think it was during the days of the Crimean War — is supposed to have said, 'This Prince Consort would do well to take a look at our Traitors Gate now and then. To be sure, it's been a long time since any kings have climbed up those slimy steps, but at the same time it's not that far back that we can't remember it. And a Prince Consort is a long, long way from being a king.'"[6]

Woldemar, as Melusine said this with a somewhat supercilious look, smiled to himself, which so piqued the countess that with a certain irritability she added, "You're smiling. Well then, I see just how right I was to deny you had any imagination."

"Do forgive me . . ."

"And now you're getting emotional. That really is the final touch. In any case, how could I be seriously angry with you! A famous German professor is supposed to have said somewhere, 'no one is obliged to be a great man.' And just as little will he have demanded a 'great imagination' as something that's obligatory either."

Woldemar kissed her hand. "Do you know, Countess, that you really are rather haughty?"

"Perhaps. But there are some people who know how to disarm me. And you are among them."

"That's in the very same tone as well."

"I don't know. But let's drop it. Rather than that, promise me you'll write me a card from Windsor or London. No, not a card, that won't do. Well then, a letter, in which you'll inform me about the English women, and whether you've found each one of those waistless reddish blondes as beautiful as people from the continent are practically always assuring you, whenever they bring up the topic."

"That will all depend on whom I'm thinking of at the moment."

"After that remark all is forgiven."

Woldemar stayed until nine. Already in the note with which he had announced his coming, he had let the ladies know that he would have to limit his visit to a brief hour. Thus he was home again in good time. On his table he discovered a note and recognized Rex's handwriting. "Dear Stechlin," wrote the latter, "I've just heard you are going to London. I overlooked it in the papers where they tell me it was announced. I congratulate you heartily for this distinction and include a card which, if it suits you, will introduce you to my friend Ralph Waddington. He is a lawyer and one of the most highly regarded leaders of the Irvingites. You needn't fear any attempts at conversion, by the way. Waddington is a refined gentleman through and through, therefore, reserved. He can be helpful to you in innumerable ways if you should be interested in informing yourself about the nature of the English dissenters, their chapels and meeting houses. He is a specialist in that field. And of course, I well know your predilection for such questions."

Stechlin put the letter under a paper weight and said, "Good old Rex. He overestimates me. Dissenter studies. I'll be satisfied if I get to see a single Quaker."

23

What Rex had written nevertheless had its good side. Woldemar, amused by the thought of seeing himself introduced to a prayer meeting by Ralph Waddington, suddenly found himself released from a certain weariness. He was glad of it, for he needed the right mood to write several more letters. It all went more easily now and by the time eleven had scarcely rolled around, everything had been completed.

Naturally, the next morning found him up early. Fritz flitted about him and helped wherever it was still needed.

"Well then, Fritz," were Woldemar's last instructions, "See to it that everything's taken care of. Don't forward anything to me. Throw away the newspapers. And these three letters, when I'm gone put them in the mailbox immediately. Is the cab here yet?"

"At your service, Herr Rittmeister."

"Well then, God be with us. Air the place out every day. And look after the horses."

And with that Woldemar took his leave.

Of the three letters, one was addressed to Stechlin. Inasmuch as it was still able to go by the first train, it arrived shortly after dinner at his father's. It read:

"My dear Papa. By the time you receive these lines, we'll be under way. 'We', means our colonel, our second ranking staff officer, myself and two younger officers. From your own days of soldiering you'll be familiar with the nature of such assignments. Once we became the "Regiment of the Queen of Great Britain and Ireland" this business of introducing ourselves over there was merely a matter of time. Being assigned to a mission like this is, of course, a great honor for me, doubly so, when I consider the names at the regiment's disposal. The days when the phrase 'a historical family' was emphasized are over. I also wrote to Aunt Adelheid about the matter as well. She'll easily work up what I myself perhaps still lack in the way of elation. And that really pleases me because, all in all, I actually do owe her a great deal.

"Let me merely mention in passing that I'd rather not be leaving Berlin at this particular moment. You should be able to figure out the reason without too much difficulty. With best wishes for your well-being, and with warmest greetings to Lorenzen, as always, your Woldemar."

Dubslav was sitting by the hearth as Engelke brought him the letter. After the old man had finished reading it through, he remarked, "Woldemar's on his way to England. What do you say to that, Engelke?"

"Always thought something like that would happen."

"Hm. Then you were smarter than I. I didn't think anything of the sort. An' now just three more days and along with his colonel and his major he'll be planting himself in front of the Queen of England, and saying, 'Here I am.'"

"Sure, Master. Why shouldn't he?"

"Fair point o' view too, I s'pose. And maybe even the right one. 'The voice of the people, the voice of God.' Well, get along over to Lorenzen and tell'm I'd like to see him. But don't say anything about the letter, I want to surprise him. Sometimes you're an old chatterbox."

Lorenzen arrived within a half hour. "You ordered . . . ."

"I ordered. Yes indeed, just the right phrase. Sounds just like me . . . . Well now, Lorenzen, pull up a chair and if Engelke didn't spill anything — he doesn't always keep his trap shut, y'know — well then, I've got some real news for you. Woldemar's gone to England . . . ."

"Ah, with the deputation."

"Then you do know about it already?"

"No, except for the one point that a deputation or emissarial visit had been intended. I read about it and have to admit I thought of Woldemar."

Dubslav laughed. "Strange. Engelke imagined something like that. Lorenzen imagined something like that as well. Only his own father never thought of a thing."

"Ach, Herr von Stechlin. That's always so. Fathers are fathers and can never forget that their children were children. But yet it all comes to an end one day. At twenty Napoleon was a poor lieutenant, and as far as standing goes, a long way from being the likes of a Stechlin. Yet by the time he was as old as our Woldemar is now, yes indeed, there he stood already between Marengo and Austerlitz."

"Now listen here, Lorenzen, you really are reaching high there. My sister Adelheid'll no doubt agree with you, by the way, and date the beginning of a new historical era from today. I'm taking it a bit more calmly, even though I do realize it smacks of a great distinction. And once he's back home again, he'll have all sorts of advantages from it. But as long as he's over there! Don't trust the whole business. No peace of mind whatsoever. Those cousins of ours over there just can't be satisfied; maybe it piques them that somewhere outside in the world there is a 'Regiment of the Queen of Great Britain and Ireland.' They'd prefer to take care of that sort of thing themselves and when others come up with it, find it nothin' but a pretension. What do you think about it? Maybe you've taken the Beefeaters to your heart because of all those dissenters. Some cardinal, who, it's true, was a gourmand as well, is once supposed to have said, 'Terrible people. A hundred sects and only one sauce.'"

"Yes," laughed Lorenzen, "when it comes to that I'll admit I'm for the 'Beefeaters,' as you say, and against the cardinal. That business about the hundred sects I'll let rest. My taste, by the way, it's not, but under any circumstances, I'm for at most only one sauce. That's the only right way because it's the healthy one. Things have to be something of themselves and if that's the case, then actually any sauce, not to mention sauce in the plural, has been judged in advance.

"But let's leave the cardinal and his outrageous remarks and take the object of his aversion instead: England. There was a time when I used to rave about it unabashedly. Not surprisingly. After all, in the entire circle I frequented, didn't we used to say, 'Good grief, if we can't love England any more, what are we supposed to love at all?' And I went along with this semi-deification honestly too. But that's a pretty long way back now. They've become terribly decadent over there, because the cult of the golden calf is continuously growing. Nothing but money grubbing and the upper class leading the pack. And so hypocritical in the process. They say 'Christ,' but they really mean 'cotton.'"

"It's true, sad t'say, least from the bit I know about it. And all in all, I've always been for Russia for that very reason. And lately all the more so. When I just think back on our Czar Nicholas and the time his uniform arrived as a gift and got put into the Garrison Church as a decoration. Naturally in Potsdam. Course, we've done away with relics, but we still have them in our own way nonetheless and looks like we just can't do without something like that, I guess. Started with Old Fritz, of course. We've got his walking stick and that three-cornered hat of his and his handkerchief. Well, maybe they could have forgotten about that. And now on top of those three pieces, we've got Nicholas's uniform too."

Lorenzen looked down in embarrassment. To say something contradictory would not do, and to agree would do even less.

Dubslav, however, continued on. "And then they're more daring there in Petersburg, and they can draw on unlimited resources, even if their best jewels have been lost in the process. Things like that happen, still just a primitive folk. I actually can't stand that gift-giving business. There's something like bribery about it and it looks just like a tip. And a tip's even worse than bribery. Doesn't suit me one bit at all. But then on the other hand there's something pleasant about after all, snuff boxes like that. When things are going fine, it's a family heirloom, and when things go bad, it's a last resort. Of course, you never do have a completely clean feeling about it."

Lorenzen remained a full hour. The old gentleman was always pleased when now and then the opportunity was afforded him for a real old-fashioned chat, and today, of course, the very best topics were at his disposal: Woldemar, England, Czar Nicholas and in between, Aunt Adelheid, about whom, to be sure, only brief remarks were dropped, but nevertheless in such a manner that, because they were mocking, they substantially increased the old man's good humor.

And his good humor still remained when at about five o'clock he took his oaken walking stick and crumpled felt hat from the hook to undertake his usual walk around the lake in the direction of Globsow. Directly along the south bank, at a place where the cliff fell off steeply, stood a stone bench, overarched by the branches of a beech. It was his favorite spot. The sun already lay below the horizon, and only the red of twilight still glowed through the trees. There he now sat and looked back on his life, the old things and the new, his childhood days and those as a lieutenant, the days shortly before his marriage when the pale young woman who would become his wife was still the favorite lady-in-waiting of old Princess Marie. All of that passed by him again, and in between his sister Adelheid, in those days still in passably good condition, but even then as hard and bitter as today, so that with her virtue she had frightened off that charming Baron Krech, simply because he still had an almost half dead "affair" and an admittedly still surviving gaming debt at his disposal. Those were the old, old stories. And then Woldemar was born and his young wife died, and the boy grew up and learned all that stupid nonsense from Lorenzen, that new business (to which there was, perhaps, something after all), and now there he was on his way to England, in Cologne by this time perhaps, and in a few hours in Ostende.

As he sat there, he stared down drawing figures in the sand with his stick. The forest was utterly silent; on the lake the last reddish glow was vanishing and from some distance away echoed sounds as if people were cutting wood. He listened with half an ear and was just looking at the narrow road from Globsow when he noticed an old woman of probably seventy who, with a basket packed with kindling wood on her back, made her way up the gently sloping path, several steps before her a child with a few gentian stems in its hand. The child, a little girl, might have been ten. The light fell in such a way that the blond tangled hair seemed to be glowing around the child's head. When the little one was almost to the bench, she stopped, waiting there for the approach of the old woman. The latter, who could well see that the child was either afraid or embarrassed, said, "Gow on ther, Agnes. 'E won't 'urt y'none."

188

The child, overcoming her fears, actually did go on, and as she passed the bench, she looked at the old gentleman with large intelligent eyes.

In the meantime the old woman had approached.

"Well now, Buschy," said Dubslav, "do you only have kindling wood there in your basket? Otherwise the forester will be after you."

The old woman grinned. "Lory, master, if yer 'round, 'e prob'ly won't be doin' noth'n."

"Well, I guess it's not really all that bad. But tell me, who's that little girl there?"

"That's Karliner's."

"Well, well. Karline's. She still in Berlin then? And is he going to marry her? Rentsch in Globsow, I mean."

"Naw. 'e don't want 'er."

"But it's his, isn't it?"

"Aye, she sez so. But 'e sez 'twern't 'im."

Old Dubslav laughed. "Well listen here, now, Buschy. I really can't blame him. After all, that Rentsch really is a swarthy fellow, you know. An' just take a look there at that child."

"Oi tald 'er all that too. An' Karliner don't know so rightly either, an' jus'alwez laughs. An' she don't need'm either."

"Things going that well for her?"

"Aye, that ya could almost say. She's alwez ironin'. All'o'm like'er alwez does ironin'. This summer in Berlin Oi wuz wid Agnes — Agnes is 'er name — an' we all went tergethr t'th circus. An' Karliner wuz as happy's could be."

"Well that makes me glad. And her name's Agnes, you say. She's a pretty child."

"Aye, that she be. An she's a good choil. She cries right arf an' she's alwez so handy wi'er littl' han's. Them kin's alwez like that."

"Yes, that's right. But you better keep an eye on her, else you'll have a great-grandchild before you even know it. Well then, eevn'n, Buschy."

"Eevn, Master."

24

Baron Berchtesgaden's coach drove up before the Kronprinzenufer and the baroness, having heard that the upstairs residents were at home, slowly made her way up the steps, since she was not good on her feet and a bit asthmatic. Armgard and Melusine greeted her with joy . "How splendid, how nice to see you, Baroness," said Melusine. "And we're expecting another visitor. At least I am. I've got such a tingle in my little finger. And when that happens somebody always comes. Wrschowitz for sure. He hasn't been here for three whole days, you know. And maybe Professor Cujacius. And if not he, then Doctor Pusch, whom you don't know yet even though you really should — an old acquaintance from London days. Possibly Frommel will come too. But above all, Baroness, what sort of weather is it you're bringing along with you? Lizzi just told me the fog was so thick you couldn't see your hand in front of your face."

"Lizzi has informed you quite correctly. A real London fog. Which naturally leads me to think of your friend Stechlin. But we'll talk about him later. Right now we're still with the fog. It was really so bad out there that I kept on thinking that we would run into one another. And at the Brandenburg Gate with those big chandeliers in between, it almost looked like a picture by Skarbina.[7] Are you familiar with Skarbina?"

"Of course," said Melusine. "I'm quite familiar with him. But I admit just since the last exhibit. And besides the gas lights in the fog, the thing by him that actually sticks in my mind is a little picture: a long hotel corridor, one door after another, and in front of one of all those doors are a pair of ladies shoes. Charming. But the main thing was the lighting. From somewhere or other there came a light that made it all golden, the corridor and those little high button shoes."

"Right," said the baroness. "That was by him. And it was that particular one that pleased you so much?"

"Yes. And it's only natural. In my Italian days — whenever I talk about 'Italian days' by the way, I never mean my married days. During my married days, thank God, I saw practically nothing, my husband hardly ever, but even then too much, I've got to say. Well anyway, during my Italian days I stood before so many 'Ascensions,' that I'm for ladies shoes in the sunshine nowadays."

"My view exactly, Melusine, my dear. Of course besides that, I'm now for Japanese as well. Water, three rush stalks and a stork in between. At my age I can talk about storks, you know. In the old days maybe I might have said crane."

"No, Baroness. I don't believe you there. You were always for what they call realism these days, whatever has tone and color. And that includes the stork as well. That's the very reason why I love you so much. Oh my, if only the natural would come back in style again."

"It's coming, Melusine dear."

Melusine's tingling little finger proved to be correct. More visitors did indeed come, first Wrschowitz and then, however, instead of the three whom she had also anticipated, only Czako.

The reception of the one as well as the other of the two gentlemen had taken place up front in the ladies' room, without the presence of the old count. The latter appeared only as they were going in to tea; he bid his guests a cordial welcome because at all times he felt the need to hear something of what was abroad in the world. Each of them took care of that in their own fashion, the countess though reports concerning the upper social sphere, Czako with promotions and demotions, and Wrschowitz by means of "critizzizm." Everything which came up for discussion had more or less the same value for the old count, but his favorite was nevertheless the court gossip which the baroness dispensed in a cheerfully and unabashedly open manner. Remarks such as "I'm sure I can depend on your discretion," were utterly foreign to her. Not only did she possess the courage of her convictions in a general fashion, but she possessed the same courage with regard to every one of her specific tales as well. To be sure, as a rule it could indeed be said that she was in urgent need of the same as well.

"Tell me, my dear friend," began the old count, "what actually is happening with this business about letters at court."

"About letters? Oh, that's getting better every day."

"Better every day?"

"Well, better isn't perhaps exactly the right word," laughed the baroness. "But it certainly is getting more and more mysterious. And anything that's mysterious simply has that particular something about it, that it takes, which is to say, that necessary charm. Why just the every-day phrase 'a mysterious woman' has something to say in its favor. Any woman who isn't mysterious is actually no woman at all, by which, of course, I personally pronounce a sort of death sentence on myself. Because I may be everything else, but I'm just not a mystery. But when all's said and done, we are as we are and so I'll just have to try to get over this particular shortcoming . . . . It's always said that 'more or less taking pleasure in slander is sinful.' But what can you call slander here? Perhaps what we get to hear about merely in bits and patches is nothing but a weak echo of the real thing, and actually amounts to too little rather than too much. In any case, however all of that may be, my nature is just inclined towards the sensational and that's all there is to it. To tell the truth, our lives run in a rather average way, in other words, boringly. And since that's the case, I feel free to add, 'Thank God, we've got scandals.' I'll admit, you don't say that sort of thing for Armgard. That girl shouldn't even hear it."

"But she hears it nevertheless," laughed the comtesse, "and she thinks to herself when she does, what strange inclinations and pleasures there are. I've got no feeling for that sort of thing myself at all.

191

Our dear baroness finds our way of life boring and chronicles of that sort interesting. I, on the other hand, find such chronicles boring and our every-day life interesting. When I catch sight of our doorkeeper Hartwig's Rudolph down below, running up the street with his hoop and those long Berlin legs of his, I find it more interesting than these so-called juicy tidbits."

Melusine stood up and gave Armgard a kiss. "You really are your sister's sister, or the product of my training, and for the first time in my life I've got to leave my dear baroness completely in the lurch. There's no value to all this gossip. Nothing really comes of it."

"Oh, my dear Melusine, that's not right at all. On the contrary, a great deal comes of it. You Barbys are all so frightfully discreet and idealistic, but for my part, I'm different and take the world as it is. A beer, a suggestive little ditty and now and then a little lynching party,[8] that's what gets the most results. What we're all going through in this case right now is just such a lynching party, a little touch of the secret court."

"Just not a holy one."

"No," said the baroness, "not a holy one. The secret court wasn't always holy either. I just saw Goethe's *Götz* again, just on account of the secret court scene. Rosa Poppe was splendid by the way. But the fellow in black from the secret court is supposed to have been much nastier in the original version — Goethe was still very young in those days — so that one can hardly read it. I'd venture to take it on though. And now I'll turn to our gentlemen friends, who — I'm not sure whether it was chivalrously or unchivalrously — have left this awkward battlefield all to me. Dr. Wrschowitz, what do you think about it"

I think exactly as you, my Lady. What we read there is like in-scriptions of runes . . . no, *not* like runes . . . (Wrschowitz interrupted himself at this point, disgruntled by his own slip into the Scandinavian realm), what we read there in letters from court — that is critizzizm. And because it is critizzizm, it is goood. Even if is abuse of critizzizm. Everything has abuse. Justice has abuse. Church has abuse. Critizzizm has abuse. But so what? Secret court is important thing. Its big knife must again stick in tree."

"Brr," said Czako, which earned him a serious look from Wrschowitz.

When half an hour later they arose from the table they again changed rooms and returned to the ladies' salon, because the old count wished to hear some music in order to convince himself of Armgard's progress. "Doctor Wrschowitz will perhaps have the good-ness to accompany you."

192

Thus followed a quatremains, and as it came to an end old Barby took the opportunity to give vent to his love for such four-handed playing, inducing Wrschowitz, whose artistic arrogance knew no bounds, to offer smiling calmly the counter proposition that one frequently encountered such a view among dilettantes. The old count, little satisfied by such "critizzizm," was nevertheless much too familiar with artistic behavior in general and Wrschowitzian in particular to be seriously put out by such remarks. He contented himself instead with a cool bow in the direction of the Doctor of Music and, taking a seat on a nearby causeuse, drew the good Baroness Berchtesgaden into conversation, knowing that her cheerful remarks never took on the character of golden indiscretions.[9]

Wrschowitz, for his part, remained standing at the opened grand piano without the slightest trace of embarrassment. Thus there was really no need to be concerned about him. Nevertheless Czako considered it appropriate to look after him and in the process ask the traditional question as to whether Herr Doktor Wrschowitz had by now come to feel at home in Berlin.

"I hev," responded Wrschowitz with brevity.

"And don't regret your having set up your tent among us?"

"*Au contraire.* Berlin a beautiful city, varry good city. Varry nice city *pour moi en particulier et pour les étrangés en général.* A varry nice city because it hez musiic and because it hez critizzizm."

"It gives me great pleasure, Doctor Wrschowitz, to hear so many good things about our city, particularly from your mouth. The Slavic world in general and especially the Czech is . . . ."

"Oh, the Czech world. *Vanitas vanitatum.*"

"It's really rare, when it comes to national questions, to encounter such a free sense of being above all such things . . . . But if it's all right with you, Doctor Wrschowitz, here we are standing like two shield bearers next to this open piano. Perhaps we could take a seat. Countess Melusine is looking our way in any case."

And after Wrschowitz had expressed his agreement to Czako's suggestion, the two gentlemen strode from the piano towards the fireplace, before which the countess had seated herself upon a fauteuil. Next to her stood a little marble table on which she supported her left arm.

"Well now, at last, Herr von Czako. But before you do anything else pull up some chairs. I noticed you two gentlemen in what was apparently an intimate conversation. If it concerned anything I might join in with, please grant me the honor. Papa's engaged himself, as you see, with the baroness, I imagine regarding justifiable Bavarian peculiarities, and Armgard's thinking about her playing and all her

193

wrong notes. How you must have suffered, Wrschowitz. Once more then, my dear Hauptmann von Czako, what was it you were talking about?"

"Berlin."

"An inexhaustible topic for scandalous gossip."

"Which Doctor Wrschowitz to my astonishment chose to pass over. Just imagine, Your Ladyship, he seemed to want to praise everything. Of course we'd only gotten to music and criticism. As for the people — not yet a word."

"Oh, Wrschowitz, you've got to make up for that! A stranger sees more than a native. Well then frankly and openly, without any inhibitions. How are the upper classes? How are the little people?"

Wrschowitz rolled his head from side to side as if considering just how far he could go in his answer. Then all at once he seemed to have made a decision and said, "Upper class, goood, lower class varry goood, middle class, *not* varry goood."

"I can go along with that," laughed Melusine. "Just lacking in a few details. How about a few of those?"

"Middle class Berliner find goood, what *he* say, but not find goood what odder says."

Czako, although feeling affected by it, nodded.

"Middle class Berliner, when odder fallow speak get convulsions. Gets hidden convulsions or not so hidden convulsions. Wid hidden convulsions is pitiful sight, wid not so hidden convulsions is insult."

"Splendid, Wrschowitz. But more. I beg you."

"Berliner always top notch. At least so he think. Berliner always hero. Berliner know everything, find everything, discover everything. First is come Borsig, then Stephenson, first is Rudolph Hertzog from Berlin, then Duke Rudolph from Austria, first gingerbread-maker Hildelbrand, then Pope Hildebrand."

"Not flattering, but pretty close to the mark. And now, Wrschowitz, one more thing, then you're off the hook . . . . How are the ladies?"

"Ach, Your Ladysheep."

"None of that, none of that. The ladies."

"The ladies. Oh, the ladies varry goood. But not specific. Specific in Berlin only the madamm."

"Now I'm really getting curious."

"Specific only the madamm. I was, Your Ladysheep, in Pettersburg, and I was in Moscoú. And was in Budapest. And was in Saloniki too. Ah, Saloniki! Beautiful ladies of Helicon, and beautiful ladies of Lebanon, tall and slim like the cedar. But no madamm. Nowhere is madamm; madamm is only in Berlin."

"But Wrschowitz, after all there must be some similarities there. When you get right down to it a madamm is still a lady, at least a kind of lady. Why the very word itself says so."

"No, Your Ladysheep, *rien de tout*. Lady! Lady think of chivalry, lady think of fancy thinks or maybe of getting divorce. But madamm think only of Rieke the maid outside and now and then about Paul. And when she speak to Paul, who is her youngest son, then she says, 'Oh Lordy, your fadder.' Oh, the madamms! Some say they dying out, odders say, they never die."

"Wrschowitz," said Melusine, "what a shame that the baroness and papa didn't get to hear this and that our friend Stechlin, who loves this sort of topic, isn't here. By the way, we had a telegram from him today. Did you get some news too, perhaps, Herr Hauptmann?"

"Today, Your Ladyship. Also a telegram. Brought it along because I thought of the possibility that . . . ."

"Please read."

And Czako read. "London, Charing Cross Hotel. Everything magnificent beyond expectations. Seven unforgettable days. Richmond beautiful. Windsor even more so. And Nelson's column right in front of me. Your v. St."

Melusine laughed. "That's what he telegraphed us too."

"I found it to be rather little," stammered Czako embarrassedly, "and in duplicate I find it even less. And a man like Stechlin, a man on an official mission! And right now even under the eyes of Her Majesty of Great Britain and India."

All agreed that it was too little. Only the old count refused to hear of it. "What do you want? On the contrary, it's a very good telegram because it's a real telegram. Richmond, Windsor, Nelson's column. Is he perhaps supposed to telegraph that he's longing to see us? And he simply isn't up to doing the likes of that sort of thing, as monstrously spoiled as he is right now. The whole pack of you'll just have to really pull yourselves together. And that includes you too, Melusine."

"Naturally, me most of all."

Engagement: Christmas Excursion to Stech-lin

25

THREE DAYS LATER Woldemar had returned and announced himself for the next evening at the Kronprinzenufer. He encountered only the two ladies, who did nothing to hide their pleasure, especially Melusine. "Papa sends his regrets at not also being able to welcome you today. He's gone to a card party at the Berchtesgaden's which he naturally can't afford to miss. That's a 'duty' that's much more strict than the kind you have. We've got you all to ourselves and that's a nice thing too, you know. There's hardly a chance we'll be getting any visitors. Rex was just here yesterday for a short stay, a bit stiff and formal as usual, and we were able to spend an hour chatting with your friend Czako last Saturday. Wrschowitz was here the same evening too. They both meet more often and get along better than I'd have imagined at the beginning of their acquaintance. Who else could possibly be coming?

"And now, sit down and empty your travel cornucopia on us — the sort of cornucopias in style these days are mostly candy holders, and that's exactly what I'm expecting from you too. You were supposed to write me a letter about the English women. And who didn't write? You, that's who, even if we're willing to consider your telegram a whole one."

Melusine laughed as she spoke. "Maybe you didn't want to insult us in our vanity. But an open and honest game is still always the best. What you didn't write about then, you're going to have to talk about now. How were things over there? As far as beauty goes, I mean."

"I saw nothing in particular that might have astonished me, or perhaps carried me away."

"Nothing in particular. Is that supposed to mean that you admired practically the whole pack of them instead, the entire totality of femininity, so to speak?"

"I could almost agree with you on that. I remember a friend once telling me years ago, you could find beautiful women anywhere in the world, thank God, but it was only in England where the women were beautiful in general."

"And you believed the likes of that?"

"It's actually worse than that, Your Ladyship. I didn't believe it, but, despite my incredulity, I've found it belatedly confirmed."

"And you don't tremble to make such an exaggeration?"

"I'm afraid I can't, as much as here of all places I feel an obligation to do so."

"No bribery."

"I'm supposed to tremble at such an exaggeration," continued Woldemar, "but, perhaps Your Ladyship, will relieve me of this bit of trembling once I've explained myself better. That England admirer I just quoted was a devotee of pithy remarks, and one ought never take such remarks literally. Least of all in a realm as delicate as this.

"There's nowhere in the world where beauties simply bloom like buttercups across an entire meadow. Truly genuine beauties have, after all, always been rarities. If they weren't such rarities, they wouldn't be beautiful, or we wouldn't consider them to be, because we'd have some other standard.

"That much is certain. But yet there are general qualities of attractiveness which determine the type as a whole, and it was this standard of not exactly astonishing, but nevertheless extremely pleasing average beauty, that was what I encountered over there."

"I'll let that pass with just this one qualification. In Papa, with whom we often argue about the matter, you'll find a fellow advocate for your opinion. Average attractive qualities. Agreed. But what is it that's expressed by that, an almost impersonal quality, the typical aspect . . . ."

Melusine started slightly at this instant, believing she heard the doorbell outside. And so it was. Jeserich entered to announce Professor Cujacius.

"Oh, for heaven's sake," the countess let slip inadvertently, and making use of the brief pause remaining to her, she whispered to Woldemar, "Cujacius . . . Professor of painting. He'll talk about art. Please, don't contradict him. He gets fired up about it so easily, or even worse."

And scarcely had Melusine gotten that far than Cujacius appeared, and with a quick bow in the direction of Armgard, strode toward the countess to kiss her hand. The latter had collected herself in the meantime and made the introductions, "Professor Cujacius . . . Rittmeister von Stechlin."

Both bowed toward one another, Woldemar with a composed demeanor, Cujacius with that superior apostle's glance characteristic

197

of him, which, even if unintentionally, nevertheless always had something provocative about it.

"Completely in the picture, thanks to Countess Melusine," he remarked with a certain air of condescension. "Call of duty. Off to England. Windsor. I really envied you, Herr Rittmeister. Such a beautiful journey."

"Yes, that it was. But unfortunately only too short, so that I was unable to dedicate the right amount of attention to more intimate things, English art for example."

"On which point you may set yourself at ease. What I personally would envy anyone on a trip of that sort is solely for its great overall impressions, the court, the lords, all those things which go to make up the history of the country."

"All of that was the main thing for me too. As well it should have been. But be that as it may, I'd have liked to go in for something artistic, specifically painting. For example, the school of the Pre-Raphaelites."

"An outworn point of view. There were a few of them whose appearance we — it's artists of my own school to whom I'm referring — whose appearance we followed with interest and even with admiration. Millais for example . . . ."

"Ah yes, that chap. Very true. I recollect one of his most important pictures, which unfortunately was sold off to America. At an enormous price too, if I'm not mistaken."

Cujacius nodded. "It's probably the highly celebrated 'Angelus.' you're thinking of there, Herr Rittmeister, a market item puffed up by dealers for which, fortunately, you ought not hold the English Millais, which is to say, the *ais*-Millais, responsible. The Millet which, as you were saying, was sold off to America for a ridiculously high sum, was an *et*-Millet, a full-blooded Parisian, or at least a Frenchman."

Woldemar grew slightly embarrassed over this mix-up, likewise the ladies, all much to the edification of the professor, whose rapidly expanding sense of superiority bloomed with ever new shoots of spirited good humor under the impression of this *faux pas*.

"And incidentally you'll forgive me I'm sure," he went on ever more radiantly, "if I briefly summarize my judgment on both by saying, 'they are truly deserving of one another.' And we'll leave it to the two great cultural nations of the West to contend with each other to discover which of them has been led around by the nose more. The Frenchman Millet is a nil, a dwarf, next to whom the Englishman comparatively expands into a giant, I say comparatively, mind you.

"Nevertheless, if I may be permitted to repeat myself, at the outset of his career he was an object of our local interest. And rightly so. Because the Pre-Raphaelite movement, whose founder and representative I consider him to be, bore within it a seed of the future. A great revolution seemed in the making. That great revolution they call retrograde development. Or, if you will, reaction. One needn't take fright at such words. Words are nothing but children's noise-makers."

"And this English Millais — whom I sincerely regret having confused with the French one — this *ais*-Millais, this great reformer, became — if I understand you correctly — untrue to himself."

"One might put it that way. He and his school declined into eccentricities. Their sense of discipline went astray, and that avenges itself in every realm. Whatever gets splotched together these days throughout the world, especially in the American and Scottish schools, which is even seeking to spread out here in our country nowadays, is the exuberant excess of an otherwise respectable movement. The train that chugged along nicely and happily under moderate steam, once it got going under full steam — and even that isn't enough — ran right off the rails. And there it lies now next to the tracks, huffing and puffing. And it's a crying shame that its firemen didn't stay at their posts. 'Such is the curse of evil deeds . . . . ' In the presence of the ladies, I'll refrain from finishing this quote."[1]

A brief pause ensued until Woldemar, who recognized that something had to be said, roused himself to remark, "When it comes to the latest things, I've actually only become acquainted with seascapes, among them the fantasies of the painter William Turner. Unfortunately only in passing. He painted the *Three Men in the Fiery Furnace.*[2] Stupendous. Something grandiose seemed to be speaking to me from his creations, at least in everything that has to do with his use of color."

"A certain grandeur," continued Cujacius with a smilingly superior look, "cannot be denied him. But every form of madness easily encroaches upon the grandiose and then regularly dupes the masses. *Mundis vult decipi.*[3] And those in England at the head of the pack. There is but one salvation. A turn-around. A return to the chaste line. These colorists are the misfortune of art. A very few of them were outstanding, but not *parceque*, but rather, *quoique.*[4] Even today, in fact, it will fall to me to speak on this very topic in a meeting of our society. To be sure, amidst contradiction, perhaps even to hooting and howling. After all, along with correct lines in art, correct forms in society have also been lost. But the more enemies one has, the more honor, as they say, and these days every post has need of its man of Worms, its Martin Luther. 'Here I stand.'[5] The most miserable wretches of all are those halfhearted ones who want to make some sort of a compromise. Between beauty and ugliness there can be no compromise."

199

"And beauty and ugliness," interrupted Melusine here, happy to be able to interrupt at any price, "was the very question we were discussing when we had the opportunity of welcoming you in our midst. Herr von Stechlin was supposed to confess all regarding the beauty of English women. And now it's *you* I ask, Herr Professor, do you too find them as beautiful as we're always being assured in this country?"

"I take no pleasure in speaking of English women," continued Cujacius. "A touch of idiosyncrasy has me in its grip there. These daughters of Albion, they sing so much, they make so much music, and paint so much. And the fact is, they haven't any talent."

"That may be. But you're not allowed to talk about that right now. Merely the one thing, beautiful or not beautiful?"

"Beautiful? Well then, no. Everything strikes one as dead. And whatever strikes one as dead, if it is not death itself, is not beautiful. By the by, I see I have only another ten minutes. How happy I would be to stay at a place where one encounters such understanding and cordiality. Herr von Stechlin, tomorrow I'll take the liberty of sending you an engraving after a picture of the real English Millais. Dragoons' Barracks, Halle Gate — I know. Day after tomorrow I'll have the folder picked up again. Name of the picture, *Sir Isumbras*. Extraordinary creation. Too bad that he, the father of the Pre-Raphaelites, didn't hold out along that line. But not surprising. Nothing holds out these days, and next thing you know we'll be counting those who are famous by days. Titian was still a delight after a hundred years. Nowadays anybody who's been painting for five years lands on the scrap heap. Your Ladyship, Comtesse Armgard, I beg most warmly to convey my regards to my patron, your father, the Count."

Doing the honors of the house as permitted by his intimate position, Woldemar had accompanied the professor as far as the corridor and here helped him with the artist's cloak he had worn in unchanged cut since his days in Rome. It was a short cycling cape. To this was added a slouch hat of silken felt.

"You know, in his own way he's really not so bad," said Woldemar, as he again returned to the ladies. "These days one can hardly take offense at the stout sense of self-importance from which he unquestionably suffers, presuming the facts more or less justify it."

"A stout sense of self-importance is never justified," said Armgard. "Bismarck perhaps excepted. In other words then, one per century."

"According to which under the best of circumstances Cujacius would be number two," laughed Woldemar. "What really is the story with him? I've never heard of him. That, of course, doesn't say much, especially after I blithely mixed up Millais and Millet. Now everything is more or less all mixed up. Is he someone I really ought to know?"

"That completely depends on the opinion you have of yourself," said Melusine. "If it's your ambition not only to be acquainted with the original old Giotto from Florence, but also all those Giottinos who go wandering about from estate to estate out there east of the Elbe these days, doing their little bit extra for art and Christianity, why then it stands to reason, you've got to know Cujacius. He's the number one fellow out there. By no means the worst of the lot, by the way. Even his enemies, of whom he's got a bushel and a peck, concede he's got a nice touch of talent. It's just that he spoils everything because of his conceitedness. And so he doesn't have any friends, despite the fact he's always talking about like-minded comrades and brought them up again today. But it's precisely these like-minded comrades who are most decisively against him. That, by the way, isn't just his fault, but also that of his comrades. It's always the ones who are pursuing the same goal who contend with one another so, above all in the realm of Christian things, even if it's not Christian dogma that's at stake, but just Christian art.

"Among our professor's favorite turns of phrase is that he 'treads the path of tradition,' which however, just garners him mockery or shrugged shoulders. One of his like-minded comrades — as if he were looking to hold me personally responsible for it — asked me full of ironic solicitude just the other day, 'Is that Cujacius of yours still treading the path of tradition?' And when I answered him, 'You're making fun of it, but doesn't he really have one?' this particular colleague of his answered: 'Certainly he has a tradition. His very own. For forty-five years now he's been painting the same image of Christ over and over again, traveling around the provinces under his care as an art-, one could almost say, church fanatic, so that it can practically be said of him, 'His Christ doth preach at every spot, yet more beauteous thereby, it's certainly not.'"[6]

"Melusine, you simply can't go on like that," interrupted Armgard at this point. "You know, of course, Herr von Stechlin, how things stand around here and that my older sister, who brought me up, well, I hope, now has to be subjected to some belated upbringing on my part."

As she spoke she extended her hand to Melusine. "He's just gone out the door, the poor professor, and already such awful things about him. What sort of consolation is our poor friend Stechlin supposed to derive from all this? He'll be thinking, 'You today, me tomorrow.'"

"I'll agree with you on every point, Armgard, just not on the last. When you get right down to it, everybody knows how others take him, whether he's loved or not, presuming he's a 'gentleman' and not a peacock. But 'gentleman.' With that I've found the way back to England again. That beauty business has been dealt with, it was only a caprice anyway. But as for everything else, which after all is much, much more important, why, we still know as good as nothing at all. How did you find the Tower? And was I right about Traitors-Gate?"

"Only on one point, Countess. In your distrust of my imagination. It failed me there completely, that is, if it didn't perhaps have to do with the thing itself, Traitors-Gate, I mean. Because at other spots I could practically sing the praises of my imagination, and most of all at that spot where, for me only too understandable by the way, you yourself lingered with such enthusiasm."

"And what spot was that?"

"Waltham Abbey."

"Waltham Abbey? But I know absolutely nothing about the place. I don't know a thing about Waltham Abbey, scarcely even its name."

"And yet I know for sure that on the evening before my departure your Herr Papa said to me, 'Melusine is the one to know that; why she knows everything about everything there, and she's more familiar with Waltham Abbey, I believe, than Treptow or Stralau."

"There you see how reputations get made," laughed Melusine. "Papa just said that without the slightest thought, simply pulled out any example that came to hand. And now just look at the implications! Let's let it pass, though, and why don't you tell me instead, what Waltham Abbey is, and where is it located?"

"It lies quite close to London, just an afternoon's journey, more or less like when one visits the mausoleum in Charlottenburg or the one in the Church of Peace in Potsdam."[7]

"And does it have something of a mausoleum about it?"

"Yes and no. There's no memorial stone, but the entire church can be thought of as a monument."

"As a monument for whom?"

"For King Harold."

"The one for whom Edith Swanneck went looking on the battlefield of Hastings?"

"The very same."

"During my London days I saw the picture by Horace Vernet which shows the moment in which the beautiful Col de Cynge is wandering among the dead. And I recall too that two monks were walking along beside her. But more than that I don't remember. And I haven't the faintest idea of what happened then."

"What happened then, why that's simply the final act of the drama. And this final act is called Waltham Abbey. Those monks you remember walking along next to Edith were Waltham Abbey monks, and when they finally found what they were looking for, they laid the king on thickly entwined tree limbs and bore him back the long road to Waltham Abbey. And there they buried him."

"And the spot where they buried him, did you visit it?"

"No, not his grave. That doesn't exist. We only know in general that they buried him there. And as I stood there on a centuries-old linden path, in the midst of grave stones right and left, and the evening bells began sounding from the church, it seemed to me as if the procession of monks came up the linden path once more, and I caught sight of Edith and saw the king too, even though branches half covered him. And as I did — although in reality your Papa and not you, Countess, is to blame for it all — I thought of you with a sense of old and new gratitude."

"And that you have defeated me. But it's only I who say so. You naturally wouldn't say a thing like that. You're not the type of man who would puff himself up over a victory, much less over a woman. Now I've learned about Waltham Abbey and I'll believe in your imagination from today on, even though you've left me in the lurch with Traitors' Gate. And besides all that, I'm sure you were also at Martins le Grand, in honor of Armgard in fact, and I'm just as sure that you fulfilled Papa's single requirement and made your visit to the Chapel of Henry VII, that wondrous achievement of the Tudors. What impression did the chapel make on you?"

"The most magnificent imaginable. I know those cones they call 'water spouts' which hang down have been found to be unattractive, but aesthetic precepts simply don't exist for me. If something impresses me, it impresses me. I couldn't get enough of them. Nevertheless, the most essential thing was something else again entirely, and didn't occur until I was standing there between the sarcophagi of the two hostile queens. I would never have thought that anything would have spoken so movingly or deeply to me as that very place."

"And what was it about that place that moved you so?"

"The feeling, 'between these two opposing forces swings all of world history.' At first, of course, we seem to have only the opposition of Catholicism and Protestantism. But on deeper consideration it goes far beyond that, because it's not bound to time or place. We have the polarity of passion and calculation, beauty and cunning. And that is the reason why interest in this affair never dies. They represent magnificent archetypes, these hostile queens."

Both sisters remained silent. Then Melusine, who felt the obligation to steer things once again into more cheerful realms, said, "And now, Armgard, tell us, for which of the two queens are you?"

"Neither the one, nor the other. Nor even for both. Certainly they are archetypes. But there are others who mean more to me. To put it briefly, Elizabeth of Thuringia is more preferable to me than Elizabeth of England. Living for others and giving bread to the poor — there alone rests true happiness. I would like to be able to achieve something like *that* for myself. But one doesn't achieve anything for oneself. It's all grace."

"You're a child," said Melusine, as she endeavored to control her feelings. "One day they'll be putting you on display on Unter den Linden. On one side they'll have those native girls from Dahomey,[8] on the other, you."

Stechlin departed. Armgard accompanied him as far as the corridor. A strained sense of embarrassment held sway between them, and Woldemar felt he must say something. "What a kindly sister you have."

Armgard blushed. "You'll make me jealous."

"Really, Comtesse?"

"Perhaps, . . . Good night."

Half an hour later Melusine sat next to her sister's bed and the two were chatting still. Armgard was uncommunicative, however, and Melusine could easily perceive that she had something on her mind. "What's the matter, Armgard. You're so distracted. As if you were somewhere else."

"I really don't know, but I almost think . . . ."

"Well, what?"

"I almost think, I'm engaged."

26

And what the younger sister had whispered to the older turned out to be true; just a few days after this first reunion Armgard and Woldemar were engaged. The old count saw a long-harbored wish fulfilled and Melusine kissed her sister with an intensity as if she herself were the lucky one.

"You really don't begrudge him to me then?"

"Oh my dear Armgard," responded Melusine. "If only you knew! I've got nothing but the pleasure of it all, it's you who's got the burden."

On the very same evening on which the engagement had taken place, Woldemar wrote to Stechlin and to Wutz. The one letter was just as important as the other, for the Domina aunt, whose disapproval was as good as certain, had to be appeased if at all possible. Of course, it was an open question whether that would succeed.

Two days later letters of reply had arrived. This time it was the letter from Wutz which carried the day over that from Stechlin. This was simply because Woldemar had expected nothing but carping from Wutz and from Stechlin nothing but delight. Neither, in fact, was the case. What his aunt wrote was not at all that bad. She limited herself to repeating the reservations she had expressed in conversation before. And what his father wrote was not all that good, at least not as appropriate to the situation as Woldemar'd expected. Naturally it was congratulatory, but even more it was a political digression. As a letter writer Dubslav suffered from the tendency of taking pleasure in lingering over irrelevancies, occasionally not seeing the forest for the trees. Thus he wrote:

"My Dear Woldemar. The die is cast, *alea jacta est*, as they used to say, although even I'm not that old-fashioned anymore, and since the two sixes are up, I can only say, congratulations. Anyway, after that conversation I had with you on the morning of October 3, while the two of us were walking around our fountain here at Stechlin — it hasn't been running for the last three days, the mice have probably been nibbling at the feeding pipe — since that very morning I've been expecting something like this, no more, but then no less, either. And so it turns out you'll be making a career for yourself, first on your own merits fortunately, and then, it has to be admitted, also through your fiancee and her family. Count Barby, with beet fields in the Magdeburg area and mineral springs in Graubünden country, it scarcely gets higher than that. Unless, of course you were to stray into Katzlerean realms. Armgard is pretty much already, but Ermyntrud is even more, in any case too much for poor old Katzler.

"Yes, my dear Woldemar, you'll be coming into money and influence and will be able to raise up the Stechlins again. Baruch Hirschfeld was here just yesterday and agreeable to everything. The Jews aren't as bad as some people make them out to be. And when you move in here, and instead of this old barn have something in chateau-style put up, and maybe even start keeping pheasants so that first Postmaster General von Stephan and then the Kaiser himself come by to visit you, well, then there's a good chance you'll be able to achieve what your old father never could — because Filesharpener Torgelow was more powerful than he was — admission to the Reichstag with a clear view of Kroll's Opera right across the street.

205

"More than that I can't say right at this moment, nor can I screw up my sense of joy. And in this relative state of composure, for the first time I feel a certain familial similarity with my sister Adelheid, whose religious conviction, when you get right down to it, runs to the view: minor nobility over high nobility, Junker over count. In fact, when it comes to your high-born friends, I feel the Junker in me stirring a bit. The rich and elegant are after all always rather special people, who of course keep up their contact with our kind, even seeking us out in certain circumstances, even though maintaining contact with those on high is in the end far, far more important to them. People are always saying, 'It's the little fellows like us, who are the ones who do everything and have what it takes to do it all.' But then when you look at it in the light of day that's nothing but the same old 'You think you're doing the pushing, but it's you who's getting pushed.' Believe me, Woldemar, we're being pushed, and we're nothing but a battering ram. Always the same old story, just like with the proles and the propers. The proletarians — when they were still the genuine article, today, I suppose, things may be different — they were always on hand just to pull the chestnuts out of the fire; but if things went wrong, old Brother Penniless went off to Spandau prison and Brother Proper climbed into bed. And when it comes to the high nobility and petty nobility, its almost the same story. Of course it can happen that an Ermyntrud marries a Katzler now and then, but actually she's more on the lookout for a Stuart or a Wasa, if the likes of them are still around. Don't seem t'be though, I guess.

"Excuse this outpouring, to which you shouldn't give any more weight than its due. It all more or less flowed right out of my pen because I was just reading again today how one of our kind — who could have been saved by the intervention of an Ippe-Büchsenstein — was shamefully left in the lurch. Ippe-Büchsenstein is naturally only a generalization. All in all, I have confidence that you've chosen rightly and that nobody will be leaving you in the lurch. In any case, a real Mark Brandenburger has eyes in his head and is practically as clever as one o' them Saxons.[9]

"As always, your old father, Dubslav von Stechlin."

It was the end of November when Woldemar received this letter. He quickly came to terms with it and by the third day he read it all with a certain elation. Every bit the old fellow. Every line full of love, full of kindness, full of drolleries. And these very drolleries, didn't they actually hit the nail right on the head? Certainly. But what was best about it all, as much as it all might fit the situation in general, when it came to the Barbys, practically none of it was fitting. They were really different, they did not seek out contact with those above nor with those below. They didn't look to make arrangements with the right or the left, they were merely people, and that they desired to be *that* and nothing more, there lay their happiness and at the same time their sense of self. Moreover, Woldemar told himself, as soon as he got to know them the old fellow would pass over to the Barby camp with all banners flying. The old count, Armgard, and above all, Melusine. She was exactly what the old timer needed. As he thought of it his heart swelled with joy.

Christmas Eve Woldemar spent at the Kronprinzenufer. Wrschowitz and Cujacius — the former naturally unmarried, the latter, because of constant bickering with his wife, divorced — were also in attendance. Cujacius had asked to be allowed to paint a crèche transparency, which when it appeared, was then set up on a side table and admired by all. The Three Kings were portraits, the old count, Cujacius himself, and Wrschowitz as the moor, the latter, despite woolly hair and pursed lips possessing a striking similarity. All sought to find an association in Mary too, and at last it was discovered: it was Lizzi who, like so many Berlin chamber maids, had a demurely coy expression about her. After tea there was music, and Wrschowitz — wishing to present the elderly count with a little token — played the Polonaise by Oginski, at the first performance of which, some seventy years past, the Polish count and composer — according to an old *on dit* — was said to have shot himself dead in the final moment. Because of love, of course.

"Splendid, splendid," said the old count, practically overflowing in his gratitude, and so completely carried away that finally Wrschowitz roguishly remarked, "The bang-bang shooting at the end I must deny myself, your Eggzellency, even so, my admooreyshun (a glance at Armgard) is varry great, so great almost as your Eggzellency's admooreyshun of Count Oginski."

Thus passed Christmas Eve.

It had already been agreed that the three of them would make an excursion to Stechlin on the second day of the Christmas season to introduce the future daughter-in-law to her father-in-law. On Christmas Eve itself, despite the fact that midnight had already passed, Woldemar wrote a few lines to Stechlin, in which he announced himself along with his fiancee and sister-in-law for the evening of the second holiday.

His lines arrived at Stechlin in timely fashion. "Dear Papa. We intend to start from here by the late afternoon train on the second day of Christmas. Therefore we'll be at the Gransee station at seven and

207

with you by nine, or not much later. Armgard is overjoyed at meeting you at last and making the acquaintance of someone she's long admired. That, my dear Papa, is something I've definitely attended to. Count Barby, who is not feeling well, which prevents him from coming along, wishes to convey his respects to you, as does Countess Ghiberti, who will be accompanying us as *dame d'honneur*. Armgard is full of fear and trembling as if she were about to take an examination. Very much without need. After all, I well know my Papa, who is goodness and love itself. As always, your Woldemar."

Engelke stood next to his master's chair as the latter, half-aloud, yet with complete clarity, read these lines. "Well, Engelke, what have you got to say to that?"

"Aye, Master, what should I say? When you get right down to it, y'know, that's what folks call good news."

"Course it's good news. But haven't you ever had it happen that good news could embarrass a fellow too?"

"Lori' Master, never get none."

"Well, be happy about it then. Then you don't know what 'mixed feelings' are. Y'see, right now I've got mixed feelings. My Woldemar is on his way here. Fine. And he's bringing his fiancee along. That's fine too. And then he's bringing his sister-in-law along and that's probably fine as well. But his sister-in-law is a countess with an Italian name and his fiancee goes by the name of Armgard, which, after all, is a pretty odd thing too. And the two of them were born in England and their mother came from Switzerland, from some spot where nobody knows for sure what it belongs to because everything's all mixed up down there. And everywhere you look, they've got property, and Stechlin's really nothing more'n an old box. See, Engelke, that's embarrassing, and gives you what they call 'mixed feelings.'"

"I s'pose, I s'pose."

"And then we've got to do our bit socially. After all, I've got to put somebody in front of'm. Well then, who'll I put there in front of'm? Not much 'round here. Course, I got Adelheid. Naturally I've got to invite her, and she'll come for sure, even though we've had snow. But then she can take a sled. For all I know her sled's better than her carriage. Good God, just the thought of that top with its great big leather patch, that doesn't make me feel any better. And then, along with all that, she thinks she 'really is somebody,' which when you get right down to it is just as well too, 'cause when somebody gets to thinking he's nothing, then he really is nothing."

"And then, Master, she is a Domina after all, y'know, an' has real rank. Why I read someplace she was actually more than a major."

"Well, anyway, she's more than her brother; a forgotten major really is a sad case. But Adelheid herself, more or less when you first get a look at her, ain't much more than just so-so. Whatever happens, we've got to have somebody else besides. Give me a suggestion. Baron Beetz and old Zühlen, who're the best, live too far away, and I don't know, but since we've got the railroad, horses have been running worse than ever. Or maybe it just seems that way. Well then, the good numbers are out. And then we're back to Gundermann again."

"Glory be, Master, not him. He's s'posed to be so dubious, y'know. Uncke told me so. Course, Uncke's always using that word, 'dubious.' But it's probably true just the same. An' then Frau Gundermann. She's the reg'lar Berlin sort. Ain't no dependin' on him, an' not on her either."

"Well now, Engelke, you're supposed to be helping me and are only making things worse. We could try Katzler, but the child is sick over there and maybe it'll die. And then of course we still have our pastor. Well, he'd be fine except that he always sits there so quietly as if he was waiting for the Holy Ghost. Once in a while he comes, but then more often than not, he doesn't. And people of that sort, who're used to somebody always saying something fancy, what are they supposed to make of our Lorenzen? He's a closed-mouth."

"But he still always keeps his mouth closed better than that Gundermann lady opens her's."

"That's for sure. Well then, Lorenzen and maybe, if their child pulls through, Katzler too. As they say, 'A scamp gives more than he's got.' And then, Engelke, ladies like that who've been everywhere in the world, you never know which way the wind is blowing with that kind. It's just possible they could be interested in Krippenstapel. Or listen to this, something else just occurred to me. What do you think of Koseleger?"

"Well, we never had him before."

"No, but necessity's the mother of invention. I don't really think much of him, but just the same he's still a superintendent and that sounds like something. And besides, he went travelin' around with a Russian grand princess and a grand princess like that is actually more than a regular princess. Well then, talk to Kluckhuhn. Have'm send a messenger. I'll write a card right away."

Katzler declined, or at least left it unclear as to whether he could come. Koseleger, on the other hand, fortunately accepted, and sister Adelheid too responded by the messenger, that she would "arrive on the second day of the holiday at Stechlin and as far as useful and proper, see to it that everything was put in order."

Adelheid was a good hostess in her way, coming from the old days when the lady of the house learned and could carry out everything, right down to slaughtering and skinning eels. Thus, in this direction Dubslav relinquished any and all fears. But when suddenly he imagined that perhaps his sister might get it into her head to recall the time-honored venerability of her nobility, or the preferences accruing to being established in the Brandenburg Mark for a good six-hundred years, then every bit of the consolation he had taken comfort in during the conversation with Engelke dropped away once more. He feared the possibility of one of his sister's "put-on highborn looks" like a ghost from the grave, and the same applied to the question of her attire. When it came to him, whether he put on his red uniform as a member of the provincial diet or his high-collared black tailcoat, he was fully aware of the old-fashionedness of his appearance. In addition to that, however, as far as his own person went, he was at the same time also aware of a certain patriarchal quality. Similar comfort could not be taken from the external personage of sister Adelheid. He knew exactly how she would appear: black silk dress, lace ruffle with tiny buttons at the neck and the seven-electoral-prince brooch. What he dreaded most, however, was that moment after dinner in which, when beginning to feel more or less comfortable, she was in the habit of putting her entire Wutzean footgear on the fireplace screen, and drawing in warmth from below.

Shortly after seven Woldemar and the Barby ladies arrived at the Gransee station and found Martin and the Stechlin sled waiting. The latter, inasmuch as it possessed a genuine bear-skin blanket, was a splendid specimen. At the same time, its bells and snow covers and even almost the horses more or less left something to be desired. But Melusine saw none of that, and Armgard even less. It was an enchanting ride; the air was still and the stars twinkled in the steel blue heavens above. So they rode amidst snow-covered fields, and when here and there their caps or hats brushed against low-hanging branches, flakes fell into their sled. In the villages life was still abroad everywhere, and the barking of the dogs, which was then answered from the next village, resounded over the fields. All three sled passengers were happy without having felt the need to converse much, and at last making a wide curve they turned up the chestnut avenue, which quickly brought them over village green and bridge to the ramp of Stechlin Castle.

Dubslav and Engelke were already standing at the main door and assisted the ladies in getting out. As they entered the roomy entrance hall, the first thing they saw was a large mistletoe hanging from the ceiling. At the same moment the stair clock struck, its scythe bearer looking down as if puzzled and almost irritated at the strange guests. Many lights were burning, yet it seemed as if everything were nevertheless dark. Woldemar behaved a bit self-consciously, Dubslav as well. And then Armgard wanted to kiss the old man's hand. But it was that which gave the latter back his tone and good humor again. "The other way round, it would become a shoe."

"And sooner or later a slipper," laughed Melusine.[10]

27

"Now there is a lady and charming young woman to boot," said Dubslav silently in his old heart, as he now offered Melusine his arm to lead her from the entry hall into the salon. "That's how women ought to be."

Adelheid too strove to be obliging. But it was as if she were paralyzed. That lightness, cheerfulness and vivacity which the young countess displayed in her every word, was a foreign world to her. And it nettled her that at the same time an inner voice constantly whispered, "Yes indeed, this lightness that you have not, that is life itself and the heaviness you do have, is its very opposite." For although she constantly preached humility, she had nevertheless not learned to overcome herself through humility. Thus everything that crossed her lips was more or less distorted, an attempt at friendly gestures which in the final analysis came down to dour rudities.

Lorenzen, who had put in an appearance, helped out as best he could, but he was no ladies man and even less a good conversationalist. Thus it came about that Dubslav looked with a sort of longing for the Chief Forester, even despite the fact that he knew since noon that he was not coming. His youngest daughter had, in fact, died and was to be buried on the coming day in a small private cemetery bordered by Christmas trees that Katzler had laid out between the garden and the forest. It was the fourth tiny daughter in a row; each lay in a kind of garden bed and had, like a seed whose sprouting was anticipated, a small wooden plaque beside it on which was inscribed its name. When Dubslav's letter was received, Ermyntrud had as usual urged Katzler to accept the invitation. "I do not wish that you withdraw from your social obligations, not even today, despite the seriousness of the moment. Social obligations are also duties. And the Barby ladies — I recollect the family — will recognize a special act of friendship in your appearance precisely because of our mourning. And that is exactly what I desire. Because the comtesse will sooner or later be our closest neighbor."

But Katzler remained firm and stressed that there were higher things than social obligations and that he thoroughly wished that this be displayed. The princess's eye rested majestically upon Katzler during these words with an expression that seemed to say, "I know I have not given my hand to someone unworthy."

Thus Katzler was missing. But Koseleger too, despite his acceptance, had not yet arrived. Thus Dubslav found himself in the strange predicament of wishing for the arrival of the Quaden-Hennersdorfer, for whom he actually had little regard. Finally, however, Koseleger pulled up, excusing his somewhat belated arrival with official duties. Immediately thereafter all went in to dinner and a conversation started up. At first they discussed the northern railway which, since the advent of the Copenhagen extension had triumphantly overcome the name of horror which clung to it from earlier days.[11] Now it was called the 'orange line' which could indeed scarcely be topped. Then they passed on to the old count and his properties in the Graubünden region, finally, however, to the family's long sojourn in England, where both daughters had been born.

This conversation was still long from being completed when all arose from the table. Thus it came about that the chat on the selfsame topic was continued during coffee, taken in a half circle around the hearth fire in the garden salon. Dubslav expressed his regret that in his youth his military service and then later circumstances had prevented him from getting to know England. It was, after all, nowadays the model country, for all parties, in fact, even the Conservatives, who found their ideal realized there at least every bit as well as the Liberals. Lorenzen enthusiastically agreed, whereas the Domina on the other hand exhibited rather clear signs of impatience. England was by no means a gratifying topic of conversation for her, which of course did not hinder her brother from dwelling upon it in the least.

"I should like," Dubslav went on, "to turn to our Herr Superintendent in this matter. Were you over there?"

"Unfortunately not, Herr von Stechlin. I was not over there, very much to my regret. And I could have so easily had the chance. But it's always the same old story. Whatever one can achieve in a few hours and sometimes in a few minutes, is the very thing one puts off, simply because it's so close. And then all of a sudden it's too late. I was in The Hague for years and from there to Dover was not much more than to Potsdam. Nevertheless it never happened, or to put a finer point on it, just for that very reason.

"I could forgive myself for never having gotten to see the tunnel or the Tower. But the life that goes on over there! If that oft-cited phrase about gaining more in a day than in the monotony of a year is fitting for any place, it's over there. Everything modern and at the same time so old, so deeply rooted, stabilized. It is unique. More than any other land is it the product of civilization, so much so, in fact, that the inclinations of its people hardly follow the laws of nature any more, but instead those of a refined cultural tradition."

The Domina felt more and more unpleasantly moved by all of this, especially when she noticed that Melusine constantly nodded in agreement to everything Koseleger expounded upon. "Everything I've heard here," she said, "can't do a thing to influence me in favor of these people. Why, simply because they're surrounded on all sides by water, it's all so cold and damp there. And the women, right on up to the very highest ranks, are practically always in a condition I really wouldn't care to identify by name in present company. At least that's what I've been told. And then when it gets foggy, they all get what they call the spleen and fall into the water by the hundreds. And nobody knows what's happened to them. That's because, as Pension Director Fix, who was there, has assured me on his word, they're not recorded in any book and don't even have what we call the Residents' Records Office. So you could practically say, they as good as don't even exist. And the way they cook and do their meat! Everything practically still bloody, especially what we here call 'Englische Beefsteaks.' And how could it be otherwise, considering they're always around savages so much, and never have any chance at all of acquiring a more refined kind of breeding."

Koseleger and Melusine exchanged knowing glances. The Domina, however, took no note of this, and went on undauntedly. "Fix is a good observer, of moral conditions too, and one of their kings had five wives, ladies-in-waiting mostly. I had to write an essay about it once when I was a girl. And he had the head chopped off one of them and another one he sent back home again. And she was a German besides. And they're not supposed to have any real nobility anymore either, because there was this war one time, during which they took turns chopping off each other's heads. And then when they were all gone and done for, they pulled in common people and gave them the old names. So when you think somebody's a count, he's really just a baker, or at best a beer brewer. But they say they've got lots of money and their ships are supposed to be good and sturdy, and very clean too, practically every bit as good as the Dutch ones. But when it comes to religion, they're splintered and by now they're even starting to turn Catholic again."

213

Old Dubslav, as his sister launched into her diatribe against England, had from the outset become resigned to an attitude of "fate take thy course." Woldemar, however, again and again endeavored to bring about a change of topic. In this he might perhaps have succeeded, had it not been for Koseleger. The latter, either because as an aesthetic connoisseur he took genuine pleasure in Adelheid's remarks, or further desiring to spin out the question of nature and morality (a hobby-horse of his), which he himself had introduced, held firmly to England and remarked, "In my opinion the Frau Domina seems to start from the position that precisely the natural being, bordering occasionally almost on the savage, is in full flower over there. And I shan't dispute that in every point, either. But along with that sort of thing, we encounter a sophistication in the way of life and society, which, despite some contestable elements, I must characterize as a supreme cultural expression.

"I recollect among other things a trial which was taking place just at the time when I was living in The Hague, about which I was daily required to provide Her Imperial Highness a report. High-life-trials meant more to her than anything and the topic at hand was so truly the expression of a refined, or if you will, over-refined cultural way of life. So fully the opposite of the ethos of merely natural type of fellows. It is, of course, a rather long story . . . ."

"Too bad," said Dubslav. "But just the same . . . if it's at all tellable . . . ."

"Oh most assuredly, most assuredly; the most harmless thing you could think of . . . ."

"Well then, my dear Superintendent, if it's really as harmless as all that, I make myself without further ado the spokesman of our assuredly curious ladies, my sister, the Domina included. What happened? How did the story go in which an Imperial Highness was able to take such a lively interest?"

"Well, if it must be then," began Koseleger slowly and as if merely yielding to pressure, "at that time there was a beautiful duchess living in London, who couldn't bear it that the years were not inclined to pass over her without a trace. Tiny wrinkles and crow's feet had begun to show. In this distress somehow she heard about a 'plastic artist' who by application of a wax paste was supposed to know how to restore a person's youth. This artist was called in and the restoration was actually a success. But then, one fine day came the reckoning, the 'bill' as they say over there. It was for a sum calculated to give a fright even to a duchess. And since the artist persisted in her demand, it finally came to the trial I alluded to, which soon took on the nature of a *cause célèbre*."

"Quite understandable," affirmed Dubslav and Melusine agreed as well.

"Numerous persons appeared at the hearings and finally competitors in this special area of 'plastic art' were also heard as expert witnesses. All of them found the demand significantly excessive, and it seemed as if victory was rapidly inclining towards the duchess. But in this very moment the artist, seeing herself severely pressured, approached the chief justice of the court and requested that he simply put a question to those of her colleagues who had testified, regarding the duration of the youth and beauty renewed by their art; a request which the chief justice immediately accommodated. The answers that followed sounded quite varied with regard to duration. But when, despite the variety of these statements, not one of the competitors ventured to guarantee it for more than three months, the accused turned calmly to the high court, and not without dignity, stated, 'My Lord Judges, my colleagues, as you have just heard, help for *a time*. What *I* achieve' — and these were her exact words — 'is 'beautifying for ever.' Everyone was swept off his feet by this statement, the high court included, and the duchess had to pay out the gigantic sum of money."

"And would something of that sort be possible in this country?" asked Melusine.

"Utterly impossible," responded Koseleger, who raved about all things foreign. "It can not occur here simply because we lack the necessary higher cultural conditions, and the corresponding general attitudes. In this dear old Prussia of ours, and above all, especially in our Mark Brandenburg, they only see the bizarre aspect of a procedure of that sort, or at the very best its grotesque element; not, however, that extraordinary measure of social sophistication absolutely required by such things to develop — regardless of whether one may smile at them or condemn them because of their refinement."

Most were in agreement, Dubslav, who always understood such things, in the forefront. At the same time the Domina spoke of *horreur*, and visibly chagrined, shook her head back and forth. Of course Woldemar renewed his efforts to turn the conversation his aunt found so disagreeable to other things, on which occasion, after touching upon the greatest possible variety of topics, he finally came to speak of Covent Garden market and English vegetable gardening. That was more to the Domina's liking.

"Ah yes, vegetable gardening," she said, "now that's a wonderful thing. One really gets true joy from that. Wutz Convent really is a garden spot. After all, our asparagus is the best far and wide, and my good Schmargendorf's grown artichokes every bit as big as a sun flower. True enough, nobody wants them particularly much and everybody always says it takes such a long time to peel off every leaf like that and you actually don't get anything from them anyway, even if the sauce is ever so thick. Our old Schimonski has much more luck with her gigantic strawberries — of course, I don't mean Schimonski herself, she can't do a thing herself, but she's got a really capable young thing — and a dealer from Berlin buys them all from her, except that the snails often eat away half of every strawberry. You'd never believe such creatures have such a refined taste. But anyway, even if it is uncertain on account of the snails, you should try cultivating something like that yourself, Dubslav. If it turns a profit it's tremendously advantageous. At least Schimonski's gotten more out of that than from her chickens, even though they lay ever so well. Because now and then they're cheap, the eggs, I mean, or then they go bad on you and the rotten ones get counted against you and deducted from the bill and there's no end to all the fighting about it."

Shortly before eleven the conversation concluded and everyone withdrew. Old Dubslav would not let himself be deprived of personally accompanying the ladies up the stairs to their rooms and there to take leave from them with a kiss of the hand. It was the same two rooms which exactly three months earlier Rex and Czako had occupied, the larger room set apart now for Melusine, the smaller one for Armgard. But as both stood before their traveling cases and superficially set to busying themselves with them, Melusine said, "This canopied bed is for me, I see. If it's all the same to you, why don't you take this place of honor instead, and leave the small bedroom to me. After all, we're still together; the door is open."

"All right, Melusine, if you absolutely prefer it that way, why of course. But I really don't quite understand you. They want to honor you, and if you refuse it, it could be noticed. After all, in a house where one is still half a stranger, one has to do everything the way it's desired to be."

Melusine went to her sister, looked at her half embarrassedly and half roguishly and said, "Of course, you're perfectly right, but I'm asking you just the same. And anyway, not a soul has to notice. Direct checking will undoubtedly be out of the question, I imagine, and I don't make any deeper impression in the bed than you."

"Fine, fine," laughed Armgard. "But tell me, what's this all about? You're usually always so easy-going. And if it should be that you're really a bit anxious here in this front room because it's so close to that hall corner, well then, we can always lock the door."

"That won't help a bit, Armgard. In old castles like this there are always secret doors. And as far as *that* thing goes," she pointed to the bed as she spoke, "all ghost stories always take place in canopied beds. I've never heard yet that ghosts approached a plain birchwood bed. And didn't you see that mistletoe downstairs? Mistletoe is sort of a remnant from old pagan times too, used by the old Teutons for sure, and probably the Wends as well, in case the Stechlins really are Wends. When I look at Aunt Adelheid, I can practically believe it's so. And the way she went on about chickens and eggs. It was all so Wendic. Of course, I don't actually believe in ghosts, although I'm not completely against them either. But however that may be, when I just think of the possibility that Aunt Adelheid might appear to me here and bring me a strawberry the snails have been munching on, it would be the death of me."

Armgard laughed.

"Oh yes, you're laughing. But did you see those eyes of her's? And did you hear her voice? And the voice, as you surely do know, is the soul."

"Of course. But soul or not, there's nothing she can do to you with her voice and she can't appear to you either. And if she comes anyway, well then, you'll just call me."

"I'd like it most if you just stayed right by me."

"But Melusine . . . ."

"All right, all right. I can well see, that isn't going to work out. Well then, something else! I saw a Bible before, or perhaps it was just a hymnal lying there, there on that small shelf where that little doll is standing. Incidentally, that's something rather odd too, this doll. Please, get the Bible from the *étagère* and put it here on my night table for me. And leave the light burning. And when you're lying in bed, keep on talking until I fall asleep."

28

Next morning they all met at breakfast. It had grown relatively late without Dubslav's having gotten impatient, as is usually the custom in the country. The same could not be said for Aunt Adelheid. "I don't find this letting people wait a long time particularly fitting, least of all when it comes to persons to whom one wishes to show respect. Or am I perhaps going too far when I say anything about showing respect?"

Thus had Adelheid expressed herself to Dubslav. When, however, the Barby ladies finally did appear, the Domina controlled herself and asked all the questions one usually asks on such first mornings. The sisters responded with complete frankness, most openly Melusine, who took the occasion to tell old Dubslav that she had not been able to do without placing the Bible next to her bed.

"Intending to read in it?"

"Almost. But nothing came of it. Armgard chatted so much — at my request, I admit. I could constantly hear the clock striking from the steps and kept seeing the word 'museum.' But, of course, that was already in my dreams. I was fast asleep by then. And this morning I'm just like the proverbial fish in water."

Dubslav would like to have confirmed this, in the process seeking out the particular fish which more or less might have rightly suited for comparison with Melusine. The glances of his sister, however, which seemed to ask, 'did you hear that?' induced him to refrain from doing so. Thus, after a few more things had been said about the vast upstairs corridor and its pictures and chests, exactly as three months before when Rex and Czako had been visiting, a program was arranged which very much resembled the one from that time: the lookout tower, the lake, Globsow, then on the way back the church, perhaps Krippenstapel as well. And finally, the "museum."

Some of it remained indefinite, however, depending upon the weather. It was only the lake they wished to see under any circumstances. Engelke was recruited to go ahead with rugs and blankets and to take a few persons along to shovel the snow, merely in case the ladies might indicate a desire to investigate the site of the funnel and spray more closely. "And if there aren't any people in our place, then go over to the mayor's office and ask Rolf Krake to help out."

Melusine, who had heard these commands being issued, was astonished to encounter the name 'Rolf Krake' in a village in the Brandenburg Mark. She soon learned the connection. She was completely enchanted by it all and said, "That is charming. Any sort of puffed-up patriotism is a horror to me, but when it takes such forms as this, couched in terms of humor or even irony, it's the best thing you can have. A man who has a nickname like that is really alive, why, he's a story in himself."

Dubslav kissed her hand. Adelheid, however, pointedly turned away; she had no desire to be a witness to such perpetual demonstrations of homage. "When somebody gets to be an old major, he's nothing but an old major, and not a young lieutenant anymore. Dubslav is twenty, twenty years retired that is."

It was around ten when they started on their way, first to climb the lookout tower. After having fittingly admired the forest landscape, looking marvelous in its snowy adornment, from its topmost level, and then safely managing the descent, they passed through the castle courtyard with its glass sphere. They then crossed the village square to turn onto the large road leading down to the lake. On the square everything was wintry silence. Only before the inn stood three persons: Engelke, who had sent the snow shovelers on ahead, with his plaid shawls over his arm, next to him Mayor Kluckhuhn, and next to the latter, Gendarme Uncke, his carbine hung over his shoulder.

"Here we are running into the all the higher authorities," said Dubslav. "I can include Engelke as well, he rules me, that actually makes'm the top man in the feudal order of things."

As he spoke they approached the group.

"Glad to run into you here, Kluckhuhn. I think you'll accompany us . . . . Your Ladyship, may I present to you our village regent? Mayor Kluckhuhn, an old veteran of sixty-four."

And now the procession arranged itself. Dubslav and Uncke brought up the rear, Woldemar, Armgard and Aunt Adelheid held the middle, and Melusine led the way, Rolf Krake next to her.

"I am happy," said Melusine, "to see you coming along on this excursion. The elder Herr von Stechlin has told me about you and that you were in the campaign of sixty-four. And I know your name too, your second name, that is. And I must say, I always enjoy hearing something as charming as that."

"Ah, Rolf Krake," laughed Kluckhuhn. "Yes indeed, Your Ladyship, 'whosoever is the injured party, should pay no heed to the mockery,' as the saying goes. Which is to say, I really can't complain about injury, I really didn't get so much of that. Wasn't even wounded. And yet something like that's to be expected, when things really get going."

"Yes, Mayor Kluckhuhn, something like that is unfortunately always closed to the likes of us, or as the people here say, so cozied in. Yet that's real life. Just spending your time sitting around tearing up linen for bandages, that's nothing much. Being in the thick of things, there's what gives life meaning. But nevertheless it must have been a pretty strange feeling when you were crossing over from Düppel to Alsen like that and that horrible ship, the *Rolf Krake*, was lying there so close by."

"Aye, that it was, Your Ladyship, a very strange feeling indeed. And now and then that *Rolf Krake* still appears to me in my dreams. An' no surprise it is, either. Because that *Rolf Krake* was like a regular ghost. And when a ghost like that gets a hold on you, you're a goner for sure . . . . And I stick to my guns, Your Ladyship, sixty-six wasn't much of an affair and seventy wasn't either."

"But the terrible losses."

"Aye, the losses were terrible, that's true. But losses, Your Ladyship, that's not really anything. Of course, for the fellow who gets hit, for him it's somethin.' But what I mean right now is what they more or less call the moral factor in a thing like that; that's what really means something, not the losses, not whether they're a lot or a few. But when some fellow clambers up an embankment an' gets up to the top an' then crawls up on 'em, with a bag a' powder an' a fuse in his hand, an' then he lights it and the whole thing goes up, him along with it; an' then the fortress or the battlement is breached, aye, Your Ladyship, that's really something. And that's what our Sapper Klinke did. He had the moral factor. I don't know if Your Ladyship ever heard of him, but that's what I'll live an' die for; it's always just the little things, there's where it shows what a fellow can do. When a battalion's got to go over the top, an' I'm stuck in the middle of it, well now, what am I supposed to do then? I've got to go along. An' pow, there I lie. And now I'm a hero. But actually I'm not a hero at all. It's all been nothing but 'you've got to' and 'got to heroes' like that are to be had aplenty. That's what I call them big wars. But Klinke there, with that powder bag of his, aye, he was just a little fellow, but he was really great. And the same holds for this *Rolf Krake*, even if it was our enemy."

Thus in historically retrospective fashion went the conversation at the head of the group, while Dubslav and Uncke, who brought up the rear of the column, remained more in the present with their topic.

"Really glad to see you again, Uncke. Haven't seen you since Rheinsberg. I imagine Torgelow is really up to top speed by now. Just like Bebel. Naturally I get my newspaper every day, but it's always too much for me, and then there's its size and that thin paper. Don't always look through it so carefully. Has he made a speech yet?"

"Aye, Herr Major, he's made a speech by now. But 'twasn't much. An' not much applause either. Not even from his own people."

"He's probably not so good at that business yet, I suppose. What they call parliamentary skills these days, I mean. But that doesn't hurt anything and it's really not even important. What's more important is what they think about him here in our Ruppin corner of things, up here in our Rheinsberg-Wutz. Well then, are they satisfied with him here?

"Not that either, Herr Major. They say he's dubious."

"Yes sir, Uncke, that's what they say everywhere. That's just the way it is. Can't be changed. In France it's always 'treason' right off, and here they say 'dubious.' There was one of our kind too, whose name I don't care to mention, they said the very same thing about him too . . . ."

"They said the same about him too. Yes indeed, Herr Major. And Pyterke, who always knows exactly what's going on, he told me that time back there in Rheinsberg, 'Uncke, believe you me, the Herr Major's raised himself a serpent on his breast there'."

"Can well imagine. Sounds just like Pyterke. Always talks so cultured. But is it true?"

"It's true all right, Herr Major. The Herr Major always thinks the best of people, because you're always sitting at home so much and are like that yourself. But for somebody who gets around a lot like me all of'm are liars. What they think, they don't say, an' what they do say, they don't mean. There's no depending on anybody any more; the whole pack of 'em's dubious."

"Yes, but so straight out like that, Uncke, that was all right in the old days. But you can't do things that way anymore. You can't just tell anybody everything straight off like that. Why, that's just what they call 'the political way of doing things.'"

"Ach, Herr Major, that's not what I mean at all. The political way . . . . Lordy, when somebody gets to being dubious in political things, well, then I've got to report him; that's in the line of duty. But that doesn't bother me much. But when it comes to what isn't in the line of duty, the things you just get to see on the side, sometimes that can really get to you — more or less just as a human being."

"But my dear Uncke, what in heaven's name is actually wrong? Listening to you, you'd have to really believe the end was just around the corner . . . . Well sure, out there in the world things don't always go just right. But here, in the bosom of the family, so to speak . . . ."

"Lordy, Herr Major, that's just it. In this bosom of the family, why that's exactly where it's worst of all. And even in the Jewish bosom, where it's always been the best."

"Examples, Uncke, examples."

"Well, just to give you one example, around here we've got that good old Baruch Hirschfeld of ours in Gransee. Pious old Jew . . . ."

"Know'm, Know'm well, too well almost. All right, he's got a son. And now and then he's of a differing opinion with'm. But there's not really much you can say about that. It's like that way everywhere in the world. The old timer sticks with the old and the youngster, well, he's a young'n plain and simple, and swaggers around a bit. I don't rightly know what party he's for, but he probably voted for Torgelow, I suppose. Well, good God, why not? Lots of them are doing it these days. You've got to get accustomed to it. That's just what politics are about."

"No, Herr Major, if the Herr Major will forgive me, but when it comes to this Isadore, it's not politics. After all, I come by every third day and look in on the old boy in his store and hear what he's always sayin' there. And the young fellow talks too and always goes on about 'the principle of the thing.' But the principle doesn't mean a thing to him. He just wants to cheat and push the old boy to the wall. And that's the kind of thing I call dubious."

Armgard, Woldemar, and Aunt Adelheid had taken the middle. As they approached the tip of the lake, all the time making their way under an archway of snow-covered beeches and oaks, their attention was drawn to what sounded like the breaking of small branches. Looking up they caught sight of two squirrels playing above them, leaping from tree to tree in a constant game of tag. The branches snapped and the snow fell down like powder. Armgard could not take her eyes from the scene, laughing as the little creatures, who disappeared momentarily, reappeared again in a flash. She did not give up watching until the Domina, not exactly in an unfriendly way but yet rather impatiently and in any case as if bored by it all remarked to her, "Yes indeed, Comtesse, they do jump about. After all, they are squirrels, you know."

A few minutes later they all had reached the bench from which one had the best view of the frozen lake. The ice appeared covered with deep snow, but in its middle a spot had been swept clear to which a narrow path had also been shoveled open. Engelke laid the blankets across the bench and the ladies, who had grown weary from the half-hour long walk which towards the end had been somewhat uphill, all took a seat while Rolf Krake and Uncke, like two shield bearers, took positions at both sides of the bench. Dubslav, however, placed himself in front and, adopting the tone of a local tour guide, played the Cicerone.

"I have the honor of presenting to you the outstanding sightseeing spot of village and Castle Stechlin, our lake, *my* lake, if you'll permit me the term. All kinds of famous nature experts have been here and have spoken out in an extremely flattering way about the lake. Every one of them said, 'it is a scientific fact,' and that's the highest you can get nowadays. In the old days they used to say, 'it says in the records.' I'll leave it an open question as to which one should kowtow more."

"Well now," said Melusine, "so this is the great moment. I'm fully informed. But as is always the case with something grand, I nevertheless do feel a touch of disappointment too."

"That's because it's winter, Your gracious Ladyship. If you had the open lake before you and were imagining to yourself, 'now the funnel is forming, and now it's rising up,' then presumably you wouldn't be feeling any such disappointment. But now! The ice makes everything silent and represses the revolutionary element. Why, even our Uncke can't note down anything. Right, Uncke?"

Uncke grinned.

"Besides, to my joy I see — we owe this too to our good friend Kluckhuhn, who thinks of everything and is always looking ahead — that the snow shovelers have also brought along a few of their pick axes. I'd calculate that ice to be no thicker than two feet and if those fellows get to it, in ten minutes we'll have a nice sized hole and the cock, if he were to feel like it, might come up from those depths of his. Care to order it, Your Ladyship?"

"For heaven's sake, no. I'm very much in favor of such stories and glad that the Stechlin family has this lake. But at the same time, I'm superstitious and don't want any interfering with the forces of nature. Nature has covered over the lake for now and so I'll beware of wanting to change anything. I'd almost believe a hand might reach out and take hold of me."

At these remarks Adelheid had grown ever straighter and taller and ostentatiously moved away from Melusine more towards the arm of the bench, where, half like the personification of good conscience, half like the divine world order, stood Uncke, once more soothing the Domina's emotional condition through his mere presence. Except that from time to time she looked questioningly, searchingly and reproachfully at her brother.

The latter knew exactly what was passing through his sister's soul. It amused him enormously, but it troubled him nonetheless also. If these feelings continued to grow, where would it all lead? The possibility of a frightful scene which might afflict his house with a disgrace never to be erased, appeared before him as he thought about it.

Heaven, however, was merciful. A grayish cast had been lying upon the landscape for a quarter hour. Suddenly flakes began to fall, first one by one, then thickly and heavily. Continuing on to Globsow was no longer thinkable under these circumstances, and so they started on their way back to the castle. A visit to the church was also called off. It would be too cold there as well.

29

The way back had been begun together, but only as far as the village road. Here they divided into three groups, each one with a different goal. Dubslav, Aunt Adelheid and Armgard went to the manor house, Uncke and Rolf Krake to the mayor's office, Woldemar and Melusine towards the parsonage. Woldemar, however, only as far as the front garden where he took his leave from Melusine.

Lorenzen had stood self-consciously at the window as he observed Woldemar and Melusine approaching his parsonage. On seeing the couple separate, however, he more or less again regained his composure. He had by now become so unaccustomed to any sort of conversation with women that a visit such as that of the countess could primarily create only a sense of embarrassment. If it absolutely had to be, however, a *tête-à-tête* with her was far more preferable to him than a three-part conversation. And so he went to the entry hall to meet her, helped her out of her coat and — feeling every shred of shyness quickly fall away — expressed his sincere pleasure at being able to welcome her in his parsonage.

"And now, my dear Countess, I ask you to make yourself as comfortable as possible here amid my books. I am, it's true, also the proud possessor of a parlor with an acceptable enough rug and a cold stove, but from the standpoint of your health, I couldn't take that responsibility upon myself. Here at least we have an acceptable level of warmth."

"Which always remains the most important thing. Ah yes, an acceptable level of warmth! From the social point of view that's almost everything and, sad to say, so rare. I know of houses where, if you'll forgive the absurdity, the cold stove never goes out. But be good enough not to insist on my taking this place here on the sofa; I don't feel myself quite yet the 'elderly lady' enough to warrant it, and moreover, I'd like to stay *en vue* of those two pictures, even though I practically know one of them well already."

"The Descent from the Cross?"

"No! The other one."

"Jenny Lind then?"

"Yes."

"So you have seen that beautiful picture in the National Gallery?"

"That too. But, in fact, only just recently, whereas I've known of your water-color copy for several months now. That was on a steamer excursion we made to what they call the 'Egg Cottage,' and the one who revealed all about the picture was none other than your pupil, Woldemar, of whom you can be proud. To be sure, he would turn that sentence around, or I'd say rather he's done so already. Because, he spoke with such affection of you, that I've loved you with all my heart from that day on as well, which is something I venture you'll just have to put up with. A lucky thing he took his leave outside and can't hear what I'm saying here . . . ."

Lorenzen smiled.

"Otherwise these confessions would have been forbidden. But since they've now been made, and one never knows when and how

224

we'll meet again, let me go on with them. Woldemar told me — you'll pardon me for my indiscretion — about your being carried away for Jenny Lind. We all sat up and took notice at that, almost envying you in fact. There's nothing more enviable than a soul that can be carried away for something. Being carried away like that is like flying, a divine uplifting motion towards the heavens."

Lorenzen was startled. Here was more than merely a charming and polite high-society woman.

"And to make a long story short," continued Melusine, "Woldemar spoke on that occasion as if he were talking about your first love." As she continued, she pointed smilingly to the small portrait of Jenny Lind. "But he also spoke of your last — no, no, not your last, *you* will always find a new one. Well then, he spoke about your being carried away for that wonderful man way down there on the Tajo, about your enthusiasm for Joao de Deus. And after he had told us everything, all of us who were present rallied around this '*un santo*' and made a secret covenant. Firstly, around the '*un santo*' and secondly around you yourself. And now I ask you, do you want to join with us in this covenant of ours, which wouldn't even exist were it not for you? Many a thing has gone wrong for me. But I believe, I am close to the day that will enable me to sense that our trials are also our blessings, and that all of my suffering came about merely that I might more firmly take hold of the staff which bears and supports us. I'm sorry to say I can't add that this staff is the cross, although it's possible that someday it might grow into it. My whole nature is that of an unbeliever. But just the same, I hope I might venture to say: I am at least humble."

"At least humble," repeated Lorenzen slowly, at the same time staring straight ahead half embarrassedly. And Melusine, perceiving with a sharp ear the doubts expressed rather clearly by the repetition of these words, continued in a suddenly altered and almost cheerful tone, "How cruel you are. But then you're right. Humble. And to think I go on praising myself for it besides! Who is humble? When you really get down to it, all of us are really the opposite. But one thing I can say, I have the desire to be."

"And even *that* counts, Your Ladyship. Except, it's got to be admitted, humility isn't enough. Of itself it achieves nothing, it accomplishes nothing outwardly. It scarcely even stimulates us."

"And yet at least it represents the first step to improvement, because it clears away egoism. Anyone who wants to work his way up the ranks, has to begin by serving at the bottom. And this much at least remains, within it is contained the solution to every question presently affecting the world. Being humble means being Christian,

Christian in my, I might perhaps even say, in *our* sense of the word. Humility shrinks from double standards. Whoever is humble is tolerant, because he knows how much he himself stands in need of tolerance. Whoever is humble sees the walls of separation crumble, and perceives the human factor in all of humanity."

"I can agree with you there," smiled Lorenzen. "But, if I read the expression on your face aright, Your Ladyship, these confessions are really only the introduction to something else. You're still holding back on the real thing and, as strange as it might sound, are combining something extraordinarily special and almost practical with your admission."

"And I'm pleased that you've sensed that. It's as you say. We've just come from your Stechlin, from your lake, the best thing you have here. I was against the ice being broken, because any form of intrusion or even merely looking in on whatever keeps itself hidden, frightens me. I respect what's been passed down to us. Along with it, of course, what is emerging too, because the very thing that's emerging will sooner or later itself be something passed down. We should love everything that's old, as far as it has a claim to our respect, but it's for the new that we should really and truly live. And above all, as the Stechlin teaches us, never should we forget the great interrelatedness of things. To cut one's self off is to wall one's self in, and to wall one's self in is death. It's vital that we keep *that* constantly in mind. My confidence in my brother-in-law is unlimited. He has a noble character, but I'm not sure if he has a firm character. He has a refined sensibility, and anyone who is refined, can often be manipulated. Moreover, he's not intellectually distinguished enough to be able to resist differing opinions, errors, or class prejudices. He needs support. It's you who have been this kind of support for my brother-in-law Woldemar from the days of his youth. And what I ask you now is, keep on with it in the future."

"If only I could tell you how joyfully I put myself at your service, my dearest Countess. And I can do so all the more easily since, as you know, your ideals are the same as mine. I live for them, and I feel it a gift of Providence to immerse myself wholly in the new where the old fails to measure up. And it's a new thing of that kind that's at stake here. Whether such a new thing should be — because it must be — or whether it should *not* be, that's the question around which everything revolves. Everywhere around us here there are a great number of excellent people, who in all seriousness believe, that whatever has been handed down to us ought to be defended like the temple of Solomon — above all whatever has to do with the church, but not, unfortunately, with what is truly Christian. In our upper classes,

226

moreover, there prevails a naive tendency to consider everything 'Prussian' to be a higher cultural form."

"It's precisely as you say. And yet to give it its due, permit me to ask if this naive belief doesn't have a certain justification?"

"At one time it did. But that's in the past. And that can't be changed. The primary difference between everything that is modern and the old lies in the fact that people are no longer put in their accorded places by virtue of their birth. They now have the freedom to put their capabilities to use in every direction and in every field. Time was, when people were lords of the manor or linen weavers for three-hundred years. Now any linen weaver has the chance to be the lord of the manor some day."

"And practically the reverse," laughed Melusine. "But let's put that rather delicate topic aside. I'd much, much rather hear what you have to say regarding the value of our way of life and our social forms, about our way of viewing things in general, the permissibility of which, as it seems to me, you so emphatically place in doubt."

"Not absolutely. If I do doubt, my doubts are directed not so much at the things in themselves, as at the huge measure of faith that is placed in them. That all these mediocre things are viewed as something special and superior, and therefore as something, if can be, to be preserved for all time, that's what's bad about it all. What once had validity, should go on being valid, what once was good, should go on being good or even be the best. But that's impossible, even if all those things, which is by no means the case, either, really did measure up to an ideal concept of power and glory . . . ."

"We've had, when we look back on it, three great epochs. That's something we have to keep in mind. The greatest, perhaps, and at the same time the first, was the one we had under the Soldier King. There was a man who can't be praised enough; marvelously suited to his times, and at the same time ahead of them. He not only stabilized the kingdom, but what's even far more important, he created the foundations for a new era, and in place of disorderliness, and self-serving individualism and capricious despotism, he set up order and justice. Justice, there was his best '*rocher de bronce*'."[12]

"And then?"

"And then came epoch number two. After the first, it was not very long in coming, and this country of ours, so completely without brilliance in its nature and history, suddenly found itself illuminated by the lightning of true genius."

"That must have elicited quite a bit of amazement."

"Indeed it did. But more in the world outside than at home. Admiration is an art too, you know. It takes a certain something to recognize greatness for what it is . . . . And then came the third era. Not great, but yet rather great after all. That was when this poor, miserable land, that had half fallen into ruin, was lit through, not by genius, but instead by enthusiasm, by faith in the higher power of the spirit, of knowledge, and freedom."

"Good, Lorenzen. But do go on."

"And all of what I've just recounted covered a century in time. We were ahead of the others in those days, now and then on an intellectual plane and morally for sure. But our *Non-soli-cedo* eagle,[13] with its bundle of lightning bolts in its claws, doesn't make lightning any more, and the enthusiasm is dead. A retrograde motion has taken over; something long since dead and buried, I've got to say it again, is supposed to bloom anew. But it won't.

"In a certain sense, of course, everything does return, but with returns of that sort millennia are passed over; the Roman imperial ages, good or bad, those we can have back again, but not that bamboo cane from Friedrich Wilhelm's 'tobacco cabinet.' Not even the walking stick of Sanssouci. That sort of thing is all over and done with. And a good thing it is. What was once progress has long since become just the opposite. The old-fashioned battles with all their battalions — even though they still keep on multiplying — they're disappearing from modern history. From real history, I mean, the kind that's worth reading about. And if they themselves aren't disappearing, interest in them is in any case. And along with interest, prestige. In their place it's inventors and discoverers, and James Watt and Siemens mean more to us than du Guesclin and Bayard. Heroism hasn't exactly run its course yet, and it won't have run its course for a long time yet, but it has already passed its own particular high point. Yet instead of coming to terms with this fact, our regime keeps trying to revive artificially something completely on the decline."

"Things are as you say. But against whom is it directed? You spoke of a 'regime.' Who is this regime? A person, or a thing? Is it the machine that's been taken over from the old times, with its cogs and gears clacking along as if dead, or is it *he*, who is standing at the machine? Or in the end, is it a certain clearly defined group, who are striving to control, to direct the hand of the man at the machine? In everything you're saying there resounds a rebellious voice. Are you against the aristocracy? Against the 'old families?'"

"First off, no. I love the old families, and I've got good cause to do so. And I'd almost like to believe everybody loves them. The old families are still popular, even today. But they are wasting and throwing away this empathy, which everybody has need of, every individual and every caste. Our old families are afflicted through and through with the misconception that 'things can't go on without them.' But nothing is further from the truth because things surely will go on without them. They're no longer the pillars holding everything up, they're the old stone and moss roof that still goes on straining and pushing down on things, but can't offer protection against storms any longer.

"It's well possible that the days of the aristocracy may come back again some day, but right now wherever we look, the sign of these times is a democratic world view. A new age is dawning. I believe a better and a happier one. But even if it's not a happier one, at least it's an age with more oxygen in the air, an age where we can breathe better. And the more freely one can breathe, the more one lives. As far as Woldemar goes, *of me* you can be sure, Your Ladyship. Leaving, of course, as a main factor, the Comtesse. For *her* it's *you* who's got to stand surety. After all, it's women who determine everything."

"That's what everyone says. And we're vain enough to believe it. But that leads us to completely new realms. For the time being, your hand to seal the bargain. And now, after this revolutionary discourse of ours, permit me to make my way back to the cottages of peaceful folk. I only took a half hour's leave from the old gentleman and I'm counting on the fact that you will accompany me, if not as far as the 'museum' itself — which according to the program is supposed to be visited — at least as far as the castle ramp."

30

Lorenzen did as was wished of him, and on the way to the manor house both of them continued to chat, even if about much different things.

"What is it actually about this 'museum?'" asked Melusine. "I can scarcely picture anything in particular to myself by it. An old cardboard sign with an inscription hangs there crookedly over the door. And the whole thing is just next to my bedroom. I was a bit afraid of it all."

"No need to be, my dear Countess. That primitive cardboard sign, which I must admit, does look odd enough, is more or less just intended to suggest that whole thing's more a kind of joke than anything really serious. A bit like collections of meerschaum pipes or snuff boxes. And it's primarily rarities of that sort you'll run across. On the other hand, though, it's really a true historical museum, despite the fact that it has only turned out to be half of what Herr von Stechlin was initially after."

"Which was?"

"Which was something more grotesque. It must well be twenty years ago now since he read in the newspaper one day about an Englishman who collected historical doors, and who for an enormous sum, I do believe it was twenty thousand pounds, had just recently acquired the prison door through which Louis XVI and later Danton and Robespierre had been led off to be guillotined. This notice made such an impression on our dear old Stechlin lord of the manor, that he decided to set up a historical collection of doors just like it too. He didn't get very far with it though, and had to be satisfied with the window from Küstrin Castle at which Crown Prince Friedrich stood when they led Katte by on the way to being decapitated.[14] But even that is uncertain, the fact is, most folks don't believe a thing about it. It's only Krippenstapel who holds firmly to it."

"Krippenstapel?"

"Yes. I see the name astonishes you. As a matter of fact, that's our teacher here. A favorite of the old master, and his advisor in that sort of thing. It was he who put the present 'museum' together, something one might view as a down payment on the 'historical doors.' Besides that somewhat dubious window Your Ladyship will find a few fantastic rain troughs and above all quite a few weather vanes taken down from old markish church towers. A few of them are supposed to be quite interesting. I don't have any feeling for things like that. But Krippenstapel has prepared a catalog."

As they continued their discussion, the two of them had reached the ramp on which Engelke stood awaiting the countess. Lorenzen took his leave. But Melusine did not wish to go upstairs to the museum immediately, preferring rather to enter the main salon and warm herself there. Engelke immediately saw to the fire, which suited the countess quite well, because she still had a few questions she wished to ask.

"That's good, Engelke, your putting on coals like that and a few pine cones too. I always like it when it burns so cheerfully like that. And it's probably cold up there in the 'museum.'"

"Aye, cold it is, Your Ladyship. But the cold, well, when you get right down to it, a body can stand that and all that dust up there, you can probably put up with that too. Dust keeps things warm. And those rain troughs and weather vanes won't hurt a soul . . . ."

"But whatever is there besides those?"

"Ah, I just mean them damned things, them spiders."

"Oh good heavens, spiders?" cried Melusine.

"Aye, spiders, Your Ladyship. But there ain't no real bad ones up there. That poisonous kind with a cross on their backs I ain't never seen around here. Just the kind they call daddy longlegs ."

"Oh, of course, those are the ones with the long legs."

"Aye, long legs they got. But they don't hurt anybody. Actually they're real timid creatures that go crawling off and hide when they hear the doors getting opened up. Only when Krippenstapel comes, then they all come out and look around. Krippenstapel, they know him real good, and now and then I've even seen him bring them some flies. Then they go right after them."

"Oh, but that's just horrible. Is he really a good person?"

"Oh, very good, Your Ladyship. And one time when I said something to him about it, he said, 'Well, Engelke, that's the way it goes, y'know, one fellow eats up the next one . . . . '"

Their conversation continued for a while until Melusine said, "Well then, Engelke, it looks like it's high time for the museum. Or else I'll arrive too late and not get to see or hear a thing. I'm nice and warm again now." And so she got up and ascended the stairs and knocked. She did not just want to walk right in.

In response to her knocking, the door was soon opened from within and Krippenstapel with his horn-rimmed glasses stood before her. He bowed and stepped back to make room, but Melusine, whose fear of him returned, hesitated for a moment, making for an embarrassed pause. In the meantime Dubslav too had approached. "I was afraid Lorenzen wouldn't give you up. His chances of having a conversation aren't very great here in Stechlin and then, on top of that, a conversation with Countess Melusine! Well, I see he was merciful. But now, Countess, have a look around, if you please. Maybe Lorenzen has already told you about the place or even Engelke."

"I'm not so completely in the dark any more; a Küstrin Castle window, a few church roof relics and along with those, some weather vanes — all objects for which you have my congratulations. Because, you know, I'm sort of in favor of the unusual too."

"For which I'm most grateful to Your Ladyship, without being particularly surprised. I knew that ladies such as the Countess Ghiberti have a feeling for things of this sort. Might I first off show you this bishop from Lebus, by the way, and over here a saint or perhaps an anchorite? The two of them, the bishop and the anchorite are quite dissimilar, especially in regard to girth — the true polarity between the refectory and the desert. When I take a look at this saint here, I'd figure him for having eaten no more than a single date per day at the most. And now, I think, we'll continue our tour. As a matter of fact, Krippenstapel was just in the process of showing Comtesse Armgard our Derfflinger dragoon with his little standard and the date 1675. If you please, Countess Melusine, just take note of the number here right under the Brandenburg eagle. It's got the effect as if he wanted

231

to bring the news of the victory at Fehrbellin. That it's a dragoon is clear; that broad-brimmed felt hat overcomes any doubt. I've taken it as my own right to consider him a Derfflinger dragoon. But my friend Krippenstapel doesn't believe a word of it, and we've been involved in a serious feud about it for years now. Fortunately, our only one. Right, Krippenstapel?"

The latter smiled and bowed.

"Our two ladies," continued Dubslav, "ought not perhaps believe, however, that I consider myself justified in putting unrestricted scientific research in irons right here in my museum. Exactly the opposite. Thus I can but repeat, 'Krippenstapel, the floor is yours.' Now then, if you please, explain to these two ladies your own opinion as to why, given certain very specific accompanying characteristics, this can *not* be a Derfflinger dragoon. Picture books from the age aren't to be had, and all those big tapestries leave you in the lurch and don't prove a thing."

As Dubslav spoke, Krippenstapel had once again taken the weather vane forming the object of contention in his hand. As he saw that the Countess nodded to him in a friendly way — as was her nature she had long since taken the 'fly-killer' she had but ten minutes ago so feared into her heart — the assertion of his point of view was not long in coming. "You see, Your Ladyship, this argument has been in the air for as long as we've had the dragoon, and Herr von Stechlin would have long since gone over to the opposing camp, in which I and Senior Teacher Tucheband stand, if he did not get constant pleasure from my scientific enthusiasm. Tucheband, one of our best and a man who does not easily miss the mark, hit it right off correctly in this question as well. As a matter of fact he took into consideration the place from which this weather vane originates. It comes from the village of Zellin in the Neumark, which in those days at least still belonged to the old Mörner family. Now the regiment which distinguished itself above all others at Fehrbellin was Mörner's Dragoon Regiment. Therefore, it's not a Derfflinger dragoon, it's a Mörner, who in great haste is bringing the news of the victory that's been won to Zellin."

"Bravo," said Melusine. "If ever I've heard a correct inference — most of them are fakes — we've got one here. Herr von Stechlin, I can't help you out. You've been defeated."

Dubslav agreed and kissed Melusine's hand, without in the least concerning himself about the disapproving glances cast by his sister, who for her part insisted they finally get around to displaying the two mills, her favorite pieces. These two mills, she assured them, were the only things in sight which could in any way justify the term 'museum.'

Indeed that was almost the case, as even Krippenstapel admitted, despite the fact that at least until quite recently nothing in the way of historical controversy — which, after all, was always the main thing — had been associated with them. Recently, to be sure, that had changed. Two Berliners, gentlemen from the Trade Museum, had gotten into an argument about the mills, specifically about their place of origin. To be sure, at the outset they had agreed that the water mill was Dutch, whereas the windmill, a regular old-fashioned German platform mill, was a Nuremberg piece; Krippenstapel, however, had merely smiled at this peace treaty. He was far too much the serious man of science not to be able to sense to what extent this so-called 'attribution' was nothing but a cover up. The outbreak of new disputations was near at hand.

These were, however, out of the question for the time being, since both sisters, Armgard as well as Melusine — like children with a favorite toy — were completely wrapped up sheer pleasure. The windmill clattered so much that it was a joy, and the wheel of the water mill, when it sparkled in the sun, gave off such a silvery reflection that it looked as if glistening water really were passing over the paddle blades. All was seen and admired, and what was not seen was accepted on faith. Nary a single spider put in its appearance, merely long gray webs hanging here and there, which, however, only seemed to add a certain solemnity. And so by the time noon had arrived they left the 'museum,' first to rest for an hour, and then to assemble together again at table. The Countess, however, before leaving the huge and chaotic room, approached Krippenstapel once more, and with a winning smile requested of him, that as soon as any relatively serious dispute regarding the two mills should flare up, he would not withhold any of the documents involved from her.

Krippenstapel promised all.

The midday meal was set for three. Lorenzen appeared a quarter hour before, however, encountering old Dubslav in a particularly stately mode of attire or, as he himself had described it to Engelke, "decked out really feudally."

"Ah, that's fine, Lorenzen, you're being here so soon. I've still got all sorts of things on my mind. We've got to do something, a regular formal welcoming ceremony. That business last evening was too little, you know. Or else maybe some sort of solemn farewell, in short, something or other that belongs in the realm of toasts. And that's where you've got to help out. You're an expert in this sort of thing.

After all, anybody who's capable of preaching every Sunday, ought to be able to give an after-dinner speech too."

"That's easy for you to say, Herr von Stechlin. Now and then an after-dinner speech is easy and it's a sermon that's hard. But it can be the other way around as well. And besides, once you just get your mind used to the idea that it has to be, it will all come off just fine. You'll see. As always, it's the heart that makes the speaker. And then these ladies, the two of them with such rare amiability and charm. And when it comes to the Countess . . . ."

"You're right there," laughed the old man, "when it comes to the Countess . . . . You're making it easy for yourself, Pastor. The Countess — if it were just a matter of her, maybe even I could pull it off. But the Comtesse, she's got something so serious about her. And then to top it off, she's my daughter-in-law besides, or at least she's supposed to become that, and so I've got to talk like a real person of standing. And that's difficult, maybe because in my imagination the Countess always seems to take precedence over the Comtesse."

Dubslav continued in this vein but it helped him not a wit. Lorenzen was not to be shaken in his resistance. And thus approached the lunch hour and with it also the anxiously awaited moment in which the speech had to be made. The oldster had reconciled himself to it after all. "My dear guests," he began, "dearest bride-to-be, most honored sister of the bride! Another word which might designate my relationship to Countess Melusine is, for the time being, not to be had in our German language. A thing I deeply regret. Because that expression is a long way from saying enough for me.

"It has only been a few hours, ladies, since I was able to welcome you at this spot, not even a full day, and parting is now upon us. In that time I have not proposed the use of the intimate pronoun *Du*, but it's in the air, and even more so on my lips . . . .

"Dearest Armgard, it looks like this old Stechlin House is to become your future home. You'll bring new life into it. Under my regime there wasn't much of that. Not even today either. I only have a clear conscience for having shown you everything that could be shown during this brief span of time, my museum and my lake. The spouting place has kept its silence, the hand of winter lay upon it. But my Derfflinger dragoon — in Krippenstapel's absence I can call him that again, you know — he spoke all the more clearly to you in its place. The year 1675 is on his standard and he's spreading the victorious news of Fehrbellin throughout our Brandenburg countryside. If I live to see it, and Krippenstapel lets me, sooner or later for my part I too will be putting a dragoon on my little turret — don't have a regular tower — and as a matter of fact a dragoon from the Regiment of the Queen of Great Britain and Ireland. And he too will be carrying the news of victory throughout the countryside. Not of Königgrätz and not of Mars-la-Tour,[15] but of a victory every bit as weighty. Long live the House of Barby and my dear daughter-in-law Armgard!"

Everyone was moved. Lorenzen most of all. As he approached the old man, he whispered, "D'you see. I knew it." Armgard kissed the old man's hand and Melusine was radiant. "Ah yes, the old guard!" she remarked. Sister Adelheid alone could not bring herself to feel particularly at home amidst such general rejoicing. All festive events simply had to be kept within the bounds prescribed by her. It was the regional trait she had which held: "Be sure there's never too much of anything, least of all homage. Or even adulation."

When they were again seated, Melusine remarked, "Krippenstapel will be disgruntled when he hears about your toast, by the way. It was, after all, actually a renewed solemn proclamation of the Derfflinger point of view. And whatever is said on occasions like this, becomes valid . . . . Incidentally, is there anybody else interested in this museum of yours?"

"Some expert now and then. Otherwise nobody."

"Which you find irritating."

"No, Your Ladyship. Not in the least. I take very few things seriously and least of all do I take my museum serious. It started with me, that's true enough, and kept me interested for a while too. Afterwards though, everything actually went right on without me. That's more or less the rule. Whenever some sort of a beginning's made, things run on of themselves. But people don't let you loose again, they hold on to you, whether you want or not. I'd have perhaps long since given it all up again, but nobody will let me. It offers some folks the satisfaction of being able to consider me a bit of an odd fellow, and others talk of at least fishing around for a certain originality. You've just got to put up with all sorts of things."

31

At five o'clock Woldemar and the Barby ladies started out so as not to miss the train which passed through Gransee at seven. It was already growing dark, but the snow provided a glimmer of light. Thus they drove over the timbered bridge and down the chestnut-lined road with its bare and ice-covered branches.

Lorenzen had stayed on at the castle and, to get warm again — it had been cold and drafty on the ramp — seated himself in the vicinity of the fireplace, directly across from old Dubslav. The latter had lit his meerschaum and looked comfortably into the flames. But he remained uncharacteristically silent precisely because a third person was present, who quite obviously wished to hear nothing with regard to the charming young women, about whom in his soul he so urgently desired to vent his feelings. This third person was, of course, Aunt Adelheid. *She* did not wish to talk. On the other hand some sort of attempt at conversation had to be made. Thus Dubslav reached out to the Gundermanns, to briefly express his regret that he had not been able to include his neighbors from Siebenmühlen. "Engelke had been so against it."

All of these regrets — as, considering the situation, could not be otherwise — came out lukewarmly enough. But the Domina was out of sorts to such an extent that even such half-hearted remarks, merely gently touching, and indeed only casually brushing the realm of cordiality, were enough to set her off. "Oh, for heaven's sake, forget about that woman. Born nothing but a Helfrich," she said. "The daughter of some old captain, who's supposed to have won the Battle of Leipzig. At least that's the story she's always telling. Horrible woman. Doesn't fit in with our kind at all. And such a loudmouth in the bargain. I can't abide it that we're always being forced to be looking at the higher-ups that way, but this Helfrich woman, I have to say it, she's not to my taste after all either. As far as I go, keeping to your own kind is the only right thing to do. Modest in your circumstances, but lines clearly drawn."

Lorenzen took care not to contradict her, attempting rather, by partially agreeing with Adelheid and her tone, to reestablish a better mood. Seeing that he was unsuccessful, however, he got up and took his leave.

And now the old brother and sister were alone.

Dubslav paced restlessly back and forth, only now and then approaching the table on which the liqueur bottles still stood, left over from coffee. He wanted to say something, but did not quite dare. Not until he had had two Curaçaos and a Benedictine for good measure, did he finally turn to his sister, who as silent as he himself, pulled her golden chain back and forth.

"Yes indeed," he said, "they're probably in Woltersdorf by now, I imagine."

"I suspect even further than that. Naturally Woldemar will let the horses run. They are, I imagine, ladies who don't much care to ride slowly."

"You say that as if you're looking to find fault, Adelheid. As if the ladies hadn't particularly pleased you in general. I'm sorry you feel that way. I'm extremely pleased with the match. Of course, the

Countess as well as the Comtesse are pampered, one can see that. But I might even say, the more pampered they are . . . ."

"The better they please you. That's just like you. I prefer our kind of people. After all, the two of them are practically foreigners."

"Well, that's not so bad."

"On the contrary. I dislike anything foreign. Just let me tell you a little story. I was in Berlin last summer with Schmargendorf and went to Josty's, because Schmargendorf, who loves that sort of thing, wanted a cup of chocolate."

"You too, I hope."

"Certainly, I do too. But I never got in the swing of it. Just sipped at it because I found myself getting so terribly worked up. Right there at the next table were sitting a man and a lady, if she actually was a lady, that is. But they were English. He was all done up in flannel with his breeches rolled up, and the woman was wearing a skirt and a blouse and a sailor hat. And the man had a greyhound that was constantly shivering, even though it was eighty degrees."

"Well, why not?"

"And between the two of them was a tray with water and cognac. And what's worse, that woman sat there holding a cigarette between her fingers, watching the smoke rings she was blowing."

"Charming. Must have made a really delightful picture."

"And I'll stake my last pfennig on it, this Melusine smokes too."

"Well why shouldn't she? You slaughter geese. Why shouldn't Melusine smoke?"

"Because smoking's for men."

"And slaughtering's for women . . . . Good Lord, Adelheid we'll never be able to agree on something like that. They say I'm moderately old-fashioned, but you, why, you're downright petrified."

"I do not understand that word, and only hope that it means something you don't have to be ashamed of. It sounds strange enough to me. But I know you just love things like that and, because you picture all sorts of things when you think of it, you certainly also love that name Melusine."

"I could just about say so."

"Just what I thought."

"Oh yes, Sister, it's easy for you to talk. Not everybody has it as good as you. Adelheid! There's a name that always fits in. And in the church records, as Lorenzen showed me just the other day, it even appears as Adelheide. With the rotten management in our house, that final -e just managed to get lost along the way. The Stechlins have always squandered everything."

"I beg you, chose some other words, if you please."

237

"Why? Squander is a perfectly good word. And besides, even old Kortschädel once told me, you shouldn't be so strict with words and especially not with names. There's many a fellow sits in a glass house. Do you think Pension Director Fix is such a nice name? And when I was still with the cuirassiers in Brandenburg, in my last year of service, right next to us we had a little man from the fire insurance company, name of Paperweight. Just think, Adelheid, if I had dealt with that fellow the way you just did with Countess Melusine, I'd have had to imagine the fellow as half a shell cap or a bullet man. Because back then, in sixty-four it was, all the paper weights were nothing but 'bullet men.' A musket ball up top and two musket balls at the bottom. And naturally a cartridge case for a belly in the middle. But that little fire insurance fellow who by chance had such a funny name, thin as a rail he was."

"Fine, Dubslav. What's all this supposed to be mean? You're giving your little birdie a nice piece of sugar for a change. I say little birdie because I don't want to get insulting."

"Kiss your hand, Madame."

"And what I have to say regarding the matter at hand is just this: I haven't got a thing against somebody being named Paperweight, and it's up to him if he wants to be a bullet man or a rail. But I've got plenty against Melusine. Paperweight, well, that's just a pure accident. But Melusine that's no accident, and the only thing I can say to you is that this Melusine is a true blue Melusine. Everything about this creature . . . ."

"Now wait just a minute, Adelheid . . . ."

"Everything about this lady, if you insist that's what she's supposed to be, is seductive. Never in my life have I ever seen such coquettishness. And then when I think of our poor Woldemar next to her. Against a Delilah like that he's lost from the very beginning. Before he even knows what's going on he's entangled, despite the fact that he's only her brother-in-law. Or maybe just because of it. And that eternal back and forth with her hips. It all goes to prove that there's some truth to that business about the serpent after all. And then the way she carried on with Lorenzen! But then, if it's possible, he's even easier to catch than Woldemar. He constantly looked at her as if she were a revelation. And she is something like that too. No doubt about it. But of what?"

Wedding

32

THE TRAVELERS WERE back in Berlin in good time. Woldemar had accompanied his fiancee and prospective sister-in-law to the Kronprinzenufer, but was forced to forgo staying at the Barby house because of a small celebration at the officer's club he wished to attend.

As the cab stopped, the old count was slowly and painfully pacing back and forth on the rug of his room. As usual when the weather turned, his foot once again tortured him with a relatively painful attack of neuralgia.

"Well then, here you are back again. The train must have been late. And where is Woldemar?"

They informed him of everything and that Woldemar sent his apologies for failing to appear. "Fine, fine. And now sit down and tell me everything. In the case of the Comte, back in those days a great deal was left to be desired . . . forgive me, Melusine. But as you can well imagine, I'd like to see that things go better this time. Woldemar doesn't give me any real concern, of course, but the family, old Herr von Stechlin. Of course, it's taken for granted that Armgard doesn't have to respond to such a delicate question, if she doesn't want to, although as a matter of experience there is a difference between mothers-in-law and fathers-in-law. The latter are sometimes more obliging than the son."

Armgard laughed. "Something as nice as that doesn't happen to me, Papa. But with Melusine, it was the same old story again. The elder Stechlin started off and the pastor followed. Or at least, so it seemed to me."

"Then I'm reassured, presuming that Melusine doesn't forget her real father because of her new father-in-law."

She went up to him and kissed his hand.

"Then I'm reassured," repeated the old man. "Melusine almost always pleases. But it's true enough, there are some whom she doesn't please. There are so many people who have a natural aversion to anything pleasant because they themselves are so unpleasant. All of those narrow-minded and puffed-up individuals, all of those who have a bigoted view of Christianity — the real thing has quite a different look to it — all the Pharisees and pretentious types, the self-satisfied and the vain, all of them feel themselves personally offended and insulted by persons like Melusine. And if old Stechlin has fallen in love with Melusine, then I love him myself already for that very reason, because plain and simple, he is a good person. I don't need to know any more about him. And what else could you expect anyway? The apple doesn't fall far from the tree, and the reverse holds just as well, if I know the apple, I know the tree too . . . . And who else was there? Relatives, I mean."

"Only Aunt Adelheid from Wutz Convent," said Armgard.

"That's the old fellow's sister?"

"Yes, Papa. His older sister. Probably ten years older and only his half-sister besides. And a Domina."

"Very pious?"

"I wouldn't say that."

"You're so closed mouth. It doesn't look as if she particularly appealed to you."

Armgard remained silent.

"Well then, Melusine, you say something. Not so pious then, that's all right too. But *hautaine* perhaps?"

"One could almost say that," answered Melusine. "But that doesn't quite fit either, simply because it's a French word. And Aunt Adelheid is eminently unfrench."

"Ah, I see. The comical sort then."

"Not quite that, either, Papa. Let's just say, backward, antediluvian."

The old Count laughed. "Ah yes, it's like that in all the old families, above all among the rich and upper-class Jews. Familiar with that from Vienna, where you can really study questions of that sort. I once frequented a large banker's house in which there wasn't merely a lot of splendor, but a lot of medals and uniforms besides. Practically too much of it all. But all at once over there in a corner — completely alone and yet almost perfectly satisfied he was — I ran across a remarkably ancient old fellow, who looked just like old Gobbo, that one who appears in one of Shakespeare's plays. And when I later asked a dinner companion, who it was, I was informed, 'Oh, that's just Uncle Manasses.' You find Uncle Manasses like that everywhere, and given the right circumstances, they can even be named 'Aunt Adelheid.'"

That the old count took it all so lightly visibly pleased his daughters, and when Jeserich soon thereafter brought in the tea, Armgard too became more talkative, relating first about Superintendent Koseleger and Pastor Lorenzen and afterwards about Lake Stechlin, which had been so completely frozen over that they had not been able to see the famous spot, and finally about the museum and the weather vanes.

It was the latter which interested the old count most. "Weather vanes. Exactly. They've got to be collected, not just old dragoons cut out of tin, but the most up-to-date silhouettes too, let's say from the diplomats' lodge. We'd be able to put together quite a pretty little gallery there. And do you know, children, it's that business of the museum that only now gives me a real idea of the old fellow along with a feeling of complete satisfaction, almost more than the fact that he liked Melusine. I'm usually not much for collectors. But somebody who collects weather vanes, that really does tell you something; he's not simply a good person but a clever one besides. Because there's something implicit in that sort of thing, something like snapping your fingers at society. And any fellow who can do a thing like that is my man. That's the sort of fellow I can live with."

They did not remain together much longer. Both sisters, relatively wearied from the day's exertions, retired early. Their conversation regarding Stechlin Castle and the two clergymen, however, and above all about the Domina, against whom Melusine violently railed out, continued in their bedroom.

"I do believe," said Armgard, "you're putting too much weight on what you call the aesthetic factor. And unfortunately Woldemar does the same. Generally he won't let a word be said against his Mark Brandenburg. But on this point he talks almost exactly as you. Wherever he looks he finds the element of beauty missing. The slightest little thing that somehow resembles it — or so he constantly complains — is nothing but an imitation. On its own nothing of that sort is capable of being born here."

"And the fact that he complains about that very thing is what I more or less treasure about him most. You think when I talk of the Domina, I place too much weight on things of this sort, which, after all, are nothing but externalities. But believe me, things of that sort are not just externalities. Anyone without finer sensibilities, be it in art or in life, such an individual simply doesn't exist for me, and when it comes to my friendship and love, with absolute certainty. There you have my program. Our entire social order, which thinks wonders of how high and mighty it is, is more or less barbarism; Lorenzen, of whom you actually think so highly, made himself absolutely clear to me in the same way. Oh, how much further ahead of us were those pagan times we so uncomprehendingly find fault with these days! And

241

as far as beauty goes, even our 'dark ages' stood higher than we do, and those executioners' stakes of theirs, as long as it wasn't you who was scheduled to be next on them, they weren't half so terrible."

"I'll yet live to see the day," laughed Armgard, "when you'll start preaching a new Crusade or something of that sort. But we've completely gotten away from our real topic, the Domina. You said her feelings were in contradiction with each other. What feelings?"

"That's easy to answer. First off, she congratulates herself on herself, then afterwards she gets angry with herself about herself. And that she had to do *that* is our fault, and she can't forgive us for it."

"I might agree perhaps, if what you're saying there didn't sound so vain . . . . I'd say, she has quite a good mind."

"That she does. For sure. They all do here, or at least most of them. But a good mind, as much as that is, is on the other hand very little, and when you get right down to it — unfortunately, I've got to use a Berlin way of putting it — this good old Domina is really nothing more than a 'fence post,' tall and pointed. And not even painted green."

"And the old fellow? *He*, at least, will stand up to your criticism."

"Oh, him, he's beyond compare, *hors concours* as they say, and even surpasses Woldemar. What would you say if I were to marry the old fellow?"

"Don't talk like that, Melusine. I know perfectly well how you mean it all. It's that high spirited way of yours again and again. But, you know, when you think about it, he really isn't all that old yet. And you, as much as I do love you, when it comes right down to it, in the end you would actually be capable of falling in love with that sort of complication, such as father-in-law and brother-in-law all in one, and if it were at all possible, all sorts of other things besides."

"At least more than in the fellow who presents these complications or might even bring them about . . . . Well then, 'be still, thou friendly element.'"

33

That was in the closing days of December. The young couple's wedding had been set for the end of February. In the intervening period, however, the old count pondered as to whether the ceremony should not perhaps be held on one of the Barby estates after all. The bride herself, however, was against it, protesting with a liveliness not usually customary to her, that she bore a particular fondness for the army, for which reason — not even taking her dear Pastor Frommel into consideration — she by far preferred the Berlin Garrison Church. That

242

in the eyes of many the latter was nothing more than a huge barn made no difference. When it came to the Garrison Church, what mattered so much to her were its grand memories. A house of God in which the Schwerins and the Zietens had once stood, and if not actually they, others who were scarcely less, a place of such historical significance would be far more preferable to her on her wedding day than the family church, the coffins of so many Barbys under the altar notwithstanding.

Woldemar was extremely pleased to find such a Prussian military streak in his fiancee, who also, one time when the future was being discussed and therefore the question of staying or not staying in the army, had laughingly responded, "No Woldemar, no retiring just yet. I'm all for freedom, but I think I'm almost even more for your making Major."

The wedding was set for three o'clock The bridal coach had appeared nearly half an hour before and stopped in front of the Schickedanz residence. Decorating its vestibule had been a pleasure the Frau Insurance Secretary would not let herself be denied. From the stairs out to the sidewalk, flower stands had been set on both sides. On them, in such abundance and beauty as if it were a May flower exhibit being held, stood Frau Schickedanz's favorites. Behind the various levels, however, all the residents of the house had taken up position, Lizzi, Frau Imme, and the entire Hartwig clan, naturally Hedwig too, who after a brief period of service in the house of Commercial Councilor Seligmann had about a week before again given up her job.

"Good God, Hedwig. Was it the same old thing again?"

"Oh no, Frau Imme. This time it was even more."

Frommel conducted the ceremony. The church was densely crowded, including the merely curious who, before the great organ started to play, had the most remarkable things to inform one another. The Barbys were actually supposed to be Italians from the area around Naples and the old count was said to have been a member of the secret society of the Carbonari in younger days, something you could see just by looking at him even yet. But then just like that he had switched sides and betrayed his sacred cause. And since in cases of that sort someone was always chosen by lot to see that justice was carried out, which, of course, the count knew perfectly well too, he had cautiously left his beautiful homeland and come to Berlin, where he had even made his way to the court. And Friedrich Wilhelm IV, who had taken a tremendous liking to him, had always spoken Italian with him.

The wedding banquet took place at the Barby residence, necessarily *en petit comité*, since even with the most skillful arrangement the large-sized middle room could hold only about twenty persons at best. By far the greater part of the group was made up of persons known to us already, at the top of the list, of course, the elder Stechlin himself. He had been happy to come despite the fact that the isolated way in which he lived had initially made the decision more difficult. Aunt Adelheid was absent. "I suppose we'll just have to console ourselves," said Melusine — with a touch of haughtiness well suited to her.

Obviously the Berchtesgadens were there, and the same held for Rex and Czako as well as Cujacius and Wrschowitz. Besides them was a young Baron von Planta, a nephew of the deceased countess, only recently moved to Berlin for the purpose of concluding his agricultural studies. Initially a First Lieutenant Szilagy, a friend and former regimental comrade of Woldemar, had joined company with him, followed later by a certain Doctor Pusch — well known to the Barbys since their London days. Across from the bride and groom sat the two fathers, or fathers-in-law, respectively. Since neither the one nor the other could be reckoned among the orators, it was Frommel who raised his glass to the young couple in a toast in which earnestness and wit, Christian values and good humor were mixed in happy proportions.

Everyone was delighted, old Stechlin, Frommel's table companion, most of all. The two gentlemen had become friends beforehand and following the completion of the official toast, when the table talk passed over into conversation with one's neighbor, Frommel and the elder Stechlin saw themselves no longer prevented from engaging in a more intimate private discussion.

"Your son," said Frommel, "as I was personally able to discover, has quite an attractive place. Might I conclude from that you've taken quarters with him?"

"No, Herr Court Preacher. Living with children that way is always a problem. And my son knows that too; he knows his father's tastes, or, if you will, his little idiosyncrasies. And so, as has always been the best thing, he's set me up in a hotel."

"And you're satisfied there?"

"To the fullest, even though it is a bit too fancy for me. I'm still a relic left over from the days of the Hôtel de Brandenbourg, where only the Frenchified atmosphere used to irritate me. Everything else was splendid. But hotels like that — since we've been blessed with Kaiser and Reich — well, they've become more or less old-fashioned, and as a result my son's set me up in the Hotel Bristol. Everything top notch, no doubt about it. And what's more, the mere name itself is enough to give me a chuckle. These days it as good as knocks any competition right out of the field. Back when I was still a Lieutenant, a long time ago I've got to admit, back in those days all the Berlin jokes had to be by Glassbrenner or Beckmann. Beckmann was the top comedian and whenever people got together and somebody would say, 'and did you hear this one from Beckmann? . . . ' we all more or less knew just what was coming. And the way it used to be with jokes in those days, is the way it is nowadays with hotels. They've all got to be named 'Bristol.' I've been racking my brains trying to figure out how of all places Bristol got to be so important. After all, when you think about it, Bristol isn't anything but a second class resort. But Hotel Bristol is always tops. Do you think there have been any people around here who've ever even seen Bristol? Not many, that's for sure. I'd say those ship's captains who sail between Bristol and New York are still pretty much rare birds in this good old Berlin of ours.

"Incidentally, with all due respect to my famous hotel, I dare say the ones that aren't so famous are usually more interesting anyhow. Those Bavarian inns in the mountains, for instance, where you've got a fat innkeeper's wife they say was once such a beauty that some emperor or king paid court to her. And then along with that, you've got trout and a gamekeeper who's just brought in a poacher or some vigilante fellow from the other side of their peaceful lake. It's places like that, there's where it's most beautiful. And if the lake gets riled up, it's even more beautiful.

"Our Baron Berchtesgaden, who's sitting right over there, would be glad to back me up on that for sure, and you, Herr Court Preacher, in the end you'll back me up as well. Because this very moment it occurs to me that you were always in Gastein with our dear old Kaiser Wilhelm, the last man who really was a good man in the truest sense of the word. And you were always right there at his side.

"Nowadays instead of a genuine good man, they've set up what they call the 'super-man.' But in actuality there really aren't anything but sub-men any more. And now and then they're the very ones they're trying so hard to make into a 'super.' I've read about people like that and even come across a few. Lucky that in my view of things they're always particularly comical types, or else you could give up in despair. And next to the likes of those, that old Wilhelm of ours! What was he like when he used to spend his summer days so quietly? Anything you can tell me about him? Something of the sort that one can really recognize him by right off?"

"I dare say I could, Herr von Stechlin. Experienced that very kind of thing with him, I did. Just a brief little story, but it's those that are always the very best. One time we had a really rainy day in Gastein. So bad the old gentleman wasn't able to get out in the fresh air, and instead of being outside in the mountains, he was forced to take his usual constitutional as well as could be managed in that gigantic living room of his. And on the floor underneath him, as he knew to be the case, lay a terribly sick man. And so, just imagine, as I enter the old Kaiser's room, I see him there pulling long runners and carpets together and laying them one on top of the other. And as he catches sight of my astonishment, with an indescribable and unforgettable smile, he says, 'After all, my dear Frommel, there's a sick man lying down there below me, and I wouldn't want him to get the feeling that I'm more or less trampling on his head up here . . . . ' Do you see, Herr von Stechlin, there you've have the old Kaiser."

Dubslav remained silent and nodded. "How I envy your having experienced something like that," he began after a while. "I knew him quite well too, that is in the days when he was still Prince Wilhelm. And then superficially later too. But his real time is his time as emperor after all."

"To be sure, Herr von Stechlin. As Schiller said, 'Man grows to match his higher purposes.'"

"Exactly, exactly," said Dubslav. "More or less just what I was thinking too. Just couldn't quite come up with it right off. Yes indeed, so he was, and we won't be getting the likes of him again. Incidentally, I say that with all due respect. I'm not one of those dissident fellows, you know. Dissidence is a regular horror to me and doesn't suit our kind. Just that now and then maybe it does after all."

In the meantime seven had come round, and at seven-thirty the train, in which the young couple planned to get as far as Dresden, that traditional first stop for every southern-bound honeymoon, was to leave. All rose from the table and while the ladies and gentlemen mingled among themselves and began to chat, Woldemar and Armgard withdrew without being noticed. Their baggage had been sent ahead an hour earlier and now the four-seated coach stopped before the Barby house. The baroness and Melusine had agreed between themselves to accompany the newlyweds and, without Woldemar or Armgard being able to prevent it, took the two back seats of the coach. That led, however, to a full-blown disagreement on the matter of rank and courtesy, particularly between the two sisters. "Of course, if we were heading for the church just now," said Armgard, "you'd be in the right. But now our coach has become just a plain old Landau again, and, four hours after the ceremony like this, Woldemar and I are simply two regular people again. And realizing a thing like that is something a person can't begin early enough."

"Armgard, you're just getting too clever for me," said Melusine.

In the end they came to an agreement, and when the coach arrived at the Anhalt Station, Rex and Czako were already there — each with a giant bouquet — withdrawing again immediately after the presentation of their flowers. Only the baroness and Melusine remained on the platform, waiting for the train's departure and chatting lively all the while. In the compartment the young couple had chosen were two other travelers; the first, a pleasant blond fellow wearing gold-rimmed spectacles, could only be from Saxony. The other, however, with a fur coat and a suitcase of Russian leather, was obviously an international type from the east or even from the southeast of Europe.

At last they heard the signal and the train began to move.

The baroness and Melusine continued to wave good-bye with their handkerchiefs. They then again entered the coach waiting outside. The weather was glorious, one of those early spring days that occasionally appear as early as February.

"It's so beautiful," said Melusine. "Let's put it to use. I think, my dear Baroness, we'll ride along the canal here and turn into the Tiergarten, and then past the restaurants at the Zelten landing as far as your apartment."

The ladies kept their silence for a while. The instant they turned off the bumpy cobble stones and on to the quiet asphalt roadway, however, the baroness remarked, "I really don't understand Stechlin's not having taken a separate compartment."

Melusine shook her head.

"That fellow with the gold-rimmed glasses," continued the baroness, "I don't take him so badly. A Saxon won't do anybody any harm and he's scarcely even an intrusion. But that other fellow with the Russian leather suitcase. He looked like a Russian, if not maybe even a Romanian. Poor Armgard. Now she's got her Woldemar and yet she doesn't either."

"Lucky for her."

"But Countess . . . ."

"I see you're astonished, my dear Baroness, to hear me say that. And yet it's only too true. Once bitten, twice shy."

"But Countess . . . ."

"I got married, as you know, in Florence and took the train to Venice on the very same evening. On one point Venice is exactly like Dresden, namely as the first stop after weddings. Ghiberti too — I still always prefer to say 'Ghiberti' rather than 'my husband.' 'My husband' really is such a horrible expression — well then, Ghiberti too had chosen Venice. And so as a result we had to pass through that big tunnel through the Apennines."

"I know, I know. Endless."

"Exactly, endless. Ah, my dear Baroness, if only someone had been with us, a Saxon or even a Romanian. But we were completely alone. And by the time I came out of that tunnel, I knew what sort of misery was in store for me."

"Dearest Melusine, how I feel for you. Really, dearest friend, truly and sincerely. A tunnel right off like that. Why it's almost like destiny, you know."

Rex and Czako had withdrawn from the station immediately after presenting their bouquets and headed for the Königgrätzerstraße. Having arrived there, Czako remarked, "If its all right with you, Rex, let's go on as far as the Restaurant Bellevue."

"Cup of coffee?"

"No, I'd really like to have something to eat. Three spoonfuls of soup, a trout *en miniature* and a chicken wing — that's too little for my condition. Truth be told, I'm hungry."

"Apparently you enjoyed yourself too much."

"No, not that either. Besides, a good conversation is filling enough, or at least for people like me, who, even if you do laugh when I say it, are more for things of the mind. And then again maybe I am a bit responsible for my miserable situation. The fact is, I just had my eyes on the countess the whole time and still can't understand Stechlin. Goes and takes the sister, he does! After all, when you get right down to it, he could have chosen either. Why, the countess's little finger, and her little toe, that's for sure, mean more to me than the whole comtesse."

"Czako, you're getting risqué again."

34

Among the wedding guests had been, as briefly mentioned, a certain Doctor Pusch, an elegant, and extremely urbane seeming gentleman with neatly trimmed sideburns, although already somewhat graying. Twenty-five years before he had come to grief on the shoals of the bar exam, and at that time had no desire to let himself be drawn into the tiresome grind anew. "The study of jurisprudence is a wearisome affair," he maintained, "and the career following thereon miserable." Thus he had gone to England as correspondent for an important Rhenish newspaper and there he had been able to make connections with the German Embassy. Things went on passably well for years. More or less at the same time when the old count gave up his London position, however, Doctor Pusch had also become fancy free again and betaken himself to America. There he found freedom somewhat freer than to his liking, however, and after first giving it a try in New York and then in Chicago, he quite soon returned to Europe. To Germany in fact. "After all, where else should a fellow live?" In keeping with such considerations, he finally took up residence in Berlin once more. He was by nature uninhibited and a little bit arrogant. The most important event of his last seven years he considered to be his change from Pilsener beer to the Bavarian lager brand, Weihenstephan. "You see, gentlemen, from Weihenstephan to Pilsener, anybody can do that. But the reverse, now that's something. Chinamen are becoming Christians, fine. But when a Christian becomes a Chinaman, that's still a matter of some importance after all, you know."

Pusch, when he again took up residence in Berlin, had also reintroduced himself at the Barbys. Melusine recollected him still, and the elderly count was happy to be able to reminisce once more about the old days, and chat about Sandrigham and Hatfield House, Chatsworth and Pembroke Lodge. Actually the somewhat expansively uninhibited manner in which the doctor took pleasure in expressing himself, by virtue of both his nature and his New York schooling, did not particularly fit in well with the practices of the old count, but there was also a certain charm in it all nevertheless, a charm which was even doubled by what Pusch knew to report from every corner of the earth. Brilliant correspondent that he was, he maintained connections with the ministries, and what to an extent weighed even heavier on the scales, to the legations. He had a sixth sense for everything.

When it came to fancy forms of address, however, he drew the line. All those telegrams had created a certain general telegrammatic style in him as well, which he relinquished only when he became expansive. In keeping therewith he maintained a regular abhorrence for such expressions as "His Excellency, the Most High Privy Councilor." Their brevity notwithstanding, titles like the Duke of Ujest or the Duke of Ratibor were still far too long for him, and so in their place he was ever ready simply to toss out the name "Hohenlohe."

In point of fact, he had a number of weaknesses. Yet these were accompanied by equally as many virtues. Thus, for example, he merely overlooked whatever took place in the way of love affairs with an almost aristocratic indifference, which suited some people very much indeed. Whether or not this process of simply looking beyond such things was but a business principle of his, or whether he found things of that sort only commonplace and therefore boring, was not easy to determine; in their place he preferred to cultivate the financial element, based, perhaps, on the view, that whoever has the finances has everything else as a matter of course, especially love.

That was Dr. Pusch. He joined up, as the party came to an end, with a group of persons who wished to spend the remainder of the 'already warmed-up evening' in a local emporium.

"Well then, where?"

"Siechen's, of course."

"Ach, Siechen's. Siechen's is for the Philistines."

"Well then, how about 'Fatty Wagner's?'"

"Even worse. I'm for Weihenstephan."

"And I'm for Pilsener."

They finally agreed to an establishment on Friedrichstraße where both were to be had.

The gentlemen who set off thence were, besides Pusch, the young Baron Planta, then came Cujacius and Wrschowitz, and bringing up the rear, First Lieutenant von Szilagy, who, as previously suggested, had formerly served in the dragoon guards, but on account of a general passion for the arts, painting and poetry at the top of the list, had but several years before retired from the service. He had not really gotten very far with his genre pictures, for which reason he had recently turned to the production of novellas, publishing an anthology under the modest title of '*Bellis perennis*.'[1] Love stories, one and all.

All five of these gentlemen, with the single exception of the young baron from Graubünden, showed themselves from the outset to be rather worked up, and anyone who overheard them would immediately have had the impression that a great deal of explosive material was piled up here. Nevertheless things went quite well at first. Wrschowitz kept himself under control and even Cujacius, who did not gladly yield the floor to others, enjoyed Pusch's blustering, perhaps because he only heard whatever suited him just at that particular moment.

Lieutenant von Szilagy, in the midst of all the questions flying back and forth — they were leaping from one topic to another with utter abandon — was queried by chance about his volume of novellas and whether he had gotten much pleasure from it.

"No, gentlemen," replied Szilagy, "Unfortunately I can't say I did. I had *Bellis perennis* published at my own expense and sent out a hundred and ten review copies to critics with a descriptive notice enclosed. That actually did get printed by a couple of papers, but only a very few. As for the rest, the critical establishment has kept its silence."

"Oh, krittikizm," said Wrschowitz. "I lov krittikizm, But goood krittikizm is keep silent."

"And yet," continued Szilagy, not quite immediately able to make heads nor tails of the somewhat Delphic expression of the good Doctor Wrschowitz, "and yet these painful feelings were nothing compared with what preceded them. Before the book's appearance, in fact, I even entertained the hope I would be able to place a few of these modest works in some party journal and when that didn't work out, in a family journal. But I failed . . . ."

"Why certainly. Naturally you failed," said Pusch. "That speaks in your favor. Listen here and take a little advice from me, because I pretty well know a thing or two when it comes to these matters. Been over on the other side, you know. Yes indeed, I might almost say I was over there on the double. First over there in England and then over there in America. They know how to do things there. Yes sir, good heavens, this blotting paper all covered with print. People make their livelihood from it and it actually rules the world. But, just the same, just the same . . . . And in the process, if I heard aright, you mentioned a party journal. Horrible! And then you even spoke about a family type journal. Horrible twice over!"

"Have you had any personal experience in this arduous field?"

"No, Herr von Szilagy. Providence has protected me from sinking that low. But I do ply my trade under the masthead, and when one lives right next door, so to speak, one does get to know to an extent what's going on with one's neighbors. Gracious me, how many a one who's poured out his heart to me, lamenting all about his sorry plight. Anybody who doesn't take it on the light side is a goner for sure. Novels, stories, detective stories. Anybody who wants to keep the masses satisfied, had better come down a notch. And if he's honestly done his best on that point, then another one after that. There's such a thing as a standard novella. Goes more or less like this: aristocratic young junior law partner and summertime reserve lieutenant, deeply in debt, loves governess of stupendous virtue. So stupendous, in fact, that if she gets put to the test, even in this most tremendously difficult realm of them all, she'd pass with flying colors. Suddenly there appears an old uncle, who wants to marry off this half derailed nephew of his to a rich cousin in a way befitting his rank. Highpoint of the situation! Conflict threatens on all sides! But just at this dire moment, not only does the cousin renounce him, she makes over half her entire fortune to her rival in the bargain. And presuming nothing else comes up, everybody lives happily ever after . . . . There you have it, Herr von Szilagy. Are you ready to compete with the likes of that?"

Everybody agreed. Only Baron Planta remarked, "Begging your pardon, Doctor Pusch, but I almost think you're exaggerating there. And what's more, you know it."

Pusch laughed. "Whenever you talk about anything like that, you always exaggerate. Anybody who parcels things out timidly, doesn't say anything at all. It's only the sharp picture, the one bordering on caricature, that has any effect. Do you think Peter the Hermit would have drummed up the First Crusade, if one day he'd only more or less mentioned to a friend when they were out picking strawberries that Christ's grave had been neglected, and somebody ought to see to a new grating for it?"

"Varry good, varry good."

"And so that's how it is, gentlemen, when I speak of modern literature. Herr von Szilagy, whom we are most fortunate to behold here in our midst, must be put back on his feet, his soul's got to be filled with new confidence. Or else with cheer, which is even better. He's got to be made able to laugh again. And if one is looking to achieve an effect of that sort, well then, you've simply got to speak out clearly and a bit imaginatively at the same time. Meanwhile, looking at it seriously as well, how do things stand with the production — I intentionally avoid the word 'creation' — or even with the consumption of most of these things!

"Let me put it metaphorically. There are all sorts of wreaths in our flower shops at present, foremost among which are those consisting of oak leaves and laurel, and in the interest of longevity, mostly woven on a tough basic wreath frame of willow. And now here you come and approach the wreath-maker intending to put in your order for a funeral or a wedding, be it for three marks, or five, or maybe for ten. Depending on the situation, she receives you with a mournful or smiling countenance. And exactly in keeping with your order, into the aforesaid basic wreath get bound a number of dahlias or water lilies, and on receipt of your most esteemed wish, even an orchid of utterly incredible composition and color."

252

"Know orchid exactly," cried Wrschowitz in tremendous ecstasy. "Violet with yellow."

Pusch nodded while at the same time continuing with rising exuberance. "And it's precisely the same with the basic novella. There it lies, complete, just like that basic wreath; not a thing's missing except the get-up, which at this point gets cordially agreed upon. On your esteemed wish a little offense against the moral tone even gets woven in. There's your big orchid, violet with yellow, as friend Wrschowitz has quite rightly emphasized."

"Under these circumstances," interjected Baron Planta, "it looks to me to be true stroke of luck that as I hear, Herr von Szilagy has several irons in the fire. What novella writing leaves to be desired for him, has to be made up by painting."

"Which, sad to say, it hasn't done up to now and presumably never will," laughed Szilagy half mournfully, "despite the fact that I've swung away from the genre painting with which I got started, and under the direction of my friend Salzmann have turned to painting ships. Now and then battles too. And as far as the blues go, I think I can perhaps say that I'm second to nobody. And besides I've just gone crazy over Gudin and William Turner. But nevertheless . . . ."

"But nevertheless without any real success," interrupted Cujacius at this point. "Which doesn't surprise me at all. Why are you wasting your time with Gudin or even with Turner? Whoever wants to paint the sea has to go to Holland and study the old Dutch masters. And among the moderns, above all the Scandinavians, the Norwegians, the Danes."

Wrschowitz gave a start.

"We've got that Melby fellow, for example. A Dane *pur sang*, who's very good and practically an important painter."

"Oh no, no," blurted Wrschowitz with ever more trembling voice. "Not varry good, not important, also not even *practically* important."

"Who is *very* important," repeated Cujacius, "important precisely by virtue of the fact that he doesn't try to pass himself off as being important. He doesn't have any false pretensions, he's straightforward, no fantasticizing, but full of mood. And when I see those pictures of his, especially the ones where the gray blue sea is crashing against a cliff, it's that specifically Scandinavian element that moves me every time, more or less like the Ossianic spell of the sea in the compositions of our splendid Niels Gade."

"Niels Gade? Nobody is talking about Niels Gade."

"I'm talking about Niels Gade. His compositions are nearly as good as Mendelssohn's."

"Vich does not make him greater."

"On the contrary, my dear Herr Doctor. To dethrone the truly great, petty arrogances of that sort won't suffice."

"Vich does not seem to prevent you, *mein Herr Professor*, from trying to dethrone the great Gudin."

"I have a perfect right to talk about painting."

"I have perfect right to talk about music."

"Strange thing. It's always personages from unregulateable border areas who are always shooting off their mouths in this country."

"I am Czech. Bud I know der is Tscherman saying. 'De Tscherman lies, venn he gets polite.'"

"For which reason, given certain circumstances, I refrain from doing that very thing."

"*En quoi vous réussissez à merveille.*"

"Now, now, gentlemen," interjected Pusch, naturally absolutely delighted with the entire tiff, "couldn't we just bury the hatchet? I've got a little proposition: meeting halfway, 'shaking hands,' as the English say. Take it all back, first one side then the other."

"Never," thundered Cujacius.

"*Jamais*," responded Wrschowitz.

And with that everyone rose. Cujacius and Pusch were in the lead, Wrschowitz and Baron Planta followed at some distance. Szilagy had cautiously headed off in another direction.

Still in great excitement, Wrschowitz endeavored to explain to the young Graubündener that Cujacius had the reputation of a rowdy. *Je vous assure, Monsieur le Baron, il est un fou et plus que ça — un blagueur.*

Baron Planta kept his silence and seemed intent on leaving his companion in the lurch. But he changed his mind when an instant later from the front he heard with ever-rising vehemence the expressions, "Cashube, Wend, Bohemian lout."

35

At the same hour in which the five gentlemen left the Barby wedding table, Baron Berchtesgaden and Court Chaplain Frommel had also started on their way, so that apart from the father of the bride, only old Stechlin was still in the bridal house. The latter — Melusine had not yet arrived back from the station — had initially withdrawn from the dining room into the deserted ladies' salon, and from there passed outside to the loggia to watch the lights reflecting on the water and to get a breath of fresh air. It was here that the old baron finally found him, and following the expression of his surprise at what from the point of health seemed a somewhat risky place to be, remarked,

"Well, my dear Stechlin, let's you and I have a little chat and get to know one another better. Your train doesn't leave until ten-thirty, so I'd say we've got almost an hour and a half."

Thus he took Dubslav's arm, to lead him over to his living room, which until then had served as the smoking room.

"Permit me," he continued, "to put my half-bandaged and half-splinted elephant's leg on a chair first. Twitched very nicely the whole time it did, and above all that standing at the altar really got to me. Please, pull your chair right over here. Everything went by so quickly during our little dinner. I'll bet you really got shortchanged when it comes to coffee. The moment the beer is passed round is always the most important in the eyes of these modern people; and so that means that the coffee hour gets a bit abbreviated."

As he spoke he pushed the call button.

"Jeserich, another cup for Herr von Stechlin and naturally a cognac or a curaçao, or better yet bring the whole Benedictine monastery — one of Cujacius's jokes, so you can't hold me responsible for that one . . . . Unfortunately, I won't be able to join you in your 'second coffee.' During dinner I had to be satisfied with a bottle of Apollinaris water deceptively set in a champagne bucket just for appearances' sake. But what can you do, after all, one doesn't want to stand out with all of one's ailments."

Dubslav followed the old count's invitation and sat directly across from his host, a lamp with a green shade between them. Jeserich entered with the tray.

"I can recommend the cognac, "continued old Barby, "connections still going back to the old days, when you could talk to a Frenchman without any constraints, and ask about a good supplier. Were you on hand back there in seventy too?"

"Yes, sort of half way. Actually scarcely even that. I was long since retired from my regiment. Just as a medical volunteer in the Knights of St. John."

"Exactly as I myself."

"A wonderful time, that winter of seventy," continued Dubslav. "Even from a purely personal point of view. At that time I had something that had been lacking in my life, if not totally, at least more than one would desire: contact with the real world. They always say the nobleman belongs on his little patch of soil and the closer he grows to it, the better it is. And that's true too. But there's nothing that's absolutely true. And so, you know, I've got to say it really was invigorating to have Old Wilhelm right there in front of your eyes every day like that. Actually got to see him only in passing, of course, but even that was a real joy to behold. They're calling him 'the Great' nowadays, and putting him up next to Fridericus Rex. Well, that sort he wasn't for sure, he doesn't measure up to the likes of him. But as a true human being he was better than he, and in my opinion in a certain sense that makes the real difference, even if there's something else required for 'greatness.' Ah yes, 'Old Fritz.' You can't put him up there high enough, yet there's one point nevertheless in which I find that we assume the wrong attitude when it comes to him, we of the nobility in particular. He wasn't so much for us as we always believe, or at least as we are always telling everybody. He was for himself and for the country, or as he loved to say, 'for the state.' But that we as a class or caste really gained something from him, that's nothing but imagination."

"Surprises me to hear that from you."

"But yet it's probably true just the same. After all, how were things really? We had the honor and permission to go hungry, go thirsty and go to our death for king and country. But we were never really asked whether it suited us either. Just that now and then we heard that we were 'noblemen,' and as such, had more 'honor.' But that was all there was to it too. In the depths of his soul he really shouted to us the very same thing he did to the grenadiers at Torgau.[2] We were his raw material and for the most part he looked at us with a tremendously critical eye. All in all, my dear Count, I find our year 1813 greater by a considerable measure, because everything that happened then had less of the command character about it and more of freedom and self resolve. I'm not one for that sort of freedom the liberal parties have patented for themselves, but I'm nevertheless for a certain measure of freedom overall. And if I'm not completely deceived, the belief's gradually awakening in our ranks as well — especially even from a purely practical, egoistic standpoint — that we'll fare best that way."

Old Count Barby was visibly pleased at these remarks. Dubslav, however, went on, "Incidentally, you must let me tell you, my dear Count, you live splendidly well here on this Kronprinzenufer of yours. A charming view, and I'll bet strangers would scarcely believe that anything as pretty as this could even be found on the banks of our dear old Spree. Where a person decides to locate, and the living quarters question in particular, are always important factors when it comes to happiness and comfort. And you especially, who were abroad for so long, were probably not without your reservations before you decided on the *visavis* of our Berlin Jungfernheide here. When it comes to the landscape, for sure, and quite possibly in regard to the people."

"Let's say for sure on that point too. I really did have that kind of reservations. But they've been suppressed. A great deal did not please me at all, when I returned here after many, many years abroad, and a great deal still doesn't please me yet. Too slow a pace everywhere. We've got too much sand in every sense around us and in us, and where there's a surfeit of sand, nothing really seems to move forward very well; it's always nothing but first this way, then that. Yet nevertheless this sand is firm under foot, not tremendously so, but secure enough. It just needs the right weather conditions, on the moral level above all, rain and sunshine at the right time, so to speak. And I believe Emperor Friedrich would have given it that sort of weather."

"I don't believe so," said Dubslav.

"Do you think, when all's said and done, he wasn't really serious enough about the whole affair?"

"Oh no, not at all, not at all. He was very serious about it, completely so. But it would have been made too difficult for him. Plain and simple, he'd have been thwarted."

"By what?"

"By his friends perhaps. By his enemies for certain. And that would have been the Junkers. They always say the Junkers aren't a power any more, the Junkers are eating out of the hand of the Hohenzollerns, and the dynasty only breeds them to have them ready at hand for any situation. And for a certain time maybe that was true too. But it's not true anymore today; today it's one hundred percent wrong. The Junker class, despite the fact that it claims it's not doing anything but patching its thatched roofs, and maybe now and then it really is, this Junker class — and in the midst of all due loyalty and respect, I'm proud to be able to say it nevertheless — has gained power tremendously in the struggles of these recent years, more than any other party, scarcely even excluding the Social Democrats. Now and then, it seems to me as if the old Quitzows[3] of blessed memory were rising from their graves again. And when that happens, when our people start to think about what they haven't been thinking about for the last four hundred years, then we can really get to see things happen. Everybody always says, 'impossible.' Ah, bah, what's impossible? Nothing's impossible. Who in this naive and utterly Philistine nest of ours called Berlin would have considered the 18th of March possible before the 18th of March?[4] Everything gets its chance, sooner or later. That should never be forgotten.

"And the army! Yes, of course. Who would say anything against the army? But every successful general is always a danger. And under certain circumstances others too. Just take a look at that old fellow there in Sachsenwald, our civilian Wallenstein.[5] When you get right down to it, God knows what he could have become."

"And you believe," interjected the count at this point, "that Emperor Friedrich would have come to grief on these sharp Quitzow rocks?"

"Yes, I do believe it."

"Hm, it doesn't sound too far fetched. And if that's so, in the end it was lucky that things turned out differently after the ninety-nine days, and we never had to face the question."

"I've often discussed this business with my Woldemar, who — I can't say anything good about it and don't care to criticize it — has a strong liberal bent. Naturally, he was for a new era, therefore for experimentation . . . . Well, in the meantime he's chosen the better part, and while we're chatting here by now he's passed Trebbin. Strange thing, I haven't traveled around very much, but whenever I've passed by that little whistle stop out there in the Mark just outside Berlin, I've had the feeling, 'Now it's getting better, now you're free.' I can say I love that whole sand box out there, just for that reason alone."

The old count laughed comfortably. "And Trebbin has never even had the faintest idea of this rapture of yours. But incidentally, you're right. Everybody more or less lives as if in a prison at home and wants to get away. And yet, I'm actually against travel, particularly against this honeymoon madness. Whenever I see persons climbing into a train compartment like that, heading for Italy, I'm always overwhelmed by a feeling of gratitude for not having to participate anymore in this 'greatest joy on earth.' It really is a form of agony and the world will get away from it again one day too. Sooner or later people will only travel the way one marches off to war or climbs aboard a balloon, merely because one's profession demands it. But not for enjoyment. And why should you anyway? There's no real reason anymore. In the olden times the prophet went to the mountain, now miracles are happening and the mountain's coming to us. You can see the best of the Parthenon in London and the best of Pergamum in Berlin, and if they hadn't dealt so leniently with our dear Greek friends, who are always bankrupt and never seem to be able to pay what they owe, one could take a little stroll on the museum island here in Berlin and be in Mycenae in the morning and Olympia in the afternoon."

"Completely of your opinion, my dearest Count. But yet at the same time a bit distressed to find you so firmly against any sort of travel. I was, in fact, on the point of inviting you to Stechlin, to my old cottage, which my good old Globsowers constantly insist on calling a castle."

"Ah yes, dear Stechlin, your 'cottage.' That's something else again. And to tell you the whole truth, if you hadn't invited me — as a matter of fact it really hasn't happened as yet, but I'm anticipating you will — I'd have announced myself. That's long since been my plan."

At this moment the bell rang outside. It was Melusine.

"Bringing the fathers, and respective fathers-in-law the warmest of greetings. Your children are presumably well beyond Wittenberg, the great city of Luther or apple pie stopover, depending on how you want to look at it, and in less than two hours they'll be pulling in to the Dresden station. Oh those happy souls! And yet I'll wager by this time Armgard's longing for Berlin. Maybe even for me."

"No doubt," said Dubslav.

The countess herself, however, continued, "Before one completely parts from one's old life, one longs for it heart and soul one more time. Admittedly, Sister Armgard will feel that sort of thing less than others. She's simply got the most kindly and best of husbands, and I could almost envy her, despite the fact that I really did get a frightful scare at the last minute when I heard him say that tomorrow morning he wants to walk with her before the Sistine Madonna. Looked absolutely radiant as he said it besides. And I find that simply unheard of. And why, you'll perhaps be asking me? Well then, in the first place, it's an insult to be looking forward to a Madonna so ardently when one has a bride or even a young wife at one's side, and secondly, because this planned visit to a gallery indicates a definite lack in organization and economic attitude which is enough to make me concerned for Woldemar's entire future. Said future lies, after all, on the agrarian side, and the right sort of organization means as good as everything when it comes to agricultural management."

The old count wanted to contradict her but Melusine did not let it come to that, continuing, "In any case — and there's no disputing it, either — our Woldemar is riding into the land of Madonnas right now, and presumably wants to make his appearance there in passably good condition, even if he's wasting his strength in Germany. And so when he's in Rome, he'll probably alter his program and have to read a Berlin newspaper in the Café Cavour instead of rhapsodizing about art in the Palazzo Borghese next door. A Berlin newspaper I say, quite intentionally, because we're getting to be a metropolis these days, and along with our press are expanding even beyond the borders of Charlottenburg . . . .

"By the way, as do our newlyweds, the baroness too sends her warmest greetings. A charming woman, Herr von Stechlin, whom especially you will very much get to like. Doesn't actually believe a thing, and pretends to be a strict Catholic. That sounds absurd and yet it's the truth, and charming at the same time. All those South Germans are much nicer than we are, and the nicest, because they're most natural, are the Bavarians."

Sunset

36

ON ARRIVING SOON after eleven at his Gransee Station, old Dubslav found Martin and his sled waiting for him. Engelke had fortunately seen to it that warm things were available, for it had become quite cold in the meantime. At first the east wind blowing in the open felt wonderful to the old man after the usual oppressive air that had prevailed in the train compartment. Soon, however, a chill set in. Even on the day before, at the outset of his journey, he had not been feeling quite up to it, a headache, pressure at the temples. Now the same condition was back again. Nevertheless, he took it lightly and looked out at the twinkling panoply of stars above him. Poplars, rising up like gigantic brooms, cast dark grotesque shadows across the road, while he enlivened the dead snow fields to the right and left with the varying images of all the day just past had brought with it. Thus he saw once more the red-carpeted marble stairs of the hotel with the head waiter in the pose of an ambassadorial attaché, and in the next instant the sexton of the Garrison Church, whom he had initially taken for a Privy Councilor invited to the solemnities. Next to these stood the pale, beautiful bride and the charming and supple Melusine. "Yes indeed, that Old Barby, when he looks at *her*, he's got it good; he can hold out. To have a good and clever person around you all the time, always to hear and see someone that smiles at you and invigorates you, that's really something. But me! For my part, regardless of whether it was my fault or not, I always got nothing more than just enough to get by. As a child because I was lazy, and as a lieutenant because I didn't quite have it. Then came a ray of light. But then she died right afterwards, she, who should have been the staff and support of my life. And through all the thirty years that have come and gone since, I've had nobody left but Engelke — who was still the best — and my sister Adelheid. God forgive me, but a consolation that woman's never been. Never anything but dry as a crab apple."

With such thoughts he rode into the village and immediately afterwards stopped before the door of his old house. Engelke was waiting there and assisted him, doing his best to unwrap him from the heavy wolf's hide. Still beset through and through by chills, he stomped his feet, and with visible satisfaction threw aside his formal hat, which, because it had pinched so, he had probably cursed a hundred times during the trip. "Ah, that's the thing, Engelke, you've made a fire," he said, immediately on entering his room. "You know what does an old fellow some good. But it's still not enough yet. Any hot water downstairs? A regular grog, that would be just the thing for me right now. Freezing right down to my bones."

"Ain't no more hot water, Master. But I can set up the warming pan. Or even better, I'll get the kerosene stove."

"No, no, Engelke. Let's not make such a big fuss. I don't go for that. And as for the kerosene stove, that least of all. You never get anything but headache from that thing, and I've got one of those bad enough already. But bring me a cognac and some cold water. If you take that more or less half and half, it's as good as if it had been nice'n hot."

Engelke brought what had been requested and a quarter hour later Dubslav went to bed.

He fell asleep immediately. Soon, however, he awake again and merely drowsed on and off throughout the night. And so the morning finally came.

When Engelke brought breakfast at the usual hour, Dubslav dragged himself laboriously from his bedroom to the breakfast table. But nothing tasted good to him. "Feeling bad, Engelke. My foot's swollen and that cognac last night wasn't the right thing after all. Tell Martin he's to go to Gransee and bring Doctor Sponholz back. And if Sponholz isn't there — the poor fellow's constantly gallivanting over hill and dale in that buggy of his, can't make ends meet without making house calls all over the countryside — then he's to wait until he comes."

Things turned out as Dubslav presumed, Sponholz was really out making calls and did not return until afternoon. He had a quick bite and climbed into the Stechlin carriage.

"Well, Martin, what's the Master up to these days?"

"Oye, Doctor, Oi might say, 'ee looks a bit changed, 'e does. Didn' feel so good las' Sund'y already, an' then 'ee 'ad to go off to Berlin, y'know. An' one thing Oi knows, when a feller's got to go to Berlin, there alwez be somethin' wrong fer sure. Oi don' know what they do there wid'n ol' feller."

"Aye, Martin, that's the big city for you. They always overdo it there, you know. And then of course there was the wedding too. No doubt they probably tippled a bit there. And the cold church beforehand. And all those fine ladies besides. The Master isn't used to things like that any more and so he wants to show off a bit and goes at it hard and the next thing you know, you catch something before you know it."

It was twilight as the little chaise pulled up on the ramp. Sponholz climbed out and Engelke took his gray coat with the double collar and the tall lambskin cap as well, in which — the only thing about him to have such an effect, to be sure — he looked like a Persian.

And so he entered Dubslav's room. The old gentleman was sitting before the fire and staring into the flames.

"Well now, Herr von Stechlin, here I am. Was out in the country. Things are getting pretty nasty. Every third person I see's coughing and has a headache. Influenza, of course. Divvel of a sickness."

"Well, at least I don't have *that.*"

"Never can tell. Anybody can get a touch of it as easy as that. Well, what's the problem?"

Dubslav pointed to his right leg and said, "Badly swollen. And now the other one's starting too."

"Hm. Well, let's take a look. May I?"

Dubslav raised his pants leg and pulled down his sock. "There's the whole mess. Can't be gout. Don't have any pains . . . . Must be something else then."

Sponholz tapped lightly with his finger around the swollen foot and then said, "Nothing of significance, Herr von Stechlin. Moderation, diet, not too much to drink, even not much water. The accursed water presses upward right off and then you get shortness of breath. And just a few drops of this medicine. Please, just keep sitting, I know my way around here." And with that he went to Dubslav's desk, tore off a piece of paper and wrote out a prescription. "Your coachman can ride right over to the apothecary shop. That will probably be the best."

In the vestibule, after taking leave of Dubslav, Sponholz again quickly slipped back into his overcoat. Engelke assisted him and as he did, said, "Well, Herr Doctor?"

"Nothing at all, nothing at all, Engelke."

Martin was still waiting with his chaise outside on the ramp and thus they quickly set off back to town from which the old coachman was immediately to return with the drops.

The winter twilight was beginning to set in as Martin returned to give the medicine to Engelke. He brought it to his master.

"Just take a look at that,' said the latter as he held the roundish bottle in his hands. "Those Gransee folks are getting fancy too these days. Everything all done up in pink tissue paper." On an attached label, however, it read, "Herr Major von Stechlin. Ten drops three times daily." Dubslav held the little bottle toward the light and dropped the prescribed number of drops into a spoon of water. Once he had taken them he moved his lips back and forth, somewhat the way a connoisseur tests a new wine. Then he nodded and said, "Yes sir, Engelke. Now we're off and running. Foxglove."

For several days in a row old Dubslav took his drops quite conscientiously and even found that things got somewhat better. The swelling abated a tiny bit. But the drops took away his appetite as well, so that he ate even less than he was allowed.

It was a fine early March day, already past lunch time. Dubslav sat at the fully open glass door of his garden salon and read the newspaper. It appeared, however, that what he was reading did not especially appeal to him. "Ach, Engelke, the newspaper's all right as far as it goes, I suppose, but for the whole day like this, it's just not enough after all. Maybe you could bring me a book instead."

"What kind of book?"

"Doesn't make any difference."

"There's that little yellow book still lying around. "No more Lupins.'"

"No, no. Nothing like that. Lupins. I've read so much about that business already. That always just keeps on changing and one thing's just as dumb the next. Farming won't be coming back on top again, or at least not through something like that. Bring me a novel instead; in the old days, when I was a youngster, they used to call'm 'tear jerkers.' Yes sir, in those days all the words were a lot better than nowadays. Do you still remember how back in the year I became a civilian I had my first frock coat made? 'Frock coat' is a word like that too, really lots better than 'tail coat.' Frock coat's got something cheerful about it, confirmations, weddings, christenings."

"Good God, Master, ain't always that way, either. After all, most frock coats is when somebody gets buried."

"Right, Engelke. When somebody gets buried. That was a good idea that popped into your head just like that. In the old days I'd have said, 'timely.' Nowadays they say 'opportune.' Ever hear of that?"

"Aye, Master, I've heard about it before."

"But you didn't understand it. Well, I actually didn't understand it either. Leastwise not so exactly. And you, you never even went to school."

"No, Master."

"All in all, be happy you didn't . . . . But, Engelke, once you've brought me that book, I'd rather move right out there on the verandah with my chair. It's like spring today. You've got to put good days like this to use. An' bring me a blanket too. Never used to be much for that namby-pamby business, but nowadays it's 'better safe than sorry.'"

In the entire triangle between Rheinsberg, Wutz Convent, and Gransee the news of old Dubslav's serious illness had spread about far and wide. And it was no doubt in connection with this that approximately at the same hour in which Dubslav and Engelke were conversing about 'tail coats' and 'opportune,' a one-horse buggy drove up the Stechlin ramp, a somewhat strange vehicle from which old Baruch Hirschfeld slowly and carefully descended. Engelke assisted him in the process and immediately reported that the old fellow had come.

"Old Baruch! For heaven's sake, Engelke, whatever does he want? After all, luckily there's nothing wrong, you know. And just on his own like that. Well, let him come up."

And Baruch Hirschfeld entered straightway.

Dubslav, wrapped up in his blanket, greeted the oldster. "Why, Baruch, what in the world's going on? What brings you here? Makes no difference anyway, I'm glad to see you just the same. Make yourself as comfortable as you can on the three slats of a garden chair. But then again, what's going on? What brings you here?"

"The Herr Major will excuse me, it's nothing at all, and nothing I'm really bringing either. I was just sort of more or less passing by, business with Herr von Gundermann, and so I thought I'd take the liberty of stopping in and asking about your health. I'm hearing the Herr Major isn't feeling so good these days."

"No, Baruch, not so good, poorly enough, you could almost say. But let's drop this not so good new business; the old things were actually better, you know, at least now and then. And sometimes I get to thinking back on all of what the two of us went through together."

"And always smooth, Herr Major, always smooth, never any problems."

"Yes sir," laughed Dubslav, "problems were something *I* never made. But had them I did, problems aplenty. And nobody knows that better than my friend Baruch. And now tell me first off, what's your Isadore up to? That great friend of the people? Is he still satisfied with Torgelow? Or does he realize that they cook only with water too? It just surprises me that a son of Baruch Hirschfeld, a son and partner in the firm, is so hot for the revolution."

"Not for the revolution, Herr Major. Isadore, if I might put it that way, he's for the good old values. But along with that, he's got a heart for humanity."

"Does he? Well, that's nice."

"And a heart for humanity, that's something we've all got, Herr Major. And if something good should come our way because of that, then we got, if I might put it that way, the dividend. Lord God Almighty, we sure can use it. And since it's dividends I'm talking about, mortgages I'll mention too. We got since last Friday a bit a' capital. Gransee people. And I'll let it out at three-and-a-half."

"Well now, Baruch, that's really nice. But at the moment I'm not in any need of it. Maybe later sometime my Woldemar. As you know, he's just made quite a rich match, and anybody who marries a pile needs a pile too. People always think, 'that's when it stops' but that's all wrong, that's when it really gets going. But whatever the circumstances, let me thank you for just wanting to come by and see how I'm feeling. Unfortunately, I can only repeat, poorly enough. But things'll keep on running for a while though. And if they don't, everything will work out nice and smooth with my son, I imagine, just the way it was between us two, even smoother yet, and maybe one day the two of you will be able to work out something nice, something solid, something big, that'll really be worthwhile. That'll be the new times then. And now, Baruch, you've still got to take a glass of sherry. At our age that's always the best thing. For you, that is, you're still in good running order. Only thing I can do is touch glasses with you."

A quarter hour later Baruch rode off in his little buggy back into the Stechlin Forest, and with little satisfaction thought over everything he had heard inside. The dreamed-of Castle Stechlin days suddenly seemed over once and for all. Everything the old gentleman had said about 'working out something together' was nothing but a feint, a slight of hand trick.

Yes indeed, Baruch felt something like disgruntlement. But Dubslav did as well. It seemed to him as if for the first time he had caught his old Gransee financial and business friend (even though he had not the least idea of his latest plans) in some secret and clandestine thing. Thus when Engelke arrived to clear away the sherry bottle, he remarked, "Not much with Baruch either, Engelke. I thought, goodness knows, what a regular saint he was, and now the old club-foot and horns have popped out in the end after all. Wanted to practically force mortgage money on me, he did, as if I didn't have enough of that already . . . . Funny, it looks like Uncke with that constant 'dubious' of his turns out to have it right after all. Anyhow, policemen like that with a carbine on their shoulder, when you look at 'em in the hard light of day, they're always the best judges of character. It irks me that I didn't realize that sooner. To have been so stupid! But that business about my 'sickness' today, that was too much even for me. Once people start asking about how sick you are it's always bad. The fact is, its all the same to everybody how you feel. Why I even knew some folks who were already looking over the furniture and the pictures whenever they started asking questions like that, and didn't have a thing on their minds but an auction."

37

The next few days too were almost summer-like. They did the old man good and made it easier for him to breathe. He began to have hope again, talked things over with the agricultural inspector and the forester, and was not only full of restored interest in things in general, but brimming once more with good cheer.

And so the middle of March approached. The sky was blue, Dubslav sat on his verandah, the little fountain before him, and watched the fluffy white clouds passing overhead. From the park he could hear the first finch calling. It might have been an hour that he was sitting there like that when Engelke arrived and announced the doctor.

"Good of you to come, Sponholz. Not to help me out. It's always bad business when somebody's finally got to be helped. No indeed. To see that you've helped me out already. These drops here, there's really something to them after all. If only they didn't taste so awful. Always have to give myself a regular kick in the pants to get'm down. And the fact that they're so green besides. Green is poison, so people say. Actually a pretty stupid idea. The fields and forests are green too, and they're really pretty much the best things there are."

"Yes, it's a specific medication. And I'm pleased too that in your case digitalis has once more shown what it can do. I'm doubly pleased because I've got to take my leave from you for six weeks."

"For six weeks. But doctor, why that's half'n eternity. Not been paying your bills so you're heading off to prison?"

"You could almost think something like that. As long as the existence of Gransee has been historically documented, there's never been a doctor away for six weeks. And the district physician in the bargain. A doctor's existence doesn't permit luxuries of that sort. After all, how does one get by in a place like this? How have we always gotten by? Always cutting boils, always carbolic bandages, always climbing into a buggy, always issuing discharge papers for some old fellow earthling or fetching a new one in. And now six weeks away.

267

How am I going to find my district when I get back? . . . . Well, maybe the Good Lord will be merciful."

"After all, He probably is the best assistant doctor."

"And the cheapest above all. The other one, whom I've had to have transferred to me here from Berlin — and good Lord, after so much paperwork — he's more expensive. And my trip will be costing me plenty enough as it is."

"But where are you off to then, Doctor?"

"Pfäffers."

"Pfäffers? Never heard of the place. What is it you want there? Why? What's the reason?"

"My wife's been plagued with rheumatism, rather advanced, not a very pleasant sort of thing any more. And when it comes to that, Pfäffers is supposed to be the last word. Swiss bathing resort with all the trimmings, and all the fancy prices too probably. One of our Granseers, to be sure, the kind you could display in a show window for money, spent some time at that rather remarkable spot and gave me a description of it. Took a look in Baedeker too, of course, and among other things found a river mentioned there named Tamina. Sort of reminds you of *The Magic Flute*, and sounds pretty good as far as it goes. But nevertheless a crazy place, this Pfäffers. As far as its being a spa, it's nothing more than a hole in the rocks, a big bake oven they shove you into. And so there you squat just like the Indians, and the vapors rise up over you boiling hot from down below. Anybody who doesn't get himself pulled together after all that can pack things up once and for all. By the way, yours truly is going along to crawl in as well. One thing I can say for sure, anybody who's bounced around back and forth through the Gransee district for nearly thirty-five years, with that east wind blowing every now and then, there's a fellow who's come by his rheumatic pains honestly enough. Funny though that the main part of it should fall on my wife."

"Yes indeed, Sponholz, in a Christian marriage . . . ."

"True enough, Herr Major, true enough. Even though that business about a 'Christian marriage' is only just so so. When I was in the service we used to have a company surgeon, regular old school. Always said, 'Yes indeed, Christian marriage, fine thing, know it well. Like ham in Burgundy wine. One part's always there, but the other's not."

"Right," said Dubslav, "those regular old company surgeons, knew that sort myself too. Terrific cynics one and all, died out these days, sad to say . . . . And you're looking to spend six weeks in a bake oven like this Pfäffers place?"

"No, Herr von Stechlin, not that long. Just four, at the very most four. Because it really puts a strain on you. But, well, once you're down there roundabouts in that area in Switzerland, you know, where they even talk Italian here and there, when you get right down to it a fellow wouldn't mind having a peek at that promised land they call *Italia*. And so we, my wife and I, plan to start from this Pfäffers place and first going over the Via Mala up to the Splügen Pass or some pass or another. And then, once we've had a look at all that splendor down below there on the other side, we'll go back the way we came, and yours truly will put on his gray overcoat again — I've had a new one made for the trip, you know — and go back to bouncing back and forth through the Gransee district."

"Well, Sponholz, really glad to hear that you'll be getting away for once. It's only when you go through the Via Mala, you've got to be careful there."

"Why, have you ever been there, Herr Major?"

"Heaven forbid. My worldly travels, given a few modest exceptions, always ran between Berlin and Stechlin. At the most Dresden and a bit of the Bavarian scene. When you sort of don't know any more where you ought to go, you naturally go to Dresden. Result: never got to see Via Mala. But a picture of it. In general, looking at pictures isn't exactly my style either, and if the museums had to live off me I'd really feel sorry for them. But then, as chance would have it, now and then you do get to see something like that after all. And in this Via Mala picture there was this rocky chasm with figures in it, by a very famous painter fellow, named Böcking, I think, or Böckling."

"Ah yes. One of them's named Böcklin if I'm not mistaken."

"Quite possibly he's the one it was. Right, even very probable. Well then, you see, Herr Doctor, there was this Via Mala there in this picture, with a little river down below and across that river ran the arch of a bridge and a procession of people, could even have been knights, just coming down the road. And they all wanted to get over the bridge."

"Very interesting."

"And then, just imagine, what do you think happens? Right next to this arch, close to the right side, all of a sudden the rock wall opens up, just the way a regular petit bourgeois opens up his shutters of a morning to take a look at what the weather's like. But this fellow at the bridge, who just by chance takes a look out the window, just listen to this, Sponholz, he wasn't some petit bourgeois fellow, but instead he's a regular dragon or something like that from what they call the dinosaur age. So far back that even the oldest nobility, the Stechlins included, couldn't hold a candle to it. And this monster, just as the oncoming procession is ready to pass over the river, he's come right up to the people and the bridge with his maw wide open. And the only thing I can tell you, Sponholz, when I looked at that, my heart stood still, because I could feel plain as could be, yes sir, one more second and he'll snap it shut and the whole crowd are goners."

"Well, Herr von Stechlin, the only consolation we've got is that as far as I know the dinosaurs have since died out. But just the same, I'd better not tell my wife that story, she passes out now and then, you know. There's always something going on in a doctor's house."

Dubslav nodded.

"And there's only one thing more I'd like to tell you, Herr von Stechlin, just go right on and continue as you are with the digitalis. If your appetite doesn't come back then preferably just twice a day. And never more than ten drops. And if you should feel unwell, my replacement has been informed about everything. You'll like him. New school, modern fellow, but yet not too much of a good thing, at least, I hope so. And in any case, smart as a whip. As far as his name goes — it's Moscheles, as a matter of fact — you shouldn't let that bother you. Born in Brünn he was, and most everybody there has a name like that."

The old man expressed his agreement with everything, even with the name, despite the fact that the latter awakened painful recollections in him. Some fifty years before he had had to play musical selections, all of which had born the name of Moscheles. But he didn't wish to make the fellow about to appear on the scene pay for the likes of that.

And so, following these calming assurances, Sponholz wished him the best and took his leave, driving off to further farewell visits throughout the county.

Two days later the Sponholz's started out on their journey from Gransee to Pfäffers. The wife, suffering greatly, was silent. Her husband, however, was in high spirits from travel fever which expressed itself, once they had arrived at the station, in an ever growing garrulousness.

Several friends, mostly lodge brothers, had accompanied him thus far. At the station Sponholz jumped nervously from one thing to another. "Ah yes, our good old Stechlin, things are only so so with him . . . . Baruch saw him too and found him a good bit changed . . . . And you, Kirstein, you'll write me of course when young Burmeister arrives; I know he doesn't really want to, it's just his father who does, even supposed to have mentioned something about 'hocus-pocus.' But we shouldn't take things like that too seriously. Inexperience, misjudgment, we're all past that sort of thing; the more enemies, the more honor, as they say . . . . But just to mention it one more time, that old fellow in Stechlin's got me worried. But we've got to hope for the best, nothing's impossible for the good Lord. And I've got plenty of confidence in Moscheles, watching him do an auscultation is a real pleasure for somebody in the know."

Thus went what Sponholz had to say from the window of his compartment even at the last minute. Everything, but of course most of all what had been said about old Stechlin, was spread far and wide, reaching even to the villages, and particularly even as far as Quaden-Hennersdorf and Superintendent Koseleger. The latter had recently been engaged in lively comings and goings with Ermyntrud and, stimulated by the princess, who was becoming more pious with every passing day, was planning an energetic campaign against the decline of faith and increase in laxity gaining an upper hand throughout the county. With this goal in mind, Koseleger as well as the princess wished to begin their campaign with old Dubslav as their 'next objective,' and they considered his asthma attack as the most suitable opportunity.

To that end could be read the following in a letter from the princess to Koseleger: "I have no desire to cast the slightest doubt on the old gentleman's upright nature. Moreover, he has something tremendously affable about him so that from the purely personal point of view I am extremely fond of him. But his principles, which admit of nothing higher than 'live and let live,' have permitted every possible kind of error and eccentricity to take root like weeds in our region. Take this Krippenstapel person, for example. And then Lorenzen himself! Katzler, with whom I discussed our plan yesterday, asked that out of consideration for the old man's illness that I at least refrain temporarily from all these things, but I have had to contradict him. It's true, illness does make one irritable and obstinate, but on the other hand it makes one equally malleable in moments of distress. And no doubt here too it is precisely these afflictions and adversities from which a blessing will arise for the patient, and whatever the case, for our district as a whole. Whatever the circumstances, however, we must take consolation in the awareness that we have done our duty."

It was a week after Sponholz's departure that Ermyntrud wrote these lines, and even before lunch next day, Koseleger, who in all essentials was of one mind with the princess, drove up the Stechlin ramp. Immediately upon his arrival Engelke entered the room where Dubslav was sitting and announced the Herr Superintendent.

271

"Superintendent? Koseleger?"

"Yes, Master. Superintendent Koseleger. He looks real well and spic–and–span as can be."

"What remarkable days we're getting lately. Today's another one, you'll see. Started off with Moscheles. Ask the Herr Superintendent to come in."

"I hope I've come at a convenient hour, Herr von Stechlin."

"Best time of all, Herr Superintendent. The new doctor was just here. And if there's even the slightest thing to this *praesente medico* business, a medicinal presence like that has got to last at least a quarter hour."

"Surely, surely. And this Moscheles fellow is supposed to be very bright. The Viennese and those Prague people know what they're doing, especially when it comes to everything that lies in that direction."

"Yes," said Dubslav, pointing to his chest and heart, "in *that* direction. But to put it plainly, when it comes to some other directions, this Moscheles fellow isn't particularly my style. He holds his cane in such an odd way and swings it so besides."

"Yes indeed, under certain circumstances one just has to accept things as they are. But then I hear too that our Major von Stechlin has more or less a philosemitic tendency."

"*That* our Major von Stechlin has indeed, because he can't abide lack of Christian charity and particularly dislikes narrow-mindedness in the realm of principles. I'm one of those people who prefer to look at the individual case. But admittedly, there's many an individual case that doesn't appeal to me. Such as, for example, this one here with the new doctor. And my good old Baruch Hirschfeld, with whom I suspect the Herr Superintendent is also acquainted, he doesn't so rightly appeal to me anymore either. I really used to put great store in him, but — maybe it's his son Isadore who's to blame — all of a sudden out pops the old club foot."

"Yes indeed," laughed Koseleger, "that always pops out sooner or later. And not just with Baruch. But, I must say all that has far, far less to do with race than it does with the particular profession. I was just visiting with Frau von Gundermann . . . ."

"And you found something like that there?"

"In a certain sense, yes. Naturally a bit different because the feminine factor was involved. The governess or, as they say, 'The Housewife's Support.' And when it comes to that sort of thing it's not at all difficult for hanky-panky to get started. And she, this very 'Housewife's Support' was still a teacher until just recently, and when it comes to women teachers, old and young, there's always a snag, as with teachers in general. Has to do with the profession. And those young university tutor-type fellows at the head of the list."

I can't recollect," said Dubslav, "of having heard of anything grossly improper in our area."

"Oh, I've been misunderstood," replied Koseleger appeasingly, rubbing his well-manicured hands with a certain contentment. "No transgressions in the erotic realm, even though it might indeed have once again taken on this, I might say, trivial secondary form with the Gundermanns — who seem to be rather plagued particularly on this very point. No, indeed, that great tutorial club foot of which I was thinking when making my first remark bears entirely different credentials: insubordination, overestimation, and as a consequence thereof, a peculiar striving to abandon the paths of salvation and seeking fulfillment of the inner being in a false scientific posturing."

"I wouldn't say I'm in favor of that; but even such a 'false scientific posturing,' I'd imagine, would have to be reckoned among the rarest of exceptions in this old county of ours."

"Not as much as you might imagine, Herr Major. Why, from your very own school here in Stechlin complaints have reached my ears about such things from church-going parents. Granted, old school Lutherans from the Globsow area. In any case, as tiresome as these people now and then may be, on the other hand they do nevertheless possess the spiritual earnestness of the true faith and, as they expressed themselves in an epistle to me, find this spiritual earnestness severely neglected in the Krippenstapel pedagogical methodology."

Dubslav rocked his head back and forth, and notwithstanding all respect due the representative of ecclesiastical authority, would have probably responded rather sharply and pointedly had not everything he heard appeared to him in a humorous light at the same time. Krippenstapel, his Krippenstapel, he who knew all there was to know about Old Fritz just as well as the catechism, but at the same time was every bit as well informed with regard to the catechism as about Old Fritz, Krippenstapel, that magnificent old beekeeper of his, corresponding member of a number of Mark Brandenburg historical societies and the soul of his 'museum,' his dear friend, this selfsame Krippenstapel was supposed to have failed to appreciate the 'spiritual earnestness of the true faith.' Indeed, in his very person that sort of pedagogical arrogance, constituting a peril to the entire community, was supposed to have erupted. True, he remembered — something which at this moment irritated him a bit — having on occasion personally made similar remarks. But that had always been by way of joking. But when two do the same thing, it's no longer the same thing. If ever that remark applied, it was here.

Thus with some effort he got up from his chair, walked over to Koseleger, shook his hand and said, "Herr Superintendent, it can't be the way you're describing it there. When it comes to regular Lutherans of the old school, there's not a single one around here, least of all in Globsow. That bunch doesn't believe a thing, so to speak. I smell intrigue here. There are others behind it. In the case of my old Baruch the old clubfoot may have popped out, but when it comes to my old Krippenstapel, it hasn't popped out yet, and it's not going to pop out either, because, plain and simple, there isn't any. My good, old Krippenstapel, I know him."

Koseleger, man of the world that he was, quickly gave in, mentioning fundamentalist narrow-mindedness and admitted the possibility of an intrigue.

"Naturally it's difficult for a person to believe in the likelihood of things of that sort in this little backwoods corner of the world. After all, 'intrigue' is reckoned quite eminently among the higher culture forms. Here in our old county I tend to believe intrigue hasn't yet gained the slightest bit of ground. But then on the other hand, it's got to be admitted just the same, that nowadays reprehensible things, in fact, even crimes and acts of vice, appear not only in the wake of culture, but instead precede it as lamentable heralds of a false morality. Just consider what we've recently gone through in our equatorial provinces. Civilization has not yet arrived and already we have its horrors. A person shudders when he reads about it and is happy for those petty and commonplace circumstances in which the will of God has mercifully placed us."

Following these words, which implied something of a good exit, Koseleger arose and the old man, for his part linking his arm in that of the Superintendent, "to support himself upon the church" as he said, accompanied his visitor outside to the ramp, and was still waving as the carriage passed over the timbered bridge. Then he turned again quickly to Engelke, who stood next to him, and remarked, "Too bad I can't bet with you Engelke. I sure feel like it. Somebody else'll be coming today, you'll see. There hasn't been a cat seen around this place for a week, but when fate's finally made its decision for us, it doesn't seem to know when enough's enough. Either you win the lottery big three times over, or bang your noggin three times. And always on the same spot."

It struck twelve as Dubslav passed through the vestibule from the main entrance. As he did, he looked up at the scythe bearer and counted the strokes. "Twelve," he said, "and at twelve it's all over and done with, and then the new day begins. True enough, there are two twelves and the twelve that's striking up there now is the midday twelve. But midday! . . . Whither have you gone, midday sun!"[1]

Pursuing such thoughts as he now often did, he reached his place before the fireplace and took up a newspaper. He scarcely looked at it, however, and while appearing to read, he actually busied himself instead merely with the question of who else might still be coming today. As he did, while thinking of Lorenzen along with others from his immediate vicinity, he came to the conclusion that even with all that new nonsense of his, Lorenzen was in the end still preferable to Koseleger and all those riches of salvation he had spoken of probably two or three times over. "Yes indeed, the riches of salvation. They're all very fine. Obviously they are. I won't be sinning when it comes to anything like that. The church can do things, it really is something, and that old Luther fellow, well, he certainly was something, that's for sure, because he was honorable and ready to die for his cause. Nearly did too. Actually, it always just boils down to somebody saying, 'That's something I'm ready to die for.' And then goes and does it too. It almost doesn't really matter for what. That somebody can just do something like that at all, sacrifice himself, that's the magnificent thing. From the church's point of view, of course, what I'm saying here like this may be wrong. But what they call 'moral' these days — there's some who even say 'morally pleasing,' but that's too crazy a way of putting it — well then, what they call moral these days, just looking only at that, personally putting yourself on the line and being ready and able to die for something, that's still the highest thing there is. Nobody can do any more than that. But Koseleger. That fellow wants to live."

And while he was still in the process of spinning out this thread in this fashion, his good old factotum had entered, to whom, merely for his own satisfaction and without further ado, he directed the question, "Right, Engelke?"

But the latter was no longer in a condition to hear anything; so great was his confusion that he merely stuttered, "Oh Lord, Master, now it's really gone an' happened."

"Huh? What?

"The, the spouse of our Herr Chief Forester . . . ."

"What? The princess?"

"Yes, Frau Katzler, Her Highness."

"Great guns, Engelke . . . . There you are. See, I said it would happen, didn't I? Knew it for sure. When a day like this gets going, it stays this way, just keeps right on going like that . . . . And the way everything's lying around here, everything messed up all over the

275

place. Take that coverlet away. Ach, what coverlet? A regular horse blanket, that's what it is; we've got to have a different one. And get rid of these green drops too, so it doesn't look like a sick room around here right off . . . . The princess, . . . Come on, hurry up, Engelke, get moving, . . . Tell her I'm pleased, tell the Frau Chief Forester, I'd be pleased if she'd come in."

Dubslav pulled himself together as well as he could. Otherwise, given his rather mournful condition, he considered it better to remain in his wheelchair rather than go to meet the princess, or by rising from his place welcome her in a more or less solemn fashion. Ermyntrud concurred with his intentions as well, and with a dignified wave of her hand let it be known that she did not wish to cause a disturbance. She then placed her right arm on the rest of a nearby chair and said, "I've come, Herr von Stechlin, to inquire about your condition. Katzler" — carefully avoiding the admittedly plebeian 'my husband,' she always called him only by his family name — "has told me about your illness and asked me to convey his respects. I do hope things are going better."

Dubslav thanked her for so much kindness and asked that she excuse the prevailing excess of disorder. "Where the womanly hand's missing, everything is missing." He went on like this for some time, resorting to every manner of cliché and turn of phrase with which he had been familiar from way back. The fact was, however, he was hardly aware of what he was saying, but instead hung entirely on her appearance, which was half nun-like, and half reminiscent of the way saints were pictured on holy cards, all of which was even more intensified by a large necklace of pale white beads complete with an ivory cross. She would have caught anyone's attention, even the most critical, and Dubslav, who — much as he fought against it — was completely in the thrall of her being a princess, for a time forgot his sickness and age and felt himself only a knight with his lady.

That she remained standing disturbed him for the first moment. Soon, however, he found it quite acceptable, because it became clear to him that it was only in this way that her 'image' had its full effect. Ermyntrud was fully conscious of this as well, moreover she was woman enough not to yield these advantages unless absolutely necessary.

"I hear that Doctor Sponholz, whom I have learned to hold in high esteem as a physician, has entrusted his patients to a young substitute while in Pfäffers. Young doctors are usually more clever than old ones, but yet less true physicians. Moreover, one tends to endow age with more confidence. Older doctors are like father confessors, to whom we gladly tell all. To be sure, they are not able to fully provide replacement for that spiritual encouragement, which in any serious illness remains, after all, the only true healing force. Physicians themselves — I spent a part of my youth in a convent for nursing nuns — physicians themselves, when they understand their profession correctly, share this opinion. So-called medications are and will remain nothing but a poor stopgap; all true help flows from the Word. But, to be sure, the right Word is not uttered everywhere."

Dubslav looked around somewhat restlessly. It was absolutely clear that the princess had come to save his soul. But whence had reached her the knowledge that his soul was in need thereof? It would indeed be worthwhile to find out something like that, and thus he took himself in hand and said, "Of course, Your Highness, the Word is the main thing. The Word is a miracle, it lets us laugh and weep, it uplifts us and casts us down, it makes us sick and makes us well. In fact, it alone gives us the true life, here and in the beyond. And this last, this highest Word, we have it in the Bible. That's where I get it from. And if now and then there's a Word I don't understand, as we don't understand the stars, we have those who interpret them for us."

"Of course. But there is such an abundance of interpreters."

"Yes," laughed Dubslav, "and whoever has to choose has the pain of making the choice. But I, personally, I haven't got a choice. Because exactly as it is with my body is how it stands for my soul as well. One helps one's self with what one has. First off, let's take my poor miserable body. Here sits this pain on me that rises up and pinches and tortures and gives me a fright, and when my fear's greatest, then I take those green drops. And if it still keeps torturing me, then I send over to Gransee and Sponholz comes. That is, if he's there just then. Yes indeed, this Sponholz is also one of the initiate and an 'interpreter.' Quite probably there are cleverer and better ones; but in the absence of those who are better, he's got to do for me."

Ermyntrud nodded in a friendly way and seemed ready to express her agreement.

"And," continued Dubslav, "I've got to say it again, just as it is with the body, so it is for the soul as well. Whenever my poor soul is fearful, I take my consolation and help as well as I can find them at the moment. And when it comes to that, then I think the closest consolation is the best. That's what comes to you the quickest, and whosoever gives quickly, gives doubly. One actually ought to say a thing like that in Latin. I send word to Sponholz, because when I need him, I've got him relatively close by. The other one, though, the physician for the soul, fortunately, I've got him even closer by, and don't even have to send as far as Gransee. Any words that come from the heart are good words and if they help me — and help me they do — then I don't ask too many questions about whether they're the so-called 'right' Words or not."

Ermyntrud raised herself higher; her smile, up to now warmly cordial, was obviously speedily disappearing.

"And besides," said Dubslav by way of concluding his confession, "what are the true Words? Where do we find them?"

"You have them, Herr von Stechlin, if you wish to have them. And you have them close at hand, even if not in your immediate vicinity. I personally have been supported and uplifted in difficult days by these words. I know he has enemies, in his own camp above all. And these enemies speak of 'pretty words.' But should I close myself to the Word of Salvation because it comes garbed in beauty? Should I reject a hand raised to bless me because it is a soft one? You mentioned Sponholz. Our superintendent stands head and shoulders above the latter without a doubt, and if it were not vain and overweening, I would believe I saw the hand of Providence in the fact that it was to this barren coast he had to be driven, just to be a help to *me*. But what he has done for me, he can do for others also. Simply put, he has what is needed for victory; whosoever hath the soul, hath the body as well."

With these remarks Ermyntrud strode over to Dubslav from her chair and bent over him as if half in blessing to kiss his brow. As she did, her ivory cross touched his breast. She let it rest there a while. Then she stepped back again, and bowing twice in majestic farewell, left the room. Engelke, who had been standing outside in the vestibule, hastened before her to be of assistance as she climbed once again into the little Katzler chaise.

When Dubslav was once more alone, he took the poker lying directly before him on the hearthstone and dug with it into the half-burned logs. The fire blazed up and a few sparks flew. "Poor Highness. It's not such a good thing after all, when princesses move in to Chief Forester's houses. They're out of their element then, and go grasping at everything they can lay their hands on so as not to drown in the day to day monotony they've gone and created for themselves. True, a better source of consolation than Koseleger she couldn't find. He gave *her* the consolation he himself needs. In any case, she can let herself be uplifted by anybody she wants. The old fellow at Sanssouci, with his 'everybody finding salvation in his own *façon*,' he had the right idea.[2] That's for sure. But then if I let you have your *façon*, you have to let me have mine as well. Don't make out you know everything better. Don't go coming here with innuendoes, first off against my good, old Krippenstapel, who never muddies up anybody's wa-

278

ters, and now even against my clever old Lorenzen, who can put the whole pack of you in his pocket. They wouldn't dare attack him personally, and so they come to me, and want to turn me against him, and think just because I'm sick, I'm sure to be weak too. But they don't know their old Stechlin very well when it comes to that and he'll just go and put on that thick markish skull of his. Even against Ippe-Büchsenstein and beads of ivory that are practically a regular rosary besides. And it will come to that yet too. Actually though, it's me who's really to blame. Let myself be too impressed by the princess's way of looking at me, and those four children's graves in the garden. But it's gradually passing away again, and it's a good thing I've got my Engelke."

Excitement had made him get out of his wheelchair and push on the call button. "Engelke, go over to Lorenzen and tell him I'd like to see him. He'll have to be the last one for today though . . . . Just think of it, Engelke, they wanted to convert me!"

"Oh, but Master, why that's all fer the best, after all."

"Good God, now he's startin' too."

38

Lorenzen did not come. He had gone to Rheinsberg where the clergy from the eastern part of the county were having a conference. Instead of Lorenzen came Doctor Moscheles, who talked about all sorts of things, first in brief about Dubslav's condition, which he found neither good nor bad, then about Koseleger, then Katzler, and finally about Sponholz, from whom a letter had just arrived. Most expansively, however, he spoke about Lawyer Katzenstein and Torgelow. "Ah yes, this Torgelow fellow," said Moscheles. "It was a mistake to elect him. And as if it had even been necessary; as if the party didn't have anyone better! But the fact is, you know, they've got a lot who are much different people." Dubslav was hardly pleasantly moved by all of this, since in the personal disparagement of Torgelow he could at the same time detect the unqualified approbation of the latter's party.

The visit had lasted about half an hour. Once Moscheles was on his way, Dubslav remarked, "Engelke, when he comes back, just tell'm I'm not home. Naturally he won't believe it, after all, he knows better than anybody that I'm tied to my room and this wheel chair of mine. But all the same, I don't like him. It was a stupid thing for Sponholz to pick this particular fellow, such a know-it-all who smells of the Social Democrat crowd and carries his cane around so weirdly in the bargain, always right in the middle. And to top it off, a red tie."

"But there's little black beetles on it."

"Sure, they're there all right, but real little ones. They make'm that way so nobody'll notice what sort of crowd he's from and where he really belongs. But I see through it anyway, even if he shows up on Kaiser Wilhelm's birthday sporting a little paper corn flower.[3] Right then, you tell him I'm not here."

Engelke did not contradict his master, even though he more or less had his own thoughts about it all. "The old doctor's away and he don't want the new one. And he don't want that fellow from Wutz either because he hangs around with the Domina so much. An' all the time he just keeps gettin' worse. He thinks, it ain't so bad yet. But it is. It's just how it was with Knaack the baker. An' Kluckhuhn was saying to me just last week, 'Engelke, believe you me, it ain't gonna get no better, I know what I'm talking about.'"

That was on Monday. On Friday Moscheles drove up again and turned pale when Engelke told him the Master was not at home.

"Well, well. Not home."

That was a bit much after all. As a result Moscheles climbed back into his carriage and, while driving back to Gransee, reaffirmed his utterly negative views with regard to the present social order. "They're all alike. What we need is a general smash up, a regular crash, *tabula rasa*." At the same time he was resolved to refrain from another visitation. "His gracious lordship of Stechlin Manor and surrounding properties and estates can just have me called when he needs me. Let's hope he spares himself the trouble."

As a matter of fact this wish was fulfilled. Dubslav did not have him called even though there was good reason for doing so, for his symptoms suddenly grew worse, and whenever on occasion they subsided, the swollen feet immediately returned. Engelke watched it all with concern. What more would he have of life if he no longer had his master? Everyone in the house disapproved of the old man's obstinacy and Martin, coming one day from the stables, and entering the adjoining low-ceilinged kitchen where his wife was peeling potatoes, said to the latter, "Oi don' know, mither, why 'e went'n throwd thet young docter out. Thet young feller's smarter n' ol' Sponholz. Y'only hav'ter 'ear what them Globsowers says 'bout Sponholz. Yes sir, ol' Sponholz, they says, e's good fer uz't goes, but aluz 'e says, 'chillern, 'e says, 'e ain't really so sick; all 'e needs is a bowl a' soup with a bit a'somethin' in't.' Aye, Sponholz, 'e kin say somethin' like thet, 'e got somethin' fer't. But not them Globsowers! Where they gonna' get a soup with a bit a' somethin' in it?"

Thus the days passed one by one, and Dubslav, who was truly feeling poorly, now himself saw that he had acted hastily in every way. Moscheles had been, after all, a genuine replacement, and if he now called in another, it would cast a shadow on Sponholz as well. And that was something he was not keen to do. In this distress he vacillated back and forth, and one day, when once again sorely afflicted and short of breath, he called Engelke and said, "Engelke, I'm feeling terrible. But don't start in with me about that doctor. I may be wrong but I don't want him. Tell me, what's the real story about old Buschy? Last fall she's supposed to have helped that field hand Rohrbecken's wife get back on her feet again . . . ."

"Aye, old Buschy . . . ."

"Well, what do you think?"

"Aye, old Buschy, *she* knows what's what. That's for sure. 'Cept that she's a reg'lar ol' witch, an' on Walpurgis Night, there's nobody knows where she is. And the girlies always go over to her place Saturdays, when it's gettin' dark, and Uncke's made a note of a few of them already and reported'm to the magistrate. But they're all arguing about it high and low, an' a few of'm even been swearing they don't know a thing 'bout it."

"I can imagine. And maybe it wasn't so bad either. And anyways, Engelke, if you think she really knows so much, when all's said and done, maybe it might just be the best thing for you to go over there or send somebody. Because those old legs of yours don't want to work so well any more, and it's slushy weather besides. And if you get sick on me too, I won't have even have a single soul left who'll take care of me. Woldemar's far away. And even if he were in Berlin, after all, he's got his duty and his troop, and can't be sittin' with his old father all day. And besides that, taking care of sick people is a tough job in general, that's why the Catholics have their own special blessing for it. Yes sir, they know about things like that. They know about them even better than we do."

"No, Master, I wouldn't say better."

"Well, let's drop it. A thing like that's always hard to pin down, and because so much is hard to pin down these days, why people have gone and made up for themselves what they call 'Boards of Inquiry.' Course nobody can quite figure out what exactly that's supposed to mean. Not me for sure. Do you know what it is?"

"Nay, Master."

"See? And you're certainly a sensible fellow, anybody can see that straight off, and you can see the sense of it too, that it really would be best if I were to send over to the old Busch woman. What people say about her is none of my business. And then I'm no girlie, either. And Uncke won't go writing out a report about me, I imagine."

Engelke smiled. "Well, Master, then I'll have a little talk with our Mamsell Pritzbur downstairs, she can send Lil' Marie. Marieken was only just confirmed last Michaelmas, but she's been there too already."

On the very same afternoon Frau Busch appeared at the manor house. She had more or less pulled herself together and was wearing her best attire, even a new black head scarf. But it could not be said that she gained much by having done so. Almost to the contrary, in fact. Whenever she came out of the woods with a sack over her shoulder or a basket of kindling wood strapped to her back, one saw nothing but an old, poor woman. Now, however, as she entered the master's room and was not quite certain why they had called for her, one could make out the cunning in her features and that she was ready for everything and anything.

She remained standing at the door.

"Well now, Buschy, come on over here, or stand over there at the window, so I can see you better. It's pretty dark by now, you know."

She nodded.

"Well, I'm not doin' so good anymore, Buschy. An' now Sponholz is away too. And that new Berlin fellow, don't much care for him. They say you put tenant Rohrbecken's wife back on her feet again that time. I've got somethin' like that too. Have you got the courage to take me on as a patient? I won't turn you in. If a body helps somebody, nothin' else matters. Mum's the word then. And you won't come out the loser."

"Oh, Oi knows that, Mast'r . . . . You wouldn't do nothin'. An' anyways folks all be thinkin' Oi kin do witch'n 'n all them kind'a things. But y'know, Oi can't do none o' them things t'all, 'n only got some lovage leaves, 'n juniper, n'some serpent's garlic. An' everythin's all on the' up 'n up, jest the way it oughter be. Them magistrates can't do nothin' agin me."

"Fine with me. And it's none of my business anyway. I'm not asking you to do anything like that. Don't much care for them magistrates myself. Now tell me, Buschy, do you want to have a look at my foot? One's enough. The other looks just the same, or nearly as bad."

"No, Mast'r. Let it be. Oi knows what it be. First it's sittin' up ther in yer chest 'n then it drops right down an' sits down 'ere. An' it's all one 'n the same thing. It's all got ter come oot, 'n once it's all oot, it won't press no more an' ya kin ketch yer breath agin."

"Good. Makes sense t'me. Got t'come out, y'say. That's what I say too. But how'll you get it 'oot?' That's the question. What have you got for remedies? What ways do you have?"

"Aye, Oi gots the rem'dies. An' once we got the rem'dies, then we kin find th'way too. I'll send Lil' Agnes over terday wi' two bags. Agnes, thet's Karliner's lil' girl."

"I know, I know."

"An' Agnes, she's ter go down ter the kitch'n ter Mamsell Pritzbur. An' Pritzbur, she's ter make the tea fer the mast'r then. Morning's from the white bag, an' evenin's from the blue'n. An all'ys one lev'l tabl'spoon full, 'n not too much wahter. But it got t'be boilin'. An' when them bags is all gone, then it's oot. The wahter takes the wahter 'way."

"That's fine, Buschy. We'll do it all just the way you say. And I'm not just a tolerant patient, I'm an obedient patient too. The only thing I want to know now is what it is you want to send me in those bags of yours, that white one and that blue one. Ain't no secret, is it?"

"Nay, Mast'r."

"Well then?"

"In the white'n there be club moss an' in the blue'n's what folks here'bouts calls cat's foot."

"Got it, got it," smiled Dubslav. And then as if to himself he added, "Well, sure. Why not? Could do some good. After all, between the two of'm lies the whole of world history, so to speak. Club moss, they make baby powder out of that, an' so the sweetness of existence itself starts off with it. And with cat's foot it all comes to an end. That's the way things go . . . Cat's foot . . . . those yellow flowers they use to make funeral wreaths . . . . Well, we'll see what happens."

On the same evening came Agnes, bringing the two bags. And what was almost beyond all expectations actually took place; things really did get better. The swelling receded and Dubslav breathed easier. "The wahter takes the wahter away." With this witches' incantation which he enjoyed citing whenever he chatted with Engelke, his hopes and vital forces acquired renewed vigor once more. He once again felt like getting around, and whenever the weather permitted in any way, he would have his wheel chair not simply pushed out onto the verandah, but even around the garden circle, where he would watch the little fountain which was shooting up its column of water once more. In fact, it seemed to him as if it were shooting even higher than before. "Don't y'think so too, Engelke? Four weeks ago it didn't want to go anymore. But now it's working again. Everything's working again, and it's really stupid to live without any hope at all. After all, what do we even have it for?"

Engelke merely nodded and placed the newspapers that had arrived on a lawn chair next to the breakfast table. At the bottom, as the foundation, was the *Kreuzzeitung*.[4] On top of that *The Berlin Post* and finally some letters. Most were open, advertisements and announcements. Only one remained still unopened, sealed, in fact, with wax. Postmark: Berlin. "Pass over that letter opener, so I can cut this one open in a respectable way. Looks like something fancy. The handwriting looks like a lady's, except that the strokes are a bit too thick."

"From the countess, I'll bet."

"Engelke, you're getting too clever for me. Course it's from the countess. There's the coronet right here."

Sure enough it was a letter from Melusine and with an enclosure. Her lines at the end ran, "And now permit me to include the letter which our dear Baroness Berchtesgaden received from Rome just yesterday. From Armgard, in fact, whose complete happiness I have really only now been able to make out from this letter and its little exorbitances, all of which are really quite foreign to her character."

Dubslav nodded. Then he took out the enclosed letter and read:

Rome, March

Dearest Baroness!

To whom would I rather write from here than you? The Vatican and the Lateran and the grave of Pius IX and if I'm in luck, I'll even be on hand when the Papal Blessing is dispensed on Maundy Thursday. You simply have to take in everything that comes your way. Going into raptures about Rome is in rather poor taste, and superfluous besides. After all, one never even comes close to the raptures of one's predecessors. So instead of that, I'll tell you about our journey.

We took the road over the Brenner Pass and were in Verona that same evening. *Torre di Londra*. Next day, what interested me most about the Montagues' and Capulets' town was a large park garden, the *Giardino Giusti*, with over two hundred cypresses, every one of them five hundred years old, and many nearly as tall as the royal palace in Berlin. Woldemar and I strolled back and forth, and as we did we wondered whether the beautiful Juliet might not perhaps have walked back and forth in the same place too. Only one thing disturbed us. As the end point of such a splendid boulevard of mournful trees, a mausoleum is an absolute necessity. But there was no such thing.

In the *Giardino Giusti* we ran into Captain von Gaza from the First Guards' Regiment, who, just coming from Naples, had seen all the glories of Italy by now. We asked him, if — as one is constantly assured — Verona really is the most Italian of Italian cities? Captain von Gaza simply laughed. "When it comes to Potsdam," he said, "one might say it's the most Prussian of cities. But Verona as the most Italian? Not on your life."

As for the much celebrated Venice, for now only this: Our hotel was located right in the vicinity of a church overloaded with baroque ornamentation: San Mosé. That there even was a Saint Moses was news to me and surprising at the same time. But then right off I thought of the two towers of our Gendarmenplatz churches in Berlin and calmed down. After all, when it comes to naming churches, a Moses always takes precedence over *gensdarmes.*[5]

I'll pass over Florence and in its place I'll tell you something about Lake Trasimeno, which we passed on our train journey. Woldemar, playing the role of a miniature Moltke, did not want to pass up the opportunity to see what kind of stuff the great Hannibal was made of, and so we got off in the vicinity of the lake at a little station which, I believe, was called Borghetto-Tuoro. It was more interesting than one would ever expect even for a layman, and even I, who usually don't have the slightest sensibility for that sort of thing, understood it all and was able to follow every detail. As a matter of fact, it seemed to me that in a high, narrow pass like that even I would have defeated the Romans just as well. The lake has a number of streams that flow into it or from it. One of its run-offs, more a canal than a river, is called the Emmissarius. That amused me no end. But another outlet struck me as even more interesting; it is called the Sanguinetto because it ran red from blood on the day of the battle. The diminutive here really intensifies the effect tremendously. The lake, by the way, is quite large, a circumference of thirty miles around and shallow. For that reason Napoleon I wanted to have it pumped out. Then they would have been able to establish a new duchy . . . .

"Well, well," said old Dubslav. "Who would have expected that from the pale young comtesse? Yes indeed, travel and going off to war, that's what broadens you, makes a different person out of you."

And he put the letter aside.

At the same time a quiet sense of contentment had taken hold of him and he reflected on how many a joy life still held for him after all. In front of him, in the trees of the park, birds were singing and a chaffinch flew down onto the table and looked him over, completely without fear. That did him uncommonly good. "Trust, that's one of the really beautiful things in life, even if it's only a little dickybird that gives it to you. Some people have nothing but black bile and are always saying everything's rooted in nothing but murder and mayhem from the start. But I can't see it that way."

Engelke came to clear things from the table.

"Beautiful day today," said Dubslav. "And the crocuses are coming out already. Actually, I didn't believe I'd get to see anything as pretty as all this ever again. And to think I owe it all to Old Buschy. Crazy world! Sponholz never had anything but those green drops of his, and Moscheles never had a thing but that interminable Torgelow fellow and then along comes the old Busch woman and just like that it's better. Yes sir, really remarkable. An' now to top it off, even if it's only on loan, I get such a pretty letter from a pretty young woman. And a daughter-in-law, besides. Yes sir, Engelke, that's the way it goes; not t'be believed. And you should have seen that chaffinch a while ago, the way he looked at me. Except when you came, he flew away. Must have been afraid of you."

"Ah, Master. Ain't no creature 'fraid of me."

"I can believe you there. And you'll see, today'll be a good day, and somebody'll come, whom we'll be glad to see. When I was feeling bad it was Koseleger and the princess who came. But today it was a chaffinch. As sure as can be, he'll have a following."

Dubslav's premonition proved correct and in the afternoon came Lorenzen. Since the old man had been drinking his cat's foot tea he had seldom put in an appearance and then only briefly. But that had been purely by chance and not intended as an expression of disapproval that the oldster was letting Old Buschy handle his recovery.

"Well, at last," remarked Dubslav by way of receiving him, as Lorenzen entered. "Where have you been keeping yourself? They always say we Junkers are supposed to be little kings. As if anyone believed that. All the little kings have a retinue that's constantly outdoing itself with homage and somersaults. But I haven't seen much in the way of an entourage like that yet. Baruch was here, that much I'll admit, and then Koseleger and the princess, but the fellow who's more or less supposed to come *ex officio*, he stays away, and at best sends over old Frau Kulicke or Elfriede with an inquiry now and then. Why a fellow could die an' molder away. And they call that pastoral care."

Lorenzen smiled. "Herr von Stechlin, your soul, this neglect of mine notwithstanding, gives me very little in the way of concern, because it can be counted among those which can do without any special recommendation of any sort. Allow me to speak purely on the human level, in fact, for a clergyman almost blasphemously. But I must. I live, as a matter of fact, absolutely firm in the conviction that, when the day finally comes, the Good Lord will be quite pleased to see you again. When that day finally comes, I say. But it hasn't come yet."

"I'm not so sure you're right, Lorenzen. In any case I find myself in my present tolerable state only through the help of Old Buschy, and whether that is particularly capable of putting in a good word for me up above is a pretty doubtful thing, as far as I can see. But let's put a delicate question like that aside. Why don't you tell me something downright nice and cheerful, even if it's really old hat, the sort of thing they used to call the 'miscellaneous addendum.' That's what I always liked best and still do today. That stuff I read there in the newspapers, the political business above all, I always know all about that already, and whatever I get to hear from Engelke, I know that too. Just in passing — and speaking only from the utterly egotistical view of the newspaper reader, of course — it's really a lucky thing that there are still so many accident cases, otherwise you'd practically never get a thing out of reading the newspapers. But you now, you read all sorts of other things, now and then even some good things — rarely, to be sure — and you have a wonderful memory for all kinds of stories about robbers in their dens and anecdotes from every corner of the world. And besides that, you're a Fridericus-Rex man, the thing I actually value in you most of all. Because Fridericus-Rex people, they all have their hearts and heads in the right place, you know. Well then, dig up any old thing of that sort, an old Zieten story, or one about Blücher. Could be about Wrangel for all I care. I'm grateful for everything and anything.

"The worse things go for a fellow, the nicer some fresh and high spirited cavalry yarn strikes you. I personally don't go in for heroism myself. Bragging about yourself is a miserable business. But one thing I can say, I love the heroic. And, thank God, that sort of thing still happens these days."

"Of course things like that still happen. But yet, Herr von Stechlin, all this business about the heroic . . . "

"Now wait a minute, Lorenzen, don't tell me you're against the heroic? You're not that far gone yet, are you? And if that were so, I'd get seriously angry."

"The goodness of your nature wouldn't allow that."

"You're trying to trip me up. But this time you won't pull it off. What is it you've got against the heroic?"

"Nothing, Herr von Stechlin. Not a single thing. On the contrary. Heroism is good and great. Under certain conditions it's the greatest thing there is. Completely in favor of the cult of the heroic I am, that is, of the genuine and real thing. But what you want to hear from me, is, you'll forgive the expression, heroism second class. *My* kind of heroism — which is to say, what I consider to be heroism — isn't to be found on the battlefield; it has no witnesses, or else always only the sort who perish along with it. Everything takes place in silence, in isolation, out of sight of the world. At least as a rule. But then of course, when by way of exception the world does get to hear about it, well, I listen carefully too, I perk up my ears, so to speak, like a cavalry horse catching sound of a trumpet call."

"All right. Fair enough. But how about some examples."

"I can oblige. First off, there are fanatical inventors, the ones who never lose sight of their goal, utterly oblivious to whether a lightning bolt strikes them or an explosion blows them sky high. Added to that are the great climbers, be it up on the peaks or down into the depths. Thirdly, there are those people who investigate the sea bed as if it were a meadow. And finally there are the explorers of all four corners of the earth, including the ones who take part in expeditions to the North pole."

"Good grief, that eternal Nansen fellow. Nansen, who because he found a pair of pants up there in Greenland he'd lost down here, got the idea that what those pants can do, I can too. And so off he went across the pole. Or at least he wanted to."

Lorenzen nodded.

"All right then, fine. It was a good idea. And that this Nansen fellow got right to work on the thing, I respect that too, even if nothing ever did come of it in the end. Still, a brilliant bit of work. Certainly. A fellow like that sits up there on the ice, doesn't see a thing, doesn't hear a thing, and if anybody comes by at all, it's at best a polar bear. And he's happy just the same, simply because it's at least a living creature. I dare say, I've got a feeling for that sort of thing. But nevertheless, Lorenzen, the guard at St. Privat really is more than just that."

"I'm not so sure, Herr von Stechlin. Genuine heroism, or to narrow it down even more, the sort that's likely to affect me personally, always stands in the service of a personal idea, of a highly personal decision. And that even holds for cases in which this decision borders on the criminal. In fact now and then for that very reason, or, what's almost worse, something that's ugly. Do you know Cooper's *Spy?* There you have the spy as a hero. In other words, the lowest of the low as the highest. It's the underlying conviction that makes the difference. That much is certain for me. But there are other examples yet, even better ones!"

"Now I'm really curious," said Dubslav. "Well then, if you can, let's have a name."

"A name: Greeley, Lieutenant Greeley; Yankee *pur sang*. And besides that, another one of those Arctic explorers."

"Which is therefore to say, Nansen Number Two."

"No, not Number Two. What he did was many years before Nansen."

"And he got farther up? Closer to the pole? Or were his polar bear encounters of an even more serious nature?"

"All of that wouldn't mean much to me. The traditionally heroic element is completely missing from his story. What takes its place is something utterly different. But this different element, that's exactly the thing that makes it all."

"And that was?"

"Well — I'll recount it from memory. I may be wrong in specific details or in minor facts . . . but in the main it's right . . . . Well then, finally, after being lost for a long time, there were only five of them left: Greeley himself and four of his men. They had abandoned their ship and so they were making their way across the ice and snow. They knew their route, in so far as there was one to speak of, and their only concern was whether the small amount of supplies they were carrying with them, hard tack and dried beef, would hold out to the next human habitation. Each was granted a maximum, and actually at the same time the minimum amount of daily provisions, and if they kept to this measure and nothing unexpected happened, it would probably be enough to last. And one of them, the one who still had the most strength, was carrying all the provisions. And so it went for days on end. Then Lieutenant Greeley realized that their provisions were disappearing faster than had been calculated, and he realized too that the fellow carrying the provisions himself was taking rations when he thought no one was looking. That was a horrible realization, because if it went on that way, all of them were done for.

"So then Greeley took the three others aside, and they talked it over. There could be no possibility of a normal kind of punishment, and getting involved in a fight was also out of the question. They no longer had the strength for that. And so finally it all boiled down to one thing, and it was Greeley who said it: 'We've got to shoot him in the back.' And soon after this court martial scene, when they got on the way again with the secretly condemned fellow at the head of the column, Greeley stepped up to him from behind and shot him down. And it turned out not to have been the wrong thing either. Their rations held out and on the day they consumed their last crumbs they reached an outpost."

"And what happened then?"

"I don't remember anymore whether it was Greeley himself who appeared as his own accuser on returning to New York, but I do know that it came to a big hearing."

"And in this hearing . . . ?"

". . . in this hearing they found him not guilty and he was carried home in triumph.

"And you agree with that?"

"More than that, I'm full of admiration. Instead of doing what he did, Greeley could have said to his companions, 'Our premise is wrong, and we all have to perish because of the guilt of one; I don't want to kill him — therefore all of us have to die.' For his own person he could have spoken and acted in that way. But it wasn't just a matter of himself alone; he had the role of the leader and commander, at the same time the obligations of the judge, and had to protect the majority of three against a minority of one. What this one person had done, of itself a triviality, was, given the circumstances, a damnable criminal act. And so against the serious crime that had taken place, he took upon himself an equally serious counterstroke. To intuitively feel the right thing in moments like that, and to do something terrible in the conviction of what is right, decisively and unshrinkingly, something that out of context runs counter to every Divine precept, to every law and to our every precept of honor, that is something which impresses me tremendously. In my eyes that's the real thing, true courage. Shame and disgrace or at least the reproach of having acted disgracefully have from time immemorial been associated with everything that is highest. Battalion courage, the courage of the masses, with all due respect for it, it's nothing but the courage of the herd."

Dubslav stared straight ahead. He was obviously in a state of ambivalence. Then, however, he took Lorenzen's hand and said, "I suppose you're right."

39

Following Lorenzen's visit Dubslav had a good night. "When you hear something out of the ordinary like that, you feel better right away." But the cat's foot tea continued to have its effect too, and what helped the patient most of all was that he was not taking the green drops.

"Listen, Engelke, in the end it'll all turn out all right after all. How do you like my legs? No more marks when I press."

"Sure, Master. It's gettin' better, an' it's all from the tea. You're right, Old Buschy knows what's what, that's what I alw'ys said. And last night when Lorenzen was here, Lil' Agnes was here too an' askin' down in the kitchen, how things actu'lly stood wi' the Mast'r. An' Mamsell told her, thing's was pretty good."

"Well that's how it should be, that the old woman's concerned just like a regular doctor and wants to know about everything. And that she doesn't come herself is even better. She's got a touch o' a bad conscience, fer sure. I think she's got quite a bit on her record, and as far as Karline's bein' the way she is, nobody but the old girl's responsible for that. And the little girl'll maybe still turn out that way too; already acts just like a little doll, she does, and that long blond tangled head of hair besides. I always have to think of Little Belle — do you remember her, when the mistress was still living? Little Belle had hair like that too. And she was the favorite too. That kind are always somebody's favorite. I hear Krippenstapel's spoiling her in school too. When the others are still staring at him working out the answer, she fires away with it. Clever little thing."

Engelke confirmed what Dubslav was saying and went downstairs to get the Master his second breakfast, a soft-boiled egg and a cup of consommé. But as he passed from the garden room into the large vestibule, he saw a coach had pulled up, and instead of going into the kitchen, he went straight back to his master to report with an embarrassed look that her ladyship, the mistress, had just arrived.

"What? My sister?"

"Aye, her ladyship, the mistress."

"Oh, we're really in for it for sure this time. Things'll really start shaking around this place now," said Dubslav, who was genuinely terrified, certain that peace and quiet were now gone for days, perhaps even weeks. For Adelheid, with her seventy-six years behind her, was not the sort to put herself in motion for trivialities, and if she had traversed the nearly twelve miles from Wutz Convent, it was not just for afternoon tea, but for an extended stay. He felt his whole condition worsen again in one fell swoop and in an instant he was once more half short of breath.

He did not have long to ponder such matters, however, for even at this moment Engelke was opening the door and Adelheid approaching him. "G'day, Dubslav. Got to see for myself, you know. Our Pension Director Fix was in Stechlin day before yesterday and learned about your latest ailment when he was here. That's how I found out about it. Before you'd personally ever let your sister know about something like this, or send a messenger . . . . "

291

"I'd have to be dead already," said old Stechlin, completing her thought and laughing. "Well, let it pass, Adelheid, make yourself comfortable and pull up that chair there."

"That chair there? Good gracious, Dubslav, the things that come into your head! Why that's nothing but a grandfather's chair, or practically one at any rate." And as she spoke, instead of the proffered chair, she reached for a small light wicker chair and settled down on it. "After all, I didn't come to you to sit in some huge, overstuffed chair full of pillows over here. I want to nurse my dear patient, but I haven't the slightest intention of being a patient myself. If things were that bad with me, I'd have stayed home. You always figure that I'm ten years older than you. Well, of course, I *am* ten years older. But what are years? The air in Wutz is healthy, and whenever I read our gravestones over there, there's practically not a single one of us who's passed on under eighty. And you're just turning sixty-seven. But I believe you didn't plan your life the right way, I mean your youth, when you were still in Brandenburg. And from Brandenburg constantly running over to Berlin. Well, we know all about that sort of thing. I was reading some statistical material just the other day."

"Ladies should never read statistical material," said Dubslav. "It's either too boring or too interesting — and that's even worse. But now — forgive me, getting up is so hard for me — ring for Engelke to bring us breakfast. You've arrived *a la fortune du pot* and will have to take what you get. My only consolation is that you've been on the road for three hours. 'Hunger is the best cook,' as the saying goes."

During breakfast, which was soon set up — the season allowed for a plate of plover eggs being put out as well — the atmosphere improved a bit. Dubslav yielded to what his fate had in store and Adelheid became less severe.

"Wherever did you get those plover eggs?" she said. "That's something new. When I was living here we didn't have any."

"Yes, the plover have just recently arrived here on our Stechlin, down there where the rushes grow, but only on the Globsow side. They don't want to come over to the other side. I thought maybe it was a hint that I ought to send a few to Friedrichsruh. But that wouldn't do; otherwise in the end I might be considered one of Bismarck's close admirers too, and Uncke would make a note of me. Anybody who sends plover eggs three times gets marked down in the black book. And I can't do anything like that just for Woldemar's sake alone."

"Good that way, too. Too much is too much. They say he even let himself be photographed together with that opera singer Pauline Lucca. And while they're carrying on like that up there in the government and now and then even at court, they're demanding morality and virtue. It just won't do. One has to start with one's self. And then, after all, he's only a human being too, you know, and worshipping any human being is idolatry. Worshipping people is worse even than the golden calf. But I know very well, idolatry's on the rise again these days and witchcraft is too, and they say — at least that's what Fix told me — you're even supposed to have sent for that Busch woman yourself."

"Yes, I was in bad shape."

"Exactly when a person's in bad shape is when one should come to know the Lord God and Jesus Christ, but not that Busch woman. And they say she brought you some cat's foot tea, and is supposed to have said 'water drives out the water.' Now you must have realized from hearing that, that that's not a Christian charm. That's what they call 'conjuring things,' or 'casting spells.' And where the likes of that all comes from, . . . Dubslav, Dubslav . . . . Why didn't you stay with the green drops and with Sponholz? His wife was a minister's daughter from Kuhdorf."

"Didn't help her any either. And now there she sits with him in Pfäffers, a Swiss health resort, and they're roasting together in a bake oven. He told me himself it's a bake oven."

The first day had passed by quite tolerably in any case. Adelheid talked about Fix, Schmargendorf and Schimonski, and finally even about Lebenius, the master mason in Berlin who wanted to establish a vacation settlement in Wutz. "My God, we'll be getting so many low class people around our village and nothing but Berlin brats with squinty red eyes besides. But green meadows are supposed to be good for that, they say, and our lake's supposed to have iodine in it, not very much, of course, but just enough so that they are able to detect it."

Adelheid went on talking at such a rate that Dubslav could scarcely get a word in edgewise. If he did succeed at it, however, she quickly interrupted him, despite her constant assertions that she had come to nurse him. Only when he steered the conversation to the topic of Woldemar did she listen with something resembling attention. To be sure, the Italian travel descriptions as such bored her; it was only at the mention of certain names, among which 'Tintoretto' and 'Santa Maria Novella' were at the top of the list, that she became visibly amused. In fact, she giggled at them almost as happily as did Schmargendorf. A genuine and not merely passing interest, albeit not of the friendly sort to be sure, she evidenced only when Dubslav mentioned the young bride, adding, "She's got something so inviolate about her."

"I suppose, I suppose. But that's all in the past after all."

"Whoever's chaste, stays chaste."

"Do you mean that seriously?"

"Of course I mean it seriously. I never make jokes about things like that."

At this Adelheid laughed heartily and said, "Dubslav, what kind of books have you been reading lately? Because you certainly couldn't have come up with something like that out of your own head. And not from your Pastor Lorenzen either. Next thing you know, he'll be founding his own sect of dissenters."

So passed the first day. All in all, despite little irritations, entertaining enough for the old man, who, suffering from his loneliness, was usually pleased to find anyone to chat with, even if not exactly the right person when it came to other matters. But it all did not last for long. His sister became more and more opinionated and domineering from day to day, and under the pretext that "her brother needed to be provided for differently," meddled in everything, including things having nothing at all to do with his care. Above all she was bent on talking him out of the cat's foot tea, and in the evening, when the little Meissen teapot was brought in, again and again ensued an agitated dispute about the Busch woman and her witchcraft.

Thus not even an entire week had gone by when it became indisputably clear to Dubslav that Adelheid would have to be sent packing. At the same time he pondered over what would probably be the best way to do it. That, however, was by no means a simple matter, since the "notice" would necessarily have to emanate from her. As little as he really cared for her, he was nevertheless too much the gentleman of form and refined hospitality ever to bring off insisting on her departure on his own.

It was approximately four o'clock, the weather fine but brisk. Adelheid wrapped her fur collar, an old family heirloom, around her neck, and was making her way to Krippenstapel to have him show her his bee hives. She was hoping in the process to hear something about the pastor, because she assumed that a teacher always has something to complain about the preacher and the preacher about the teacher. Every rural noblewoman considers this to be so. The bees she was more or less simply prepared to put up with.

Darkness was falling, and when the Domina was finally out of the house, it was a free hour for Dubslav who did not wish to hesitate much longer in setting his trap.

"Engelke," he said, "you might go down to the kitchen and send Marie to Old Buschy. Marie know's what's what on that score. And then she can tell the old witch Lil' Agnes is to come along up here tonight to sleep and always be around whenever I need something."

Engelke stood there with an embarrassed look.

"Well, what's wrong with you? Are you against it?"

"No, Master, I ain't actu'lly against it. But I sleep right next door too, y'know, and then it's as if I wasn't there for nothin' anymore, and was as good as replaced already. And that child can't do all the things that's got to be done, y'know. After all, Agnes is still only a wee little thing."

"Aye, that she is. And you're to stay in the next room and do everything like always, But Agnes is to come nevertheless. I need that child. And you'll soon see why too."

And so it was that Agnes indeed came, but not until quite late after Adelheid had gone upstairs to bed, not even suspecting what intrigues were being spun against her in the meantime. But everything depended on that very sort of secrecy. In fact, precisely as Schiller's villain Franz Moor — whom he otherwise resembled but little — Dubslav had devised that surprise and consternation had to be integral parts of his plan.

Agnes slept in an iron bedstead set up in the adjoining room. Dubslav, just as his sister, had not caught sight of the somewhat outlandishly dressed child when she put in her appearance at the manor house; she wore a long sky blue woolen waistless dress, to which were added high buttoned shoes and long red stockings — all things Karline had given her already last Christmas. Back then, on Christmas day in fact, the child had actually dressed herself up in all her finery, but only quietly and for herself alone, for she had been embarrassed to show herself thus in the village. Now, on the other hand, when she was to assist in caring for the master himself, now the right time had come for such things.

The night passed quietly. No one was disturbed. Not until seven did Engelke enter and say, "All right now, lil' gal, git up, 'tis sev'n already." Agnes was out of bed like the wind, ran a horn comb with a few missing teeth she had brought with her through her tightly curled long blond hair, preened herself like a kitten, and then put on her sky-blue jumper, red socks and high-buttoned shoes. Immediately thereafter, Engelke brought her a pitcher of coffee with milk, and when she was finished, she took her knitting and went into the large

295

room next door, where Dubslav was already sitting in his easy chair awaiting his sister. For at eight they took their first breakfast together.

"Well, Agnes, that's fine that you're here. Have you had your coffee yet?"

Agnes curtsied.

"Well then, sit yourself down over there at the window, so you can see better at your work. I see you've got your knitting things with you. Such a little thing like you always has to have something to do, else you get silly ideas, right?"

Agnes curtsied again and seeing the old man had nothing further to say, went over to the designated window at which stood a longish oaken table and began to knit. It was a very long stocking, fire red, and considering its narrowness, intended for herself.

She had hardly been at work very long when Adelheid entered and approached her brother seated in his easy chair. In the prevailing dim light it turned out she did not catch sight of the guest at the window. Not until Engelke entered with breakfast and the suddenly opened door let more light into the room, did she notice the child, and said, "Why, there's somebody sitting over there. Whoever is that?"

"That's Agnes, Old Buschy's grandchild."

Adelheid maintained her composure with effort. When she had once again come to herself, she said, "I see. Agnes. That child of Karline's?"

Dubslav nodded.

"That's a surprise t' me. And where have you been keeping her hidden, since I've been here? I haven't laid eyes on her the whole week long until now."

"You couldn't have either, Adelheid. She's only been here since last night. It wasn't working out any more with Engelke, at least not in the long run. After all, he's just as old as I am. And always up at night and up and down and turning me over and lifting me up. I just couldn't put up with that any more."

"And so you had Agnes come to you? Now she's supposed to turn you over and lift you? That child? That little mite? Haha. The stories you're always making up for yourself."

"Agnes," said Dubslav at this point, "you might take a run down to the kitchen to Mamsell Pritzbur and tell her I'd like a stuffed pigeon for lunch today. But not too lean and not too little stuffing, and make sure it doesn't taste like stale rolls. And then you can stay down there with Mamsell and have her tell you a story, about the *Shepherd and the Princess* or the *Fisherman and his Wife*. You know *Red Riding Hood* by now, I imagine."

Agnes stood up, strode unabashedly to the table where bother and sister were sitting, and once more made her curtsey. As she did, she held her knitting and the long stocking in her hand.

"Who are you knitting that for, eh?" asked the Domina.

"For me."

Dubslav laughed. Adelheid too. But there was a difference in their laugh. Agnes, of course, took no note of this difference, but rather looked about herself without the slightest trepidation and strode from the room to carry out the order down in the kitchen.

Once she was out of the room, however, Adelheid's crabbed laughter was repeated. But then she said. "Dubslav, I simply do not know why you've taken on this particular kind of help as long as I'm here. I am you sister and a noblewoman of the Mark. And Domina of Wutz Convent besides. And my mother was a Radegast. And the Stechlins, over there in that crypt under the altar, as far as I know, they put great store in their good name and gave themselves as much honor as any one of them could rightfully lay claim to. And here you go taking that child of Karline's right into your own room and putting her on display at your window almost so everybody can get a good look at her. How did you ever come by that child? Woldemar will certainly have reason to be pleased about that, and his wife will too, who has something 'so inviolate' about her. And Countess Melusine! Well, she'll be pleased no end, I'll bet. And has the right to be too. But I'll ask the question again, how did you ever come by that child?

"I had her come."

"Haha. Very good; 'had her come.' The stork brought her to you from those green fields out there and naturally was sure to see to the red legs at the same time. But I know you better than that. The people around here always act as if you were morally superior to old Kortschädel. As for me, I can't see it, and I'd be glad to let you have my opinion on the matter. But I don't care to put distasteful words into my mouth."

"Adelheid, you're getting all upset. And I ask myself, why? You're a bit against Old Buschy. Well that's all right, a person can be against Old Buschy. And then you're a bit against Karline. Fine. A person can be against Karline too. But I can see it in your face, the real thing that's upsetting you, it's not old Buschy and it's not Karline either, it's nothing but those red stockings. Why are you so dead set against those red stockings?"

"Because they're a sign."

"That doesn't say anything, Adelheid. Everything's a sign. What are they a sign of? That's the important thing."

"They're a sign of insolence and impudence. And whether you feel like laughing or not — because the way a blade of grass bends is how you can make out best which way the wind is blowing — they are a sign that every shred of reason has departed from this world and that every social barrier is disappearing more and more. And you support it all. You think wonders of how safe and sound you are, but you're not safe and sound and can't be, because you're caught up in all kinds of nonsensical schemes and vain ideas. And when they butter you up, or get to you through one of those hobbies of yours, then without a second thought you just let the things that really matter most in the lurch. They say there's a lot of your kind these days, for whom their wittiness and their know-it-all-attitudes are more important than their religiosity and their creed. Because they're their own creed all unto themselves. But believe you me, behind that sort of thing hides the tempter himself, and where he leads to in the end, that you know — that much will still have stuck with you, I'm sure."

"So I hope," said Dubslav.

"And because you are the way you are, you're pleased that this little fashion plate — just like Karline already — is wearing her red stockings and knitting new ones for herself in the bargain. But I'm telling you one more time, these red stockings, they're a sign, a banner held on high."

"Stockings aren't held on high."

"Not yet, but it can come to that too. And then we'll have the real revolution, the revolution in morality — what nowadays they're calling the 'final revolution.' And I simply don't understand you, that you don't have the good sense to see that, you, a man of good family, of loyalty to throne and Reich. Or who at least imagines he is."

"All right, all right."

"And you go riding around, when they want to elect that Torgelow person or Katzenstein, and you give those speeches of yours, even though you really can't speak well at all . . . . "

"Right you are there. But I didn't give any, either . . . ."

"And give your speeches for king and fatherland and for the good old values and against freedom. I don't understand you with that eternal 'against freedom business' of yours. Let them do whatever they want with that whole stupid freedom business of theirs. What's freedom anyway? Freedom isn't anything at all; freedom is when they all get together and drink beer and start up some paper or other. You served with the cuirassiers and must know, after all, that Torgelow and Katzenstein, it doesn't make the slightest difference which one, the likes of them won't shake us, not us, and not our faith and not Stechlin and not Wutz either. Those Globsowers, so long as they're

298

nothing but Globsowers, they can't shake anything at all. But once Old Buschy's grandchildren, because Karline probably has had a bunch of them by this time, once they start wearing those high buttoned shoes and their red stockings, as if that's just the way things are supposed be, yes indeed, Dubslav, then it's all over. As for freedom, just let me repeat it again, there's not much to that; but those red stockings, they *are* something. And you I don't trust one little bit and that Karline person even less, of course, even if maybe it is a while back by now."

"Let's just say, maybe."

"Oh, I know your tricks. You want to joke it all away, that's the way you are. But our convent isn't so far removed from the world, that we don't know what's what too."

"Why else would you have that Fix of yours?"

"Not a word against him."

And in great agitation the conversation broke off. But on that very same afternoon Adelheid took leave of her brother and drove back to Wutz.

But Stay a While - Death - Burial - New Days

40

WHILE THE ACRIMONIOUS scene between brother and sister was being played out upstairs, Agnes was down below in the kitchen with Mamsell Pritzbur, telling her about Berlin where she had visited her mother the previous summer. "They had a thing there," she recounted, "called the aquarium. There was a snake lying there that was thick as a leg."

"But have you ever really seen legs?" asked Pritzbur.

"Oh now, Mamsell Pritzbur, I certainly ought to've seen legs by now . . . . And then, on one other day, we were in an animal park, but a real one, I mean, with all kinds of animals in it. And they called it the 'Zoological.'"[1]

"Yes, I've heard of that place too."

"And in the 'Zoological' there was this real little lake, lots smaller than our Stechlin, and standing there in the lake were all kinds of birds. And one of them stood on one leg, just like a stork."

When the kitchen girls heard the word 'stork', they all came closer.

"But the legs on that bird, I suppose it was more than just one bird, they were lots bigger than stork's legs, and lots thicker around and redder too."

"And they didn't do anything to you?"

"No, they didn't do anything to me. Except when they'd been standin' there like that for a while, then they stood on the other leg. And I said to my mother, 'Come on, Mother, that one over there is always looking at me funny.' And so we went to another place where they had a bear."

The child continued recounting all sorts of things. The serving girls and even Mamsell Pritzbur enjoyed having Agnes, who also performed some of the songs her mother Karline always sang when she was ironing. She danced too as she sang, lifting her sky-blue dress delicately, exactly the same way she'd seen at the amusement park in Hasenheide.

And so the afternoon approached, and when it was already beginning to get dark, Engelke asked, "Aye, Master, what'll we be doin' wi' Agnes? She's still down there wi' Mamsell Pritzbur, an' the girlies is all watchin' 'er when she sings n' dances. She'll prob'ly turn out somethin' like Karline. Should she be goin' home or should she be stayin' here?"

"Of course she's to stay here. I really enjoy seeing that child. You've got a nice face, Engelke, but I'd enjoy looking at something else now and then besides you. How that lil' girlie sat there, just as straight as a princess; I just kept lookin' on and watching her for a good quarter of an hour or so, the way those knitting needles kept going and that red stocking dangling back and forth there next to her. Haven't seen anything as pretty as that since Christmas, when the count's family was here, the pale comtesse and the countess. Did you like her too?"

Engelke grinned.

"Well, I can see that. That's that then, Agnes stays. And she can get up during the night now and then and bring me a glass of that tea, or whatever else I might need, and you, you good old soul, you can get a good night's rest. Ah, Engelke, life really is hard, y'know. I mean, when it's going downhill. Before that, it's pretty good, as far as it goes. Do you remember when we used to ride from Brandenburg to Berlin? In Brandenburg there was never much doin', but in Berlin, there it was all right."

"Aye, Master. But now it's comin'."

"Aye, now it's comin'. Now it's cat's foot time. They didn't have anything like that yet back in the old days. But I won't say anything, or else Old Buschy will get mad and you've got to stay on good footing with old women. That's even more important than with the young ones. And just as I said, Agnes stays. I really do enjoy seeing something dainty as that. She really is a charming child."

"Aye, that she is, but . . . ."

"Ah, cut out your buts. You say she'll turn out like Karline. Could be. And then maybe she'll even be a nun. You never know."

And so Agnes stayed with Dubslav. She sat at the window and knitted. One time during the night, when he was feeling really poorly, he wanted to call the child. But on second thought he refrained. "That poor child, what good would it do if I disturb her sleep? And she can't help me anyhow."

A week passed in this manner. Then old Dubslav remarked, "Engelke, this business with Agnes, I just can't go on watching it anymore. She sits there knitting every morning. Why the poor little creature's going to die here for sure. And all just because an old sinner like me wants to see a friendly face. It can't go on like this. We've got to do something for the child. Don't we have some kind of book with pictures in it or somethin' like that?"

"Aye, Master, we still have them four volumes we had bound at bookbinder Zippel's in Gransee last Christmas. Actually it wasn't anything but 'n 'Agricultural Journal,' and everybody who's ever won a prize is in it. But Bismarck's in it too and so's the Kaiser."

"Right, right. That's fine. Give that to her. And you don't need to tell her not to fold down the pages, she won't do anything like that."

And so indeed it was that the 'Agricultural Journal' lay out on the next morning and Agnes was as happy as could be to have something other than her knitting and to be able to look at the pretty pictures. For there were castles in the book and little ponds with swans floating on them. And in one picture, an insert it was, even hussars were to be seen. Engelke brought a new volume every morning and on one occasion even Elfriede put in an appearance. Lorenzen had sent her over from the parsonage to inquire about Dubslav's condition. "Naturally she can look at the pictures too," said Dubslav. "Probably it will be fun for her too, and maybe while they're at it she can explain things for the little one, Agnes, I mean. And that'll make it just as good as a school lesson."

Elfriede was quite prepared to do so. And so now the two children stood next to one another and paged through the book, and the little one absorbed every word the older one told her. But Dubslav was also listening and was not certain which of the two interested him more. In the end, however, it was probably Elfriede after all. For she had that melancholy charm of all those who are to be called away early. Her delicate, almost incorporeal body seemed to say, "I'm dying." But her soul was aware of none of that. It emitted a radiance and said, "I am alive."

The picture books lasted for several days. Then Dubslav said, "Engelke, that child is starting all over from the beginning again. She's been through all four volumes twice, thick as they are. I see we've got to give this place the once-over for something new. That's a phrase from thieves' language, y'know. That's how low we've sunk. Wait a minute, I've just had a good idea. Bring down one of our weather vanes for her. They're just lyin' around like that, an' when I'm dead an' gone and everything gets assessed — what they call 'putting things in order' — then Reuter the coppersmith'll come over from Gransee and tally it all up at seventy-five pfennigs."

"But, Master. Our Woldemar."

"Oh sure, Woldemar. Woldemar is a good fellow, of course he is. And the Comtesse, his young wife, she's good too. Everybody's good; I didn't mean it as bad as all that. A fellow just talks that way now and then. But this much is true for sure, that collection of mine upstairs is good for spider webs and not much else. Collecting is crazy in general. And if Woldemar doesn't bother with it any more, it's nothin' but the restoration of good old common sense. Everybody has his own particular screw loose, and I've had mine. But don't bring everything down all at once. Just bring the mill and the dragoon."

Engelke did as he was ordered.

On the first day, as can be imagined, Agnes was completely taken by the dragoon, which years ago, when they took him from his church tower in Zellin, had been freshly painted: black hat, blue coat and red breeches. But the little girl soon wearied of the dragoon's bright colors and then it was the mill's turn. That lasted longer. Most of the time — once it was put into motion — the child needed only to blow to keep the mill arms moving fairly quickly, and the scraping of the somewhat rusty spindle remained a continuous joy and delight for her. Those were happy days for Agnes. But almost happier still for the old man.

Yes, old Dubslav took pleasure in the child. But as beneficial as her presence was to him, in the long run it was not much different after all than if a golden flower had stood at the window, or a goldfinch had been singing. He enjoyed seeking her out with his eyes, but when one week and then another had passed, he began to perceive a certain languor, so strong that he thought back almost longingly to the days when sister Adelheid had made herself obnoxious to him. That had been extremely unpleasant, but notwithstanding that, along with everything else, she possessed a keen mind, so that in everything she said there was something one could argue about, or to set off an entire fireworks of suggestive or witty remarks. That had always been one of the most important things of all for him. One could reckon Dubslav among the most peace-loving individuals in the world, but nevertheless he did love little frictions too, and even downright irritating occurrences were preferable to him than none at all.

No doubt about it, the old squire of Castle Stechlin was longing for company, and it was truly a festive day whenever visitors arrived from far or near. One day — it was already getting dark — Krippenstapel put in his appearance. He had donned his best coat and held a covered, painted jar in his left arm.

"Well now, that's nice of you, Krippenstapel. Glad to see that you're looking in to check now and again whether our museum up there still has its commander-in-chief. Commander-in-chief, I say. After all, it's you yourself who's the real director. And now here you come with an urn besides. Dug up somewhere or other by your friend Tucheband for sure. Or is it just a tureen? Good God, Krippenstapel, you didn't go off an' cook me a bowl of sick man's soup, did you?"

"No indeed, Herr Major, no soup. Not at all. But yet to a certain extent it is somethin' like that. Matter of fact, it's a honeycomb. Picked it out from my hives at noon today and permitted myself to bring you my best honeycomb. Sort of something like the medieval tithe. The tithe, if I might be permitted the remark, was actually even a finer thing than money."

"Just what I think too. But people these days don't have any sense for something refined like that. Always everything in cold cash and then more cash on top of that. Oh, money's such a common thing. When you don't have any, that is. If you've got some then it's pretty good, far as it goes. And that you thought of your old patron right off, a word, incidentally, that's maybe a bit too high-flown and doesn't rightly express our relationship. Lorenzen won't take it amiss, I hope, that when I call myself your 'patron,' I promote you, so to speak. But this business with the honeycomb. Genuinely pleases me. But I probably won't be allowed to dig into it. It's always, 'None of that.' First Sponholz forbade me everything, an'now it's old Buschy. So now I'm actually just living on club-moss and cat's foot."

"But maybe in the end it will all turn out right," said Krippenstapel. "I know of course that a layman can't meddle in a regular treatment. But maybe honey'll be an exception. Genuine honey is like good medicine and it's got the complete healing power of nature."

"But isn't there maybe something in it, that it would be better wasn't?"

"No, Herr Major. I see the bees swarming and gathering lots of times, and I see where they do their swarming and where it is they gather. First off are the lindens and the acacias and the heather. There you have it, those are innocence itself, I don't even have to say anything about it. But then you ought to see the bees when they land on a poisonous flower, let's say on a monkshood for example. You know there's lots of poison in every monkshood, especially in the red ones, but in the blue ones too though,"

"Monkshood, I can well imagine. And how do the bees act there?"

"They never take the poison, they always just take the healing power."

"Well, you ought to know, Krippenstapel. And on your responsibility I'll have a good taste of it and Old Buschy will just have to put up with it and be content for better or for worse. Incidentally, just thinking about that old woman naturally puts me in mind of the child too. There she is, sitting at the window. Well now, come on over here, Agnes, and tell us that you've been learning something here too. As a matter of fact I've been giving her books with all sorts of pictures in'm, including since day before yesterday a book about the gods. One of those still from the good old respectable times, that is, with every one of the gods decently dressed. And she's learning pretty well from it, I think. Right, Agnes?"

Agnes curtsied and returned to her place.

"And then I gave the child our dragoon too, and the windmill. In other words our best pieces, that much is true. But I imagine our museum director won't get upset over this particular intrusion. In fact, it's actually better. The child gets something from it instead of the spiders. But what's your Senior Teacher in Templin been up to lately? Has he found anything new?"

"Yes, Herr Major. A coin site."

"Ah, that's always the best. *Georgstaler* or something like that, I suspect. Thirty Years War. A horrible time, y'know. But that they went and buried so much from fear and misery actually turns out to be a blessing too. Is it anything much?"

"However you take it, Herr Major. Looked at from the practical and secular point of view, it's not particularly much. But from the scientific standpoint it's actually quite a bit. As a matter of fact, three Roman coins, two from Diocletian and one from Caracalla."

"Well at least they fit together. Diocletian was the fellow with the Christian persecutions, as I recollect. But I think when you get right down to it, it really wasn't all that bad. We've always had persecutions. And sometimes the ones who are persecuted get to be on top."

As he said that the old man laughed. Then he called Engelke to take the honey out. Krippenstapel, however, took his leave, his empty tureen carefully nestled in his arm.

41

Dubslav had been genuinely pleased by Krippenstapel's visit as well as by his gift because it was, after all, the best thing that loyal old soul was able to bring him. He insisted therefore — even though Engelke, who had a prejudice against anything sweet, was against it — that the honeycomb be placed on the breakfast table every morning.

"See, Engelke," he remarked after a week had passed, "my feeling better again, that's from the honeycomb. You've got to eat every speck of it, you know, wax and all. He told me so himself. It's just like the apple peel. That's the way nature wants it done an' it's a regular sign from nature that's got to be respected."

"I'm more for peeling them myself though," said Engelke. "When you get to see all that's on them sometimes . . . "

"Good grief, Engelke. I don't know. You've been getting so refined lately. But I'm still real old-fashioned. And besides, along with everything else I really do believe that the true 'complete healing power of nature' lies in the wax, almost moreso than in the honey. Incidentally, Krippenstapel's become so awfully cultured these days too and he's got so many refined turns of phrase, that one about 'complete healing power of nature,' for example. But he's still he's a long way from being as refined as you, I'll take an oath on that. And I'll bet that he doesn't peel any pears either."

Dubslav remained in this good mood for quite a while, more and more convincing himself that he actually could have spared himself the torments of all the other things. "After all, if it's got *everything* in it, then it's got club-moss and cat's foot in it too and, of course, foxglove as well, or, the way Sponholz puts it, 'digitalis.'"

Engelke, of course, did not want to hear the slightest bit of this sort of sophistry. His master, however, did not let himself be deterred by any such doubts and instead continued, "And then, you know, Engelke, it makes a difference from whom a thing comes. The cat's foot comes from old Buschy, but the honeycomb's from Krippenstapel. In other words, behind the honeycomb there's a good spirit and behind the cat's foot there's an evil one. And you can believe me, a great deal in life depends on mysteries of this sort, and when Lorenzen gives me that paw of his, it's a completely different thing than when Koseleger offers me his hand. Koseleger's got such soft fingers and he wears a gigantic ring on his fourth."

"But, after all, he is a superintendent."

"True, superintendent he is. And he'll be climbing higher up too. If it were up to the princess, he'd get to be pope. And then we'd all want to get an indulgence from him: but I'll not give much."

While Dubslav and Engelke conducted this conversation, Agnes sat at the window as usual, listening with half an ear. Although she understood little, she nevertheless understood just enough. Krippenstapel was a good spirit and her grandmother was an evil one. But all that meant nothing more to her than if she were being told a fairy tale. She had heard so much in her life by then and was probably destined to hear many, many other things as well. Thus her facial expression remained the same. She merely day-dreamed, and the fact that she had such a nature was actually the very thing about her that so captivated the old gentleman. The gaze with which she looked upon humanity was different from that of others.

Engelke had withdrawn to the adjoining servant's room, a bright radiance fell from the verandah through the balcony door and gave the relatively dark room somewhat more light than usual. Dubslav held the *Kreuzzeitung* in his hand and was swatting at a horse fly which buzzed around him again and again. "Damnable creature," he said, as he prepared to swing at it again. Before he could strike, however, Engelke appeared and asked if Uncke could speak with the master.

"Uncke, our old Uncke?"

"Aye, Mast'r."

"Why, certainly. Finally get to see a sensible person again. Wonder what he's bringing with him. Maybe an arrest someplace. A nest of democrats he's cleaned out."

Agnes perked up her ears. An arrest! A nest of democrats cleaned out! Now there was something even better than a fairy tale about good and evil spirits.

In the meantime Uncke had entered, his chin whiskers and mustache as usual firmly waxed. He remained standing near the door and saluted in a military fashion. Dubslav, however, called to him, "No, Uncke, not over there. My hearing won't reach that far, not to mention my voice. And anyway, I presume you're bringing some news. Something official. Over here then. And if it's not something really official, just take that chair there."

Uncke came closer but did not take a chair. "If the Herr Major will excuse me, I'm here just . . . . Old Baruch Hirschfeld was telling me, and Old Buschy was telling me . . . ."

"Aha, about my feet."

"Yes sir, Herr Major."

"Right, Uncke. Would to God things were better. Every time somebody new comes, I think, 'This'll do it.' But nothing works any more, helps just for three days. Old Buschy doesn't help any more, and Krippenstapel doesn't help any more, and Sponholz hasn't helped for a long time already; he just goes touring around like that all over the world. Nobody left but the good Lord."

Uncke accompanied these sentiments with a nod of his head which was intended to express his respectful attitude — although nothing more than that either — towards the good Lord. Dubslav took note of it and was amused. Then he went on in rapidly increasing good humor, "Yes indeed, Uncke, we've gone through many a good day together, you and I. Think back on it with pleasure — you're still one of the old timers. And Pyterke too. What's he up to?"

"Ah, Herr Major, still on the job he is, dashing as ever," and as he said that he pulled himself up straighter, as if at least to offer a suggestion of the superior dignity of his colleague.

Dubslav took it in this manner and said, "Yes sir, old Pyterke, naturally, always way up there on his horse. And you, Uncke, you've always got to hoof it like a country postman. But that has its good side too. Walking keeps you loose, riding makes you stiff. And lazy too. And any way you take it, Shank's mares are still always the best. You never have a downfall with them. But these days everybody wants to be up there on his high horse. That's what they call the 'sign of the times.' Have you heard that expression yet, Uncke?"

"Yes sir, Herr Major."

"And the Social Democrats, they want to be up on their high horse too, just like Pyterke, only a lot higher. But a thing like that doesn't happen right off. Good things take time, as the saying goes. And Torgelow, even if he can talk a lot maybe, he's still a long way from being in the saddle. Tell me, what's he actually been up to? That Torgelow fellow, I mean. Are the common folk more satisfied with him these days?"

"No, Herr Major, they're still not yet satisfied with him. He wanted to make a speech in Berlin the other day and actually mentioned something about it to Count Posadowsky.[2] And it was so dumb that it embarrassed the others. And so they signaled to him, 'Torgelow, you just keep quiet for now. That's not the way things work around here'."

"Right," laughed Dubslav, "and where that fellow stands now, I was actually supposed to be standing. But it's better this way anyhow. Now Torgelow can show he can't do anything. And the others too. And when they've all shown it, you never can tell, then maybe we'll be in line again and come out on top one more time and everybody'll get a bonus. You too, Uncke, and Pyterke too, of course."

Uncke smiled and put two fingers to his temple.

"For the time being though, we'll just have to wait and see and prevent what they call the 'revolution' and make sure that our Globsowers are satisfied. And if we're smart, maybe we'll pull that off too. Don't you think so as well, Uncke, that there are little things we can do?"

"Yes sir, Herr Major, there's little things we can do all right. Already being done."

"And which ones do you mean?"

"Music, Herr Major, and later closing times."

"Yes sir," laughed Dubslav. "That's the sort of thing that helps. Music and a schott'sche, then the girls are happy."

"And," said Uncke by way of confirmation, "when the girls are happy, Herr Major, everybody's happy."

Uncke had to promise to come by again some time. It never came to that, however, for Dubslav's condition rapidly worsened. No more visitors were accepted, and only Lorenzen had admittance. But mostly he came only when called.

"Strange," said the old man while gazing out at a spring day, "this Lorenzen fellow isn't actu'lly a regular pastor at all. He doesn't talk about redemption and not about immortality either. Almost seems, as if he considered somethin' like that too good for every day use. Maybe it's somethin' else though too, and in the end he doesn't know much about it himself. At first I was a bit surprised about it because I always told myself, 'Well sure, a fellow with cassock and collar like that, when you get right down to it, he ought to know about that sort of thing; after all, he's got his three years' studying behind him and he's preached his probationary sermon, and a consistorial councilor or maybe even some general superintendent has laid hands on him and told him and a few others 'Go forth and teach ye all nations.' And when you hear something like that, well then, then you expect a fellow knows how things actually stand with you too. It's just the same as with the doctors. But in the end you put yourself in their hands anyway and prefer those doctors who honestly tell you, 'Listen, we don't know anything either, we'll just have to wait and see.' Good old Sponholz, who's probably passed that bridge with the ichthyosaurius by now, he was practically that sort of fellow and Lorenzen is for sure. Known him nearly twenty years now and to this day he never tried to fool me one single time. And to be able to say that about somebody, why that's really the most important thing of all. That other business, . . . right, good heavens above, where's it all supposed to come from anyway, when you get right down to it? It's been a long time since anybody's stood on Mount Sinai, and even if anybody had, what the good Lord said up there doesn't unlock any great riddles either. It's all been mostly concerned with this life; 'thou shalt' this and 'thou shalt' that, and more often still 'thou shalt *not*.' Actually it all sounds as if some Nuremberg magistrate had been making proclamations."

Just afterwards Engelke entered, bringing the mail. "Engelke, you might send Marie over to Lorenzen — I'd like to have him come over."

Lorenzen did in fact come and pulled his chair over to the old man's side. "Nice of you, Pastor, that you've come right over. I see again how all good things are rewarded right off down here below. You should know, as a matter of fact, that I've already been thinking about you quite a bit today, and — to the extent it's possible, have come to some pretty firm conclusions regarding your character, which, of course, vacillates like so many other things. If talking weren't to a degree difficult because of my asthma, I'd be capable of slipping into some kind of indiscretion against myself and give away what I was thinking about you. I've got, as you of course well know, a natural inclination for telling everything, for just chattering in general. Old Kortschädel, who otherwise never distinguished himself with the use of French words, once even called me a *'causeur.'* But, of course, that's a long time ago now, and completely over and done with. In the end even the old children's nanny in us finally dies."

"Don't believe it. You at least, Herr Stechlin, are proof there's always an exception."

"I'll take that for what it's worth and use it to justify myself at the same time. Did you read in the papers how they've been badgering poor Bennigsen lately?[3] I don't like it, even if Bennigsen isn't exactly my man."

"Nor mine. But whatever he may be, one thing he is, and that is an idealist, what they call an 'Excelsior-man'. And in this part of the country, when it comes to the Junkers from East of the Elbe — begging your pardon, you're among them yourself, of course — whoever's always ready with a cheerful 'Excelsior' is a dubious character from the start and an object of deep distrust. Any higher-set goal, any willingness that goes beyond a sack of potatoes, finds no support, certainly no credence. And if anyone actually does something altruistic, they just say he's casting a sprat to catch a mackerel."

Dubslav laughed. "Lorenzen, you're back on you hobby horse again. But I'm to blame for it myself, of course. Why did I ever bring up Bennigsen? That brought up the whole topic and your joust for Bebel and Co. (you're certainly not far from it, that's for sure) could commence. But just so you'll know, I've got my hobby horse too, and it goes like this: King and Crown Prince or the old times and the new times. And there's something I've been wanting to talk with you about for quite a while, not theoretically but Brandenburgish-practical-like, more or less with a particular regard to my immediate future. Because in my case it's practically, 'What thou doest, do quickly' . . . ."

Lorenzen took the old man's hand and said, "Different times are coming for sure. But one shouldn't start too soon with questions about what will come and what will be. I don't see any reason why our dear old King of Thule[4] won't be reigning around here for quite a while yet. Quaffing his last drink and throwing the beaker into the Stechlin, we've still got plenty of time for that."

"No, Lorenzen, it's not going to be much longer. The signs are there, more than enough of them. And just so everything goes the way it's supposed to, I'll soon be hitting sixty-seven as well, and when a real Stechlin hits his sixty-seventh year, then he goes to death and the grave. That's more or less a family tradition. I wish we had a different one, because we human beings are really cowardly and would really rather go on living this miserable life."

"Miserable life! Herr von Stechlin, you've had a very good life."

"Huh, if only that's true! I don't know if all the Globsowers think that way. And *they* bring me back to my main topic again."

"Which is?"

"Which is: Dearest Pastor, see to it that the Globsowers don't get too high and mighty."

"But Herr von Stechlin, those poor people . . . ."

"Don't say that. Those poor people. That was true once, but these days it doesn't fit any more. And such a shaky character as my Woldemar, and as my dear old Lorenzen — from whom, you'll pardon me, the lad has all that nonsense — such shaky characters, instead of barring the door against them, meet that Torgelow bunch half way and say, 'Why sure enough, Töffel, you're actually right as rain,' or, what's even worse, 'Sure, sure. Jochen, Let's do it just like that.'"

"But Herr von Stechlin."

"Yes, Lorenzen, even if you do put on such a good face, it's true nevertheless. The whole of history is being poured into a different mold and when they have another election one of these days, Woldemar will go riding around telling them all over the place, 'Katzenstein's the right man.' Or somebody else. But they're six of one or half dozen of the other — if you'll forgive the rather modern expression.

"And then, when the young mistress has guests or maybe even gives a ball, I'll tell you exactly who'll show up in this old barn here, which'll be renovated by then besides. First off, Minister von Ritzenberg'll be invited, who, because he was put on ice under Bismarck, has had a real rage at the old boy from Sachsenwald from a long way back. He'll open the Polonaise with Armgard. And then there'll be a professor, a class-room socialist. Not a soul will know whether he wants to straighten out society or put it out of joint. And he'll be leading some female aristocrat with short hair — who writes, of course — in the quadrille. And then joining in there'll be an Africa explorer, an architect and a portrait painter. And when they have an intermission after the first dances, they'll present a *tableau vivant* in

311

which a poacher gets shot dead by some nobleman or else they'll perform some French play that lady with the short hair translated, one of those so-called adultery plays, in which some lawyer's wife gets glorified because she shot her husband dead as a doornail with a pocket revolver. And then come some musical pieces in which some piano player goes sweeping up and down the keys with his long mane. And in an adjoining room others'll be sitting, leafing through an album with nothing but celebrities; first off, of course, old Wilhelm and Kaiser Friedrich along with Bismarck and Moltke. And right in their midst, comfortable as can be, Mazzini and Garibaldi and Marx and Lasalle, who are at least dead, and Bebel and Liebknecht right next to them. And then Woldemar will say, 'Just take a look at Bebel there. My political opponent, but a man of conviction and intelligence.' And then when a nobleman from the imperial residence steps up to him and says, 'I'm surprised, Herr von Stechlin — I expected to see Count Schwerin[5] here,' Woldemar'll say, 'That gentleman and I have lost touch.'"

The pastor laughed. "And *you*'re talking about dying. Anyone who can talk that long will live for another ten years."

"None of that, none of that. I'm holding you to it. Will it be coming to that or not?"

"Well then, it will surely *not* come to that."

"Are you certain?"

"Absolutely."

"Then tell me what *will* come, but honestly."

"Well, I can easily do that; and you yourself pointed the way for me right at the beginning when you spoke of the 'king and crown prince.' This polarity naturally exists everywhere and in all stations of life. There will simply always be days when the people are on the lookout for some sort of a crown prince. But as surely as that's true, the other point is even more so: that crown prince everyone's on the lookout for never lives up to what's expected of him. Sometimes he tips over at the outset, and in a fit of suddenly awakened piety declares his desire to go on reigning in the sense of his beloved and late lamented predecessor. As a rule though, he makes a passably honest try at making a new beginning, and even actually pulls out a program from his pocket that's intended to assure the happiness of his people. But it's just not for very long. As Schiller put it, 'Thoughts with each other easily reside, but things in narrow space collide.'[6] And in half a year this innovator will be steering for the old paths and byways."

"And that's what Woldemar will do too?"

"That's what Woldemar will do too. At least very soon he'll feel like more or less halfway heading back to the old ways."

"And naturally you'll oppose this feeling. You put it into his head that something totally new has to come. Even a new form of Christianity."

"I don't know if I said anything like that, but if I did, this new form of Christianity is precisely the old one."

"Do you believe that?"

"I do believe it. And what's better, I feel it."

"Well fine. That business of a new Christianity is *your* affair, I'm not going to interfere with you there. But as for the other business, there you've got to promise me something. If he thinks it over and comes around to the view that the old Prussia with its king and army, despite all its ailments and moth-eaten old tales, is still better than that of recent date, and that we old timers from the Cremmen Pike and Fehrbellin, even though we're not in such good shape, still have more heart for the Torgelow crowd than all the Torgelows put together, if it ever comes to that sort of reconversion, *then*, Lorenzen, don't do anything to hinder the process. Or else I'll haunt you. Granted, pastors don't believe in ghosts, but when they do come knocking, they get the shivers too."

Lorenzen put his hand on Dubslav's hand and stroked it as if he were the old man's son. "Every bit of that, Herr von Stechlin, I can gladly promise you. I educated Woldemar as was incumbent upon me. And you, in your good sense and the goodness of your nature, did nothing to hinder me. Now your son is a distinguished gentleman and is old enough to stand on his own. There is a time for speaking and a time for keeping silent. But if you take control of him and me from up above there, and maybe even feel like haunting me, don't lay a burden on me that's not my due. It won't be I, who'll be guiding him. That's been seen to already. The times will have their say, and along with the times, the new house, his pale young wife, and perhaps too the beautiful Melusine."

The old man smiled. "True, true."

42

So the conversation went. And thus, when Lorenzen got up to leave, the old man felt as if he had been restored and looked forward to a good night with plenty of sleep and little in the way of anxiety.

But it turned out differently. The night passed badly, and when morning came and Engelke brought breakfast, Dubslav said, "Engelke, get rid of the honeycomb. I can't even look at that sweet stuff any more. Krippenstapel meant well. But it's not any good, and that whole business about the complete healing power of nature isn't any good."

313

"I think you're wrong there, Master. It's just that the honeycomb can't do nothin' 'gainst the power it's against."

"By which you mean, I suppose, there's no remedy against death. Right, that's probably it. I think so too."

Engelke said nothing.

An hour later a letter arrived, which, despite its having originated from extremely close by, had nevertheless been sent through the mail. It was from Ermyntrud and dealt with the asylum for neglected children planned by Koseleger and herself. At its conclusion it stated that, when — hopefully within a short time — her wishes regarding Dubslav's improving health had been fulfilled, Agnes, Old Buschy's grandchild, might, she trusted, be the first to be taken in for moral healing at the aforesaid asylum.

Dubslav turned the letter back and forth. He read it again and then said, "Oh, this farce . . . 'when my wishes for your improving health have been fulfilled,' . . that simply means 'pretty soon when you'll be looking at the grass from underneath.' People are all egoists, princesses too, and if they're pious, they've got their own special jargon to boot. Let it stay like that too, it's always been that way. If only they had a bit more confidence in the common sense of others."

He stuck the letter back in its envelope as he spoke and called to Agnes. The child came.

"Agnes, do you like it here?"

"Yes, Master, I like it here."

"And it's not too quiet for you?"

"No, Master, it's not too quiet for me either. I'd like to stay here for ever."

"Well then, you'll stay too, Agnes. Just as long as it's possible. And afterwards, well, afterwards . . ."

The child knelt down before him and kissed his hand.

Dubslav's condition worsened quickly. Engelke went up to him and said, "Master, shouldn't I send to town?"

"No."

"Or to Buschy?"

"Yes, do that. An ol' witch like still always knows what's best to do."

Tears came to Engelke's eyes.

Dubslav, as he noticed it, quickly struck up a different tone. "No, Engelke, don't get afraid of your old master. I was just talking. Old Buschy's not to come. It probably wouldn't do me any harm, but when you're practically looking into your grave like this, you've got to talk differently, you know, or else people'll say things about you after you're gone. An' that's not the kind of thing I'd want, not for my own sake nor for Woldemar's either . . . And then there's Adelheid, she just popped into my head too . . . . In the end she'd probably come right after me, just to save me. No, Engelke, no Old Buschy. But give me some more of those drops again. They're a little bit better than the tea after all."

Engelke left and Dubslav was alone once more. He felt the end approaching. "The self is nothing — one's got to fill himself completely with that idea. It's an eternal law fulfilling itself, nothing more. And this fulfillment, even if it is called 'death,' shouldn't make us fearful. Calmly accepting this law, that's what makes a moral human being and ennobles him."

He pursued these thoughts for a bit and was glad he had overcome all fear. But then more waves of anxiety came nevertheless and he sighed, "Life is short, but the hour is long."

It was a difficult night. Everyone remained up. Engelke ran back and forth, and Agnes sat in her bed peering with wide eyes through the half-opened door into the sick man's room. Not until dawn was breaking did it become more tranquil throughout the house. The patient dozed weakly and Agnes too fell asleep.

It was probably past seven — the trees of the park behind the front garden were already bathed in bright sunshine — when Engelke came to the child and awakened her. "Git op, Agnes."

"Is 'e ded?"

"Nay. E's sleepin' a bit. An' I b'lieve, 'e ain't got it sittin' so ona breast."

"I'm so 'fraid."

"Don't have ta be. Could ev'n be e's slept 'imself better agin . . . An' now, git op an' put a cloth on yer hed. It's still a bit cool out there. An' then go out in the garden an' if yer find somethin' pick 'im a bit a crocus er whatever else ther' be."

The little girl passed quietly through the balcony door to the verandah, and made her way towards the round flower bed to look for a few flowers. She found all sorts of things. The best were the snow drops. Then she walked back and forth a few times, the flowers in her hand, watching as the sun rose higher across the way. She shuddered from the cold. At the same time a feeling of life came over her. Then she again entered the room and walked to the chair where Dubslav sat. Engelke, his hands folded, stood next to his master.

315

The child approached and laid the flowers on the old man's lap.

"They be the first," said Engelke, "an prob'ly they'll be the best o'em too."

43

It was early Wednesday morning when Dubslav quietly and painlessly departed this life. Lorenzen was called. Kluckhuhn too arrived, and an hour later a local messenger was on the way to bring the news of the old man's death to those living closest in the county, above all to the Domina, then Koseleger, the Katzlers and finally to the Gundermanns.

On the next day two letters arrived at the Barbys, one from Adelheid, the other from Armgard. Adelheid provided the count's family briefly and formally with notice of her brother's passing, while at the same time informing them that the funeral would take place Saturday at noon. Armgard's letter, however, ran as follows: "Dear Melusine! We'll be staying here until tomorrow — one more time for the Forum and once more the Palatine. I'll be drinking from the Trevi Fountain on this very day, that means you'll come back again and, as everybody knows, for anyone leaving Rome that's the greatest consolation of all. Then we're off to Capri, but in slow stages and among other places we'll be staying half a day at Monte Cassino, where — forgive my erudition — the whole system of monastic orders is supposed to have gotten its start. I love monasteries even if they aren't the thing for me personally. We'll be touching Naples only briefly and are heading right for Amalfi, unless we prefer Ravello, which lies somewhat higher up. And only then by way of Sorrento to Capri, the real goal of our trip. We won't be staying at Pagano's, where, with all due respect for art, there are too many artists, but somewhat further down at about the half-way mark. Some people here have recommended it to us. We'll be there by this time next week for certain. See to it we find a letter from you waiting for us. Before then we're as good as unreachable, a condition I always wanted for myself as a child and pictured as being something extraordinarily poetic. Kiss my dear old Papa for me. And send a thousand greetings to Stechlin. But above all, see to it that you go on being what you've always been, the sister, the mother (but never the auntie) of your blissful and always and always tenderly loving, Armgard."

Armgard's letter scarcely received its due, since both the old count as well as Melusine were totally taken up with considerations as to whether it might not be possible to reach the young couple some-

316

where by telegram, despite Armgard's assertions to the contrary. But it could not be done, they were forced to give up and content themselves with making their own personal arrangements for the journey to Stechlin. The old count's health was not of the best, thus his absence from the funeral was sorely desired on the part of the family physician. But that was utterly unthinkable. And thus early Saturday morning father and daughter started out on their way to Stechlin. Jeserich was also brought along to be on hand just in case. Splendid weather held sway but the air was sharp. Thus despite the sunshine they shivered from the cold.

In the old manor house at Stechlin things looked greatly changed on the day of the funeral. Usually so quiet and secluded, everything today was hustle and bustle. Innumerable coaches appeared and took their place on the village square, most of them quite close to the church. It stood in blazing sunshine so that one could easily make out the tall gravestones fixed into its fieldstone wall which had lain in the nave before its restoration. Of ivy there was none, only elder bushes which were beginning to sprout, and in between bushes of mountain ash grew around the choir.

The deceased had been laid out in the house vestibule, which had been transformed into a hall of greenery by palms and laurels. Adelheid did the honors, and her advanced years, but even more her sense of self-importance, enabled her to carry out the role which had become her responsibility with a certain dignity. From Berlin, besides the Barbys, father and daughter, had also come Baron and Baroness Berchtesgaden as well as Rex and Captain von Czako. Rex looked as if he wanted to say something at the grave whereas Czako contented himself with displaying the socially acceptable average measure of mourning.

But the Berlin guests were lost, of course, among the contingent which the county itself had assembled. The selfsame gentlemen who — scarcely half a year earlier — had come together on election day in Rheinsberg and who on that occasion, apart from a few exceptions, had actually been more amused than irritated by Torgelow's victory, were again assembled today: Baron Beetz, Herr von Krangen, Jongherr van dem Peerenboom, von Gnewkow, von Blechernhahn, von Storbeck, von Molchow, von der Nonne, the majority of them, as was usually the case, with extremely critical countenances.

Director Thormeyer had also come, *in pontificalibus*, bedecked with so many decorations and medals that he far outdid the provincial nobility. A few poked one another in fact, and von Molchow re-

317

marked *sotto voce* to von der Nonne, "D'ya see there, Nonne, looks like that 'Battle of the Butterflies'[7] show we've been reading about in the papers every day."

But despite these mocking remarks, Thormeyer would have remained the chief object of every eye had not the noble Lord of Alten-Friesack, scorning every form of decoration, and merely berobed in a high-collared and absolutely primeval mourning coat, presented him with competition that carried the day. The Wendic idol-like cast of his head again today proved to be the decisive factor in his favor. With a pagoda-like air he merely nodded hither and thither, and seemed to address even the eldest of the assembled nobility with the question, "What business have you here?" He considered himself in fact — whereby he followed an inherited familial tradition — to be the sole truly legitimate inhabitant and representative of the entire county.

Those were more or less the chief mourners. All stood closely packed, and von Blechernhahn, who, when it came to 'dash' almost approached von Molchow, commented, "Curious to see what that fellow Lorenzen will come up with. Leans toward that liberal Göhre crowd, y'know."[8]

"Right, Göhre," said von Molchow. "Strange the way chance rolls the dice. Life always comes up the best jokes after all."

Further this somewhat uninhibited discussion did not go, for just as Molchow was letting loose his arrow, general attention was directed toward that place in the entry hall where the coffin lay in state on its catafalque. In point of fact, it was at this very spot and clad moreover in a marvelously well-fitted tail coat trimmed with satin lapels, that at this very moment Attorney Katzenstein put in his appearance. Having laid a gigantic Gransee wreath at the foot of the coffin, with the sense of repose only a good conscience can impart, he then strode toward Adelheid, before whom he bowed in his most respectful manner. The latter displayed her best demeanor and thanked him. From various sides, however, one could softly make out the word 'affront' while a Katzensteinean colleague, only recently gone over to Christianity and Conservatism, standing in the immediate vicinity of the noble Lord of Alten-Friesack, murmured smilingly to himself, 'crafty rascal.'

And now it was time.

The procession came to order. A military band from the nearest garrison took the lead, then came the Stechlin peasants, who had requested permission to bear the coffin. Servants and maids from the household carried the wreaths. Then proceeded Adelheid with Pastor Lorenzen, immediately followed by the entire body of mourners, many in their uniforms of office. Outside one could see that a large number of common folk had formed a guard of honor. It was the people from Globsow. At election time they had all voted for Torgelow, or at the least for Katzenstein, but now that the old timer was dead, they were predominantly of one opinion, "Far'z it went, he wuz dern good."

The music sounded wonderful, and little girls strewed flowers about, and so it was that they made their way up the gradually ascending church yard, threading between the graves, heading finally in the direction of the age old low church portal. In front of the altar they placed the coffin on a stone slab fitted with a special lowering device, beneath which the vault of the Stechlins was located. The church's nave and lofts were filled to overflowing; even in the churchyard outside people stood shoulder to shoulder.

And now Lorenzen approached the coffin to say a few words over him, whom — despite all their differences of opinion — he had so dearly loved and revered.

"'Whosoever walketh in his uprightness shall enter into peace; they shall rest in their beds.'"[9] To walk this path was the endeavor of him at whose bier we now stand. I'll not give a picture of his life, for the sort of a life it was is known to all who have appeared in this place today. His life lay open like a book; nothing in it was hidden, for nothing needed to be. When one saw him, he seemed to be of the older generation, old too in the way he viewed the times and life itself. But for those who knew his true nature, he was not an oldster, although to be sure, not of the new generation either. Rather, he possessed something which lies far beyond all temporal things, something which has always been of value and always will be of value, a heart.

"He was not a program nobleman, not a nobleman according to the traditional mold. But instead he was a nobleman in the sense of that which encompasses the best of all things, that something which goes by the name of noble-mindedness. He was really and truly free. Knew it too, he did, even though he often disputed it.

"Kneeling before the golden calf was not his way. So it was that he was impervious to what brings unhappiness and ruins the lives of so many others, envy or a bad reputation. He did not have a single enemy, because he himself was the enemy of no man. He was goodness itself, the embodiment of that wise, old saying, 'Do unto others as you would have others . . . . '

"And so that leads me to the question of his religious convictions. In that regard he had less of the word than of the deed. He held to good works and was truly that which we should call a real Christian. For he had love. Nothing in human nature was foreign to him, be-

319

cause he felt himself to be a human being, and was always aware of his own human failings. Everything which our Lord and Savior once preached, and to which He attached His promise of salvation — all of that was his, he was a peace-maker, merciful, and pure of heart. He was the best we can be, a man and a child. Now he has gone to his father's dwelling and there he will have that heavenly rest which is the blessing of all blessings."

A few of those present glanced at one another at this concluding turn of phrase. Most noticeable was Gundermann. His attitude of half agreeing, half rejecting called forth again at this point a smile amongst the "ancient and venerable" here assembled — who apparently ascribed to themselves, but not to him, the right to be critical. Then in upraised voice followed the prayer and final blessing, and as the organ set in, the coffin on its lowering stone descended slowly into the vault. A moment later as the now ascending stone closed the vault opening with a peculiarly clattering noise, could be heard from the direction of the church door first a violent sobbing, then the words, "Now h'it's awl owver, Oi wanna go too."

It was Agnes. They led the child from the kneeling bench on which she was standing, to take her, with the encouragement of those around her, outside to the church yard. There for a time she wandered weeping amidst the graves and then made her way down the street towards the woods.

Old Buschy herself had not ventured to attend.

Among those standing outside in the church yard were von Molchow and von der Nonne. Each awaited his coach which could not immediately drive up because of the dense crowd. Both froze bitterly in the sharp wind blowing across from the lake.

"I don't know," said von der Nonne, "why they didn't hold the services in the house, where they could at least have heated things up. Why, the temperature inside there wasn't fit for a human being at all. And now to top it off, out here."

"Sad but true," said Molchow, "and I'll prob'ly wind up with a head cold besides. And now and then a fellow can even die from a thing like that. And when you're in Berlin — it's even worse. I know, because I just recently took part in something like this there too. They've got something they call a viewing room there, a sort of chapel with bible sayings an' laurel trees, and behind it all, they've got a few singer people hidden. But when you get to see them afterwards, they look pretty well fed."

"Seen it, seen it," said Nonne.

"Well, the singing," continued Molchow, "that's all right, I suppose. In the end you can put up with it. But that floor and the draft through the open door. And if that were the only thing you're in for. But if you're really unlucky in the winter, you wind up standing right next to a hot iron stove. And when I say that thing's steaming, that's still not sayin' enough. And you can feel sorry for the preacher too. He's more or less not speaking for a soul. I mean, who can really pay attention when you've got such a draft or an oven steaming like that? The only thing I know is that it always makes me think about the three men in the fiery furnace. Half iceberg, half baked apple like that. Not the thing for me."

"Right, the Berliners," said Nonne. ". . . Not t'be believed."

"Not t'be believed. And then they actually imagine they got the best of everything. And there's many a one of 'em that really believes it too. But hell'll get the last laugh."

"I say there, Molchow, control yourself. That bit about Berlin, that's all right, I suppose. But to go on right here like that about hell, right here in the middle of a Christian church yard . . . ."

Soon thereafter the church yard had emptied and everyone who lived in the county round about was on the way home. Only the guests from Berlin, who were compelled to await the next train from Rostock which would pass through Gransee, had returned to the manor house, where in the meantime a snack had been prepared. Rex and Czako as well as the Berchtesgadens first took a glass of wine, then a cup of coffee. A moderately lively conversation sprang up between the old Count and Adelheid, in which the count recalled the good qualities of the deceased. Since sister Adelheid, however, like so many sisters, harbored all sorts of doubts and reservations with regard to the deeds and doings of her brother, the conversation soon turned to the children. It was lamented that they had not been able to be present at such a beautiful ceremony. To be sure, there was also an almost diametrically opposed regret here and there expressed that the young couple would undoubtedly have to break off their sojourn in the south. The old count, in the goodness of his nature, found everything Adelheid had to say quite reasonable; Adelheid's feelings on the other hand were satisfied in the recognition that she actually found the old fellow much nicer than expected.

44

Melusine had returned from the church to the manor house and first devoted herself briefly to her friends the Berchtesgadens, then to Rex and Czako. Following that she made her way to the parsonage to express her thanks to Lorenzen, and to have another brief conversation with him about Woldemar and Armgard, essentially a repetition of everything she had discussed with him during her Christmas visit. Thus she chatted the time away far beyond her intentions, and when at last she returned to the manor house, she encountered there that restless atmosphere of readiness for departure which no longer permitted the serious pursuit of any topic whatsoever. She confined herself, therefore, to a few words with Aunt Adelheid.

That they could not abide one another was as certain to the one as to the other. Simply put, they were antipodes: a woman of the convent and a woman of the world, Wutz and Windsor, above all, a narrow and an open nature.

"What a man your Pastor Lorenzen," said Melusine. "And luckily enough still unmarried as well."

"I would rather not emphasize that point and find it all the less praiseworthy. It contradicts the example given by our man of God Martin Luther and no doubt contradicts nature as well."

"True, commonplace nature. But there are exceptions, thank the Lord. And those the ones who are truly chosen. Taking a wife is an everyday event."

"And not to take a wife is a risky business. And one has all that gossip from people besides."

"One always has gossip. It's the first thing one must become indifferent to. Not pridefully, but lovingly."

"I'll allow to that. But the love of a natural person reveals itself at its best in the family."

"Yes, that of a natural person . . . ."

"It would seem to sound, *Frau Gräfin*, as if you were taking the part of the unnatural."

"In a certain sense that's true, *Frau Domina*. The decisive point is whether one reckons upwardly or downwardly."

"Life reckons downwardly."

"Or upwardly — as the case may be."

It all sounded rather strained. For as easy-going and cheerful as Melusine was, there was one tone she could not bear, that of moral superiority. Thus there was the real danger of seeing these sharp exchanges continue. But the announcement that the carriages had driven up put an end to any such peril. Melusine broke off the discussion and merely briefly made known that she intended to write a letter from Berlin tomorrow morning as early as possible which would presumably arrive in Capri at the same time as the newlyweds. Adelheid was in agreement, and Melusine took Baron Berchtesgaden's arm while the old count took that of the baroness.

The top of the carriage pulling to a halt before the door was pushed back, and soon the baroness and Melusine had taken their places while the two gentlemen occupied the rear seats behind them. Thus they passed down the willow-lined boulevard already blooming with catkins leading in an almost straight line to Gransee. The weather was glorious. Of the cold prevailing in the morning, nothing more could be felt; the sky was an even gray, only here and there a spot of blue. Smoke hovered on the silent air and the sparrows chirped cheerfully on the telegraph wires. From the green fields of budding grain larks rose into the sky.

"How beautiful," said Baron Berchtesgaden, "and yet you always hear talk of the unpoetic barrenness of these regions."

Everyone agreed, especially the old count who soaked up the spring air and again and again expressed how content this hour made him. His ardent feelings made a deep impression on all.

"I thought, my dear Barby," said the Baron, "that I had done the utmost possible in my homage to your Brandenburg countryside in the spring. But I see that I'm nevertheless still far behind you. You've driven me from the field."

"Yes," said the old count, "and it's probably fitting that I do. After all, I'm the next in line who will have take leave of it."

Rex and Czako followed in a light hunting chaise. The two dappled ponies, little Shetlanders, shook their manes. That they were coming from a funeral could not be readily made out from the vehicle.

"Rex," said Czako, "You can put on a different face again now. Or are you trying to make me believe that you're really that depressed?"

"No, Czako, I wouldn't put on that clumsy a show. And even if anything like that occurred to me, under no circumstances in front of an audience named Czako. Anyhow, you just want to unburden yourself to me. It's you who's depressed, and when I think it all over, it looks to me as if that Chateau Lafitte didn't agree with you. It had the effect — you know, I still gratefully remember the old boy's *Bocksbeutel* from our visit in October — as if Aunt Adelheid had brought it with her from the convent."

"Rex, why, it looks as if you've been transmogrified and are talking almost in my style. It really is remarkable, you know, no sooner do people get that provincial nest of a Berlin behind them than they begin to talk reason again."

"Much obliged. But no fancy tricks with the main business. I'm still asking, why so glum, Czako? Because it's beyond a doubt that you're glum. Well then, if it's not the Lafitte, it can only be Melusine."

Czako sighed.

"Well, there we have it. Facts of the case determined, although I don't quite understand your sighing. After all, you haven't got the slightest reason for doing so. Overall situation on the contrary extremely favorable."

"You're forgetting, Rex, the Countess is very rich."

"That doesn't complicate matters, merely makes them easier."

"And besides that, she's as sharp as they come."

"Which you are too practically, at least now and then."

"And then the Countess is a countess, in fact she's even a double countess, once by birth and then once more through marriage. And then, besides that, these devilishly aristocratic names, Barby, Ghiberti. What chance does a Czako have? My dearest Rex, one has to have the courage to look the facts straight in the eye. I make no secret of it, Czako has something of the lower ranks quality about it, sort of like Reserve Private Schultze. Do you know that delightful ballet *The Bumpkin and the Beauty?*[10] There you've got the whole story. Melusine is pure Beauty."

"Conceded. But what harm does that do? Italianize yourself and sign your name Ciacco from tomorrow on. Then you're right on that Ghiberti fellow's heels, regardless of his being a count."

"*Sapristi*, Rex, *c'est une idée.*"

45

The young couple, following planned short sojourns, first in Amalfi and then in Sorrento, had arrived in Capri. Woldemar asked about letters but learned that nothing had arrived.

Armgard seemed annoyed. "Melusine usually never lets me wait like this."

"That's only made you pampered. She pampers you in general."

"Perhaps. But if it's all right with you, we'll talk about that another time, not today. I'd say for confessions of that sort we've really not been married long enough yet. After all, we're still on our honeymoon."

Woldemar soothed her. "There'll be a letter tomorrow. Well then, let's make our peace with one another and if you're up to it, climb up towards Anacapri. Or if you don't feel like climbing, let's stay where we are and find ourselves a good lookout spot right here."

It was on the front balcony of their hotel, situated on the middle slope, that they engaged in this conversation. Since the efforts and exertions of recent days had been rather considerable, Armgard was ready, at least for today, to pass up Anacapri. Thus she was satisfied to climb up to the flat rooftop lookout with Woldemar and there, in view of the beauty spread out before them, spent a happy hour. Fishing boats crossed over before them from Sorrento, the fishermen singing their songs, and the sky remained clear and blue. Only across in the distance from the cone of Vesuvius rose a thin column of smoke, and from time to time it seemed as if one could make out a dull rumbling and thundering.

"Do you hear it?," asked Armgard?

"Certainly. And I happen to know too that they're expecting an eruption. Maybe we'll even get to see it."

"That would be magnificent."

"And in the process," Woldemar continued, "I can't get rid of the presumptuous idea that if things get going in a serious way over there, our Stechlin will do its bit too, even if only on a modest scale. After all, it is an upper-class relationship."

Armgard nodded. And coming from the edge of the water, where Sorrentine fishermen were just tying up, could be heard:

Tre giorna son che Nina, che Nina
In letto ne se sta . . . [11]

As prophesied, on the next day a letter from Melusine arrived. This time, however, it was not addressed to her sister but to Woldemar.

"What's wrong?" asked Armgard, who did not fail to notice the emotions which Woldemar attempted to suppress as he read.

"Read for yourself."

And he gave her the letter announcing the death of the old man.

The thought of arriving in Stechlin to attend the funeral was of course out of the question. The day of the burial had already passed. Thus they agreed to make their return journey slowly and in stages, passing through Rome, Milan and Munich, staying — for both of them yearned to be home — no longer than a day in each place. From Capri Woldemar took but a single souvenir with him, a wreath of laurel and olive branches. "This is something he truly earned."

Their last stop was Dresden, and it was from here that Woldemar directed a few lines to Lorenzen:

"Dear Lorenzen,

We've been in Dresden for half an hour and I write these lines in full view of the ever beautiful panorama one gets from the terrace, that never fails to have its effect even on the most jaded. We intend to leave here as early as possible tomorrow and will be in Berlin by ten and Gransee by noon. I want first to see our good old Stechlin and then to lay a wreath on the coffin. Please see to it that a carriage is waiting for me at the station. If I were to be met by you personally as well, that would be what I would wish for most. One can chat so well on the road. And from whom could I learn more detailed or dependable details about his last days than from you who no doubt passed them with him? My wife sends her warmest greetings. As ever, your old, faithful and grateful friend,

Woldemar von St."

At twelve the train stopped at the Gransee station. Woldemar could even make out the carriage from the coupé, but in place of Lorenzen, Krippenstapel had come. That was at first somewhat disconcerting, but he quickly saw it from its good side. "Maybe Krippenstapel is better after all, because he's more open and less circumspect in some things. Lorenzen, even if he'd smile at the expression, has a diplomatic tendency."

In this instant followed their welcoming by the 'bee father,' who had in the meantime approached them, and all three entered the carriage which had its top laid back. Krippenstapel made apologies for Lorenzen, who 'had been prevented from coming because of a wedding.' Everything would have been in perfect order had our splendid old museum director refrained from improving the appearance of his external personage before undertaking his trip to Gransee. That, however, had seemed improper to him; consequently he sat across from the young couple done up in a narrow string tie and a large protruding dickey. The tie was so narrow that not only the edge of the shirt which served to hold the stiff collar in place was half visible but also, alas, his Adam's apple, which, popping out from a wedge-shaped opening, was now constantly moving up and down like something totally uncontrollable.

The embarrassment felt by Armgard, whose eyes — unwillingly, of course — fixed continuously upon this play of nature, would have increased from minute to minute were it not that Krippenstapel's artless behavior ultimately helped her over it all.

It turned out, moreover, that his artlessness matched his garrulousness. He recounted everything about the funeral and who all of the

326

local county aristocracy had been in attendance. Then came the turn of Thormeyer, Katzenstein, the Domina and finally, "Lil' Agnes."

"We'll have to take care of the child," said Armgard.

"If you insist, of course. But it will be more difficult than you imagine. Children of that sort, regardless of all the pedagogical clichés, have got to be left to their own resources. The more perilous path, if anything good is to be found in them at all, is the better one every time. Then they make something of themselves from their innate character. But whenever any sort of compulsion is applied to bring about such a turn-around, usually nothing comes of it. Nothing but hypocrisy and pretense are born that way. One's own free choice outweighs a hundred pedagogical principles."

Armgard agreed. Krippenstapel, however, continued with his report and told them about Kluckhuhn, Uncke and about Elfriede. Sponholz was expected back next week and Koseleger and the princess were heart and soul together, especially — and this was the very latest — since collections were being taken up for a rescue shelter. Contributions were eagerly being made by the nobility. Only Molchow had refused to participate: "Things like that only make for confusion."

At two they arrived at Stechlin Castle. Woldemar strode through the deserted rooms, lingered for a brief time in the death chamber, and then went to the church vault to lay the wreath on his father's coffin.

Late in the afternoon Lorenzen appeared and first expressed his regret that because of official duties he had not been able to come; Tenant farmer Zschocke had gotten married again. He then remained for the entire evening and related all sorts of things, at the end what he solemnly had had to promise the old man.

Woldemar smiled as he listened. "It looks like the future lies with *you*."

And with these words he extended his hand to Armgard.

46

Armgard felt comfortably at home in the remoteness from the world that held sway in the house at Stechlin. But the thought of spending the rest of her days here was for the present far from her mind. Thus, shortly after a week had passed she returned to Berlin, where in the meantime Melusine had seen to everything, even to renting and furnishing an apartment not far from Woldemar's barracks.

It was located on Belle-Alliance Square. When the young couple moved in to this apartment, the winter season was already nearing its end. The spring parades were beginning, and soon thereafter the races, in which Armgard took avid interest. Yet the pleasure she derived from these things was less than she had imagined. Neither the metropolitan hustle and bustle nor the military atmosphere, neither sport nor art continued to maintain the enduring appeal she had initially expected. Thus, before the peak of summer had come, she said, "I've got to admit it to you, Woldemar, to a certain extent I'm yearning for Castle Stechlin."

He could not have heard anything that would have pleased him more. What Armgard said came straight from his heart as well. Amiable and unassuming as he was, it had long since become clear to him that he was never destined to become one of the celebrities of the general staff. At the same time that old markish Junker nature, something he had imagined himself free of, gradually began to stir in him. Every new day cried out to him, "The good soil of home, that's what gives you freedom, it's what's truly best after all."

Thus he submitted his resignation. They were loath to let him go, for he was not simply well-liked at the post he occupied, but truly beloved. When his retirement was at hand a regimental farewell dinner was given in his honor, and the commanding officer, who was especially well-disposed toward him, spoke in his address of the "wonderful days spent together in London and Windsor."

Throughout this time those little stresses and cares inevitably associated with a move to the country naturally confronted the young couple as well. One of the first of these concerns was finding a suitable chamber maid. Lizzi had refused because she did not care to do without the big city and its "culture." As luck would have it, however, it turned out that Hartwig's pretty niece was once again unemployed, and so it was she who was engaged. Melusine directed the negotiations. "Of course, I really don't know if you'll like it out there, Hedwig. I do hope so, though. And in any case, there are two things you *won't* be having. No more servants' lofts and no more 'pestering' as they say here. Or at least no more of it than in the end you care to have."

"Oh, that's not much," Hedwig assured her, half modestly, half mischievously.

On the twenty-first of September the young couple hoped to move in to Stechlin, and all preparations were made to do so. Mayor Kluckhuhn rounded up all the veteran's groups in the neighborhood — those who had been at the storming of Düppel on the right flank of course — while Krippenstapel collaborated with Tucheband on a welcoming poem to be recited by Rolf Krake's oldest daughter. The

Globsowers even went them one better and prepared a speech in which the young master was to be hailed as "one of their very own."

All of that was for the twenty-first.

On the day before, however, a letter from Melusine arrived at Lorenzen's. At the end it read:

"And now, dear Pastor, this one thing again. Tomorrow morning our young couple will be moving in to the old manor house, my sister and my brother-in-law. On this occasion I would ask you to keep in mind the pact we made during those days at Christmas. It is not necessary that the Stechlins live on forever, but long live

the Stechlin."

Notes

Book One: Castle Stechlin

[1] Lisbon: the Lisbon earthquake, 1755.

[2] The Swedish invasion: Sweden occupied part of Brandenburg from 1672 to 1679.

[3] Corps de loggias: Middle structure of a castle.

[4] Pomeranian: Pomerania, a region northeast of Prussia with Slavic cultural ties, today part of Poland.

[5] Boitzenburgs, Bassenburgs: Well-known Prussian aristocratic families.

[6] Gerson: Berlin fashion house frequently mentioned by Fontane as a symbol of bourgeois materialism.

[7] A red stripe: In contrast to the black and white Prussian flag, the imperial German flag incorporated a red stripe. Red is also the color of the Socialist movement.

[8] Ministerial Assessor: Czako describes Rex in German as a *Ministerialassessor*. The rank of *Assessor*, a favorite with Fontane, is essentially that of a candidate for a bureaucratic position. As a member of the nobility, Rex is in a junior post in government service.

[9] Frundsberg's day: An era of mercenary soldiers in the 15th and 16th centuries. Among their most famous leaders was Georg von Frundsberg (1473–1528).

[10] *"pour combler le bonheur."* "to top off their good luck."

[11] Queen of Great Britain and Ireland: It was customary in the imperial army to name exclusive regiments after foreign royalty. The Dragoons Guard Regiment Nr.1 carried this appellation since 1889 and counted a number of German princes as well as the Prince of Wales (later George V) in its ranks.

[12] *à la suite*: An honorary position of being on regimental lists entitling the recipient to wear the regimental uniform without participating in active duty. Usually reserved for high-ranking princes.

[13] Parquet of kings: An expression by the French actor Francois Joseph Talma, who at the invitation of Napoleon, performed before assembled royalty at the Congress of Erfurt in 1808.

[14] Alexander: The Prussian *Kaiser Alexander Garde-Grenadier Regiment* Nr. 1, Berlin. Named after Czar Alexander I since the days of the Wars of Liberation.

[15] Solingen or Suhl: Well-known German knife and razor producing towns.

[16] "descended into hell": Fontane also took issue with this phrase of the Apostles Creed. In a letter to Georg Friedlaender (29 Nov. 1893), he wrote, "'Born of the

Virgin Mary, . . . descended into hell, sits at the right hand of God,' there's nothing more to be made of that. Not even painters dare to deal with it."

[17] The Order of the Prussian as well as the Wendish Crown: Medals of honor created by the Prussian and Mecklenburg royal houses. Fontane had received both.

[18] Schiller: *Wallenstein*, Prolog, verse 59, translated by Charles E. Passage, New York: Frederick Ungar Publishing Company, 1958, 4.

[19] St. Crispin: Roman martyr and shoemaker, a patron saint of those who work with their hands.

[20] Franconia: Northern Bavaria. Stöcker actually owned a farm in Southern Bavaria.

[21] Priest from Wörishofen: Sebastian Kneip (1821–97), Catholic priest, founder of a hydrotherapeutic institute and inventor of a water cure much admired in the age.

[22] Niemann: Wagnerian tenor appearing in Berlin between 1866–1888; Antonietta dell'Era: prima ballerina of the Court Opera between 1879–1909.

[23] Potiphar's wife: Genesis 39:7–12, Egyptian woman who attempted to seduce Joseph.

[24] Causeuse: Sofa with a diagonal divider allowing two persons to converse while sitting back to back.

[25] Alexanderplatz: Berlin square, the nexus of commerce for lower class Berliners.

[26] "A good impulse over a good constitution": Friedrich Wilhelm IV, Prussian king who refused to institute a constitutional monarchy during the Revolution of 1848.

[27] Russian church . . . . Russian houses: Alexandrowka, a settlement in Potsdam of 13 Russian style houses and a Russian church, built in 1826 to memorialize the close relationship between Russia and Prussia.

[28] Nicholas: Czar Nicholas I (1796–1855), strongly conservative anti-revolutionary Czar from 1825.

[29] The Holy Alliance: Concluded in 1815 between Russia, Austria and Prussia to guarantee the "new order" of Europe by suppressing liberal movements.

[30] Großgörschen: Battle at which Napoleon defeated the Russian and Prussian armies in 1813.

[31] "Brotherhood of arms of organ grinders and mouse trap peddlers": alluding to the alliance between Germany, Austria and Italy in 1882. Organ grinders playing Italian opera melodies were a common sight on the streets of the Second Reich, as were Italian peddlers selling mousetraps.

[32] Preobashensk, Semenow, Kaluga: Russian garrison towns.

[33] When goodly words . . .: Schiller, *Das Lied von der Glocke*. "Wenn gute Reden sie begleiten,/ dann fließt die Arbeit munter fort." ("When goodly words its company be, then flows the task with cheer").

[34] *Waldmeister's Honeymoon,*: Comic epic by Otto Roquette, a companion of Fontane in the literary society, *Der Tunnel über der Spree*.

[35] Initially favorable to the Christian-Socialist movement, Emperor Wilhelm II removed Stöcker as Court Preacher in 1890. In 1896 the emperor showed his displeasure with Stöcker's movement asserting, "Whosoever is a Christian is social already; Christian-Social is nonsense and leads to arrogance and intolerance, both of which run completely counter to Christianity. Our good pastors should concern themselves with the souls of their parishioners and foster love of neighbor, but keep their noses out of politics, because it's none of their business."

[36] The old and new faith: Allusion to the last work of the German theologian, David Friedrich Strauß (1876), which viewed Christianity in a strongly materialistic matrix.

[37] Reference to scandals at the court of St. Petersburg in the 1860's associated with Auguste Stubbe.

[38] Outlying rural sections of Berlin.

[39] Görbersdorf: Open air asylum in Silesia for tuberculosis.

[40] Dzierzon's method: Johannes Dzierzon (1811–1906), a Catholic priest, viewed in Germany as founder of modern beekeeping whereby honeycombs are permitted to grow on moveable wooden frames.

[41] Heine's Asra: Heinrich Heine (1799–1856), *Der Asra* concludes, "Und mein Stamm sind jene Asra, Welche sterben, wenn sie lieben." ("And my race are the Asra/ Who die when they love").

[42] Wrangel: Karl Gustav von Wrangel (1613–76), Swedish commander defeated at Fehrbellin who appears in Schiller's *Wallensteins Tod* as Oberst (Colonel) Wrangel. 'Father Wrangel': Friedrich von Wrangel (1784–1877), Prussian Field Marshal, notorious as commander who in 1848 dissolved the Prussian National Assembly on order of Friedrich Wilhelm IV, and who in the Danish War threatened to burn a Danish village for every German house bombarded by the Danes.

[43] Uckermark, Mecklenburg: Regions to the northeast and north of Berlin.

[44] *Toujours perdrix*: ("Partridge every day"): Complaint of French king Henry IV's confessor, who at royal command received partridge at meals daily following reproaches regarding the king's infidelities.

[45] The Great Elector: An equestrian statue of Great Elector Friedrich Wilhelm by Andreas Schlüter, originally on the bridge before the Royal Castle in Berlin, currently in the forecourt of the Charlottenburg Palace in western Berlin.

[46] Co-hermit: Bismarck, who had made such a remark in 1848, lived alone on his estate near Hamburg following the death of his wife in 1894.

[47] Round bottle of green glass with a short neck: In German, *der Bocksbeutel*, the characteristic container for the dry white wine of the Main River region.

[48] Fat fellows: Shakespeare's *Julius Caesar*, I Scene 2.

[49] New Land for All: A proposal for redistribution of large estates popular at the time.

[50] Several Prussian generals had been from the von Katzler family.

[51] Landbook: Holy Roman Emperor Karl IV acquired the Mark Brandenburg in 1373 and by recording property rights in his *Landbuch*, sought to end local feuding and provide a record for taxation.

Book Two: Wutz Convent

[1] "That foreign word": velocipede, the original designation for a bicycle.

[2] Lipa: position on Austrian line near Königgrätz, where on 3 July 1866 Prussia defeated Austria.

[3] Seven Electoral Prince: princes of the Holy Roman Empire who traditionally elected the emperor.

[4] Pope: Pius IX (1846–1878) in 1870 declared the dogma of papal infallibility at the First Vatican Council and engaged in the prolonged *Kulturkampf* with Bismarck concerning church rights in the German state. At the time of the novel Pope Leo XIII was reigning pontiff.

[5] Irvingite: Dissenter sect founded by Scottish cleric, Edward Irving (1792–1843), which took hold in Germany after 1848 and included many high-ranking members of the Prussian military.

[6] Hus or Ziska: Jan Hus (1369–1415), Leader of Hussites, Czech Protestant reform movement before Luther. Jan Ziska, (1360–1410): Hussite leader.

[7] Hunyadis: Johann Corvinus (1387–1456), Hungarian warrior, whose second son ascended the Hungarian throne as Matthias I in 1458.

[8] Sweetheart's snack: German: *Vielliebchen*: A playful custom by which persons of the opposite sex shared a piece of intergrown fruit. On next meeting each was required to address the other as *Vielliebchen*, a term meaning something like "sweetheart." Whoever forgot was required to pay a forfeit, usually a kiss.

[9] Wendic divinity: The Wends were a Slavic race inhabiting the Mark Brandenburg.

[10] Old man's milk: From Latin "vinum lac senum," wine is the milk of the old.

[11] Our Blessed Mother's Milk: German *Liebfrauenmilch*. A popular Rhine wine blend.

[12] Käthchen von Heilbronn: chief character of drama of the same name by Prussia's greatest dramatist, Heinrich von Kleist (1777–1811), in which the heroine expresses her love for the knight Wetter von Strahl in a dream beneath an elder tree.

[13] Esterhazy: Prince Schwarzenberg: Esterhazys were among the eldest aristocratic families of Hungary. Prince Karl Philipp of Schwarzenberg: Austrian Field Marshal and Ambassador to Napoleon I., conducted negotiations for the betrothal of the Austrian emperor's daughter Marie Louise to Napoleon in 1810. The festival on the occasion ended with a fire in which his sister-in-law was among the dead.

[14] Fontane indulges in a bit of 'word' play with the German word *Wortlaut* (wording), *Wort* (word) and *Wert* (value), with obvious allusions to Nietzsche's *Umwertung aller Werte (Revaluation of All Values)*.

[15] The Halle Gate: Like the Brandenburg gate, one of the original entrances to Berlin, located on the southwestern perimeter of the city.

[16] Mars-la-Tour: Decisive engagement in Franco-Prussian War on Aug. 16, 1870 near Metz, in which the French attack was defeated by Prussian troops, including the Regiment of Dragoon Guards.

[17] First Guards Regiment: Premier regiment of German Army, dating back to days of Soldier King. Famed because of their requirement for being over six feet tall as "die langen Kerls" ("the tall fellows") and for their brass helmets still worn as part of their parade uniform under the Kaisers.

[18] The old prince: Prince Chlodwig von Hohenlohe Schillingsfürst (1819–1901), one of Bismarck's successors, who had to contend with Wilhelm II's wish to exercise absolute power.

[19] Melusine: According to French legend, Melusine was a mermaid and the primal mother of the family of Lusignan. Surprised by her husband in her true form, she disappeared, reappearing whenever the family or realm were threatened by misfortune. Fontane was fascinated by the motif of an elementary creature who sought to live and love as a human, but was unable to forswear her elfin nature. Apart from this novel, he treated it elsewhere, as in the story *Ellernklipp* and the fragmentary *Ocean von Parceval*.

Book Three: To the Egg Cottage

[1] Kronprinzenufer: Literally, Crown Prince's Bank, a street along the Spree near the Reichstag. Not rebuilt after the Second World War.

[2] Stadtbahn: Berlin's elevated tramway, one of the first on the European continent.

[3] Rittmeister: The ranking officer of a cavalry squadron, equivalent to the rank of Captain.

[4] Stage figure: Armgard in Schiller's *Wilhelm Tell*.

[5] Talers: Equivalent to 3 marks.

[6] Regiment Garde-du-Corps: A cuirassier regiment evolving from Frederick the Great's personal body guard, considered the most prestigious in the German Imperial Army.

[7] Freiherr: German title equivalent to baron.

[8] Niels Gade: (1817–1890), Danish composer, student of Mendelssohn and Schumann.

[9] Oginski: (1765–1833) Popular Polish composer. *Erlkönig*: Goethe's famous ballad in the setting by Schubert. *The Bells of Speyer*: ballad by Maximillian Freiherr von Oer set by Karl Löwe. *The Old General (Der alte Feldherr)*: operetta by Karl Holtei, a work prominently mentioned in a number of Fontane's works, especially *Irrungen, Wirrungen*.

[10] Saatwinkel, Grunewald: Regions then surrounding Berlin. Now part of the city.

[11] *Ut min Stromtid, Us der Franzosentid*: popular novels in Low German by Fritz Reuter (1810–1874).

[12] Prince Heinrich: Armgard distinguishes between the brother of Frederick the Great and the still living younger brother of Kaiser Wilhelm II.

[13] Lake Lucerne: Allusion to the founding of the Swiss Confederation and Schiller's drama *Wilhelm Tell*.

[14] The Quirinal: Following the Vatican Treaty in 1870, which terminated the civil power of the papacy, the Quirinal Palace, formerly a papal summer residence, became the palace of the Kings of Italy.

[15] Johann Julius Wilhelm Spindler (1810–73): Founder of a dye works and laundry company, later German's first dry cleaning plant. The works were so extensive as to give the entire district its name.

[16] damp-wallers: *Trockenwohner*, tenants living at reduced rates in dwellings having newly-plastered walls which, because they were damp to the touch, were considered unhealthy at the time.

[17] *Säkerhets Tändstickors*: safety matches.

[18] Swedish Nightingale: Jenny Lind (1820–1887), world famous soprano.

[19] Sedan, Düppel, Crossing to Alsen: Prussian victories. At Sedan (1–2 September 1870) the Prussian army defeated the French in the Franco-Prussian War; The storming of Danish fortifications at Düppel (18 April 1864) and the crossing to Alsen (29 June 1864), were decisive moments in the Austrian-Prussian war with Denmark.

[20] Joao de Deus: Portuguese poet and pedagogue of whom Fontane evidently learned while writing *Der Stechlin* through an obituary in *Das Magazin für Literatur* in February 1896.

Book Four: Election in Rheinsberg-Wutz

[1] Rolf Krake: Danish iron-clad which on the morning of 18 February 1864 threatened Prussian pontoon bridges at Flensburg and engaged Prussian land batteries. In his book on the war between Denmark and Prussia, Fontane described the engagement: "As 'Rolf Krake' passed through the narrows of the Flensburger Gulf between Hollnis and Brunsnis . . . it took fire from the battery at Hollnis without deeming it worthy of reply. Once the firing line of Hollnis was behind it, it made full steam and because of the lifelessness of its deck, eerily glided like a great floating coffin towards the batteries at Alnoer. Expecting the worst, we saw her take up a position just 1400 paces from Aloner and open up a cannonade with the batteries and against the bridge." (*Der Schleswig-Holsteinsche Krieg im Jahre 1864*, 120). The battle — erroneously considered by Fontane, who was unfamiliar with the American Civil War, to be the first between an iron-clad and land batteries — was a standoff and the Prussian bridge survived.

[2] St. Elizabeth (1207–1231): married at 14 to the Landgrave of Thuringia, is supposed to have fed 900 poor daily with bread and who was portrayed in this role by

the popular 19th century painter Moritz von Schwind (1804–1871) in the famous Wartburg Castle near Eisenach.

[3] Illustrated news portfolios: Gustav Kühn's *Ruppiner Bilderbogen*, describing important events in cartoons for the semi-literate. Published in Fontane's birthplace throughout the nineteenth century.

[4] Lazy Grete (*die faule Grete*): Name applied to a gigantic canon belong to the first of the Hohenzollerns in Brandenburg, Burgrave Friedrich IV (around 1415).

[5] *Fortiter in re . . . .*: "Strong in the cause, but mild in the form," a well known saying of the fourth General of the Jesuit Order, Claudio Aquaviva.

[6] Koseleger. The German word *kosen* implies affectionate caressing or fondling, while *Leger* is a substantive derived from the verb *legen*, to lay or place. The name thus suggests obsequious behavior.

[7] Frederick the Great: Alluding to a remark made by the king in 1781 when he saw his subjects stretching their necks to read a lampoon of his person which had been hung too high.

[8] Prince August (1779–1843): Prussian Chief of Artillery in the Wars of Liberation, Prince August became infamous for his relationship to a leading women of the French demimonde, Mme. Récamier.

[9] Gustav Kühn's illustrated portfolios: See p. 124.

[10] *veau en tortue*: a veal dish.

[11] *Heil dir im Siegerkranz:* (Hail to thee in Victor's Crown) German imperial hymn. Its melody is the same as *God Save the King.*

[12] building with four towers: The newly-built *Reichstag* (Parliament) in Berlin, opened in 1894 and symbol of the emerging democratic process of the Second Reich.

[13] Gretna Green: Village in Scotland allowing marriages of under-aged parties without parental consent, recognized in Prussia following an 1855 decision of the Supreme Tribunal.

Book Five: Mission To England

[1] Zelten: Recreation area on the Spree at the northwest end of the Tiergarten, featuring beer gardens, cafes and dance halls, much loved by Berliners. Not rebuilt after World War II.

[2] Emin: Eduard Schnitzer (1840–1892), German physician and traveler who as Mehmed Emin Pascha was Governor of the German East Africa from 1878 to 1889, murdered at the instigation of slave dealers.

[3] Astrakhan, Colchester: both port cities, the former famous for its caviar, the latter for oysters.

[4] Derfflinger, Blücher, Wrangel: Prussian generals. Georg von Derfflinger (1606–1695), one of the generals of the Great Elector at the Battle of Fehrbellin. Gebhard

Leberecht von Blücher, (1742–1819), commander of Prussian troops in the War of Liberation. Wrangel, also infamous for mixing the German dative form *mir* with the accusative *mich*, a characteristic of Berlin dialect.

[5] Princess of Wales: Dagmar, Thyra: Daughters of King Christian IX of Denmark. Princess Alexandra was married to the Prince of Wales, later Edward VII, Dagmar to the Russian Czar Alexander III, and Thyra to Duke Ernst August of Cumberland.

[6] Coburgean meddling . . . Prince Consort: Prince Albert of Saxe-Coburg-Gotha (1819–1861), husband of Queen Victoria, bore the title *Consort of her most gracious Majesty*. Highly revered after his death, he encountered distrust during the Crimean War, when it was thought he had Russian sympathies.

[7] Skarbina: Franz Skarbina (1849–1910) Berlin genre painter.

[8] lynching party: Fontane refers to *Haberfeldtreiben*, a form of Bavarian rough justice that died out at the end of the nineteenth century. Masked men (*Haberen*) made noise and threats outside the dwelling of someone, who although legally unencumbered, was felt to have violated local laws or morals.

[9] "golden indiscretions": An allusion to the poem *Für meine Söhne* by Theodor Storm. "A bloom of nobelest character/ is discretion: yet at times like summer storms refreshing / are golden indescretions. (Blüte edelsten Gemütes/ Ist die Rücksicht: doch zu Zeiten/ Sind erfrischend wie Gewitter/ Goldene Rücksichtslosigkeiten.)

Book Six: Engagement; Christmas Visit to Stechlin

[1] Quote: From Schiller's *Die Piccolomini*, in Charles E. Passage's translation, "That they spawn further deeds and always evil ones" In German the verbs 'fortzeugen' (to continue procreating) and 'gebieren' (to bear), are employed, words not considered appropriate for the Victorian salon.

[2] Turner: *Nebuchadnessar at the Mouth of the Burning Firey Furnace.*

[3] Mundus . . .:From *Das Narrenschiff* (*The Ship of Fools*) by the German humanist Sebastian Brant (1458–1521). In English, "The world wishes to be deceived, well then, let it be deceived."

[4] *parceque . . . quoique*: Not 'because' but 'regardless.'

[5] "Here I stand, I cannot do otherwise:" Luther's response to Charles V. at the Diet of Worms.

[6] His Christ doth preach . . .: German: "Es predigt sein Christus allerorten, ist aber drum nicht schöner geworden." A parody of a line from Goethe's *Faust* (*Schülerszene*), "Das preisen die Schüler allerorten, /Sind aber keine Weber geworden," roughly, "Tis praised by students of every spot, but made weavers thereby, they are certainly not."

[7] Mausoleum in Charlottenburg, Friedenskirche (Peace Church) in Potsdam: In the mausoleum at Schloß Charlottenburg King Friedrich Wilhelm II and Queen Luise as well as Emperor Wilhelm I and Empress Victoria were interred.

[8] Girls from Dahomey: 5000 armed girls made up the body guard of the prince of Dahomey. In the 1890's at the Panopticum on *Unter den Linden*, a group from Dahomey was on display.

[9] Märker . . . Saxon: Dubslav comments humorously on differences in personality between historical antipodes, the Prussians and the Saxons, i.e. the Germans of the Northeast against those of the Southeast.

[10] Slipper: In German the symbol for being henpecked.

[11] Name of horror: *Mordbahn*, "murderous line." Construction costs ruined many stockholders.

[12] 'rocher de bronce': Fr. "rock of bronze," from a remark by the Soldier King, Friedrich Wilhelm I.

[13] '*Non-soli-cedo*' eagle: The eagle and motto of the Prussian coat of arms, "I do not yield to the sun," implying Louis XIV of France.

[14] Küstrin Castle . . . Katte: From a window at Küstrin fortress, Frederick II, while crown prince, was compelled to witness the execution of his friend Lieutenant Hans Hermann Katte (1704–1730), after their attempted flight to England was discovered.

[15] Königgrätz, Mars-la-Tour: Prussian victories. The former on 3 July 1866 against Austria, the latter on 16 August 1870 in the Franco-Prussian War.

Book Seven: *Wedding*

[1] *Bellis perennis*: Lat. Daisies.

[2] Torgau: Where Frederick the Great cried to retreating grenadiers, "Rogues, do you want to go on living forever?"

[3] Quitzows: Old Brandenburg family which resisted the rule of the Hohenzollerns from its outset, thus symbolizing the independence of the Prussian aristocracy from Hohenzollern domination.

[4] 18 March 1848: Outbreak of revolution which nearly toppled royalty throughout central Europe. Fontane's experiences are related in his autobiography *From Twenty to Thirty*.

[5] Sachsenwald: After his forced retirement, Bismarck withdrew to Friedricksruh in the Forest of Saxony (Sachsenwald). Wallenstein: Allusion to the hero of Schiller's trilogy, who betrays the emperor.

Book Eight: *Sunset*

[1] Midday sun: Allusion to *Evensong*, (*Abendlied*), a famous poem by the 17th century poet Paul Gerhardt. The next line reads, "Night has driven you away." (Die Nacht hat dich vertrieben).

[2] "Everyone may find salvation, each in his own façon:" famous remark by Frederick the Great in a letter of 22 June 1740.

[3] Corn flower: The favorite flower of Emperor Wilhelm I, a symbol of Hohenzollern rule.

[4] *Kreuzzeitung:* Roughly, *Iron Cross News:* because of the symbol on its masthead, the common name of the *Neue Preußische Zeitung*, leading conservative newspaper espousing the cause of the government and Prussian aristocracy. Despite fundamental disagreement with many of its policies, Fontane worked at the paper's English desk during the 1860's.

[5] Gensdarmes: Allusion to the French (Huguenot) and German (Lutheran) cathedrals on the Gendarmenplatz (now Platz der Akademie), named after the Regiment gensdarmes of the old Prussian Army. See, Fontane's *Schach von Wuthenow*.

Book Nine: But Stay a While: Death: Burial: New Days

[1] Animal park . . . "Zoological": A play on words. In Berlin, the central park, formerly a royal hunting preserve, is called the *Tiergarten* (animal park) while the *Zoologischer Garten* is, of course, the zoo.

[2] Count Arthur von Posadowsky-Wehner (1845–1932), Secretary of the Reich Treasury in 1893 and Reich Interior Ministry in 1897.

[3] Bennigsen: Rudolf von Bennigsen (1824–1902), Chairman of the National Liberal Party in the Reichstag, supported Bismarck in his struggle against the Catholic Church (Kulturkampf) and was known for his readiness to compromise.

[4] King of Thule: An allusion to Goethe's famous ballad of a lover's loyalty unto death from *Faust I*.

[5] Count Schwerin: Presumably Count Hans von Schwerin Löwitz (1847–1918), member of the German Conservative Party in the Reichstag, concerned chiefly with agricultural affairs.

[6] Ideas live easily . . . things . . . collide: Friedrich Schiller, *Wallensteins Tod,* (Act II, 2): ("Leicht beieinander wohnen die Gedanken, doch hart im Raume stoßen sich die Sachen.") Fontane slightly misquotes Schiller by using the word *eng* (narrow) in place of *hart*.

[7] Battle of the Butterflies: alluding to a highly controversial drama of the day by the Naturalist playwright Hermann Sudermann.

[8] Göhre: Paul Göhre (1864–1930), Protestant theologian and politician of Wilhelmine era who sought to bring a Christian tone to the workers' movement.

[9] Freely transcribed from Hosiah 57,2.

[10] *The Bumpkin and the Beauty: (Der Kurmärker und die Pikarde),* (1859), popular Singspiel by the Berlin actor and writer Louis Schneider.

[11] *Tre giorno . . .:* Old Italian folk song: It's been three days since Nina has not been in her bed . . . .

William L. Zwiebel is Professor of German Language and Literature at the College of the Holy Cross, Worcester, Massachusetts. His annotated translation of Fontane's *Irrungen, Wirrungen* was published in *The German Library*. His book *Theodor Fontane*, treating the author's life and novels, appeared in 1992. ❏